Victor

The Women who Wouldn't Leave

An Aria Book

First published in the United Kingdom in 2023 by Head of Zeus,
part of Bloomsbury Publishing Plc

9 7 5 3   2 4 6 8

A catalogue record for this book is available from the British Library.

ISBN (PB): 9781804544754
ISBN (E): 9781804544716

Printed and bound in Great Britain by
CPI Group (UK) Ltd, Croydon CR0 4YY

Head of Zeus
First Floor East
5–8 Hardwick Street
London EC1R 4RG

WWW.HEADOFZEUS.COM

The Women who Wouldn't Leave

Also by Victoria Scott

Patience
Grace

For Teil, Raphie and Ella, always.

PART ONE

— 1 —

June

Constance

It was 5 a.m. The sun was just glinting over the horizon, inching off the starting blocks of another scorching day. The air was saturated both with the scent of baked bracken and the sweet song of the dawn chorus, and the earth beneath Connie's feet was pockmarked by the impact of hooves into dense mud; spring's adventures fossilised by summer.

She picked her footing with care to avoid twisting an ankle or bruising a knee – both of which she had done in the past few weeks. Despite having spent most of her childhood marching through these fields, she now felt like a stranger to them, and them to her, and her bruises and aches were confirmation of this. Or perhaps it was just her age. Were you already over the hill at twenty-nine, she wondered. How bloody depressing to think her best years might already be behind her, given what a mess she'd made of her life so far.

Connie halted her ambling abruptly. She could make out several dark shapes on the other side of the field. There were cows resting in a circle around their water trough, she was sure of it.

Adrenaline shot through her. Her stomach lurched. Her mouth went dry. She shut her eyes to try to stop the memory recurring, but it did anyway. It was too powerful to ignore or suppress.

She can't breathe, even though she keeps trying to take air in. She's trying to find room for some oxygen to ward off the asphyxiation which will surely come. She is panicking, truly panicking now. And the pain – the pain is searing. She has never known pain like this. And so, she decides to surrender. For this is a fight she is going to lose – is already losing.

Connie opened her eyes to try to break the spell, and sprinted for the gate. They were probably sleeping, she knew that, but it didn't matter to her. Her fear of them was real, and she had a good reason for it. What she had been through was not easy to forget.

She arrived at the gate, panting, unhooked the catch and slammed it shut behind her, mindful of the need to make sure the livestock didn't escape. She'd read in the local paper that someone had actually died driving into a cow on a single-track, high-banked road in Worcestershire last month. They'd been in a normal car, not one of those Chelsea tractors the wealthy second-home owners drove, and both the cow and the driver had met each other with extreme force – glass, bones and bonnet folding up on contact. The result had been a tangled, bloody, raw mess, one she was sure the fire brigade would not forget in a hurry, and neither would that woman's family, the poor sods.

Often, visitors to this forgotten part of Worcestershire were sent down these old sheep tracks by navigation apps, the programs naively assuming this route was both passable for cars and a handy B-road shortcut, rather than a dirt-strewn dug-out populated by slow-moving tractors and overconfident locals with ageing cars which wore scratches as a badge of honour. Yes, these roads needed to be treated with respect and approached with caution. And that was something the council planners, keen to meet their government-set target for new homes, had definitely failed to account for in recent years. At least, that's what her mum said, and she read the local paper and cared about these things.

A nearby village now had thirty brand-new houses built on

its outskirts, almost all of which were far from affordable for local people, despite promises made at the planning stage. The village's new residents, tempted into the area from cities like Hereford, Worcester and Gloucester by the prospect of a larger garden, a garage and an extra bedroom, all had at least two cars per household, and the village's narrow, winding roads, two-class primary school and two-doctor GP surgery were all struggling to keep up with the surge in numbers. Her mum had been trying and failing to get an appointment with a doctor for two weeks now. Apparently you had to log on to the website at 8 a.m. sharp every morning to request an appointment, or you would find yourself—

There was a terrible noise, a deafening screech like a banshee, and Connie's thoughts evaporated.

Her head whipped left just in time to see a tractor tyre on a collision course with her head. And just as she had when that raging bull had charged at her, she shut her eyes and waited for the impact.

'*Why don't you look where you're bloody going?*'

Connie's heart was going like the clappers. A man was shouting at her. She didn't want to look at him, she really didn't, but she knew she was going to have to, or he'd probably tell everyone he knew that she was crazy, and she'd gone through enough of that kind of shit already.

She glanced up at the tractor driver. She recognised him immediately as Dean Collins, a ruddy-faced man in his twenties whose dad ran a local farm. He'd been a good few years below her at school, but she remembered a freckly, ginger-haired kid who'd once come to school on dress-up day in a black plastic bin liner with random bits of loo roll stuck on it (he'd been a fly, apparently). No one had said anything mean, though, not that she remembered anyway, probably because they all knew that his dad spent most of his time at the Farmer's Arms and his mum worked twelve-hour days as a cleaner to keep him and his brothers fed and her husband in beer. Did he remember her? Probably not. She looked very different now. She hoped he didn't, anyway.

'*Are. You. Deaf?*'

Connie took a deep breath, shook her head, threw herself against the hedge and closed her eyes, willing him to start up the engine and move on. She went out walking at this time every day so that she could avoid people. The last thing she wanted to do was engage in a conversation, or a row, or anything, in fact, with another human. All she needed to be happy, she now knew, was a daily walk, comforting TV and booze. It was her new recipe for unfettered joy, a magic combination she wished she'd discovered years ago.

'*Fine*,' he said. She heard the tractor splutter back into life and the giant tyres begin to turn.

She opened her eyes when the sound of the diesel engine began to fade. Dean was heading down the lane at some speed towards a large grassy field where, she suspected, he was going to be making hay. Quite literally, she thought, as the sun shone. The nature of an English summer was such that you never knew when the next deluge was going to come, even during a hot spell like this one. Farmers knew to grasp an opportunity when it presented itself.

As Dean disappeared around the corner, Connie inhaled deeply and breathed out to five slow beats. She'd learned that trick from a counsellor she'd gone to see to appease her mum. That counsellor had told her that it would slow her heartbeat and calm her down. It did seem to help, particularly at night when she woke up after a nightmare, her mind polluted with screams, locked doors she could not escape through and fights she would never be able to win. She would lie there with the covers thrown off, the streetlight making her swirly Artex ceiling look like a labyrinth, her heart feeling like a thrashing serpent hunting for prey. But if she counted her breaths, both in and out, she would feel them come under her control, like she'd suddenly become an accomplished snake-charmer.

Once she felt her heart begin to slow, she resumed her walk. She checked her watch; it was now 5.45 a.m. She had just under a mile left to go. She'd be home before 6.15 a.m., just in time to miss Mr and Mrs Chicken. Those weren't their real names, of course, because she'd never spoken to them and had deliberately avoided meeting anyone since she'd moved back here. So she'd given people random names based on what she thought they did for a living, and she reckoned this pair worked at a nearby chicken processing plant.

Connie could see their house from her bedroom window, so she knew they were on day shifts this week. It must be a punishing schedule, she thought, all that toing and froing, however nice it might be to be able to work the same shifts in the same place. From the gap between her roller blind and the window frame, she could see they looked pale and a bit beaten. She thought she'd feel a bit like that too, if she spent her working hours washing and gutting chicken carcasses.

Connie looked up as she passed the sign that marked the beginning of the village. It said, 'Welcome to Stonecastle', with a little picture of a grey stone keep; which was optimistic, she thought, given that all that was left of the ancient building was a grass mound and a few heavy rocks the locals hadn't been able to lift and take away for use to build their own homes in the intervening centuries.

Next she passed the bus stop, which had neither a shelter nor a seat and offered only six services a day – three in the morning and three in the afternoon – and then a boarded-up pub, The Old Swan, whose death certificate had been drafted by the indoor smoking ban and signed and stamped by the fact that it had failed to introduce food. On the other side of the village there was another pub, the newly christened The Plucky Duck, which had been bought out by a chain a couple of years previously. It was now painted gunship grey throughout, served food on pieces of slate and offered a tasting menu and a bottomless brunch every Saturday. It was rammed at weekends, its car park packed with utility vehicles, four-by-fours and electric sports cars.

A few minutes later, she rounded the corner into Roseacre Close. It was home to eight semi-detached houses, all built in the 1950s by a local council eager to provide decent homes for local workers. How times have changed, thought Connie.

She walked at pace past Mr and Mrs Chicken's place on the corner, to make sure she avoided bumping into them. Then she passed its adjoining semi, which was currently occupied by a woman she'd nicknamed Mrs Posh Hospital and her son, Master Skiver.

She reckoned that Mrs Posh Hospital worked as a nurse at a private clinic in Gloucester. Her mum, Ellen, had told her she'd moved in about a decade ago, when her son had been about six. In that time he'd gone from being a cute, blond chubby child to a surly, chubby spotty teenager who rarely left the house, except when his mum drove him to the bus stop to wait for the school bus, which wasn't every day. Sometimes, Connie saw him returning about twenty minutes afterwards. Clearly he felt education wasn't his bag.

Connie kept her head down as she passed the houses to the left. First there was the home of Mr Hoarder and his much younger lodger, Mr Road Fixer. Their front garden was full of old cars, sofas, sinks and doors. She suspected Mr Hoarder went out in the middle of the night and brought home other people's fly-tipped furniture as if it were treasure. Mr Road Fixer, meanwhile, when he wasn't working for the local council mending potholes, seemed to spend most of his time shagging random women, if the scenes she'd witnessed in the wee hours were anything to go by.

Then there was the woman Connie had named Little Miss Perfect. Little Miss P was a young single mother with an unfathomably perfect figure and two meticulously turned-out little boys, who lived in the semi that was attached to Mr Hoarder's house. She was lucky to have been given that house,

Connie thought; old Keith, its previous resident, had died suddenly and Little Miss P must have topped the council's list. She wondered how long she had been on that list. It was apparently incredibly long and very inflexible, with people being told to take the house they were offered, wherever it was, or to go back to the bottom of the queue. That meant people often ended up miles away from their families, their kids' schools and their workplaces.

The contrast between the two houses was striking. Little Miss P's front garden was sparse but tidy, and Connie could see, by craning her neck to look down the side passage next to her house, that she'd left her washing out in the back garden overnight. A luminous yellow G-string was glistening with morning dew.

Connie was nearly home. To the right of her were two more semis. Colonel Mustard – so-called due to the military quality of his moustache – and his wife Mrs Mustard lived in the one on the right. They were both in their eighties and quite clearly devoted to each other. They always walked out of the house holding hands. And to their left lived Ms Yoga Mat, a woman in her sixties whose constant companion was a very angry Alsatian actually named – because Connie regularly heard her shouting at it – Snuggles. Ms Yoga Mat seemed to run some sort of exercise class for other older women, because a group of them pulled up in cars every Wednesday morning in comfortable clothes and trooped in for an hour or so. She had a very beautiful front garden, one of those that looked unplanned, but you just knew its planting had been laid out to within an inch of its life. It was completely different in style to Connie's own back garden, which was pruned and edged meticulously.

Finally, Connie had reached her own front door. Well, their own front door. Or maybe just her mother's? It was, after all, her mother who paid the rent to the council, so it was probably just hers, frankly.

As Connie fumbled for the keys in her jeans pocket, she glanced at the front window of old Matilda's place. Matilda was the only neighbour Connie genuinely knew the name of, because she had known Matilda – or rather, known *of* her – since childhood.

At that moment, Connie saw movement in the curtains in Matilda's front room. It had been just a twitch, the sort of movement she'd have written off as being caused by the wind, if the air hadn't been so incredibly still.

What on earth was that mad old bird doing up at this time of day, Connie wondered. She had nothing to get up for, surely, unless it was to shovel up the poo produced by her multitude of cats and random menagerie of other smelly animals, and to lob it over theirs and Ms Yoga Mat's fences, something she did fairly regularly – mostly, Connie suspected, under cover of darkness. Yes, she was either doing that, or digging up yet another part of her garden to grow things.

From her mum's bedroom at the rear of the house, you could see into Matilda's back garden – if you could actually call it a garden. It was a holy mess, frankly. There were several random lean-to sheds which Connie presumed her neighbour kept her animals in, various bits of old metal and plastic strewn around, and then piles of earth, surrounded by high wire fences, in which a random collection of crops seemed to grow quite well. It amazed Connie that anything could grow in that mess, but grow they had, year after year, apparently, according to the season.

Matilda had been their neighbour since Connie's mother Ellen had been allocated their home by the council in the 1990s, and so she had probably been living there many years before that. She was an odd woman, Connie thought. An outsider; definitely a loner. She was almost never seen outside, was prone to screaming at any children who played near her front door, and had an unknown number of animals living with her, whose number only seemed to grow. Connie knew that Matilda threw food out into her back garden for her animals twice a day. Well, they all heard it, everyone on the estate, as the cockerel made a huge racket when he was hungry, and the goats were incredibly vocal around feeding time. Not to mention the cats, who seemed to view her mother's garden as a toilet. *Jesus*, she thought, it was like living on a bloody farm.

When Connie had been a child, the other kids at school had been too scared to walk past her house in case Matilda cast a spell on them and turned them into toads. Now, Connie wasn't so much scared of her as disgusted. Just by standing outside you could see that the house was packed to the brim with crap – both living and dead, she suspected. What on earth did that woman do with all of the animals when they died, for example? She never came out, so... Connie shivered at the thought. What sort of person lived in that kind of squalor? The house was dilapidated. Her mum had apparently written to the council several times over the years asking for them to visit the house and fix its roof, gutters and leaky windows on health grounds, but no one had ever replied, and nothing had ever been done.

Connie took a deep breath, put the key in the lock, turned it and pushed the door open. Their house, by contrast, always smelled nice. Her mum was very house-proud, which was both a blessing and a curse.

'Good morning, love,' shouted her mother from the kitchen. Connie walked through and saw that Ellen was already dressed in her carer's uniform – her sleek brown hair neatly tied back, her feet clad in flat black comfortable shoes, her legs in blue trousers, her torso in a white shirt and a blue tabard, with pockets for things like latex gloves and tissues. There was a lot of call for those sorts of things in her mother's job, and Connie was impressed she could cope with it. Connie wasn't keen on dealing with her own bodily fluids, let alone anyone else's.

'Morning,' she said, making her way towards the cupboard which held the mugs and the tea bags.

'Shoes off, Con.'

Connie looked down at her muddy boots. She had not yet reacquainted herself with her mother's high standards. She sighed inwardly, smiled outwardly and walked back to the front door, where she took them off and put them on a plastic mat which had been placed there for exactly that purpose.

'Good walk? Did you see anyone out?' her mother asked.

'It was OK. Peaceful,' replied Connie.

'I do wish you'd at least take my phone, so you could call me if you needed to. What if anything happened to you? There's hardly anyone about that early.'

'You mean like being viciously attacked by a hay bale? Or verbally abused by a duck?' said Connie, keen to avoid their conversation returning to dark places.

'Very funny. Anyway, next time, if I'm home, take my phone. Or even better, get one of your own.'

Connie ignored her mother's suggestion about getting a phone. She simply didn't want one any more. No good could come from having one.

'By the way, you didn't trespass again, did you? I had old Mick on the phone yesterday, complaining you'd been walking through his wheat.'

'Nah,' lied Connie, taking a tea bag down from the cupboard. 'I won't go there again.'

'Good,' said Ellen, pulling her daughter in for a hug. Connie had to stop herself from bristling, and tried to reciprocate by rubbing her right hand up and down her mother's back. It was taking her a long time to get used to physical contact again.

Ellen snatched her car keys from the counter and picked up a reusable mug filled with tea. 'I've got to head off, love. What are your plans for today?'

'I thought I might catch the bus into Gloucester and have a wander.'

'Sounds good.' There was a brief pause, which Connie knew was because her mum was working up the confidence to ask her something difficult. 'You know, love, I do think that getting a job again might be good for you, you know,' she said, after a couple of seconds of dead air. 'Maybe have a look at the adverts in the shop windows while you're there? Or online, when you get back? It would be great to get you back to your old self a bit, wouldn't it?'

Connie didn't reply. She threw her tea bag in her mug and stared at it. Her mum *knew* how she felt about her old job in PR, about the world of pain that lifestyle had brought her. She also knew that Connie was still unstable, still damaged. It wouldn't be fair on an employer, frankly, would it, to take her on? She didn't even trust *herself*.

'OK, well, let's talk about it later? Hope today goes well. And if you do go into town, could you see if you can get me some of that hydrocortisone cream from Boots, the one percent stuff? My eczema is flaring again.'

'Yeah, course,' said Connie, trying to crack a smile so that her mum would stop nagging her. She filled up the kettle and put it on to boil.

'Great. See you later then, love,' said Ellen, kissing her daughter on the cheek, grabbing her handbag, which was hanging over the bottom of the stair rail, opening the door and slamming it behind her.

As soon as she was sure her mother had gone, Connie put the teabag and mug away, switched the kettle off and climbed upstairs to her bedroom.

It was a small room overlooking the close, just about big enough for a single wooden bed with faded floral bed linen and matching curtains that had been bought from Laura Ashley in about 1995, a pine bedside table and a wonky white melamine wardrobe with a small television perched on top.

Connie opened the wardrobe door and fumbled in the murky darkness beneath her hanging clothes, an area home to a ramshackle pile of assorted shoes, a couple of spare handbags and several bottles of vodka. She pulled one of the bottles out, sat down on her bed, grabbed the remote control from her bedside table and selected Netflix. It took a few seconds to load, and only another few seconds for her to find what she wanted to watch, because for the last few months, she had watched just one thing – *Gilmore Girls*. That was because it depicted a mother and daughter who were clever, beautiful and successful, who lived in a world populated by kooky characters and where, despite any really rather vanilla challenges the characters faced, everything always ended happily. And that was what she desperately needed right now: a happy ending.

As the familiar titles began to roll, she opened the bottle of vodka and took a swig.

Then another.

And another.

Within twenty minutes, Connie could no longer sit upright, so she lay down, threw the bottle in the direction of her wardrobe and closed her eyes.

No, she would not be going into town today.

Not today.

In fact, she had no intention of ever going there again.

— 2 —

July

Matilda

Brian was making a din, which meant that it was time to get up.

Matilda rolled over on the mattress, its wonky springs digging into her wasting muscles as she did so. Then she pulled her knees as far up as they would go – not particularly far, to be honest, these days – hauled herself over onto her front, and pushed herself up onto all fours, pain shooting down her back leg as she did so. Blinking sciatica, she thought; blinking sciatica in my blinking ancient back.

After what felt like an eternity, she managed to roll over the three or four inches onto the dimpled lino floor and raise herself to standing using the solid oak dining table for support. She stood there for a minute or so while her breath and heart caught up, and smoothed down her long, black cotton dress, which had stuck to her in places. It had been a hot and sweaty night.

It was then that she saw Constance, Ellen's girl, through the net curtains. She pulled them aside gently and looked her up and down in the dim morning light. She had been such a lively thing when she'd been young; so full of joy. She'd often seen her skipping off down the pavement, or heard her playing hide and seek with friends through the fence, her delighted cries a constant reminder of her own loss, long ago.

Matilda let the curtain fall back and set off on her slow journey to the kitchen. Constance had changed beyond recognition, she thought. She was older, of course, but the spark she used to have seemed to have gone out of her, too. Not to mention the fact that she was looking *far too thin*, she decided, holding onto the stacks of boxes, books and newspapers either side of her to help her stay upright because her ninety-year-old hips and knees were no longer reliable. 'It's just not *safe* to be like that,' she muttered, as she continued her slow journey through the house. 'That girl is *so scrawny* and out at silly hours, traipsing all over the place at all hours. *Anything could happen to her.*'

Why didn't Ellen do something about it, she wondered. Tell her to stop? Although Constance must be in her twenties, she now realised; her grasp of the passing of time was loose, verging on completely absent. That was partly because she could no longer see the lounge clock, and the one on the kitchen wall had run out of batteries a decade ago. Not that she cared much for time. She went to sleep when she was tired, woke up when she was rested and ate when she was hungry. And anyway, she had the animals. They functioned as her alarm clock.

Yes, the girl *must* be in her twenties, maybe even late twenties, so an adult, you'd think. She could be a mother right now, in charge of little lives, but instead she was living back with her own poor mother, and behaving like *that*. Well, there was nothing she could do about the world outside, she thought, the idea her own familiar mantra. Yes, that was something Matilda had accepted a long time ago. She needed to stop being distracted by that poor girl next door and her odd habits, and just focus on the things she *did* have control over: namely, maintaining a roof over her head and keeping herself and the animals alive, all things she was proud that she'd managed to do for so long by herself. Yes, this was her sanctuary. She was safe here.

'*I will say of the Lord, He is my refuge and my fortress, my God, in whom I trust*,' recited Matilda, the familiar lines from Psalm 91 tripping off her tongue as she reached the kitchen, their contents a salve to her soul.

The galley kitchen was perfectly large enough for her needs, and the cabinet doors, which had been white when she'd moved in, now appeared yellow, their surfaces sticky. Not that Matilda cared. Years of scrubbing surfaces until her skin had bled had rid her of any desire to maintain high levels of cleanliness, when she had no one barking at her. And she didn't cook much these days anyway. She left a ring clear on her hob for heating things, had a tin opener that she stored in her saucepan, and one cup, bowl and spoon, and those were sufficient for her needs. When she wanted to eat, she just went into the hall and selected an unopened can. Whether it was tinned peaches, tomato soup or stewed steak, Matilda didn't care. She ate everything she had, and never left a drop. Afterwards, she washed the can out (if Brian or one of his hens wasn't sleeping in the sink) and put it back where she'd found it. Tins, she knew, were useful for storing things like pens and keys and receipts, and it didn't do to send stuff like that to landfill, to pollute the planet. After all, the countryside she could see from the fence at the end of her garden was being threatened enough.

The view out of her kitchen used to be an uninterrupted one of undulating fields divided by ancient hedgerows, but she could now see a development of new houses in the far distance, built on the site of a disused rural petrol station, spilling out beyond its original boundaries on all sides. Those houses, clad in fake white stone, had been designed, she assumed, to mimic the chocolate-box charm of the Cotswolds, which were about twenty miles away. In reality, however, the new houses looked like gigantic rectangles of lard, and she felt angry every time she looked at them.

It all seemed a bit ridiculous. After all, the red brick her own home was built from was far cheaper and still nice to look at. But what did she know? She had never kept up with trends, and her only windows on the world these days, now she could no longer get to the TV, were her beloved radio set and the free newspaper that came through her door every week. Recently the latter seemed to mostly contain adverts selling science-fiction-sounding things like *earbuds*, *vapes* and *electric scooters*. She no longer understood the world, she thought, and that was fine. Good riddance. It had never understood her, either.

Matilda leaned against a box on the counter – it contained buttons, she remembered, some of them quite rare and so colourful – and yanked open a cupboard door. Inside was a collection of the vegetables she grew in the garden, which were plentiful at this time of year, and which she stored in bags in one of the sheds during the winter, to try to preserve them for as long as possible. She grabbed a handful of runner beans and courgettes, aware she might lose her balance if she bent over too far. Her lower back was prone to giving up on her with regularity, and her stomach muscles were a distant memory. Mission accomplished, she hugged the vegetables to her chest using her left arm, and leaned forward to open the back door, which was never locked and which also never really closed properly, because its hinges were loose.

A fresh summer breeze brushed her face as she moved out onto the back step, a welcome sensation after what had been an airless, sweaty night.

'Brian! Jennifer! Ruth! Helen! Come and get your breakfast!'

There followed a symphony of squawking, rustling and clucking, and a cockerel and three hens emerged, racing each other to be first to bag their vegetable prize. Matilda threw the food down on the earth by her feet – the goats ate every blade of grass that deigned to make an appearance – and watched them pecking at the vegetables, a smile on her face. Her animals, her *beloved* animals. They were uncomplicated in personality, simple in their needs and ample in their affection.

'Now – Eddie, Clarrie. Where are you?'

Matilda clung to a fence post next to the door – that particular fence was necessary to protect her latest crop of carrots from the animals – and took a tentative step down into the garden, worried that her knee might give way at any moment. Then, she spotted Eddie. He was walking up from the end of the garden, where he'd been eating the grass on the other side of the fence. But where was Clarrie? She looked left and right, assessing the runner beans as she did so – they were growing well, and the next crop would be ready to be picked in a few days – and the tomatoes on the right, which were climbing with vigour up cane wigwams.

Then, a white furry face emerged from behind the tomato plants.

'Clarrie! There you are. Come over here, I've got some food for you, too. I wouldn't miss you out.'

Clarrie was a five-year-old crossbreed, born to one of Matilda's favourite goats, Jill, who had been a mix of white and brown and a great milker. She'd been an intelligent goat, apparently capable of knowing when Matilda needed company and when she didn't, and Clarrie had inherited this trait from her. She was incredibly independent and didn't seem to like Eddie much (except in mating season), and sometimes, Matilda thought, she seemed more human than goat. Which was ironic, given how much Matilda tried to avoid actual humans.

Matilda turned to her right, and, propping herself up against the wall as she went, walked over to the old outside toilet, which was now a storehouse for animal feed. She opened the door, braced her left arm on her leg and bent down as far as she could go, far enough so that she could scoop grain out of the sack which was resting on the toilet seat.

She stood back up, the scoop in her hand, and shuffled slowly along to the feeding trough she'd made out of several old paint cans. She deposited the grain in there and watched as Eddie and Clarrie cottoned on and ran towards it, their tiny fluffy tails bobbing as they did so.

Once she'd made sure they'd both had enough to eat, she worked the rest of the way through her morning chore list: fill up the water troughs, put food out for the cats, and scoop up any poo on the paths and put it either on the vegetables to act as fertiliser; or, if she didn't have room for it on the beds, she'd toss the occasional one over the fence. Until recently she had only thrown it into the field at the end of the garden, but now that she struggled with her mobility, she had taken to chucking it over whichever fence was nearest. It was biodegradable, anyway, she reasoned, and neither of her neighbours went into their gardens much, so she was sure they wouldn't notice a poo or two among their hedges and shrubs.

Forty-five back-breaking minutes later, Matilda was satisfied her morning tasks were done. She ached all over and her stomach was telling her it was breakfast time. What might it be today, she wondered, as she hobbled back in the direction of the house. Corned beef? Tuna? Oxtail soup? The world was her oyster, she thought, chuckling to herself at the absurdity of that statement. She hadn't left the county in over seventy years.

When she reached the back door, Matilda grabbed hold of the frame, hauled herself upwards and, with significant effort, raised her right foot high enough to clear the threshold. Once inside, she pushed the door closed behind her and walked slowly and carefully to her cans in the hall. As she did so, a memory came to her of rows of long tables and the clicking of cutlery against cheap porcelain, and she shivered. *No*, she thought; never again. Leaving there was the best thing I ever did.

She'd reached the door that led into the hallway. The walls on each side were lined with tin cans, some of them full but the majority empty, and she was careful not to lean on them too much because they were liable to topple. She wondered, for the fourth time that morning, where she'd left her umbrella. She thought it had been beside her on the floor while she slept, but she hadn't had it since and heaven knew whether she'd ever find it again. She had a few more umbrellas about, however, and they were all as useful to lean on as each other. She'd find one of them eventually.

Matilda was out of breath by the time she made it to the hall. She could feel her heart thrashing away like mad, and the heat in the house was oppressive. She needed to choose something to eat for breakfast and get out of here, back into the garden where it was cooler. Yes, she thought, I'll just pick one of these ones nearest to me. Dean had brought them a year or two ago now, and they probably needed eating. She examined the stack in front of her. Some of the labels were a bit dusty, but she could still make out what they said. Tomato soup? Hmm, no, she thought, not this morning. Oxtail? No, she didn't feel like that today. Baked beans with sausages? Bingo. Yes, that was proper breakfast food. It was several rows down, though, so a little tricky to access. Matilda lifted up her left arm, reached forwards and grabbed onto a stack of cans to the left, aware she needed support to achieve her goal.

It was a second or two before she realised her mistake. She had pressed too hard on the top can, which was unevenly balanced on the stack below. She watched as, almost in slow motion, a cascade of cans poured down upon her. She was forced back by the blow, falling into the stack of cans behind her, which shifted and then began to tumble.

Then a series of heavy objects fell on her head, and there was darkness.

— 3 —

July

Constance

'Fucking hell! *Will somebody please stop those fucking things making that fucking racket*,' yelled Connie, aware as she did so that as she was the only one home, no one was going to hear her. She took one of the pillows out from under her head and clamped it over her ears, but it was no good; she could still hear the bloody goats. She had been trying to get to sleep now for several hours, but the noise from next door was so distracting, even her nightly vodka hadn't sent her off.

Connie opened one eye and checked her clock. It was 11 p.m., at least three hours past her usual bedtime. She went to bed early every night so that she wouldn't feel too shitty getting up at 4 a.m., and usually she was well and truly away with the fairies by eight. Tonight, however, she was having no such luck, which was particularly bad because they'd made a racket yesterday, too, for several hours after dark. That meant that two nights of not enough sleep beckoned for Connie, and she knew very well that this was bad, bad news, because Connie needed her sleep. The lifestyle he had encouraged her to lead had deprived her of it, and she realised now that this had been part of the reason for her downfall. Her mental health, which even on good days teetered on the brink, plunged her into darkness when she was tired. Genuinely, a good night's sleep was all that stood between her and Armageddon.

Right, she thought. *Right.* I am going to have to do something about this.

Connie sat up, swung her legs over the side of the bed, and formulated a plan. It wasn't a very complicated one. It simply involved banging the hell out of next door's front door, and yelling through the letterbox. Matilda needed to get her bloody livestock under control, and clearly she needed a prod to make her do it. Maybe she should try writing a letter to the council, too? Surely she could persuade them to move Matilda on for reasons of hygiene or nuisance.

Connie paused for a moment and listened to the noise more closely. It *was* odd, though. This was the first time in her memory that the animals next door had bothered them after dark. Why were they making such a din now, she wondered. It was genuinely strange. Maybe a fox had got into one of the enclosures, or something? She needed to find out what the issue was, so that she could sleep in silence.

Connie made her way downstairs, reached for the house keys from the hook beside the front door and put them in the breast pocket of her pyjamas. Getting locked out would be very bad, because her mum was on a night shift.

She opened the door and stepped out, catching her breath as a small figure ran just a few feet in front of her across the path, towards the road. It took her a few seconds to realise it was a fox. Maybe it had come from next door, and the animals would go to sleep now? That would be nice, Connie thought, continuing to follow the fox, which was now under the streetlight. The streetlights in their small estate would be on for only another hour. The council had decided to switch them off at midnight a while back, to save money. It didn't bother her, because she never went out any more, but she supposed people who had a social life might not like coming home in the dark.

The fox was staring at her. It was a young one by the look of it, but despite its youth it certainly had no fear. What are you thinking, little fox. Are you wondering why the scary-looking lady is out of her house at this time of night? Well, I'm wondering that too.

What the hell am I doing, she thought. I should be in bed, not imagining a conversation with a bloody animal.

But then the goats started screaming again. So it wasn't a fox, she realised. Well, not this one, anyway. As she walked down her path and turned in the direction of Matilda's front door, the fox tiptoed away.

'Mat-tillllI-daaaaaaah.'

Connie was leaning down, shouting through the old woman's letterbox.

There were no lights on in the house, so she wasn't awake. Unless she reads by candlelight, Connie thought. But even if she was asleep, why wasn't she coming to the door? Connie wondered if she might be deaf. She probably was, at her age. How old was she? In her eighties? Nineties? One of those, anyway. Oh well, she'd just have to keep shouting until she woke her up. She had already tried hammering on the door, and that hadn't roused her.

'Mat-till... *oh fuck*,' she shouted, as someone tapped her on the back and she shot out of her skin.

She spun around to find Mr Road Fixer, Mr Hoarder's lodger, standing behind her. She hadn't seen him this close up before. He was just a little bit taller than her, maybe five foot eleven, had closely clipped dark brown hair and was dressed in jeans and a short-sleeved shiny grey shirt. He looked wet. Connie wasn't sure whether it was the material, the shadow from the streetlight, or whether he was actually soaked with sweat. She also wondered whether he was just going out, or just coming home. But then she caught a strong whiff of alcohol, and concluded that it was the latter.

'Is something wrong with Matilda?' he said.

'I don't know,' snapped Connie, aware suddenly that she was wearing only her pyjamas and no underwear, and that her wayward, curly dark brown hair was in a very messy top-knot, and that she probably had yesterday's mascara decorating her cheeks. She wrapped her arms across her chest. 'She's probably just asleep and deaf as a doornail. I'm here because of the goats.'

'The goats?'

'Yeah, can't you hear them?'

They both stood there in silence. Actual proper silence, because the goats had apparently shut up. Connie swore under her breath.

'I can't hear anything.'

'I promise you, they've been at it for hours. Screaming, they are. Bloody screaming.'

'Well, there's nothing now.'

Connie gave Mr Road Fixer a withering glare.

'Do you think I'd be out of bed and over here for nothing?'

Just then, one of the goats let out a screeching cry, as if mourning its soulmate.

'Ah, I see,' he said, scratching his chin. 'Yeah, that sounds like a distress call to me.'

'Do you speak goat, then?' asked Connie, her voice dripping with sarcasm.

'Yeah, actually I do, as it 'appens. My aunt used to keep goats.'

'Oh, right. Well, what are they bloody saying?' said Connie, her hands tensing up into small fists.

'They're probably 'ungry. Or injured.'

'Right,' she said, rolling her eyes. 'So do you have any bright ideas about how to fix this?'

'Well, we need to get to them,' he said, walking back down Matilda's path and turning right.

'Where are you going?'

'To your place. She's not answering the door, is she? And 'er side gate is locked. So we need to get into your garden and then over the fence. Something's up.'

Bloody hell, thought Connie, as she followed him down her garden path and towards their side gate. I just want to go to bed. I don't like people and I don't like animals. I just want you all to go away.

She watched as her neighbour pushed the catch down and walked through their garden gate as if he owned the place, before grabbing one of their plastic garden chairs and placing it next to the fence.

'Can you give me an 'and?' he asked.

'Doing what?'

'Blimey, you special or something? I just want you to 'old the chair for me while I climb over.'

Connie bristled. 'There's no need to take that tone with me,' she replied, sounding, even to her ears, like a trussed-up character from a Jane Austen novel. She knew her face was now the shade of beetroot; it always went that colour when she was angry. Luckily, however, they had no light in the garden, so Mr Road Fixer couldn't see it.

'Yeah, OK, sorry Posh Spice. Right. I'm going over,' he said.

'*Posh Spice*?'

'Keep your 'air on. It's only a little nickname. You don't sound like the rest of us, do ya?'

Connie lit up with rage, because he had accidentally nudged the enormous chip on her shoulder.

'I grew up here too, you know. I went to the local school, put up with the shitty council maintenance of this estate, the disappearing local shops, the crap public transport. There's nothing posh about me, all right? I just moved away for a bit. Picked up a different way of speaking. That's all.'

'Whatever. Suit yourself,' he said, pulling himself up on the wall.

Then Connie heard a thump. She turned around, and he was no longer beside her.

'Are you OK?' she said, tempted to just walk away and leave him there.

'Yeah, fine. Fell on a pile of soil. At least, I 'ope it's soil...'

Connie smiled, despite herself. 'Right, let me see. I need to turn the torch on my phone on. 'Ang on a sec.'

Connie waited, tapping her fingers on her forearms.

'Right. We 'ave light. Yeah, so... Christ, it's a bit of a mess 'ere. OK, so there are a couple of goats 'ere, and... *Shit, they're coming for me.*'

Then there was a yelp, and Connie panicked. She climbed up on the chair and peered over the fence.

'Mr Road...!' she shouted into the darkness.

There was a moment of silence, and Connie thought the worst.

'Who the fuck is Mr Road? I'm Jamie, Posh Spice,' he said, laughing. 'And I'm fine, thank you for your concern. They're just nibbling at me. They're 'ungry, definitely 'ungry. Let me see if I can find them some food first.'

Connie watched as Mr Road Fixer – Jamie – walked around the garden searching for food, finally discovering some behind the door of the outside toilet.

'*'Ere, little ones. 'Ere. Food,*' he called, his voice soft. Connie's eyes had adjusted now, and she could see the goats were almost throwing themselves at their meal.

'Look, they're starving, bless them. Do they cry like this often, the goats? I 'aven't 'eard them before, although I suppose we're a couple of 'ouses over,' he said.

'No,' replied Connie, still hanging onto the fence in front of her. 'I honestly haven't heard them make that noise before, except for last night, when they were making the same racket.'

'Shit. They might've been without food for two days, then.'

Connie tried to remember if she'd seen Matilda around yesterday. She'd noticed her every day, several times, for all of her early childhood, scrabbling around in her back garden, shovelling, scattering, picking, all of that stuff. And she'd spotted her fairly regularly since she'd moved back home a couple of months ago, although definitely less often these days, now she was knocking on a bit. But had she seen her yesterday? She couldn't really remember. She was losing track generally. Her formulaic routine and lack of a job meant that there were no identifying features to tell the days apart.

'Yes, maybe.'

'Didn't you wonder, yesterday, with the noise?'

His voice was accusatory. Connie's hackles rose.

'Unlike you, I'm not an expert on goat psychology,' she replied. 'I had no idea.'

'Have you seen 'er outside? Matilda, I mean?'

'Dunno,' she said, making an effort to drop her new accent, and return to the Worcestershire lilt of her youth. But it sounded strange in her mouth, foreign.

'OK,' he said, suddenly walking towards the house.

'What are you doing?'

'I'm going to check inside, Connie,' he said. 'If she's not feeding the animals, then I reckon something's wrong with old Matilda.' From her position standing on the chair, looking over the fence, Connie watched as he walked to the back door and turned the handle. He was far braver than her, she thought. There was nothing on heaven or earth that would persuade her to go inside that hovel.

It took Connie a moment or two to register that Jamie had used her name, and she hadn't given it to him. She was about to call out to ask him how he knew it, when he yanked Matilda's back door open and walked in. Then she heard him take a few steps forwards, before retreating at speed.

'*Call an ambulance*,' he shouted, taking big gulps of fresh air now he was back in the garden. 'I think she's dead.'

— 4 —

July

Matilda

There was a fly circling above Matilda's head. It was a bluebottle. It made sense that it had sought her out, she thought. They were attracted to dead bodies.

She'd seen them do it many times, like when one of the goats had had a stillborn kid and she'd left the body out until the morning, not to mention the many times the foxes had got into the chicken run. That was always a truly horrendous mess, the result of pure savagery. Yes, nature was cruel, that was certain, but at least it was predictable; it conformed to a rule book that was rarely changed. Bluebottles, you see, always chose dead bodies as the place to lay their eggs. Forensic scientists relied upon this very fact to judge how long it had been since someone had popped their clogs. Except this time, they wouldn't know, because it wasn't going to land on her, not if she could help it, she thought. She might be dead, but she still had her pride.

Hang on a second, she thought. If I'm dead, where is heaven? Am I there? Will I be stuck in heaven with all of the flies I've swatted throughout my life? That, surely, would be a bit like... hell?

She tried to raise her hand to swat at the bluebottle, but it seemed to be tethered to something, and she couldn't get it to move. So she tried another tack.

'Shoo,' she said, as loudly as she could manage. It came out more like a whisper, but she was still pretty impressed, given that she was deceased. She had always believed in spirits, of the soul continuing on earth after death, and this was proof of it. 'Shoooooo. Go away. Land on another dead body. This one's taken.'

'Matilda?'

It was a woman's voice, an unfamiliar one. Mind you, what am I saying, thought Matilda. Every voice, except my own, is unfamiliar to me these days.

'Matilda? Are you awake?'

Matilda became aware of an object to the right of her. It was blurry, very blurry, but she thought it might be human. But then, it might be an angel. Could it be Gabriel? Or Michael? Or Uriel? Or Raphael? Raphael, the healer, had always been a favourite of hers, and given her comfort. She had prayed and prayed to him when she had lain in a rigid metal bed in a large room in the darkness, surrounded by many others, but still very much alone.

Matilda tried to speak again, but it came out as more of a murmur.

'OK, OK, don't try to talk or move. You've got a mask on your face, and some lines in your arms. You've been poorly for a while, Matilda, very poorly. You hit your head and then you got severely dehydrated. But you're in hospital now and you're OK. Try to rest.'

So I'm in hospital, thought Matilda. Not dead. But how on earth did I end up here?

She wondered how anyone could have found her and called an ambulance. It seemed incredibly unlikely. She'd always known that when her time came she'd probably be discovered months after she'd died, by which time she would be a shrivelled-up prune, just rags and bones, and she'd been fine with that, honestly quite fine. But she'd always thought that she'd have warning, that she'd know she was on the way out, so she'd have time to ask Dean, the farmer's son she bought feed from, to come and take the animals before she had breathed her last.

Hang on a minute, she thought. The animals.

Horror swept through her. They could be starving by now. They need me. I'm all they've got, and I've let them down. I'm a selfish, selfish woman. They were right about me after all. I am mad.

'Howww long...' she said, her mouth straining against the mask, which was pumping cool oxygen into her lungs.

'You came in last night,' the woman replied.

So she'd only been here for a night. But when had she fallen? When had she been knocked out? Matilda had no idea how long she'd been lying there. She thought she'd heard Brian crowing at least once, perhaps even twice. Had she been out of it for two days? Oh my goodness, she thought. They won't be able to survive much longer, not in this heat. She'd left water out, but...

'The... ani... mals...' she said.

'Sorry, lovely, I can't quite hear you properly,' the woman replied.

'The ani... mals...' she said again, twisting her body and trying to sit up, but she found that she simply couldn't. She didn't have the strength.

There was a silence, and someone lifted the mask from her face.

'Try again now. What is it you're trying to say?'

Matilda looked straight at the woman, who was only about ten inches from her face. She was coming into view a bit now, although her glasses would have made her a lot clearer. She was young, she thought, maybe about thirty, with brown straight hair in a ponytail.

'The. Ani... mals,' she said again, her voice now barely a whisper. It felt like she was using the large scrapings of energy from a very empty tank. 'My... animals.'

'I don't know anything about any animals,' the woman

said. 'Do you have pets? If so, don't worry love, I'm sure the neighbours have taken them in.'

Matilda doubted that most sincerely.

'No. I... have... animals,' she said, a jolt of adrenaline giving her a reserve of energy she didn't know she had. 'They need food. Call... Dean...'

She could see that the nurse wasn't really taking this seriously. She probably thinks I've got a Bichon Frisé or an ageing Siamese, she thought. She has *no idea.*

The nurse was fiddling with a drain in Matilda's right hand, not looking at her. She needed her to understand that this was a matter of life and death. Literally; if the animals went, Matilda would go too. She couldn't live without them. So she took a chance, and raised her own hand just enough to grab hold of the nurse's arm. It worked. The nurse looked up at her in shock, and Matilda used her last burst of energy to say what she needed to say.

'*They need food*, do you hear... Feed the animals.'

Seeing that the nurse had heard her and was nodding, Matilda let go of her arm and sank back into the sheets. A wave of exhaustion came over her, and this time she was powerless to resist. She hoped the nurse would listen and get Dean, or the RSPCA, or whoever it might be, to look after her darlings. Because they were part of her... her lifejacket in a tempestuous sea... and anchor...

As she began to lose consciousness she felt the nurse stroke her arm, just as her mother had done when she was small and couldn't sleep because of the bombing.

'That's it. You rest, Matilda. I'll tell them. I'll let them know.'

— 5 —

July

Constance

Connie had got back from her walk a couple of hours ago, downed some vodka, and was watching the final episode of season two of *Gilmore Girls*. She had been craving some resolutions, some happy-ever-afters, even though, as in all serial dramas, the unravelled threads would be jumbled up once more, come season three.

And then the doorbell had rung.

Connie had sat up abruptly on her bed and put her head in her hands, holding her breath. Could it be him, she wondered. Had he decided that today was the day to come and expose her for what she was? Her heart was thrashing in her chest. She considered running away, sprinting down the stairs and out into the garden and the fields beyond, but she knew he'd hear her if she did that, and he could run faster than she ever could.

The bell rang again.

'*Hello? Can you hear me?*'

It was a woman's voice, shouting.

Connie relaxed a little. So it wasn't *him*. But if it wasn't him, who was so bloody determined to see her? And why wouldn't they go away? She realised her TV had been on quite loudly until a minute or so ago, and wished she'd turned it off earlier.

'*Hello?* I need to talk to you. Please come down.'

Who the hell was it? No one ever came to the house when her mum was out, except delivery people, and they never stayed long. She hit pause, swung her legs off the bed and tiptoed to the window, where she peered through the crack in the curtains.

Shit.

It was the police.

Suppressed, unwanted images flashed through her mind in quick succession: of her hands being held behind her back; of screaming, screaming over and over again, until she had grown hoarse; of the eyes of strangers boring into her and condemning her.

She wondered whether she could get away with ignoring them.

But if she did, they would break down the door, wouldn't they? They did that. Depending on what they were here for. And what was that? It couldn't be about... that... could it? That was all done with.

Then she had a sudden realisation. They've come because I've been trespassing on the fields, she thought. Maybe Dean or someone else saw her and reported her? This was not good. Not good at all. How bloody, bloody stupid she'd been. She had come here to fade away into anonymity, and now she'd undone all of her efforts.

The doorbell rang once more.

Connie felt, not for the first time that year, that she was well and truly beaten. She got out of bed and shoved her hair into a loose ponytail. As she walked down the stairs, she took in every detail of her childhood home: the school portraits of her that were hanging on the walls; the green carpet which had worn through in several places, perilously close to the carpet gripper; the slim white bookcase in the downstairs hallway which contained all of her childhood favourites. Had she been wrong to come back here? Perhaps, she thought. Perhaps. Home was supposed to be a safe place, but then, she had long lost sight of where her home actually was. And if she didn't know where her home was, how on earth could she be safe there, or anywhere?

Connie took a deep breath and opened the door, to find the police officer walking away up the path. Should she close it quietly and walk away, she wondered. Maybe they'd leave her alone?

No. They obviously knew where she lived now. There was no point putting it off, only to have to face it all later.

'Hello?' she said, her voice quiet and questioning.

The police officer turned.

'Oh hi,' she replied. 'I'd come to the conclusion that you'd gone out and left the TV on for the family dog, or something. Your neighbour over there definitely seems to need to do that for hers.'

Ah yes, the infamous Snuggles. He looked like he wanted to eat everyone, all of the time, even when he was asleep. Connie couldn't imagine the officer would have lingered long outside Ms Yoga Mat's front door.

So she's been to Ms Yoga Mat's place to look for me, thought Connie. Must have been confused by their lack of house number. They really needed to put it back up, she thought. It had fallen off when the door slammed in the wind, and was currently resting down by a flower pot next to the front step.

'No, we don't have a dog,' she said. 'We don't have pets. I'm... allergic. Sorry,' she said, thinking: *shut up, Constance, you're gabbling. She'll sense your guilt.* 'I just couldn't hear you, I'm sorry. It was on too loud. Apologies.'

'Yeah, no worries,' the officer said, returning to the front door to talk to Connie. 'I'm sorry to bother you on a Saturday morning, it's just we have a problem and I've been asked to try to solve it.' Connie put on her most concerned face, the one she felt was most appropriate when discussing the local farmer's spoiled wheat. 'The thing is... are you friendly with the lady next door?'

Connie was so shocked she almost spluttered. So they aren't

after me, she thought. Relief flooded through her. Thank heavens for that.

'*Not friendly*, no,' she replied. 'She's… not very into people? She shouts if you come too close to her front door, keeps herself to herself, that sort of thing.' Connie was warming to her theme. Now she knew that she wasn't about to be arrested, she felt like she could talk about Matilda all day. 'I've only really seen her at a distance in the garden, and then of course last night when she was being carried away on a stretcher. I'm really sorry she's dead, of course, poor thing. She must have had a strange and lonely life.'

The police officer blinked.

'She's not dead, madam,' she replied. 'She's poorly, though, and she's in hospital, and will be there for a while, so I'm told. But no, she's not dead.'

'Oh. *Oh, good*,' said Connie, genuinely experiencing relief at the news, and then feeling surprised at her reaction. They were neighbours, yes, but she had never spoken to Matilda at all. They weren't friends, or even acquaintances. She had even been afraid of her as a child. But there was something about the old woman's decision to cut herself off from the world that she sort of respected. Connie was equally keen to avoid all other humans, after all.

'She'd been there a long time, poor love,' said the officer. 'Really awful in this heat. I'm amazed she survived.'

Yes, that must have been horrendous, Connie thought, putting herself in Matilda's position. What if *she'd* fallen, and she didn't live with her mum? No one would find her for days. No one would miss her. No one at all.

'Yeah, how horrible,' she said, feeling sorry for herself almost as much as she felt sorry for the lonely old woman next door…

'Anyway, the thing I've come about is the animals.'

Connie's empathy for Matilda evaporated into thin air. Now they were onto a subject she really couldn't face thinking about.

'The animals?'

'Yes, madam. You'll be aware of course that Miss Reynolds has, erm... a large collection of animals.'

'Yeah. They make a racket and they stink.'

'Yes, I can imagine they do. Anyway, the thing is, obviously Miss Reynolds can't look after them while she's in hospital, and we've been unable to locate any next of kin. Do you know if she has any?'

'Not that I know of. We've never seen anyone go into her house, ever, so... if she does, they're definitely not close.'

'Right, I see. The thing is, normally, a social worker or someone like that would be given the job of trying to sort out things here. Because obviously, Miss Reynolds needs... help, with the animals and other things, too. But the issue is that it's the weekend, and a social worker can't come out until Monday, we don't have any more weekend cover due to budget cuts. So instead, they've sent me. And we've called the RSPCA, but they can't come out until Tuesday at the earliest. We need someone to feed them until that happens. And we... I... wondered if you might?'

From somewhere deep inside Connie's brain came an image of a hoof heading for her head. She could still feel the blow to her stomach, and how it felt to fall down, face down, the ground rising to meet her.

'Are you OK, Miss...'

Connie was clutching her head with both hands, hoping that if she squeezed hard enough, she could rid herself of the images that kept coming. It took her a few seconds to realise what she was doing, and that she was doing it in company.

'Sorry... Yes, I'm OK,' she said, fighting to stay present, to not collapse within herself. 'It's a... migraine.'

'Oh, I get those, you have my sympathies,' said the officer. 'Alternate paracetamol and ibuprofen, and lie down in a dark room.'

'Yeah, thanks, I'll do that,' said Connie, retreating back into the hall, hoping the police officer would get the hint.

'So will you do it? Will you feed the animals? I'm told all the food is there, you just need to give it to them twice a day. The side gate is now unlocked.'

'I really don't know...' said Connie, as she pushed the door a little, to signal that she was done with this particular conversation.

'Please? It's only until Tuesday. Monday, maybe, if the RSPCA turns up sooner. I don't want to go back to the woman with the Alsatian, and I was on nights last night and my shift finished two hours ago...'

Oh, for fuck's sake, thought Connie. This is why I hate people. I'm getting a guilt trip from a copper.

'Look, I can't, OK? I just can't...' said Connie.

The police officer's face fell. Connie felt guilty for making her shift longer, of course she did, but her need to shut the door on the world, coupled with her fear, was too much to make her say yes.

'OK then. I guess I'll see if any of the other neighbours can do it. But I tried a couple on the other side of the road already, and they seem very elderly and infirm...'

'Who's infirm?'

Connie, who was about to shut the door and exhale a sigh of relief, looked up to see her mother walking down the path, coming home from her own night shift.

'Oh, hi,' said the officer. 'I was just telling your... sorry... I'm not sure of your relationship?'

'I'm her daughter,' said Connie, who was now shifting her weight from one foot to the other.

'Right, yeah, I was just telling your daughter that the couple over the road are too infirm to look after the old lady's animals, and the other woman next door's dog tried to eat me, so I'm not sure about her, but...'

'Whose animals? You mean Matilda's? Did something happen to her?' said Ellen, reaching the front door, giving Connie a quick kiss on the cheek and putting her handbag down on the floor.

'Yes, she went into hospital last night. I believe your daughter...'

'Constance. Connie. My name is Connie.'

'Yes, I believe Connie actually called the ambulance for her.'

'Did you? Wow, well done you,' said Ellen, rubbing Connie's back as if she was a toddler with wind.

'Yes, and the thing is, Mrs...'

'I'm a Ms. I'm Ellen. Ellen Darke.'

'Yes, the thing is, Ms Darke – she can't look after the animals while she's in there, obviously, and we need someone to take care of them until the RSPCA takes over on Tuesday.'

'Oh, we'll do it,' said Ellen, without so much as a pause. If Connie had been younger or braver, she'd have jabbed her mother in the ribs at that moment.

'You will?'

'Yes, of course. It's only for a few days, right?'

No, no Mum, don't say we can do it. I can't. I just can't. And I know you mean for me to do this, not you. And I can't.

'Yes.'

'Well, that's fine. Will you tell us what to do?'

I'll tell you what I'm going to do, Mum, I'm going to run away where you'll never find me, that's what I'm going to do.

'Well, errr, I'm afraid I don't know too much about it, but I'm told there's food there for them. And I guess the rest is probably researchable on the internet?'

Connie could see that the officer was doubting even herself with that last statement, her clear desperation to shove off breaking through.

'Yes, that's fine, we'll cope,' replied Ellen.

'Great. Wonderful. I'll let control know. Thank you,' said the officer, who was already walking up the path at speed in the direction of her patrol car, probably worried they were about to change their minds.

Connie felt sick. She retreated into the kitchen and waited

until her mother had waved the officer off and shut the door before she let her know how she felt.

'*What the hell do you think you're doing, Mum*? You know how I feel about animals now. I can't do it. I just can't. And you're on nights the next couple of days, aren't you?'

Ellen ran her fingers through her hair and pulled her blue tunic over her hips, before retrieving a bowl, spoon and box of cereal from the cupboards.

'Connie, I really think it's time we talked about this phobia of yours,' she said, still with her back to her daughter. 'You used to love animals when you were small. You used to drag Grannie's little Billy into your bed at night. I don't really understand where this has come from.'

'You know where it's from, Mum,' said Connie, clutching her head, which was still throbbing. 'It was the... bull. And it's everything about them, now, all animals, that I can't stand... It's the smell, the noise...' She felt a shiver run through her. 'I just can't be near them. Any of them.'

'I think it's more than that,' said Ellen, taking the milk out of the fridge and turning towards Connie. 'I think...'

'I don't need your amateur psychology, Mum, thanks. You're a carer, not a doctor.' Connie saw her mum wince and, for the second time that morning, felt a surge of guilt run through her. 'Sorry, I didn't mean...'

'Yes, I'm sure you didn't,' she replied, sounding and looking a lot less furious than Connie would have been had the situation been reversed. 'Look. I think you need to go back to that counsellor.'

'Mum, I'm done talking. I've said all I can say.'

'I don't think you have, love. I really don't think you have.'

Connie refused to look at Ellen. Instead, she stared pointedly at the floor, her legs splayed wide – a stance she'd got very used to as a teenager, when she'd been rowing with her stepmother about curfews, her allowance or her latest school report.

'Look, go upstairs, Connie,' Ellen said, pouring milk into her bowl of cereal. 'I'll feed the animals. I'll go now, and then I'll get my sleep afterwards. And I suppose I'll feed them before I head out tonight, too. We can't let Matilda down.'

Connie hated the tone she was using. It reminded her of the tone she had used when she hadn't done her homework, or when she'd failed to hoover the stairs, or scrub the bath after use, or when her room had been messy in the morning. But she was an adult now. Surely her mother should be treating her with some respect?

Jesus, she should never have come back here. She had thought she would feel safe and cared for, but actually it felt to Connie like she was a child again, and that hadn't exactly been a picnic, either. Ellen just didn't seem to understand how dead she felt inside. She seemed to think talking about things could help, but frankly, Connie was long past that. It was like Ellen just wanted to ignore the elephant in the room, even though it was so enormous it was asphyxiating them both.

'*Look*. I'm broken, Mum, all right? I might look to you like I'm still functioning properly, but I'm not. I'm falling apart. I can't cope with myself, let alone a garden full of animals. I can't just pretend that everything is fine. So just give me a break. Please.'

Connie didn't wait to hear what Ellen would say in response. She ran up the stairs and slammed the door of her room, as she had countless times more than a decade previously. And once she was back in her room, she did just as she had then. She threw herself down on the bed, dug her nails into her pillow and attempted to cry her anger and despair away.

— 6 —

July

Matilda

The woman in the corner of the ward was shouting for her mother. Judging by the way she looked, Matilda reckoned that this particular woman's mother hadn't been around for a good quarter of a century at least, but there was something about being in hospital, she thought, something about being so entirely reliant on others, that made you regress back to your childhood.

If Matilda closed her eyes, she could picture her family's tiny front room in their terraced house in Croydon, with its tiled fireplace, its herringbone parquet floor and prints of rural scenes hanging from the picture rail. She could also picture a little girl of about two sitting cross-legged by the fireplace. She was trying to stack coloured blocks, but each time she tried more than three, the tower fell. In her mind's eye, Matilda kneels down opposite the toddler, and places one block on top of her short stack, and then another, and then another. Matilda sees the girl's face smile in wonder as the tower soars upwards, and her heart swells.

Yes, thinks Matilda. So this is what love looks like. This is what love *is*.

Matilda opened her eyes. She rarely thought about her own early years now. She kept herself busy so that she wouldn't have to. Her daily routine was a brilliant brick wall she'd constructed to keep her memories at bay. But being in here, devoid of any purpose, meant that chinks of light were beginning to break through that wall, and she was deeply unsettled by that. She didn't want to remember her mother stroking her arm as she read to her, or the freezing cold dormitory with the thin brown blankets, or the hand she clasped so hard her fingers went numb, or the sweep of rough black cotton as the cane came down, cutting the air like a knife.

What she wanted to think about, actually, was her animals. How were they, and who was feeding them? *Were* they being fed? She had spent most of the previous night lying awake worrying herself sick. The nurses knew about that, and they'd promised someone would come to talk to her about it today. She was impatiently awaiting their arrival. She wondered if they'd lied to her to try to placate her, and the thought made her feel furious. She might be old, but she absolutely was *not* a child who needed to be told little white lies. Why did so many people resort to treating pensioners like infants? It was so desperately insulting.

They'd been like that earlier that day, when two of the nurses had launched at her with flannels, hot water and a hairbrush. They'd talked her through it as if she was an imbecile, all 'Ooh, Miss Reynolds, you'll feel so much better when this is done,' and 'How soft your skin is, Miss Reynolds.' What utter rubbish. Matilda knew that her skin felt like leather and that her hair was knotted, greasy and lank, and she knew that she smelled a bit, and that that was why they were doing it. Why they felt the need to lie was entirely beyond her.

Apart from the animals, the only other thing she could bear thinking about today was her sole indulgence in life, *The Archers*. She'd been listening to the radio soap since she was a teenager. Ambridge, as all locals knew, was actually set in Worcestershire, which went by the name of Borsetshire in the show, for some reason Matilda couldn't fathom. The accents in the show sounded like the people she used to hear talking in the Stonecastle shop – back in the days when she'd gone in, that was. And despite the fact that she'd spent her earliest years near London, the local Worcestershire accent was an immense comfort. It seemed to her to be part and parcel of the nature all around her, of the farmers who worked the land, the hobby gardeners who tended their delicate blooms and the smallholders who nurtured their bees so they would produce delicious local honey. When she listened to *The Archers*, she felt at home, she felt safe, and she felt comforted.

Matilda strained for the controller she'd been given, the one with the button to summon help, and pressed it. A minute or so later, one of the nurses arrived at her bedside.

'Can I get you something, Miss Reynolds? Are you in pain?'

Matilda was in pain, actually, but she wasn't going to make a fuss about it. She was sure it would pass. She had never been one for pills.

'I'm fine, thank you. I just wondered whether you have a radio set in here?'

The nurse looked thoughtful.

'We have radio stations on the TV,' she said. 'You know, the TV set you have here –' she pointed to the square thing on the end of a long metal arm – 'you can listen to the radio stations without any credit, I think.'

'Does it have BBC Radio Four?'

'Yes, I *think* so,' said the nurse, who Matilda estimated to be about nineteen. She clearly doesn't listen to the radio, does she, thought Matilda. Imagine that; a life with no radio! She could not envisage her own life without it.

'Do you have headphones with you?' asked the nurse.

Matilda gave the girl a withering stare. She had never owned a pair of headphones.

'No.'

'Oh. Well, I think we have some we can share out. We took them in during Covid, infection control, you know, but there's some in a cupboard somewhere. Let me go and look.'

The girl seemed unaware of Matilda's disdain for headphones, which she realised was probably just as well. She nodded her thanks and closed her eyes. She didn't want to have a conversation with anyone in here, so she tried to look asleep most of the time so they wouldn't bother her. And if she could somehow listen to the radio all day via these headphones, then perhaps she could switch off from this place entirely.

'Miss Reynolds?'

Sleeping was obviously not going to be in her near future, however. She looked to the right, where a young man was standing. Well, young was of course a relative term. Pretty much everyone was younger than her. He was probably in his early thirties. He had a funny twirly moustache and a pointy beard, and he was wearing a tight blue shirt, its short sleeves showcasing two arms absolutely covered in tattoos.

Matilda hated tattoos. She thought they were ugly enough in the young, but absolutely diabolical on ageing skin, bringing to mind a toddler trying to draw a picture on a prune. What was it about this generation, and their refusal to consider a life beyond tomorrow, she thought. Had young people always been like that? Matilda considered her own childhood. Had she and her friends only lived for the now? Possibly. During the war they'd not even known if they'd be alive the following day. But then of course, they'd also all been taught that they'd live forever in the afterlife. They'd known that even if their current life was full of horror, their next one would be OK. What must it be like to have no hope of the hereafter? Lonely and rudderless, she decided.

Matilda looked again at the young man beside her bed, and concluded that he definitely didn't look like a professed Christian. But then, you could never tell. She had looked like one, once, and look at her now.

'Yes, I am she,' she replied.

'Hello, Miss Reynolds. May I sit down?'

'If you like.'

The man looked to be squirming, which suited Matilda fine,

because she had taken an instinctive dislike to him. She did that with people. Well, she'd *done* that with people, back in the days when she'd actually left her house.

The man pulled out the grey plastic chair beside Matilda's bed and sat down on it, turning it slightly so he could see her face.

'Thank you. Well, the thing is, Miss Reynolds... Matilda... Can I call you Matilda?'

'No.'

'OK then. Miss Reynolds. I'm Daniel Symonds. I'm a social worker. I've come to talk to you about your living conditions.'

'What about them?'

'When the paramedics came out to you, they said they found your house to be very cluttered.'

'Did they,' said Matilda, her voice deadpan. She was refusing to look at the silly man.

'Yes, they did. They said that you have so many things in your house that you aren't able to access your bedroom any more, and that you're sleeping on a mattress on the floor of your living room.'

'It's easier to sleep down there than to climb up the blinking stairs.'

'I see. How are you washing yourself, Miss Reynolds? The bathroom is full of things, too.'

'What were they doing looking up there? They had no right.'

'They were concerned about you, Miss Reynolds. We all are.'

'Are you, now?'

'Yes, we are. We are also worried about how you go to the toilet, and how you cook and eat.'

'I climb up the stairs when I need to. And I have plenty of food. I have stocks that last months. I am not starving.'

'I'm not saying you are, Miss Reynolds. But we are worried that your conditions are unsanitary.'

Matilda's head swivelled in the social worker's direction.

'*How. Dare. You.*'

'Miss Reynolds, I am only being honest. I am afraid your

house is in such poor condition now, we are going to have to inform the housing department. You are a council tenant?'

'Yes, of course I am. You know that. Roseacre Close is all council housing. But it's my house. I have never missed a rent payment, I can promise you that. You can't throw me out.'

'We don't want to throw you out, Miss Reynolds. We just want to help. We need to let the housing team know, so that they can come and check you haven't got any issues with the house. Sometimes hoard... people who have lots of possessions end up having infestations of pests, or issues with damp.'

'The house is perfectly fine. Perfectly. I do not need any interference from you. If they come and let themselves in, it will be trespass. I will not let them.'

'They are your landlord, Miss Reynolds. We are giving you notice now that we are coming to inspect the house tomorrow. It's the council's right to do so, and I would say in your own interests, too, as they'll have to pay to fix things for you if there are any problems. It will make your home nicer to live in.'

'Will it, now? I can't imagine how.'

'Well, let's see. They might be able to adapt your house a bit to get around it more easily. Also, Miss Reynolds, I need to talk to you about the animals.'

'Yes?' Her head snapped up. 'How are they? Are they OK? Is someone looking after them?'

'I'm told that one of your neighbours is helping in the short term, Miss Reynolds. But in the long term, we have two issues. One, we are not sure you'll be well enough to look after them when you are discharged from here, and two, we're worried that the animals constitute a nuisance to neighbours, which is a violation of your tenancy agreement.'

Matilda felt bile rising in her throat.

'You are an evil man, Mr... whatever your name is. I could tell that from the minute you walked in here. You have the devil in you, I'm sure of it. You came in here with the determination to have my animals put down, didn't you, and you're determined you're going to do it. But I won't let you,' she said, trying to push herself up in the bed, and to move her legs over the side. 'I just will *not*.'

'No one is going to put them down, Miss Reynolds. But some of them may need to be... removed.'

'Removed? You will not take my animals from me, young man. They are part of me. They are my... joy. They are my... friends... They are my...' The rest of the words Matilda wanted to say were swallowed up by the tears which were surging out of her eyes and down her face.

'Please calm yourself, Miss Reynolds. Nothing is decided yet. If you let us help you with the house, maybe you will be able to keep the animals...'

'*You absolute... devil...*' she shouted.

'Miss Reynolds! Miss Reynolds! Is there something wrong?'

Matilda could see one of the nurses running to her bed. It was the young, sweet, slightly gormless one, the one who didn't know what a radio set was.

'What's happened here?' the nurse asked the social worker. Matilda had now succeeded in slinging her right leg off the bed, but it was stuck at a jaunty angle. However, she was so upset, she just didn't care. The nurse lifted Matilda's leg back onto the bed and plumped up her pillow behind her, to try to persuade her to lie back down. 'You shouldn't upset her. She's been very poorly.'

'I'm sorry. I'm one of the social workers. My new boss sent me to talk to Mat... Miss Reynolds about her living situation. We want to help her.'

'Well, I'd suggest you come back another time,' the nurse said. 'When she's calmer. I can see you've upset her.'

'Right, yes, I will. Honestly, I didn't say anything bad to her.'

The young man seemed to be blushing, and Matilda was glad. He deserved to squirm.

'You want to take... you devil... You will never...' said Matilda, lying down and mumbling incoherently due to the mucus now pooling in her nostrils and throat. Matilda closed her eyes, and instead of seeing Daniel Symonds, she was seeing the shadow of a man through opaque glass, and that man was rapping at the door. She was huddled on the floor behind a chair, whispering, '*Shhh, my love, quiet now. Shhh, my darling. Shhh.*'

'*Go.* Please go,' said the nurse, and he sighed, stood up and walked away.

'He's gone now, Miss Reynolds,' said the nurse, who was now checking that the lines in Matilda's arms were still in place. 'He's gone. I won't let him come back until you're better.'

Matilda felt exhausted. She closed her eyes again and tried to block out the noises around her: the woman at the end, still shouting for her mother; the machine that helped the woman to her left breathe; the squeaking of the tea trolley in the next ward.

'Yes, you have a sleep,' said the nurse. 'But also, here are the headphones you asked for. I found some,' she added, putting something that felt like wire in Matilda's hands. 'I'll plug them in now – there, done – and I'll turn the system on and try to find Radio Four for you. Then it'll be ready when you want it. OK?'

After the young woman had walked away, Matilda fumbled for the wires and felt two small buds at each end. Without opening her eyes, she put one in each ear – and she had to push quite hard, as the bally things were so small – until she could hear something. It was the pips, the hourly beeps that told her it was 5 p.m., and thus time for one of her favourite programmes, PM, to start. That meant she had an hour and a half of news and discussion ahead of her, which she might dip in and out of, depending on how much politics they covered, followed by half an hour of comedy and then, blissfully, *The Archers*.

As she listened to the calm, well-paced headlines, she felt her breathing slowing down and her heart rate begin to ease. So, what actually happened there, she thought. *What on earth* happened there? That boy, man – was he telling me that they're going to send me into a home, and sell all of the animals? And which neighbour is looking after them? It had better not be that feckless girl. She seems to be a complete layabout. A disgrace.

— 7 —

July

Constance

The music begins, and the couple on the screen kiss – madly, deeply, truly. Obviously it won't last, thought Connie, as they're on that never ending TV drama roller coaster, but for this moment at least, everything is perfect. *Absolutely* perfect. Despite it being at least the fifth time she'd seen this particular episode, Connie felt the warmth of that moment spread through her, starting at her toes and working up her body to her fingertips.

Did people have moments like that in real life, she wondered. Did they actually, because *she* hadn't, even when she'd had someone kiss her passionately. Maybe they'd said something jarring, or they'd smelled a bit funny, or she'd not really been into it, or she'd been embarrassed to be seen kissing in public. No, she'd never, ever had a perfect moment like that, and she ached to. Deep down, of course, she also knew that expecting her life to be as perfect as a TV show was completely stupid, but nevertheless, she wanted it to be. It was crazy, frankly, that despite the shitshow she'd experienced over the past few years, she still harked after perfect, impossible romance.

As the credits for the episode began to roll, Connie's finger hovered over the 'next episode' button. Did she have time to watch another one, she debated. Because she should really be looking on the internet for work. Her mum had told her she expected it, and she needed to show she was trying, even though it was a token effort. She was worried that if she didn't, her mum might chuck her out. After all, Ellen's salary was low, and she had recently started to make noises about the cost of hot water and paying for her food – not that she ate much, frankly. But yes, she needed to do something small today to show that she was at least trying to make some money of her own, so that she could stay here for as long as it took for her to right herself. If she ever actually managed to do so.

She hauled herself out of bed and walked downstairs to the lounge. Her mum's laptop was on the coffee table. Connie sat down on their battered black leather sofa and pulled it towards her, flipping it open. As she did so, her eye caught something moving in her peripheral vision. It was brown and white and it was moving at speed.

'What... the...' she said, realising now what it was she was seeing.

There was a goat in their back garden.

Connie's response was immediate. Her heart started to beat like the clappers, and her palms began to sweat.

'*Shoo*,' she yelled automatically, despite the fact that she was inside and the bloody thing couldn't hear her. She rushed over to the French windows, turned the lock and ran out into Ellen's manicured, lovingly tended garden in her bare feet. 'Shoo! Go home!'

It must be one of the goats from next door. Her mother had fed them last night and that morning, and she obviously hadn't closed the gate properly.

'Shoo,' she said, running towards the animal and hoping it would move away from her. She needed it out of the garden, and fast. Memories of her encounter with the bull were at the forefront of her mind. She needed to get it back in the direction of their side gate and around the corner into Matilda's garden. But how the hell was she going to herd it back there? She needed some kind of sheepdog. Or a goat dog. Were there any goat dogs, actually? Did goats respond to dogs? Bloody hell, thought Connie; I'm losing it. I don't even own a bloody dog.

Connie surged towards the goat and made the loudest, most frightening sound she could manage, but the goat stood its ground. Instead of running away, it bleated at her, a whole-mouth bleat that showcased a full set of yellow teeth.

What she needed, she decided, was a rope that she could use as a lead. She could lasso it and lead it back next door. Yes, that would work. She cast around her, but no rope was forthcoming. Then she looked down at her dressing gown, and realised the cord around her waist would be perfect. She pulled it off and walked towards the animal, which was staring straight at her, as if issuing a challenge.

'There, there, pretty pretty,' said Connie, her hands shaking, not at all sure why she was trying to charm the goat with pleasant adjectives. She kept expecting the goat to turn and run at any moment, but it didn't, and before she knew it, she was standing right next to it, holding the cord just above its head. All she needed to do now, she thought, was to lean over and lower it down in a loop very slowly, and then she would…

'Ooooooffff.'

Just as she'd been about to do it, the goat had jerked away and she'd completely miscalculated her centre of balance. She'd fallen over, flat on her face, on the lawn.

'Sweet Jesus,' she said into the warm earth beneath. 'What the hell am I *doing*?' She lay there for a few moments, a smile on her lips at the sheer absurdity of the turn her morning was taking.

And then she let out a piercing shriek as something, or someone, touched her on the back. She rolled over at high speed, expecting to see Jamie, or maybe her mum. But it wasn't, of course. It was the bloody goat. It was now looming over her, its breath honking of grass and stomach juice and God knew what else, and its hooves were within inches of her face.

'Fuck,' she said, in a whisper, so that she didn't make things worse. 'Fuck…' In her mind, she could see the huge bull running at her. She would feel the impact in seconds. She closed her eyes and waited for everything to be over.

But it wasn't a kick or a punch that came for her – it was a lick.

She opened her eyes. The goat was an inch away from her nose. She took in its brown hairy ears, which stuck out at right angles from its head, and the streaks of dark chocolate fur that ran down its nose, and the feathers of fur that protruded from its chin. And then something amazing happened. Instead of fearing it, she laughed. A real belly laugh, too; something she hadn't done for a long while. Afterwards, she would struggle to explain why, except for the obviously ludicrous nature of the scene. She was lying on the grass, in her pyjamas and an open dressing gown without a cord, staring up at the jaunty face of an apparently affectionate goat with honking breath.

'Hello,' she said, once her laugh had subsided. The goat blinked. Connie noticed the short, straight brown eyelashes it had, which were similar to hers. Hers never grew any longer, and never curled. 'My name's Connie. What's your name?'

Shit, she thought. Now I'm trying to have a conversation with a goat. This day just keeps getting odder and odder. She stared at it for a few more seconds, before reaching out to pat it. It didn't even flinch when she curled her hand down its nose. It just stood there, its breath even, its body still.

'Aren't you a friendly little thing?' she said, pulling herself up to sitting. As she did this, the goat retreated a few steps and then lay down and curled up in front of her. In this position, with her above it and the goat below, Connie felt all residual fear melt away. She leaned forward and sniffed the goat's head, and inhaled the combination of hay, earth and that whiff that was undeniably goat – a smell she was accustomed to already, living next door to what amounted to a smallholding. It usually repulsed her, but today she felt differently about it. Close up, the goat smelled slightly sweet, if anything, and as she patted its coarse brown hair, she felt her breathing slow and her soul swell. This was how she felt when she was out walking in the fields, she realised. It was a peace she had never experienced in London, and it was why she had come back here. There was undoubtedly solace to be found in nature. She had discovered that as a kid, when she'd slammed the front door shut and gone on lengthy walks to try to diminish her anger and confusion. Natural things didn't argue with her, or abuse her, or shut her down.

Connie stared intently at the goat, which was still lying down in front of her.

'Are you going to argue with me?' she asked. 'Are you going to tell me to shut up?'

And then she laughed again, another full, unselfconscious laugh, both at the ridiculousness of talking to a goat, and at the sheer joy of no longer being frightened. In fact, she laughed so hard, she collapsed into the goat's stomach and then stayed there, listening for, and feeling, each of its breaths. And then, within a few minutes, she fell into a deep, easy sleep.

'Constance? Connie?'

Connie opened one eye and saw that her mother was standing by the French windows.

'Oh Mum, *hi*,' she said, trying to get up without support, but realising too late that she needed it, and ending up having to use the goat as a prop. 'What... what time is it?'

'It's noon. I've just nipped back in for a sandwich. What the... Why... A goat?' Ellen looked like a woman who'd just pulled back the curtains to discover the world had turned turtle.

'I was wondering the same thing,' said Connie, grinning. 'I ran in to try to get it out. It's from next door, obviously. You must have left the gate open...'

'I didn't. I definitely didn't,' said Ellen, walking towards her daughter and the wayward goat. 'But yes, it's one of Matilda's...'

'Oh well, anyway, yes, the goat came in here somehow and I tried to catch it but then I fell over and it licked me, and then, well... I don't know. Something magic happened and I wasn't frightened. Anyway, it's quite nice, the goat. And then I fell asleep.'

Connie could see her mother thought she was mad, which wasn't that unexpected, really, given that Ellen already spent most of the time telling her she needed to both take medication and see a therapist again.

'You fell asleep? Next to... the goat?' Even Ellen was smiling now.

'Yep,' said Connie, walking towards her mother in a post-nap daze, leaving the goat standing sentry-like where she'd been sleeping. 'It was hot.'

'Right, yes,' said Ellen, pulling Connie in for a hug. 'Well, I'm very pleased you have found a way around your phobia.'

'It's a real fear, Mum,' said Connie, bristling.

'Yes, fear. I'm glad. Very glad,' said Ellen, refusing to let go. They stood there for a moment, embracing in the garden, the only sound the rhythmic mastication of the goat.

It took Connie a few moments to register what that meant. Shit, she thought. Which of Mum's pampered plants is the goat eating?

'*Constance. It's eating my hydrangeas*,' said Ellen, who had clearly come to exactly the same realisation at exactly the same moment.

Connie turned round slowly and eyed the goat, which had its head deep in a large bush covered in beautiful blue flowers. 'Oh dear. I suppose we need to take it back.'

'I'd say we do,' said Ellen. Connie could feel her outrage building, and realised that she had to act fast before her mum lost her rag.

And then Connie realised something else. Mum thinks I'm going to refuse, thought Connie. She thinks I'm not brave enough to do it. She thinks she'll have to do it herself. She thinks I need medical help to do anything other than sleep, eat and drink. But she's wrong. Right now, oddly, I do feel brave enough.

'Yeah, I'll take it,' she replied. 'Do we have any rope?'

'Come on, Rory,' said Connie, as she led the goat along the path. She'd decided to name her after her favourite character in *Gilmore Girls*. It seemed to suit her.

The goat trotted along beside her without tugging at the rope, which it had accepted without question. When Connie reached the gate that led to Matilda's garden, she was surprised to find it closed.

'How on earth did you get through here?' she asked Rory. 'Did you jump? Dematerialise?'

'Who're you talkin' to?'

Connie jumped. She hadn't heard anyone coming down the road, but she turned to find Jamie, the neighbour who had climbed over their garden fence the other night, standing behind her. He was wearing his work clothes: bright yellow fluorescent trousers with reflective strips on them, and a baggy grey T-shirt that might once have been black.

'Oh, hello again. No one. Just the goat. Rory the Goat.'

'Rory, is it? How did *Rory* get out?'

I will not rise to the bait, thought Connie. I don't care if he thinks I'm mad. I am, anyway, aren't I? So if I just act unfussed, he'll go away more quickly, and I can continue having a nice, calm time with Rory.

'That's what I'm trying to work out,' she replied. 'Mum has been feeding the animals while the old lady is in hospital, but the gate seems to be shut, so… Any ideas, goat whisperer?' Connie couldn't resist the dig, despite her best efforts.

'Dunno. An 'ole in the fence?'

'We don't have any holes. Mum maintains the fence like it's a piece of furniture.' This was true. Ellen had once taken a week's leave to fix, fill and paint it.

'Maybe your mum left the gate open, but it blew shut?'

'Maybe,' replied Connie, doubting this most seriously, but deciding that it really wasn't worth the argument. 'Look, I've got to get Rory home and I've got to feed her, so…'

'Rory? Isn't that a boy's name?'

'Not always,' deep breaths, thought Connie, deep breaths, 'she's named after my favourite TV character – Lorelai, Rory for short. From *Gilmore Girls*. Don't expect you've ever seen it.'

'No, actually, I was just watching that yesterday.'

'Really?' Connie said that just a second before she realised he was joking. Just shut up and let him leave, she thought. You are making a fool of yourself.

'Nah.'

'Yes, well, whatever,' she replied with her most middle-class London voice, deciding he didn't deserve her toned-down efforts, which she had been trying to put on to fit back in. Who was she kidding? She had never fitted in anywhere. 'Look, I've got to be getting on. Posh Spice needs to give the animals their dinner,' she said, employing her most withering stare.

'OK, then,' he replied, and Connie turned away from him and opened the gate, which was closed but luckily unlocked. She was about to shut it behind her when Jamie spoke once more. 'What do you do for work, by the way… Connie? When you're not 'andling goats?' he asked.

'I'm between jobs,' she replied, answering, if anything, a little too quickly, she felt. She was glad the gate was blocking his view of her face. She hadn't had to use this line before and she suspected her expression might give the lie away. 'I resigned from my last post but haven't found anything new yet.'

'Nice. A rest. Sounds great. I'm just 'eading off for mine. A late shift.'

Connie nodded and pushed the gate back open a crack, knowing that carrying on a conversation without looking at him was a bit rude. She was still hoping that he'd push off, however. She'd come back here to keep away from people, not to get to know them better. Maybe he's trying to find more stuff out about me so that he can gossip with the neighbours and his mates, Connie thought, and the very idea of that made her feel sick. She didn't want any more people knowing her business.

There was an awkward silence. He probably expects me to reciprocate and ask what he does, doesn't he, she thought. That's the next thing. He doesn't know that I've already figured it out. Connie knew what everyone did in this estate, because she'd been watching them coming and going for these past few weeks. She hadn't had anything else to do.

'OK, great then. See you later,' she said, pulling the gate closed slowly, keen to keep her distance, and waving goodbye with a pasted-on smile.

'Connie,' he said, and she was forced to open it again, damn him. 'Do you know when Matilda will be out of 'ospital?'

'No, no one's said.'

'Oh, right. I can 'elp you feed the animals? Must be a lot to do on your own, like.'

'No, don't worry, I've got it covered,' she said, annoyed at his determination to talk to her. This was feeling more and more like an interrogation, and she'd had enough of those.

'OK, suit yourself. Come and knock on our door if you need anything. Martin's usually in, even if I'm not.'

'Right,' she replied, letting the gate shut and walking down the side passage in the direction of Matilda's back garden.

'Right then,' Jamie replied over the gate, his voice jolly, and apparently not at all bothered by her rudeness. He obviously can't tell when someone's not interested in him, she thought. He's probably so used to women falling at his feet and chasing him home that he's unable to compute that there might be at least one who isn't spellbound by his blue eyes and tousled brown hair. Connie was proud, actually, about how uninteresting she found him. She didn't need *any* man back in her life *ever* again.

Connie walked into Matilda's back garden with Rory by her side. As the other animals ran towards her and she felt absolutely no fear when they did so, she realised she was, for the first time in a long time, smiling.

— 8 —

August

Constance

'Rory! No! You *cannot* eat me. Eat the food. Look, I've put it on the floor for you. Eat. The. Food.'

It was 8 a.m., and the sun was well and truly up and ready for another day of baking Worcestershire's already parched earth. It hadn't rained for at least a month now. Connie wiped the sweat off her forehead with her arm, noting the dust that came off with it. This was messy, hot work.

Connie hadn't gone out for her early morning walks for a week. Instead, she'd walked next door and spent a good hour every day replenishing the water troughs, checking for eggs in the hen house, watering and picking the runner beans and the courgettes, and brushing and stroking the many, many cats. (She had lost count, as lots of them looked the same. She had also run out of names from *Gilmore Girls*, so she had ended up just calling them all Cat.)

After all of these chores had been done, she'd then set about tidying up a bit: pulling out weeds, picking up poo and chucking it over into the farmer's field at the end of the garden (it was good fertiliser anyway, she reasoned). Restoring order like this made her feel good, she discovered, as did watching things grow, both animals and vegetables alike.

After her morning's work was done, she'd sit down on the

back step and watch everything she'd tended to eat, play, grow and sleep, with Rory by her side. Sometimes, she'd fall asleep on her, as she had that first strange morning in her mother's garden.

How calm she felt in Matilda's smallholding, how relaxed, had come as a complete surprise to her. This odd twist of fate felt like a gift. This was, she now realised, the medication she had needed all along. She didn't need the chemicals everyone had told her she should take, after all. And she had thought previously that the solution to her problems was to avoid everything that was living and to drink herself into oblivion to dull the pain caused by the living, but she had now realised that in fact it was just humans she had to avoid. Other living creatures were fine, it turned out.

'Hello?'

Connie sat up, startled. Who the hell was this, she wondered. No one ever came to see Matilda.

'Yes?' she replied, standing up and brushing herself down just as a smartly dressed woman in her mid-fifties and a younger man with a hipster beard emerged from the side passage.

'Oh, hello,' said the woman.

'Hi,' replied Connie with force, angry that her moment of bliss had been interrupted. 'I'm Connie. I live next door. You are?'

'We're from the council,' said the woman. 'Well, social services, to be more precise. I'm Caroline, and this is Daniel. We're here to see how Matilda Reynolds has been living. We have received some letters from local residents about her set-up here.' So they did receive her mother's letters after all, thought Connie, wondering why it had taken them so long to act upon them. 'So we are here so that we can... work out how to... best support her.'

'Oh, great. Mum – Ellen? Ellen Darke? She wrote the letters. She's worried about Matilda's health. Mum's a carer, you see. She sees a lot of elderly people...'

'Right, yes,' replied Caroline, her face sporting a smile that stopped before it reached her eyes, which were casting around the back garden.

'You've been looking after the animals, have you?' Connie could tell that this Caroline couldn't quite work out why a well-spoken Londoner like her had found herself mucking out Matilda's animals, and frankly, she couldn't blame her. But also, Connie didn't feel like explaining, particularly to this woman, who also seemed out of place and in fact rather caustic.

'Yes, I have. They're doing very well. The chickens are laying every day, I've brushed all of the cats and Rory the goat is—'

'Great,' the woman said, interrupting Connie's flow.

'Yes,' replied Connie, disturbed by the woman's minimalist communication style, which reminded her of her old boss, and that wasn't a good thing. Connie felt her insides begin to churn. Out of the corner of her eye, she could see the man who'd come with her, Daniel, was looking uncomfortable.

'Well, don't let us stop you,' said the woman, ushering Daniel towards the back door. 'I assume this is still open?'

'Yeah, I think so,' said Connie. 'I haven't been in, though. I just put the vegetables I pick on that bench at the end of the garden—' she said, pointing to a pile in the distance that resembled a bounty worthy of a harvest festival.

'Good. Right. OK,' said the woman, as Daniel pulled the back door open. 'Oh, by the way… Connie. Are you OK looking after the animals for a bit longer? The RSPCA say they are under particular pressure at the moment, and with the animals being cared for here, it seems less urgent.'

Connie didn't even stop to think.

'Of course. I can look after them for as long as needed. Forever, if you need that.'

The older woman had an expression on her face that Connie struggled to read. Was she surprised? Pleased? Uneasy? It was impossible to say. Connie reckoned that this Caroline woman would be excellent at poker.

'Not forever, no. But for a bit. Thank you.'

'Do you know when she'll be out of hospital?' Connie asked.

'Not sure yet. Not immediately,' replied Daniel, speaking for the first time since he'd arrived. 'I visited her a week or so ago, and she seemed quite poorly.'

'Oh, right. Thanks,' replied Connie. 'I'll keep on feeding them until she comes back, then.'

Caroline and Daniel made their way into the jungle that was Matilda's house, and Connie went back to stroking Rory, who was enjoying both the attention and the morning shade.

Connie hadn't realised how much her happiness had hung on that final answer from the social worker, but when she had heard 'Not immediately' she had felt her spirits rise. It's like an addiction, this, she thought; the most healthy one I've ever had.

— 9 —

August

Matilda

'Good morning, Miss Reynolds.'

Matilda pulled her headphones out of her ears with great reluctance. Standing in front of her was that silly boy she'd met before, Daniel, along with a woman in her fifties who had a severely cut, angular, sleek silver bob. She seemed to be wearing an entire department store's worth of chunky jewellery, and the bright pink dress she had on was, in Matilda's opinion, far too clingy on the bust.

'Hello,' said Matilda, coughing as she did so. She was still feeling a bit rotten, if truth be told. Tired. Old. Achy. Her back was playing up still. And she had problems down below, too, but she was nonetheless managing to go to the toilet by herself, despite the nurses' best efforts, so that at least she was able to keep private. Sharing her bodily functions with all and sundry was not something she relished, but it seemed to be de rigueur in here. That poor woman in the corner had to have a bedpan, and two nurses had to stand there and help her use it several times a day. It must be deeply humiliating for her, Matilda thought. She hoped that if she ever lost control of her faculties, someone would just take her out and have her shot, like they did to old nags at the races.

'Hello. I'm Caroline, Miss Reynolds. I'm the head of social

services at the council. And this is Daniel. I believe you have already met.'

'Caroline what, may I ask?' Matilda believed firmly in surnames.

'Caroline Goodman, Miss Reynolds. And this is Daniel Symonds.'

Matilda looked this Daniel boy up and down. His shoulders seemed to be halfway up to his ears, almost touching his pointy beard. He doesn't want to be here, does he, she thought. Good. Go away, matey.

'Very well,' replied Matilda, modelling herself on a matriarch in a play by Oscar Wilde. 'What can I do for you, Miss Goodman?'

'Mrs Goodman.' Oh, it's like that, is it, thought Matilda. I see. 'Miss Reynolds, can we take a seat?'

'If you must.'

Matilda shuffled back up her bed a bit, so that she could try to look down on this strange pair. She was a relatively tall woman – she'd been taller than most of her peers – and she had learned long ago that height equalled power. She preferred this Caroline woman sitting down, if truth be told.

'So, Miss Reynolds, I believe that Daniel told you on his last visit that the council was going to inspect your home?'

'Yes.'

'Well, in the event, I went with him. I'm the new head of the department, by the way. I've been put in post to… sort things out a bit. So I accompanied Daniel yesterday.'

Matilda wondered why someone of management grade had felt it necessary to visit a rural council house. Surely that sort of work would be beneath her?

'Did you now?' Matilda replied, her voice dripping with sarcasm.

'Yes.'

'You went into my house without my permission?'

'The council is your landlord, Miss Reynolds. We gave you enough warning.'

Matilda's throat tightened.

'You should have waited until I got out of here.'

'Miss Reynolds, I have to tell you that we don't think you will ever move back into that house. It's simply not safe for you.'

Every muscle in Matilda's body went rigid.

'What?'

'The house is not safe for you. It's infested with rats and mice, and there's damp.'

Matilda knew about the rats – every place in the country had rats, if not indoors then definitely outdoors. But… damp?

'Damp?'

'Yes, Miss Reynolds, damp. When you have so many possessions in a small space with no air moving around, and you don't have heating, you get damp.'

'I have the fire on in the winter.'

'Do you? We tried to turn on your gas fire, but it didn't work. And you don't appear to have central heating. I can't imagine how the housing department missed you off the modernisation list. It's something I can only apologise for.'

When Matilda had moved into the house, it'd had a back boiler – a gas fire with a water heat exchanger fitted behind it which filled her hot water tank and a few radiators. But it had stopped working long ago, and she hadn't wanted to give the council any reason to come into the house, so she'd never reported that it was broken. Not to mention the fact that she'd ignored all letters they'd sent her for at least forty years.

'Miss Reynolds? Can you hear me?'

'Yes. I'm not deaf, you know.'

'So yes, anyway, you have damp. We need to send a surveyor in, actually, to check it's not also a problem with the construction.'

'There's nothing wrong with the house. It's solid, well built, will still be there long after I've gone.'

'So you say, Miss Reynolds, but even so. We are deeply concerned that you are not safe in that house, and that your current state is partly due to the conditions you were living in.'

'You can't get rid of me. I've got rights.'

'Miss Reynolds, when you moved in, the council had no idea you were going to run a smallholding out the back. This constitutes, by its noise and smell, a nuisance to other properties, and this is a violation of your contract with us. That gives us grounds for eviction. But we don't want to do that. What we want to do is to offer you alternative accommodation, somewhere more suitable, where we can give you support.'

Matilda was staring straight ahead. She refused to look at the evil woman beside her bed. There was absolutely no way she was ever going to move. She would leave that place in a box, and under no other circumstances.

'Miss Reynolds? What do you think?'

'No.'

'No to what?'

'No. I will not be moving.'

Caroline Goodman appeared to be hyperventilating. And the man with her, that Daniel creature, seemed to be physically shrinking, Matilda thought. Good. She was glad that at least someone was embarrassed by this display.

'Goodbye,' said Matilda. She sat staring straight ahead, waiting for Caroline's response, although none came. The two trolls skulked out a minute later, after they'd gathered up all of their things and what was left of their dignity.

As she saw Mrs Goodman's shiny pink rear head out of the door, she felt the first tears start to fall. She would not leave that house. Could not leave that house.

Because it held all of her secrets.

PART TWO

— 10 —

August

Constance

As Connie scattered grain for the chickens, she heard a rumble of thunder in the distance. She looked over the fence and saw a massive dark cloud forming over the distant hills. Rain, finally. It had been so long since they'd had any rain. She'd been watering the vegetables twice a day for the past two weeks, almost to the point of drowning them, desperately trying to give them protection from the searing midday sun.

She reached down and patted Rory, who was, as ever, her shadow. She found herself looking forward to their reunion every morning. It had been a long time since someone had been so glad to see her. As she stood back up and surveyed the fruits of her labours – happy, replete animals and bright green foliage on the fruit and vegetables – she allowed herself a moment of self-congratulation. No one, including her mum, could have foreseen how well she'd rise to this challenge. She certainly hadn't.

She'd spent more than twenty years of her life thinking that the whole world was against her, and she realised now that being in the concrete jungle of central London hadn't helped that at all. The rhythm and feel of her city days were getting increasingly hard to conjure, and that was a relief. She now couldn't comprehend the draw the capital had had on her, and the way she had willingly succumbed to it. She hadn't been herself there, and her regular use of mind-altering drugs had only been part of that. She'd been, what? Hypnotised? Bribed? Delusional? All three, perhaps.

Maybe she should have realised before now how much nature, the environment she'd grown up surrounded by, had meant to her. After all, she had gone on those daily dawn walks instinctively. She had obviously known, subconsciously at least, how much she needed to be around nature. It had turned out that actually there were *some* things she could find harmony with, and that discovery had changed everything.

After the past two years of hell, her expectations for the rest of her life had frankly been minimal. Retreating to rural Worcestershire had been instinctive. Everyone, including Him, had expected her to disappear afterwards, and she'd been OK with that. She'd been glad of it. She'd needed to feel safe. And she'd been satisfied, for a while at least, to live her life behind closed doors, through the characters on the TV screen and that vivid, dreamy version of herself that existed after about three swigs of vodka. She'd been too frightened of the world outside to want to be part of it again.

But then this had happened, this random twist of fate, and here she was, covered in dust and mud, her hair a halo of frizz thanks to the humidity, with giant sweat circles under her arms, and despite all that, with a smile on her face. And given she'd thought at one point that she'd never be able to smile again, that was definitely something worth celebrating.

It was during the second roll of thunder that she heard the car reversing in the drive. She thought nothing of it until she heard a voice she recognised, a voice she'd heard yelling from the other side of the fence or through her front door many times during her childhood.

'I'm fine. *Fine, do you hear me*? Just give me my stick.'

Shit. It was Matilda.

No one had warned Connie that she was coming back. She'd

assumed that social services would come and sort the house out a bit, clear it a little, before she returned to it. That's what her mother had asked for in those letters. She hadn't thought that Matilda would just – turn up.

'Wait, Miss Reynolds... I'll just get your wheelchair,' a man's voice said.

Panic took hold of Connie. The peace she had been feeling was suddenly shattered, and she realised that this entire little world she'd made for herself was now hanging in the balance. If Matilda was back, she wouldn't be needed any more, would she? So she wouldn't be able to see the animals again. The thought of being separated from them made her physically sick.

She needed to find a way to keep this going.

Then she had an idea.

It'll take her a couple of minutes to get here, thought Connie. I can use those minutes. I'll make this place look so good, she will want me to come back and help. Because she needs help, doesn't she?

Connie ran around the garden brushing up straw, scooping up poo, and moving the bench that had been at the end of the garden further up, so that Matilda could see the vegetables she'd managed to grow and store. She checked all of the chickens were in the henhouse, refreshed the cats' water and bowls of dried food, and finally walked over to where the two goats, who she'd named Rory and Lorelai, were standing, munching on some grass that was growing through the fence.

'Stop pushing me. I'm going to walk from here. I need to be able to walk,' said Matilda, her voice getting louder and louder as she was pushed down the side passage. Connie looked up as the footrest of a wheelchair came round the corner into the garden. She took a deep breath and composed herself. She had worked hard here and she knew she had a great deal to be proud of.

'*Hell*. What on earth happened here?' asked Matilda, her eyes sweeping around the garden, finally landing on Connie. Connie examined Matilda, too. She looked very different to when she'd last seen her. She had clean hair, for a start, and it was brushed and tied back in a ponytail, not greasy and loose and hanging around in lank chunks that looked like slugs. She was also wearing some kind of velour tracksuit,. definitely something she'd never ever have worn previously. Connie surmised that they'd probably had to cut her old outfit off her.

'And why are *you* here?' Matilda asked Connie, before twisting round in her chair to address the man who was pushing her. 'You can go now, thank you.'

'Are you sure, madam?' asked the taxi driver, who was in his early seventies, by Connie's reckoning. Probably working in the gig economy to supplement his pension. He was missing several front teeth and had a very wispy combover. He also looked incredibly exhausted, something Connie wasn't surprised by at all. She imagined a journey in the car with Matilda would tax anyone.

'Quite sure.'

'OK,' he said, before swivelling and walking back up the path without looking back. He must be glad to be free of this particular fare, thought Connie.

'You can go, too,' said Matilda.

Connie felt like she'd been slapped.

'But… I've been looking after the animals while you've been away.'

This was the first time she'd talked to Matilda, ever. She couldn't believe that this was how she was being spoken to. After all, she'd been helping her. Keeping these animals alive. Making things better for them than she'd managed!

'Yes, I can see that,' replied Matilda, who was eyeing Rory at Connie's side. 'Clarrie! Eddie!' she called, holding out her arms, anticipating the goats' return.

So that's what they're called, thought Connie. I prefer my names.

Matilda's face, which had lit up with a smile briefly when

she'd called for the goats, was now scowling. The goats had not gone to her, and Connie could see this had upset her. But inside, Connie was glowing. The animals had chosen her. *Her.*

'Clarrie?' Matilda called, her voice now quieter, less certain. When the goat still refused to move, she cast her eyes back over the garden, and Connie could see that she was taking in the healthy vegetables, the swept paths, the watered and weeded earth, the bounty of picked vegetables on display on the bench.

'You moved the bench,' said Matilda. It was not a question, but a statement.

'Yes, it seemed a good place to put the vegetables I picked, and I wanted to show you...'

'You should not have done that,' she said, her voice quiet and deep, as if something had caught in her throat.

'I'm sorry, I just thought it would be better there. I can put it back.'

'No. Just go.'

'I'm sorry?'

'I think you heard me. I didn't ask for your help, and I don't require it.'

'But Rory...' Connie said, reaching down and patting the goat. She was going to say 'Rory needs me,' but even she knew that this wasn't true. The truth was, she needed Rory.

'Rory who?'

'I didn't know what you called the goats, so I made up names for them.'

'She is Clarrie, Constance. She's a doe. A female?'

'You know my name?' replied Connie, astonished, and frightened. She had bargained on no one around here really knowing much about her, and she had stupidly ignored the mad woman living next door, who undoubtedly knew much more about her than she'd ever be able to fathom.

'Of course I do. You spent your early childhood next door. I must have heard your poor mother calling you, and telling you off, thousands of times.'

Connie remembered long, lonely summer days when her mother had been working and she'd been left a list of chores to complete, and she'd avoided doing them, in favour of long walks with her favourite book. Ellen had never been pleased.

'Oh.'

'Yes. Right. Anyway, time for you to run along now.'

Matilda was still in her wheelchair and had not yet managed to stand up. Connie knew that there was no room in her house for a wheelchair, and wondered how on earth she thought she was going to manage. Surely they couldn't have sent her out of hospital like that, without an assessment, or someone to help her?

'Are you sure you'll be OK? Do you need me to find you a stick or...'

'Just leave. Leave now. I don't need you. I don't need anyone. We need to be left alone...' she said, before a pause. 'Me and the animals.'

Connie looked down at Rory, and felt tears welling in her eyes. Shit, she thought. *Shit*. I can't deal with this. Not now. Not after everything.

'Bye,' she said, stooping down and kissing Rory on the head, before walking slowly towards the side gate, keeping her eyes to the floor to avoid looking at Matilda. Every muscle and sinew in her wanted to stay with the animals, but not with that woman, not with that witch.

As she pushed open the gate and walked around to their front door, tears started rolling freely down her cheeks. By the time she'd found her keys and pushed the door open, she was struggling to see, and by the time she had reached her bedroom, she had lost the ability to stand.

As she crawled across the floor of her bedroom and hauled herself up onto her bed, Connie allowed the darkness to flood back in. The only good thing in her life had just been taken away, and without it, she had lost the ability to fight.

*

An hour later, Connie had assembled the two things she needed on her bed. Firstly, she had a new bottle of vodka. It was sufficiently large that she thought she was unlikely to need it all. Secondly, she had a full box of her mother's antidepressants. Ellen had never told Connie that she took them, but it was hard to keep secrets in such a small house. Connie had clocked them a while back. It was ironic, really, that her mother had been nagging her to take these bloody things for so long, and she was now finally going to do it.

It had taken her several hours to process what had happened earlier that day. Her separation from the animals, the only thing that had broken through her eternal darkness, had cut her very deep. Having that new part scythed off was like someone giving you that final push when you were clinging onto the end of the diving board with your toes. There would be no going back.

Connie wiped her eyes and nose with her sleeve and stared down at the bottle and the box, feeling nothing but numbness. She picked up the box of tablets and methodically popped out twenty-eight, enough for two a day for two weeks. Except she was going to take them all now, and she did that in groups of seven, swigging vodka down her throat as she did so, willing the tablets into her system, begging them to get to work.

And then she thought of something.

She wanted to see the animals for one last time. She didn't want to go outside and risk someone stopping her, but if she went to her mum's bedroom window, she thought she might be able to see the goats, at least.

She walked the few steps from her room to her mum's and approached the window, wondering as she did so how long she had left. How long would it take for her to lose consciousness? She had no idea. She wasn't a scientist. She'd been shit at science, in fact. Shit at pretty much everything.

Connie reached the window and looked out at Matilda's

garden, and then she felt a surge of shock run through her. She could see the goats all right; they were standing around a large purple puddle on the ground. But it wasn't a puddle, it was Matilda. She was flat on her face in her back garden. How long had she been there? Was she still alive? It had been hours since she'd last seen her.

Shit, thought Connie. *Shit. So do I stay here and let these take effect, or do I leave Matilda there?* No one would find her, she realised. At least, not until her mother got back from work.

Oh my God. My mum is going to find me. How had she not even considered that? *She's going to find me in here on her floor, and the empty packet in my room, and she's going to blame herself and she's going to have to live with that for the rest of her life.*

What. Am. I. Doing. I have lost my mind.

Connie acted on impulse. She ran down the stairs to the kitchen and yanked the phone handset off its cradle. She dialled 999.

'999 Emergency. What service do you need?'

'An ambulance. I need an ambulance. Actually, maybe two ambulances.'

'Can you tell me where you are?'

'Roseacre Close in Stonecastle. Number three. And the other woman who needs help is at number four. She's in the back garden. Please hurry.'

'Is the patient breathing?'

'I'm the patient. One of the patients. I've taken… Lots of tablets. But I don't want to die. Please hurry.'

'OK, we're sending someone as quickly as we can. What's your name, love?'

'Connie. I'm… Connie.'

'Is your front door unlocked?'

'I'll go and unlock it now.' Connie walked to the front door and put it on the latch. As she did so, she felt a burning in her windpipe and a wave of nausea swept over her.

'Is that done, Connie?' the call handler asked.

'Yes.'

'Can you tell me about the other patient, love?'

'Er, yes. She's called Matilda. Miss Reynolds. She's very old. She's fallen in her garden. I don't know if she's breathing or not…'

'All right love, don't worry, you've done the right thing. Someone will be with you soon. I'll stay on the phone with you until they come, OK?'

'OK,' said Connie, sinking to the floor. Her legs had begun to shake.

'What have you taken, Connie?'

Connie started to reply, but she felt vomit rising in her throat and she retched. She remembered that she hadn't eaten anything today. Did that mean the tablets were absorbed more easily? I need to be sick, she thought. I need to get those tablets out of me, fast.

She threw the phone down on the floor and stumbled into the downstairs toilet, before putting her fingers down her throat. As she brought up a foul-tasting acid that burned in her mouth, Connie prayed that it would be enough.

Please let the ambulance make it in time, she thought.

Please God.

Please.

— 11 —

August

Matilda

'I thought we'd see you back here pretty soon.'

Matilda took her headphones out with great reluctance when she saw who it was that was interrupting *Woman's Hour*. That Mrs Goodman woman, that supercilious chief social worker with the attitude and the ego, was standing right beside her bed.

'You should not have discharged yourself,' she added, her hands on her hips, looking for all the world like she wanted to be bally Superman. 'You were not well enough to go home.'

'Well hello, Mrs Goodman. I'll be leaving just as soon as the physio is happy I can use my sprained wrists. I was lucky that it is just that. I can still walk. I'll be fine.'

That wasn't really how she felt, of course. In reality, she felt about as awful as she ever had, but there was no point admitting that to Mrs Goodman. She needed to get back home, and the only way to do that was to lie through her teeth, even though she knew that lying was a terrible sin.

'You were fortunate that your neighbour saw you and called an ambulance.'

'They have always kept an eye out for me,' she said, lying once more. This was getting easier every time, she thought.

'That's nice. However, Miss Reynolds, they will not be able to fix the damp in your house.'

'I do not have damp.'

'We sent a surveyor round yesterday, Miss Reynolds. We had arranged for them to go after our inspection, remember? Anyhow, they have found significant issues with the house. Significant enough that we don't think it's safe for you to return to it. In fact, we think there may be an issue with the construction of all of the houses in Roseacre Close. We're going to investigate.'

Matilda was dumbstruck. What significant issues? She'd lived in the house for seven decades, and it had never given her a moment of trouble. She'd thought there might be isolated damp in some of the walls, maybe, but not significant enough to warrant her moving out.

'Why are you so determined to get me to move out, Mrs Goodman?' she asked, smelling a rat, as she had done at the beginning, when she'd wondered why a manager would get involved in house inspections. 'What's in it for you?'

She observed the other woman's face transition from white to pink. So she doesn't like being challenged, thought Matilda. That's worth remembering.

'Nothing, Miss Reynolds. I – we – simply want for you to be safe and in a healthy environment.'

'A smaller one, a cheaper one, perhaps?'

'Nothing of the sort, Miss Reynolds. But I am giving you warning that we will be notifying you very soon with details of a proposed move for you. I'm telling you this now so that you have time to make the required arrangements for the... animals. We will find you somewhere more suitable, I promise you that.'

'You will remove me from that house over my dead body,' replied Matilda.

'Miss Reynolds, you are very lucky to be in social housing. The waiting list for such accommodation is very long. And we are offering you a new social housing contract, not throwing you out on the street.'

'*You. Will. Not. Move. Me*,' shouted Matilda, feeling her heart race in her chest.

'Matilda?'

She looked up and saw that someone else had arrived beside her bed. Thankfully, it wasn't that useless drip Daniel again. This time, it was Ellen from next door.

'Hello,' Matilda said, not sure how she should address the woman she'd lived next to for twenty years but had never actually had a conversation with.

'Hello,' said Mrs Goodman, looking Ellen up and down as she did so. Ellen was looking very smart today, Matilda thought. Very presentable. She was a handsome woman, definitely, a capable one, too, bringing up that girl on her own.

'Oh, hi. I'm Ellen Darke. I'm Matilda's neighbour.'

For once, Matilda didn't at all mind being called by her Christian name.

'I see. I'm Caroline Goodman. I'm the head of social services at the council. We're talking to Mat... Miss Reynolds about rehousing her somewhere more suitable.'

'Are you?'

'Yes. We are concerned that she is not able to manage by herself.'

Ellen looked from the social worker to her neighbour and smiled.

'I'm sure things must be tricky after a fall, but can't you arrange for carers to visit? I work for the council doing that, helping old folk so that they can stay in their homes. I'm sure I could help Matilda out if she wanted me to.'

'Her house is not... in a suitable state,' said the social worker. 'As I'm sure you know. And the animals...'

'I'm sure we can help her clear things up a bit,' said Ellen, still smiling at Matilda and not looking at Caroline Goodman at all. 'We all stick together on the estate.'

Matilda said nothing. This conversation was getting on perfectly well without her.

'Right, well. I'm afraid our inspection of Miss Reynolds' house has found significant problems which will take a long time to resolve.'

'There's something wrong with her house? We share a common wall, so if there is, I need to know about it, too.'

'As I was explaining to Miss Reynolds, I am going to put it all in a letter which will explain our findings and propose a suitable move for her. This will be forthcoming in a couple of weeks.' The social worker leaned down to pick up her leather handbag from the chair beside Matilda's bed. 'It was nice to meet you, Ms Darke,' she said, sounding absolutely like she didn't mean it. 'I'll be in touch soon, Miss Reynolds.'

Matilda watched as she strode out of the ward, her red bag swinging from her shoulder. Then she looked over at Ellen.

'Thank you,' she said somewhat huskily, before clearing her throat. 'Thank you for that.'

'Oh, that's fine. I know that sort, I've met them a lot in my time. They talk down to the old people I look after, and it makes me furious. Sometimes it's relatives that behave like that, would you believe, and other times it's people from the council or social services, and they should definitely know better.' Matilda nodded. 'You know, I'd heard there was someone new in charge of social services. One of my clients was talking about her the other day. Her reputation precedes her, not in a good way. She's been parachuted in, apparently. She's supposed to shake them up, and save money, I think. She's a slasher.'

Matilda nodded. 'Yes. As I say, thank you. They seem determined to get me out, but I will not go.'

'And neither should you. By the way, I am so sorry, I just realised I didn't ask whether it's OK for me to use your first name. I always do that at work. It's only polite.'

'It's... fine.' Matilda looked at her neighbour, who was still smiling. It appeared to be genuine, she thought. It was a long time since somebody had called her by her first name, but she was prepared to make an exception this time. 'I need to say thank you… also… to your daughter,' Matilda said, stumbling over the words, because it was a long time since she'd had a pleasant, ordinary conversation with another human. Or even a reason to be grateful. 'I believe she called the ambulance for me.'

'Connie? Yes, she did.'

'How is she? They said she also needed… medical treatment.'

'She's OK, thank God. I've just come in to visit her, actually, that's why I'm here, but I came into this ward first to bring one of my ladies some of her favourite chocolates.'

Matilda examined Ellen's face. Behind her smile, she saw dark rings around her eyes, which were creased and tired.

'Your ladies?'

'One of my clients. I'm a carer.'

'Ah yes, as you were saying. I see.'

There was an awkward silence.

'So I'll just head off, then. I can see you're busy listening to something.'

'Yes, I…' Matilda grasped at her headphones and tried to smile. She was out of practice at this.

'Oh, but before I go… I meant to say I'll feed the animals for you, all right? While Connie is in here. And when she's better, she can take over again. She loves them, did she tell you? It's really brought her out of herself, going over there. It was… so healing for her.'

Matilda watched Ellen's face as she spoke. She was almost begging her with her eyes, she thought. She was *begging* her to allow her daughter to keep interfering in her garden and with her animals. Matilda was going to have to think about that. She wasn't at all sure. She needed to be convinced that Constance could be both respectful and responsible. She hadn't allowed anyone into her house, or her life, for decades. Even letting someone into her garden was a huge step. But Ellen was being sincere, she could see that. The tears that were forming confirmed that.

'Yes... thank you,' Matilda replied, careful not to confirm or deny Ellen's daughter the opportunity to return to her back garden, despite her mother's impassioned plea.

She needed to accept Ellen's help for now, anyway. She didn't want Clarrie, Eddie, Brian, Jennifer and the rest of the gang to starve.

— 12 —

August

Constance

Connie heard her mum coming into the ward before she saw her. She was greeting all of the nursing staff like old friends, enquiring after spouses, kids, new and old lovers. You could tell she was paid to look after people. She had the gift of the gab, all right.

'Hello love,' Ellen said, when she finally made it to Connie's bed in the corner. 'How are you doing today? Any better?'

Connie wondered how to play it today. Should she pretend that everything was fine, like most other days? She did her best to do that, because it was easier for her mum to hear. She'd put her through enough already.

She'd let the darkness inside her escape only a couple of times since they'd pumped the tablets out of her. Once, she'd screamed out in fear when a male nurse had been leaning over her to fix a line in her arm. And on another occasion, she had wept throughout her mum's visit and been unable to speak. Neither of them wanted to go back to that. She'd struggled to regain her composure afterwards, and her mum had looked physically ill.

'Feeling a lot better today, thanks,' she said. So it was decided. She'd do her best to pretend again. It was far easier that way.

'You do look a bit better.'

Connie supposed that she might. After all, she had been in here for more than a week, and she'd been fed three square meals every day, without a side order of vodka. They'd also pumped her stomach out thoroughly so that the tablets she'd taken hadn't had much chance to do damage. Not that they really would have done, she'd since discovered; overdoses of that particular drug were rarely fatal. Had she known that, deep down? Was that why she hadn't even looked it up? Had she not really wanted it to work? Probably. She'd been in the depths of despair, that was certain, but it hadn't taken much for her to realise her mistake. There was comfort in knowing that even in her darkest hour, she had still wanted to live. It was a starting point, at least. That was what the new counsellor they'd started her with had told her that morning, in fact.

'So now that we have established that you still want to live, how do you want to live?' the counsellor had asked.

The problem was, Connie had no idea how she wanted to live. Since she'd moved back home, she hadn't given the slightest thought to that question. How did you decide that sort of thing, after what had happened? How did you pick yourself up and start again, when you had been to hell and somehow managed to come back? In truth, since she'd moved back home, she had been trying to remain alive while actually not really living; in effect, she'd turned herself into a ghost.

Like every other counsellor and doctor she'd had in the past two decades, the counsellor had also tried to persuade her to go on antidepressants. She'd said no, obviously. She wanted to retain at least some degree of control over herself.

'Any idea when they're going to let you out?' her mother asked. She was now sitting on the side of her bed.

'Soon, they said,' Connie replied, not wanting to tell Ellen that they were reluctant to because she was refusing to take the medication they had prescribed.

'Great,' said Ellen, smoothing the blanket down over her daughter's legs. 'Oh, by the way, I saw Matilda just now.'

Connie's head snapped up.

'Did you?'

'Yes. She's in a ward just down the hall. She said to thank you for calling the ambulance,' said Ellen, her chest rising and falling with the deep breaths Connie had noticed she often took when she was near her. 'Social services seem to be trying to evict her, the poor woman. At her age! I've said I'll help her.' Connie raised an eyebrow. Matilda and her mother had never been friends, or even acquaintances. 'And she also said that she was fine with you looking after the animals after you get out. She'll be in here a bit longer than you, I think.'

Ellen wasn't looking at her. Instead, she was methodically straightening and stroking the blanket, as if her hand was a hot iron and Connie's legs were the board.

'I'm so sorry, Mum.'

'What for?' said Ellen, looking at her now.

Connie remembered her mother standing outside her father's house under a streetlight, shouting up at her bedroom window. She had been begging, begging her to come home, so loudly that she could hear her shouts through her double-glazed window.

I'm so sorry for not coming down and letting you in. For not coming back when you asked me to. And then for coming back far too late, and burdening you with what I've become. Connie wanted to say all of those things, but that level of honesty felt like too much, today.

'For everything...'

'Don't be silly. You're not well, are you? We just need to get you better.' Her mother's tone was emphatic, determined, a little forced.

If only it was that simple, Connie thought. If only she could just click her fingers and erase the past two years – or perhaps even the past twenty years. Was that what she'd been trying to do, when she'd taken the pills? To hit the reset button on life?

'I know, Mum. And I will try. I promise.'

Ellen leaned over and pulled Connie into an embrace. The warmth of her arms and the feeling of her breath on her neck reminded Connie of her childhood and, without warning, she began to cry.

— 13 —

September

Matilda

It was twilight when the taxi pulled up outside the house. Matilda could see the bats swooping around the eaves, and a lone fox was standing proud under the streetlamp, like a West End performer relishing their spotlight. She nodded in the fox's direction – it didn't do to get on the wrong side of that particular animal – and watched as it took her in and then sauntered off out of the close.

Matilda reached for the stick they'd given her at the hospital. As she pulled the handle and the car door swung open, she inhaled the unmistakable scent of the end of summer; cut grass, last-ditch barbecues and petrichor, the smell of the earth after rain. After a searing, relentless August, the weather had finally broken in the past few weeks, and the grass she'd seen from the taxi on the way home had certainly seemed relieved to receive it.

As she pushed herself up to standing – something she'd been practising with the physiotherapist a great deal this week – she allowed herself to smile. She had desperately missed being here, and the fact that she had actually been officially discharged this time was an added bonus. However, it did also mean that the hospital had arranged for district nurses to visit her, and she was due an assessment for daily carer visits, too.

She wasn't at all keen. She didn't want any of that fuss and she didn't want her space invaded, but she also knew that if she refused all help, the council would have even more of a case to make her move on, so she had decided to pick her battles.

'Shall I bring this to the door?'

Using her stick for support, Matilda swivelled around to see the taxi driver, a young man this time, brandishing the plastic bag they'd given her for her belongings. She nodded.

She hadn't had much when they'd taken her in – just that purple tracksuit they'd provided her with, a pair of gifted new knickers and her old sturdy boots – but she'd been given a lot more things in hospital, and it had seemed wrong to leave them there. Her stash now included a toothbrush, some special toothpaste she had been told she had to use now to save what was left of her teeth, some fancy soap in a plastic bottle, a pack of new white cotton briefs, some huge grey flannel pyjamas and a portable radio which the nurses had gifted to her as a leaving present. She felt guilty now about all of the bad things she'd thought about them. They'd been all right really, in the end. Just a bit... young. And that wasn't their fault, after all.

When she'd reached the front door, she rummaged around in the pocket of another new tracksuit – a further donation from the hospital – and pulled out her keys. Once she'd managed to find the lock in the semi-darkness, she inserted the key and turned.

As she did so, she heard a door slam, and saw movement on the other side of the wall which separated the front gardens of her house and the one next door.

'You're back! I told Connie you might be coming back today,' said Ellen, walking out of her garden and down towards Matilda.

Ellen had become something of a regular visitor to Matilda's ward in recent weeks, and Matilda had begun to warm to her, despite herself. She had deliberately avoided getting to know her for decades, but it turned out that her neighbour was exceptionally patient and kind. She had, for example, put up with many awkward silences when she hadn't felt like speaking. Matilda was glad they'd made the connection, because she had decided that it might be a good idea to have at least one ally. Particularly because she was expecting a letter from the council to be waiting inside for her, and she knew enough about herself now to realise that she might need someone to help her fight back. She'd been closed off from the rest of the world for so long precisely because she couldn't cope with its challenges. While she'd put up a good fight with that horrible Caroline, the social worker, she'd been exhausted afterwards and the thought, the very idea of being made to move out had made her feel physically ill. Yes, as strong-willed as she might be, her body was undoubtedly weak, and her brain was not as sharp as it had once been. She needed help, but not from all and sundry. Just Ellen would do.

'There you are. Look at you standing up! You're doing so well. Do you want a hand getting up the step?'

'No, I'm fine, thank you, Ellen.'

'Shall I help you carry your bag in?'

'No, thank you.'

'No worries. I'll be just a second then,' she said, walking back up the path and turning into her own front garden. What on earth was she doing now?

As Matilda raised her right foot and planted it next to the pile of post which was sitting on the tiled floor beyond, bracing herself against the doorframe to lift herself up and into her home, she heard a rustling. Ellen was coming back towards her bearing two large supermarket shopping bags.

'I went out to get you some basics this morning,' she said. 'Just to get you settled back in. I've got you some milk, some juice, some bread, cheese, that sort of thing. Shall I bring it in?'

'No thank you, Ellen.'

'It's fine, I won't stay, I'll just put it in the kitchen for you.'

For the love of all that's holy, Matilda thought, *please stop*, Ellen. Just *stop*.

'Thank you very much for that, Ellen, but I've got food. I'll be fine. I can feed myself. I am not starving.'

Ellen retreated a few steps and stood behind Matilda as she flicked the hall light on. It was then that Matilda saw the exact spot she'd spent God knew how many days stuck in, her body broken, her brain not far behind. Latterly, she'd been unconscious, but she could still remember. Hundreds of cans were strewn across the floor, covering almost the entire area, except for a small patch, which was where she must have been lying. Was she really that small? Perhaps she was. The thought shocked her. She had once been a strong woman, a woman who took up space, a woman who was noticed. And now she had shrunk to the size of a small dog.

Looking around, she could also see several dark-coloured stains among the cans. The stains were either vomit, or blood, or urine, or possibly faeces. Even Matilda, who was used to the odours that came with her own choice to live the way she did, felt her stomach turn. Partly it was the smell that bothered her, and partly the memories that came with those smells. She'd thought that she would die right there, among the baked beans, tinned tomatoes and sardines, in that tiny air pocket in her baking, bursting house. She had urinated there, certainly. She had felt, frankly, as if she had been turned inside out down there, as if all of her organs had been removed from her body and laid out before her on display, with a surgeon pointing out each piece and its particular weakness.

'Shall I just help you pick those things up so that you can get through?' asked Ellen, her voice light, deliberately so. Matilda could only imagine what Ellen was really thinking, but she was glad that she was trying to hide her disgust. Even Matilda was finding it all a little hard to absorb. It was interesting, she thought, the perspective she'd gained since she'd been away; when you lived around things constantly, you no longer really noticed them, but after several weeks in the clinical cleanliness of the hospital, her house's familiar odours and clutter were bothering her a little. Not enough to have a clear-out, mind you. For that was something that would cause her great pain. But perhaps a little tidy-up might not go amiss.

'Yes, please, Ellen, that would be helpful.'

Ellen put the bags of food down just inside the door, against a stack of boxes, and walked over to the scene of Matilda's fall.

'Golly, Matilda, you poor thing,' she said, picking up the tins and piling them up behind her in neat columns. 'This lot must have felt like a tonne of bricks.'

Matilda tried to shut the memories of that moment out, but they came at her anyway: the pain as they'd pierced and bruised her fragile skin; that feeling of being punched, repeatedly, when you could not fight back; that acceptance of her own pathetic weakness.

'Yes. They did, rather.'

'Well, the main thing is, you're back now, and that's great. Let's get you settled back in.' Ellen had finished piling up the tins, so she returned to the door, picked up the bags and walked through to the kitchen, turning sideways as she did so to make sure she didn't cause any more of the tins to tumble.

'Right, so... Where shall I put these?'

Matilda looked around her and saw, at that moment, what Ellen was seeing. Her white porcelain sink was now almost entirely brown and full of animal feed and her sole plate and mug were encrusted with dirt. Every surface was stacked and packed with boxes, bags and piles of paper. Some of the cupboard doors were open, others apparently closed but not actually able to shut properly due to their overwhelming contents. And the floor, which had once been black and white chequered lino, a floor she had once swept meticulously every day, was now sticky, dusty and the colour of brick dust.

Oh, Miriam, she thought. *Oh, Miriam.* I couldn't cope without you, I just couldn't, could I? I said so, and I was right.

'*Matilda*? Oh, you poor darling. Please don't cry.' Matilda wasn't just crying, she was sobbing. Massive gasping sobs were escaping her mouth, and she had no control over them at all. 'Let me find you a seat.' Ellen left her to go into the sitting room. Matilda knew what she'd find there. She'd find her bed, or rather, her nest: a stained mattress on the floor wedged against the legs of the old dining table, topped with a jumble of old blankets. She lived like an animal, she thought. An animal. *Oh, Miriam.*

'Here you go,' Ellen said, returning with one of the dining chairs. Matilda knew she'd have had to shift her mattress, her bedding and several large plastic crates of newspaper to get to it, but she was grateful her neighbour made no mention of it. Ellen placed the chair down on the floor in between the kitchen units and took Matilda's arm as she lowered her into it.

They remained there in silence for a short while, Matilda trying to breathe deeply to regain control of her emotions, with Ellen standing beside her, silent and still, maintaining her distance – something Matilda welcomed. As her tears subsided, she heard the kitchen tap dripping. It had been doing that for at least a decade.

'Do you know what I think we'll do?' Ellen said, finally. 'I have an old camping bed in my garage. I'll pop and get it and we can make it up for you in the sitting room. It'll be easier for you to get in and out of.'

Matilda nodded. For the first time in a very long time, she was deeply grateful to have the company of another human being in her house.

Matilda woke to the sound of a cockerel crowing. It had been several weeks since she'd last done so and, despite her tiredness and the persistent ache in her back and her belly, she was overjoyed to hear it. The animals needed to be fed, she thought. That meant that order had been restored.

She threw off the floral duvet which was on loan from Ellen, swung her legs over the side of the camp bed, grabbed her new walking stick and pushed herself upwards.

Her progress from the sitting room to the garden was painfully slow, and it took at least five minutes for her to reach the back door. When she did so, she took a moment to look through the glass, taking in the sun rising over the distant new housing estate, the freshly harvested field of oilseed rape beyond the fence, and the disordered, glorious chaos of her back garden.

Several minutes later, she turned the handle and opened the door. What followed was a thump, a cry and an expletive. Matilda hobbled out into the back garden, leaning heavily on her stick, to find Ellen's daughter spreadeagled on the earth beneath her feet.

'What on earth are you doing here?' Matilda asked.

'Feeding… the… animals,' said Connie, panting in pain as she pushed herself up to standing, and then trying to brush mud off her trousers, only spreading the brown stain further. The recent rain had turned the garden into a quagmire. 'Mum said you might still need some help, so here I am. I always come early in the morning. It's my favourite time of day, actually.'

'Is it?'

Matilda wondered whether Connie's blue trousers were expensive, because if so, it had definitely been unwise to wear them to feed two hungry goats, four chickens and a whole load of cats in a garden recently doused with heavy rain.

'Yeah, it is.'

She's feisty, this one, Matilda thought. Connie was standing just a foot or so away from her, and they were about the same height, so her glare was boring directly into Matilda's eyes.

Odd that a girl with so much spirit had tried to take her own life. What darkness lurked there behind her obstinate demeanour, she wondered. Something particularly pernicious, no doubt. Something that must have seemed insurmountable.

Just for a moment, Matilda looked over Connie's shoulder towards the bench at the end of the garden, and remembered a pitch-black night lit only by the moon, when she had stared into the deep hole in the sodden ground and wished to God that she could climb into it and rid herself of that horrendous, all-consuming pain.

She hadn't done so, of course. The nuns had taught Matilda that suicide was a mortal sin. Although she'd read that the Pope had recently changed his mind on that, she wasn't particularly sure that God had. And whether or not it was a sin, it was, in her opinion, a selfish thing to do. What an awful, devastating thing it would have been to allow Ellen to find her lying there, her only baby, lifeless on the bed she'd slept in as a child.

Matilda regained her composure. She needed to be firm with the girl, she decided. She was in need of guidance.

'Fine. Good. Carry on,' she said.

Connie shrugged her shoulders, tipped her head down to the right and left and stretched her neck as if she was an athlete readying for a race, then walked towards the outside toilet to get the morning's feed.

'You're getting a bit low on mineral salt lick,' Connie said as she lifted a bale of hay from a pile shielded from the weather by a large strip of corrugated plastic that Dean had found for Matilda at the tip. 'And you'll need some more hay soon. Rory and Lorelai are hungry.'

'Clarrie and Eddie,' said Matilda, walking a few steps into the garden before finding she didn't have the energy to go any further. She watched the girl spread hay in the goat's feeding trough and replenish the water. '*They're called Clarrie and Eddie.* They're a boy and a girl.'

Connie nodded, smiled and walked over to Matilda.

'Shall I help you sit on the bench over there? I would bring it over for you but I remember you're not very keen on that?'

'Yes, leave it... I will walk over to it slowly. Thank you,' Matilda said, keen that Connie should not touch her. She'd had far too many medical staff manhandling her already. 'By the way – do you have experience with goats? You seem to know what to feed them,' she said, wending her way down the garden towards the bench.

'Oh, no. I just used YouTube,' replied Connie. 'And a bit of Google.' Matilda had not the slightest idea what either of those things was, but she decided not to probe further. The less conversation she had to engage in, the better.

When she arrived at the bench, Matilda lowered herself slowly and sat down with a sigh. Had it been this hard to get about before her accident, she wondered. It had certainly been difficult and exhausting for at least the past five years. She'd taken longer and longer to get dressed and up every day, and eventually she had started to sleep in her clothes and eschew the kitchen sink, which had become the only way she had to keep clean. She had become a slut and a slattern, as her mother would have put it. Her mother had looked down on any woman who wasn't on her front doorstep by 8 a.m. scrubbing away until the stone shone. What would she think of me now, Matilda thought. She would have been astonished by pretty much everything that she had done, most likely, and not in a good way. When she'd held her firstborn in her arms, she was unlikely to have wished Matilda's life choices upon her.

Matilda looked across to the left, where Connie was picking runner beans with a wooden trug and a kitchen knife, neither of which she recognised as her own. It was quite hard to believe that this girl had only just been released from hospital. She looked healthier than she had in a long while, far healthier than she did after those dawn walks of hers. She had colour in her cheeks and a spring in her step. Ellen had been right, she thought; her daughter does love my garden. Despite her instinctive secrecy, Matilda felt pride that someone else was able to appreciate her labours.

'You've kept the animals and the garden well,' Matilda said, the guilt she felt about their previous meeting bubbling to the surface at last. She knew that Connie had tried to take her own life immediately after she'd thrown her out of her garden, and had felt terrible about that ever since she'd found out. And also, Connie had called the ambulance that had saved her life. That didn't mean Matilda wanted to be best friends, of course, but she felt that some pleasantries were what was required. Even though that didn't come naturally to her.

'Thank you,' said Connie, turning around briefly from her task, beaming. 'Thanks.'

'I don't like your choice of names for the goats, mind. You might be coming around here every day, but you mustn't think that gives you the right to rechristen Clarrie and Eddie.'

Matilda saw Connie examine her face, trying to decide whether she was joking or in earnest. She allowed herself a small smile so that Connie could see it was the former.

'Ha, no. Sorry. I had to call them something, though, and I just thought Rory… I mean, Clarrie… was such a lovely animal.'

'I agree,' said Matilda, forcing herself to continue the conversation, because she could see that Connie was enjoying it. She mustn't ever be responsible for someone else's demise ever again. It was not something she wanted on her conscience. She already had enough to deal with.

'Would you like a cup of tea?' asked Connie. Matilda was astonished by the offer. She knew that the girl had not yet set foot in her house, but she also knew that Ellen would have told her what a state it was in. 'I'll go next door to get it,' Connie added, reading Matilda's mind. 'Mum's bought Jammie Dodgers.'

'Thank you. That would be… nice.'

Connie smiled and ran up the path and through the gate, leaving Matilda alone.

Miriam, Miriam, Matilda thought. Is she OK? Do you mind that she's here?

Matilda looked around her. Everything she could see was ordered, sated, peaceful; it seemed that the animals at least were happy to have her here. It was a huge thing, having someone else share her space, but for now, at least, it did seem to be a harmonious match. She was prepared to let it continue.

'Here you go,' said Connie, reappearing a few minutes later bearing a tray, which she carried over to the bench and laid on the floor next to it. 'I have two cups of tea – I put milk in, I hope you don't mind – and half a pack of Jammie Dodgers.'

Matilda accepted the tea, which was presented in a mug not a cup, and which was considerably stronger than she'd usually make herself, but decided she was prepared to overlook it. Connie held the biscuits out to her on a white ceramic plate and Matilda took one. It was a long time since she'd had any biscuits. They didn't have a long enough shelf life to warrant a place in her food stores.

'So where do you get your animal feed from?' asked Connie, as they both sat on the bench sipping their steaming tea. 'I never see you leave the house, and Mum says the same, and she works at all hours.'

'I don't,' Matilda replied. 'A local farmer's son, Dean, brings it and leaves it outside, and I pay him cash. Dean's dad used to supply it, and now he's almost retired Dean has taken over. I pay him for his time, of course.'

'Oh, right. And how about your own food?'

Matilda took a bite of her biscuit.

'I give Dean a list and he gets my pension out from the post office for me, and then he goes to the cash and carry, and buys provisions for me once a month. Everything I have is long-life, so that's fine. And I have fresh eggs, goats' milk and vegetables from the garden, as you know.'

They sat in silence for a minute, the only sounds the sipping of tea, the loud crunching of two hungry goats demolishing their breakfast, and human jaws clicking as they chewed on their biscuits.

'Why did you shout at me when I was a kid?' Connie asked, avoiding Matilda's gaze. Matilda had been hoping that they would never have to discuss this. It was a risk she'd taken when she'd allowed her to stay. If she had been Connie, she'd never have raised it. What did they teach young people these days?

Were they told that no subject was off limits? Were they told you should probe into someone's darkest places with wilful abandon?

Watch out, it's the witch!

Did you know she's got the severed head of a small child under that dress? That's why she looks so fat. She carries it around as a trophy.

Her face is so ugly you'll turn to stone the minute you see her.

My dad says that she has rats living in her hair.

Have you seen the mad woman she keeps locked up in her attic? She only comes out at night, and the only thing she eats is snakes and worms.

'You and your friends were unpleasant to me,' Matilda replied, after a long pause.

'I never said anything to you.'

'You were in groups with children who did, and you didn't correct them.'

'You never spoke to me, though, ever. You just glared at me and turned away. I was frightened of you. And how was I supposed to speak up for someone I didn't even know? I was a kid. A little kid.'

Matilda didn't feel like trying to see it from Connie's perspective. She was far too hurt to do that.

'It was a long time ago,' Matilda said, picking up another biscuit.

'Yeah, it was. They were wrong to say those things about how you looked, though. About being a witch, and that stuff. I am so sick to death of people judging women for the clothes they wear, or their hair, or you know, their bodies…'

Matilda said nothing. This was not just about her own appearance, that was clear. She could see that the young woman was in pain, and that what she'd just said held meaning for her. She instinctively felt that Connie would prefer silence, so they sat there together for a while, listening to the goats, chickens and cats eating the final scraps of their breakfast.

Connie drank the last dregs of her tea before standing up and putting her cup back on the tray.

'I'll help you back up to the house when you're finished,' Connie said, not looking at Matilda. 'Just let me know when. I'll keep on gardening until you do.'

Matilda watched her walk away towards the courgettes, and then she remembered.

'Constance – would you mind going to get the post for me from behind the front door? I believe there is a letter there I will have to read.'

— 14 —

September

Constance

'They say they're going to evict her, Mum.'

Ellen was sitting at the small wooden table at the end of their kitchen counter, eating her breakfast, a poached egg on a slice of wholemeal toast.

'I thought as much, from that conversation I heard them having with her in hospital.'

'What did you hear them say?' said Connie, as she clicked the kettle on to boil for her second cup of tea of the day.

'I was only there for the end bit, to be honest, but it didn't sound too friendly. I suppose they feel she's taking up a council house they could use for a family? That's my guess. They have a huge list of people waiting, and they're trying to get people to move to places that reflect the size of their family.'

'But she's been there for practically forever.'

'Yep. But she's living in a terrible mess, isn't she? It's not healthy. She needs room to move around. I mean, what if she needs a wheelchair? She'll never manage. And she can't even keep herself clean.'

'They've cleaned her up a bit, since she's been in hospital,' said Connie, filling her mug with hot water. 'I sat next to her on her bench just now, and I didn't even have to hold my breath.'

'Well, thank heavens for small mercies,' replied Ellen.

They both laughed because, although the joke was in bad taste, it was also, unfortunately, true.

Connie needed a laugh. Her conversation with Matilda had been incredibly intense, and she was still smarting over the comment about how she'd never stopped her friends from taunting her. It was true, of course, that she hadn't. But Matilda had genuinely frightened her, and she'd always been so… different, wearing old and shapeless clothes, rarely brushing her hair and smelling of the animals, and body odour, and God knew what else. She had looked like a cross between something out of Roald Dahl's *The Witches* and a tramp, and that had been a toxic combination for a child. She had definitely been 'other', the sort of woman society believed should have no right to exist. After all, women were supposed to marry young, have children, scrub up well, keep their weight down, colour their hair, shave their legs and make polite conversation, weren't they? And that was why Connie had apologised for those taunts about her appearance. Lord knows, she thought, she had learned her lesson on that one at least.

'Why are you so keen to defend her, Connie? You always told me you hated that she lived next door, with her smelly animals and her flying poo. I'd have thought you'd be pleased that they're trying to move her on.'

Connie dumped her tea bag in the bin and took a seat next to her mother.

'Yeah, I know. But I'm… not really a great example of an ordinary, functioning member of society myself, am I? Someone needs to stand up for people like me. And as you know, I've got very close to her animals since she went into hospital, and they are… Urgh, I can't really explain it…' she said, staring into her mug, watching the light brown liquid she'd just swirled with a teaspoon eddy and flow. 'They're a sort of medicine.'

'Well, at least that's one sort of medicine you're actually prepared to take,' said Ellen, giving her daughter a piercing look.

'What's that supposed to mean?'

'I know you're not taking those pills they gave you from the hospital. I emptied the bathroom bin this morning, and several of them fell out of a hole in the bottom.'

'Oh.' Damn it, I should have found a better place to dispose of them, she thought.

'Yes. *Oh*.'

'They said they wouldn't let me out of hospital if I didn't agree to take them.'

'I see. Then why aren't you taking them, Connie, if the doctors think they will help you? Why do you always refuse to take antidepressants? You have depression, love. You have always had it, since you were a child. It's a fault in your make-up, something you have no control over, and this medication might give you that, mightn't it?'

Connie thought of her mother's very obvious mental health issues: her obsession with cleanliness that had defined their day-to-day lives when she'd been a kid, the perfect lawn she had been discouraged from standing on, the kitchen she'd been discouraged from even walking through, the routines they'd had to go through every day just to leave the house. But Connie wasn't like that, was she? She was normal that way. She didn't have OCD. Tablets wouldn't help *her*.

And then Connie remembered some very dark days when she'd been a teenager.

'I want to go home. Let me go home.'

'What you need is help, Connie.'

'No, I will not stay here. You can't make me.'

'I'm afraid we can.'

Why did everyone think everything could be fixed by medicine and talking? That horrible place had only made things worse. Connie stared into her tea. She did not want to talk about this.

'Because I don't trust pills, all right? I took a few different ones when I was in London and they made me… mad.'

'Illegal ones?'

Connie shrugged. 'Some of them. Not all of them. Some of them I think came from doctors.'

'Connie, love, these are legally prescribed antidepressants that have a strong record of helping people out. Please consider taking them.'

Connie didn't want to say any more. She couldn't, *didn't* want to talk about why pills now made her want to vomit. Part of her wished she hadn't been so honest with her mother about everything. It might be easier if she didn't know the truth. But at least she was the only one who knew, and she trusted her not to share her secrets.

'So, back to Matilda,' Connie said, eager to change the subject. 'I was wondering if we could help her. You know, try to get the council off her back?'

Ellen raised an eyebrow.

'Is this about the animals, Connie?'

She knows me too well, Connie thought. And yes, part of it was that she wanted to keep her daily routine going, as it was making her feel so much better. But it was also about making amends to a woman she'd ignored and demonised since childhood.

'A bit. But mostly it's just about trying to look after a lonely, poorly old woman.'

'OK. But how?'

'Well, the letter said that they'd carried out a visit to her house when she was away – I think I saw them going in one morning – and that they think she has damp and that the house is uninhabitable. They also said that she was causing a nuisance with the animals. I wondered if we helped her clear it up a bit, make it cleaner, sort out the animal shelters and hutches so everything is more ordered, chuck some bleach around in the house, that sort of thing, I wondered if that might help change their minds.'

Ellen put her knife and fork down and sat back in her seat.

'Goodness me,' she said, chewing her final mouthful of toast.

'What?' said Connie.

'I'm just not sure how we've gone from you holing up in your room and drinking all day – yes, Connie, I'm your mother, I clean thoroughly, I know about the vodka –' Connie let out a gasp – 'to you wanting to help clean out our friendly local hoarder's home?'

Connie wrinkled her nose and took a deep breath.

'Do you want to know why? I feel guilty. I feel bad that I, *we*, have lived next to a lonely old woman for more than twenty years and never spoken to her. I feel guilty that my friends used to hurl abuse at her through her letterbox. And yes, there's a small part of me that knows that if Matilda and her animals go, I won't get my daily dose of happiness from them any more. And I know how ridiculous that sounds, but there it is. That's the truth.'

Ellen got up and took her plate and mug to the sink.

'I get that, Connie, and I admire your honesty,' she said. 'But couldn't I get you a pet? A cat, maybe? You've always wanted a cat. Wouldn't that have the same effect?'

'Mum, you have always refused to let us have animals in the house.'

'I could be persuaded, if it really made you feel better.'

Connie looked at her mother in astonishment.

'Thanks, Mum. That means a lot. I know how hard it would be for you.' Ellen shrugged and pretended to be really interested in the washing-up. 'I'll see whether the local shelters have any cats that need homes.' Connie saw her mother flinch, but she said nothing further, and she loved her for it. 'But even if we got a cat, I'd still miss the animals next door, and the gardening. It turns out I love making things grow, and I love the routine of it all. And I know that Matilda, well, she's too old to move. It's cruel. She deserves to stay in her own home.'

'I'm just thinking, love,' Ellen said, scrubbing her mug with a washing-up brush, 'that it might be very hard to get Matilda to agree to accept any help, that's all. I've worked with people like her. They don't want someone to tidy things up or throw their things away. They want to keep all of their stuff. That's the problem.'

'But why do they do what they do, Mum? People who hoard?'

'Well, it's complicated, love, is the answer. I did some reading before, when I was looking after a client who hoarded, and I read that it's now recognised as a disorder. Some scientists think it's due to a fault in the brain, and others reckon it's down to stress, horrible things happening in someone's life, that sort of thing. I think it's a reaction to anxiety, really, like refusing to leave your house, or being frightened of crowds. It's a way of controlling things, when life has got too much.'

Connie took another sip of tea and wondered what had happened in Matilda's life to make her how she was. Had she been like this as a child? Unlikely. When had it started?

'Was she like this when you first moved in?' Connie asked.

'Honestly, I don't know,' said Ellen, who was now drying her mug with a tea towel. 'Possibly. I never went inside her house, you see. I saw her in the village shop at the beginning, sometimes. But by the time you left, she wasn't leaving the house at all, and I saw more and more things, boxes, bags and books, stuff like that, appearing at the windows. I guess it was all quite gradual.'

Connie drank the last dregs of her tea and stood up and joined her mother at the sink.

'I still want to try and help her,' said Connie, turning on the tap to wash her mug.

'I think that's really admirable, Connie. It really is. It's lovely that you want to help. I just think you might find it hard to persuade her.'

'Do you think I could try, though?'

'You could certainly try. And if she agrees, I will help you. It'll be a big job. An enormous job,' she said.

'OK, then,' said Connie, taking the tea towel from her mum and drying her freshly washed mug. 'Wish me luck.'

— 15 —

September

Matilda

Matilda was already awake and sitting on the garden bench when Connie arrived to tend to the animals the following morning. She hadn't slept very well. Her lower back was really very painful now, and her whole middle felt lumpy and swollen. That was her fault, she supposed, for eating so much hospital food. She had gorged herself on it, not being used to three regular meals a day, plus dessert and snacks. It had been a long time since someone had made food for her and delivered it on schedule, and she'd taken advantage of it a little too much.

'Good morning, Constance,' she said, as her younger neighbour walked down the path. She was wearing different trousers today – these were tighter, and black – and a loose white linen shirt through which Matilda could see her bra.

'Good morning, Matilda,' said Connie, walking over to the bench. 'Did you sleep well?'

'Yes, fine, thank you.' Matilda was keen to avoid conversation as much as she could. She had never been any good at it. However, she did have something she needed to ask. 'Constance – before I forget – I am due a delivery from Dean this week. He always comes and picks up a list from me on the tenth day of the month, and brings the goods a few days later. I am writing my list. Can you let me know what you think I need for the animals, given that you have been looking after them of late?'

Connie looked pleased to be trusted. 'Yes, of course. I'll write a list when I get home and put it through your door. OK?'

Matilda nodded.

'But, child, I wanted to say. I'm very grateful if you have time to help me, but please don't feel you have to keep coming. I am sure you have... other things you want to do.'

'No,' replied Connie, her face unreadable. 'No, I really don't.'

'But surely you must have friends... or work?'

'I left all of that behind when I moved back home. I left my job in PR – that's public relations, you know, press releases and events and stuff,' she said, noting Matilda's confused expression, 'and came back here. And as you know, I was very unhappy. Really unhappy. Not really fit for work. But the animals have cheered me up, they really have. So I'd like to keep coming, if that's OK?'

'You may. Of course you may. You are being... a great help. I'm not as capable as I used to be, sadly.'

That was an understatement, of course. Matilda had been unable to open a can for supper the previous night, as she could not work out how to use a can opener, hold a can and hold her stick at the same time. She was now ravenously hungry, and was considering whether raw courgette might be an option.

'Have you had your breakfast already?' asked Connie, as if reading her mind. 'If not, I was going to have a crumpet with some jam. Would you like some? I could bring some over?'

'That would be lovely,' said Matilda, trying not to look as keen as she felt. She was salivating.

'Great, I'll go and get it in a minute,' she said. 'But first, I wanted to ask you something.'

'Oh yes?' asked Matilda, desperate for her breakfast to arrive as quickly as possible.

'I was thinking about that letter you received yesterday.'

Ah yes, Matilda thought. The one that said I am a public

nuisance with a damp house, and that I need to be moved for my own safety. That letter.

'I was thinking I might be able to help you.'

Matilda looked up at Connie, with her open, honest face, her deep brown eyes and her dark brown hair, which was tied back in a neat ponytail. She looked like she was in earnest, but Matilda couldn't quite believe what she was hearing.

'Help me?'

'Yeah. I was thinking about that stuff they said, about the house being damp, and I wondered if maybe we could see if we can fix your heating, and whether we can move things away from the walls a bit so that air can circulate more.'

'Are you an expert on damp?'

'I've been watching more videos on YouTube,' said Connie.

I really must find out what this tube is and where I can buy it, Matilda thought. It sounded useful.

'And with the animals, I thought maybe if we secured their pens and things a bit more so that they can't get out when you don't allow them to, and we tidy up a bit, you know, and clean the kitchen a bit, maybe...'

Matilda didn't reply immediately, because she was feeling a mix of emotions. Hunger, obviously – she wished this damnable girl would get on with bringing her food – but also embarrassment and a small but undeniable dose of gratitude. That letter from the council had shaken her up, there was no getting away from that. That was why she usually refused to read post. She was frightened for the first time in a long time, and she had spent hours lying on that camp bed last night trying to think of a way out of the mess she was in, but she simply couldn't. But maybe Constance was right, and this might help? Maybe if they did some superficial things, just for now, to make the house look more 'acceptable', maybe they'd leave her alone?

Connie had the same look in her eyes that Ellen had had when she'd asked if she'd consider letting Constance continue to look after the animals. It was a beseeching look. Imagine that! She was begging her to let her help. What a thing! It would almost be funny, if the stakes weren't as high as they were. Previously, she'd never have thought of letting anyone touch her belongings. But she was facing an enemy she had no idea how to fight, so – needs must, frankly.

'That would be very helpful, thank you, Constance,' she said, running her hands down the legs of her tracksuit, which was beginning to show signs of wear. How many days had she worn it for now? Three? She really must try to find one of her dresses, she thought. But heaven knew where they were.

'Really?'

'Yes, really. But –' said Matilda, rubbing her forehead – 'I need to approve everything. I want to be here, watching, and you need to ask me before you throw anything out. OK?'

'OK,' said Connie, her face alight with what Matilda felt might be purpose, or possibly triumph. Or both.

What have I done, Matilda thought. Have I made a terrible mistake?

'Right, so I'll finish feeding Rory…'

'*It's Clarrie.*' For God's sake girl, stop taking liberties, Matilda thought. I might change my mind. 'Why did you call her Rory, Constance?'

'Oh. She's a character in a TV show I like. Rory, short for Lorelai. It's a show called *Gilmore Girls*. An American show, about a mother and a daughter. They're both really bright but both have a lot to learn about life, relationships and stuff.'

'I see.' Matilda didn't really see, but she didn't really want to hear more about it, either, so she let it go.

'Why did you call her Clarrie?'

Matilda's eyes widened.

'Have you never listened to *The Archers*, girl?'

'No. What's *The Archers*?'

'Heavens forfend, you *are* a different generation, aren't you? *The Archers* is a radio drama on BBC Radio Four, about a rural community in what is basically Worcestershire. So, here – around here. It's been going for more than seventy years.'

'Oh.'

'There's a new episode every weekday. Clarrie and Eddie Grundy are a lovely couple, one of the mainstays of the show.'

Matilda looked up to see Connie laughing.

'Why are you laughing? I think they're perfectly good names for two very fine goats…'

'Oh, I get you. I quite like Clarrie, it suits her,' replied Connie. 'I just thought it was funny that we both chose to name them after fictional characters we like. Maybe we've got more in common than we realised?'

Matilda raised her right eyebrow. Then she looked at Connie. She was smiling, and it suited her.

'I doubt that very much,' Matilda said, her voice harsh but her face betraying that she felt otherwise. 'But what we do have in common, I think, is a desire for breakfast. When were you thinking about getting those crumpets?'

— 16 —

September

Constance

Connie was pacing. Her limbs felt like they needed to move. Her brain was obviously busy firing signals in all directions, including at her feet and hands, and walking was making her feel better.

Connie was feeling more energised than she had in months, or possibly even years. She hadn't even had anything to drink that morning. She had a task to do, something big, something difficult, and she really, really wanted to do it well, because if she did, she would get to help a vulnerable old lady stay in her home. She was also aware she was motivated partially by her own self-interest, but the fact that she'd be helping Matilda too made her feel less guilty about it. If she succeeded, it would be win–win.

She ran through her mental to-do list. She needed storage boxes, possibly crates; she needed cleaning equipment; she needed bin bags, or maybe even a skip; she needed someone who knew about back boilers; and she needed someone to perform some carpentry magic on the wonky, Heath-Robinson-type animal housing in the garden. No biggie. I can do this. Definitely.

But how? She didn't know anyone here, because she'd made sure of that. And she'd have to actually talk to people and risk outing herself in the process. Oh shit, she thought: can I really do this? Am I a fool to try?

No, she decided. No, I will do this by keeping it small. I'll ask Jamie. Yes, that's what I'll do. I'll ask Jamie, and then he can ask Mr Hoarder – or whatever his landlord's real name is – to help, too. He said they were happy to, and their garden is so full of junk, surely one of them will be handy with a saw and some nails?

Connie picked up her house keys, shoved them in her back pocket and walked out of the house before she could change her mind. She turned right at the end of their path and lengthened her strides as she approached Jamie's house. She took a deep breath as she rapped on the door twice.

At first, there was silence. Connie wondered if maybe Jamie was at work, but it was a Sunday morning, and she didn't think he worked on the weekend. Then there was a rustling, and what sounded a bit like a yelp, and then someone walked towards the door. It opened a crack and Jamie peered out, his eyes squinting at the sunlight which was now pouring into his house. As he pulled back the door, it became obvious that he was clothed only on the bottom half of his body.

'Oh, I'm sorry. Did I wake you? I thought you'd be awake by now,' Connie mumbled, trying not to look at his torso, which suggested he spent quite a lot of time at the gym.

'Yeah, sorry, long night,' he said. 'Or early morning, really. Sorry. Let me go and get dressed. Can you wait a minute?'

Connie nodded, still somewhat blinded by his abs. She obviously wasn't going to be invited in, was she, but she was fine with that. She had no intention of giving him the impression that she wanted to spend time with him in private, and her hard-won instinct for self-protection told her to avoid getting close to him, or any man, ever again.

Jamie smiled a bright white grin, pushed the door shut and Connie turned around and examined his front garden, which was absolutely jam-packed with junk. In one corner, a trailer was lying on its side, its tyres ripped, its undercarriage rusted. In another, there was a large bath, which was now providing a home to offcuts of wood, a stainless steel sink and a considerable amount of ivy. The grass underneath it all was barely able to grow, but where it did flourish, it was long, up to knee-deep in places. Were these really the people to help her clear Matilda's place? After all, they needed some of that medicine here.

'Done,' said Jamie, emerging from the house with a white T-shirt and a grey hoodie now covering his chest. Connie sighed with relief.

'Great.'

'What can I do for you? Do you need 'elp with the goats?'

'Sort of,' replied Connie, looking around the garden as she spoke, in an effort not to give Jamie the wrong idea.

'Oh yeah, so I should explain. This is all Martin's.'

Ah yes, *Martin*. Jamie's landlord's real name was Martin, thought Connie. Unlearning the fake names she'd given her neighbours was going to be hard.

'Oh, right.'

'Yeah. 'E likes tinkering with things, fixing things, upcycling things.' Excellent, thought Connie. Bingo. 'Although 'e's not very good at finishing the things 'e starts. 'Ence all this crap in the garden. I know it's an eyesore. 'E does promise to clear it, but as you can see... 'e never does.'

Less promising sounding now, thought Connie.

'So you were saying, about the goats?' said Jamie.

'Yeah, well, it's about Matilda, really, and the animals,' said Connie, her arms folded across her chest. 'She's back home from hospital but she's quite weak, and she got a letter from the council that's really rattled her. They're threatening to have her evicted for being a "nuisance" or something, saying that the animals are a nuisance, too. They also say that they're coming to inspect the house for building defects, and she's been told she has damp. I thought we could help her tidy up a bit, make her place a bit more... acceptable, you know? So that they don't make her move.'

'And you're 'elping 'er?'

'Yeah.'

What *is* it with this guy, she thought. Why is he so… difficult?

'Why?'

'Because it's a nice thing to do.'

'Right.'

Jamie was smiling. The cheek of him.

'Why are you looking at me like that?'

'Because you're finally outside my 'ouse in normal daytime hours, 'aving a normal chat, and talking about 'elping one of our neighbours. It's just nice, that's all.'

'What do you mean, normal daytime hours?'

'Because you usually walk past at dawn.'

It had never occurred to Connie that anyone would see her out at that time of day. The whole point of her morning walks was that she was alone, away from the world. She wanted to be able to choose when she interacted with people, and she was supposed to be spying on her neighbours, not the other way around. The fact Jamie had seen her was unnerving.

'Coming back from a night out, were you?' she said, her attempt at humour feeling very forced.

'Nah, I don't sleep well,' he replied. 'Some nights I don't sleep at all.' Connie nodded, because she couldn't think what to say. She had always assumed that he would sleep like a baby, after his shifts doing hard physical labour. 'Are you the same? Is that why you're up at dawn?'

'No, I usually manage to get to sleep. But I prefer that time of day. It's quiet. Peaceful.'

'You like being alone, don't cha?'

Connie nodded again. Shit, she thought, I look like a stupid bloody nodding dog. Talk, Constance. *Talk about something else.*

'So will you come and help me sort Matilda's house out?'

'Now?'

'Well, social services are coming back on Friday, Matilda says, so definitely soon.'

'Cool, yeah, OK. Right. Do you want me to ask Martin? 'E's quite 'andy, as I say, although 'is follow-through is often lacking.'

'Is he in?' said Connie, craning her neck in the direction of the front door.

'Oh, no, 'e goes to Mass early on a Sunday. 'E'll be back soon, though. We always 'ave a roast dinner together afterwards.'

'That's nice,' she said, taken aback that Martin, aka Mr Hoarder, was a church-going guy who liked a square meal. She'd had him down as a TV dinners, atheist sort. 'Shall we walk over to Matilda's now, anyway, and see what you think? Would be good to get your opinion.'

'You're assuming I know what I'm doing with a drill, I suppose,' he said, as they walked the short distance to Matilda's garden.

'Don't you?'

'Well, my father walked out on me when I was five, and my mother didn't 'ave time to teach me any DIY,' he said, continuing to walk straight ahead.

'I'm sorry,' said Connie, feeling the weight of her previous assumptions bearing down on her. She'd thought she was so clever, nailing down the jobs and aspirations of the residents of Roseacre Close. She'd assumed Jamie was an all-round practical guy, a hands-on, odd-job, turn-his-hand-to-anything sort of bloke.

'Nah, I'm only pulling your leg,' he said. 'Well, not about my dad walking out, but I do know 'ow to wield a drill. Martin's taught me everything I need to know, pretty much. 'E's the father I never 'ad.'

Connie had assumed that their relationship was purely transactional – that Martin needed to rent a room for more income, and that Jamie had simply filled that role. But she'd been wrong, and that was both heartening and shocking for Connie. It was nice, she thought, welcome, in fact, to be pleasantly surprised by someone for a change.

'Right, let's see what we've got,' said Jamie, walking down the passage beside Matilda's house. 'Wow, OK, yes, this place looks even worse in daylight.'

Connie stood next to him and surveyed the garden. Matilda was nowhere to be seen – she had taken to napping a lot during the day now. She seemed really tired since she'd been discharged from hospital. It was probably best she wasn't there right now, anyway. Watching someone assess the pathetic state of your infrastructure would probably be very depressing, if not infuriating.

'So the chicken 'ouse looks like someone's 'ad a terrible nightmare and tried to build it,' he said, inspecting the ramshackle combination of random wooden slats and chicken wire that Brian and his posse slept in every night. 'And are these the shelters for the goats?' he added, picking at the cracked plastic sheeting which served as Clarrie and Eddie's roof. There were also some ageing shelters for the cats and an unwieldy and open compost heap.

'All of the animal feed is currently kept in here,' Connie said, opening the door to the outside toilet. 'But I was wondering whether we could make something more permanent, and let this just be a toilet? It would be easier for Matilda to get to, and she could wash in here too, if we could get her some hot water.'

'Oh yeah. Did you say 'er boiler is broken?'

'I think so. She told me she hasn't had any hot water for a long time. She's got an old back boiler, apparently, but it broke years ago.'

'Jesus. 'Ow 'as she coped in the winters? Bloody 'ell.' Connie and Jamie stood in the garden in silence for a moment, both reflecting on the incredibly challenging, basic, lonely existence Matilda had been living right under all of their noses. 'I'll ask Martin about the back boiler. I 'ave a feeling 'e used to 'ave one when 'e was a lad. I might know 'ow they work, and 'ave an idea 'ow to fix them.'

'That would be brilliant,' said Connie. 'I think having heating and hot water would make a huge difference to social services' decision.'

'What about the 'ouse? What needs doing in there?' Jamie asked.

Connie walked over to the bench and sat down on it.

'That's a whole other world of difficulty, unfortunately,' she said. 'There's at least two if not three decades of clutter in there. You can't get into the bathroom, the kitchen is mostly unusable, and you can't even get up the stairs.'

'We're going to need some 'elp,' Jamie said, sitting down next to her on the bench. Connie turned towards him, surprised at his use of the word 'we'. 'What?' he said, shrugging. 'I'm on board now. I 'ave a couple of days off. I feel like we should do this. I like a challenge.'

'Yes, I suppose we're going to need more help,' said Connie, looking around her. 'Do you think Martin will be up for it?'

'Yeah, I reckon so. 'E's retired now, and I think 'e could do with something to do. 'E gets bored. And it's probably easier for 'im to finish a project that isn't 'is own. But we'll need more 'elp than that.'

Connie bit her lip.

'But I don't know anyone else around here,' she said.

Jamie laughed.

'But you grew up 'ere!'

'Yeah, I know. But I left when I was twelve, didn't keep in contact with anybody, and I only came back a few months ago, and since then I've been... keeping my head down.'

Jamie was still chuckling to himself. This infuriated Connie.

'Seriously. I just know Mum, you, Matilda and Dean – the latter only to look at, and he almost ran me over in a tractor once, so I suspect he's not that keen on me.'

'Oh dear,' said Jamie, who was still laughing, to Connie's annoyance.

'It's not funny! Almost being run over is... not funny.'

'Nah. Sorry. I was just laughing at 'ow you could really think that. Lots of people 'ere remember you.'

'Do they?'

'Yeah. Martin does, for one. 'E remembers you walking to school with your mum past 'is door, and bringing bonfire toffee round to share that you'd both made too much of on Guy Fawkes.'

'Oh.'

When Connie had made the decision to move back in with her mum, she had done so in the firm belief that no one in Stonecastle would remember her, because she had been such an unmemorable child who had left as soon as she had the passport to do so.

'And you know the old couple over the way, Brian and Jocelyn? She was Brown Owl for a bit. Do you remember 'er from when you were in Brownies? Because she remembers you. She says you were very quiet and very polite. She told me that last week when I popped round to 'er with some shopping.'

Ah, so that couple who were so devoted to each other, that pair she'd christened Colonel and Mrs Mustard, were actually called Brian and Jocelyn.

'You coming with me to Donna's? You know, Donna the nurse?' Ah yes, thought Connie. Mrs Posh Hospital. 'Yeah, she works at an 'ospice.' *Oh*. ''Er son Tom is doing a plumbing course. I reckon 'e might be useful.'

— 17 —

September

Matilda

'That's it, just turn it the other way – *no* – the other way – that's right. That'll do it.'

Matilda watched with amusement as two men she had spoken to for only the first time that morning tried to wrestle a huge old trailer and full-size bath through her side gate. The plan, apparently, was that they were going to use both of these items to store her animal feed, hay and gardening supplies, thereby allowing the outside toilet to become a toilet once more, although exactly how they were planning to carry out this feat, she had absolutely no idea.

When they'd finally brought both through, the two men – one younger and tousled, the other older, greying and more gnarly – wiped the sweat from their foreheads with their forearms and stood staring at the objects they'd deposited in the garden, as if they might magically transform themselves through the power of thought.

From her perch on the bench, Matilda reflected on how she was feeling, seeing these people, who were essentially strangers, on her property. She had thought that she'd feel violated, as she had when those numbskulls from the council had entered to 'inspect' her house, but this time she'd given her permission, and it felt different. And since she had welcomed Ellen and then Constance into her life, it felt like significantly less of an effort to let others in. Strictly on a case-by-case basis, mind you. But more than anything, she knew that doing this was the price she had to pay to be able to live out her days here, and so it was more than worth paying.

The older man walked over to where Matilda was sitting. He was tall and slim with closely clipped grey hair and a well-trimmed beard.

'Hello, Miss Reynolds,' he said. 'I'm Martin. I live up the way, you know, at number one? I remember seeing you walking past a lot in the early days. Back when my wife was alive. Do you remember Janet?'

Matilda didn't remember Martin or his wife, but she felt it would be impolite to say so.

'I do, Martin...?'

'Larton. Martin Larton.'

'It is nice to see you again, Mr Larton.'

'And you, too. Janet always used to say that we should ask you round to our place for cake and tea, but we never did, and I'm sorry about that. And now, well, I'm not as good at that whole guest thing as Janet was.'

Matilda, who was rarely prone to emotion, felt a lump rising in her throat.

'No matter,' she said.

'I'm glad. Anyway, now, Miss Reynolds, we need to ask you... Where would you like your new feed store?'

Matilda surveyed the farmyard that passed for her garden.

'I wonder about putting it where the lean-to is now, do you see? Up against the toilet building?'

Martin looked in that direction and nodded. 'Yes, I think that needs to come down anyway. It doesn't look safe.' He looked embarrassed, when he realised what he'd said, and who he'd said it in front of. 'No offence meant, Miss Reynolds.'

Matilda looked over at the lean-to, which she'd put up single-handedly one night, armed with a hammer, a random collection of nails, a lot of determination, but absolutely zero finesse.

'None taken,' she replied. 'It's done its time, I think.'

'Yes, I think so,' said Martin. 'Jamie – let's take these over there, and I'll go and get my tools.'

Matilda looked at Jamie. He was a good-looking young lad, she thought, although she had never been a connoisseur of the type. He was tall, had strong-looking broad shoulders and a very wide jaw, which she had always thought was a rather neanderthal feature, although it didn't seem that way on him. How old was he, she wondered. Perhaps mid-twenties? And why was he renting a room from Martin in a council house miles out of town, at his age? It was inconvenient for his work, his social life – his everything, surely? Yes, he was interesting, she decided; and so was Martin. And then Matilda smiled, because it had been a long, long time since she last found a man to be anything other than disturbing or frightening.

'Martin?'

Matilda squinted into the sun, and saw another young man walking into her garden.

'Ah, Tom,' said Martin, smiling broadly. 'Nice to see you again, young man.'

Tom was a different kettle of fish to Jamie, Matilda thought. He was short, round about the middle, with the remnants of adolescent acne still making their presence felt on his face. He was also struggling to smile and was mostly looking all around the garden, and not at Martin.

'Yeah, thanks, Mr L,' he said. 'Mum said you 'ad something that needs fixing?'

Matilda couldn't work out whether Tom was anxious or just awkward, but he certainly looked uncomfortable to be there, surrounded by people he hardly knew.

'Yes, Tom, yes. It's an interesting one for you, this, one of those back boilers that we used to have in the sixties.'

Matilda saw Tom's face transform.

'Oh, like the Baxi Bermuda?'

'Exactly so.'

'I'd love to 'ave a look at it,' said Tom, beaming. 'But I'll 'ave to ask my mate Gaz to come and 'elp me do the gas work that's needed, that's the thing. I met 'im at college. 'E's qualified already, see. But yeah, I can see what needs doing first.'

'Of course. That's great. Jamie, would you mind taking Tom into the house, to show him where it is?' Martin asked, still smiling.

'Yeah, course. Follow me, Tom,' said Jamie.

As the two young men walked up towards the back door, Martin walked nearer to Matilda.

'Young Tom is autistic,' he said. 'He's really struggled in mainstream school and never really got on with schoolwork, but it turns out he absolutely loves tinkering with things, and Donna says that he's doing really well on his plumbing course. He's absolutely loving it, and making friends, it seems, too. So I thought this would be a good project for him.'

Matilda suddenly felt a rush of emotion so strong that she struggled to stop herself from letting out a sob. Instead, she rubbed her eyes with vigour, hoping Martin wouldn't notice.

Oh Miriam, if only you'd been born now, she thought.

'Tired?' he said, looking at her.

'Yes. I don't like that camp bed much. But it would be rude to tell Ellen that, I know.'

It was the first excuse that had come to mind. She didn't actually mind it, if truth be told. It was far easier to get out of than a mattress on the floor.

'Yes, well, Connie said that she's going to try to clear your front room a bit today, so we can put a single bed in there,' he said. 'Then you won't have to climb the stairs, and you'll be able to have the heat from the fire, and you can use the outside toilet to wash. I'm going to ask Tom and his mate to put a shower in there. That's the plan, anyway.'

'Constance is clearing out my front room?'

'Yes, I believe so...'

Matilda didn't wait for his reply. Instead, she pushed herself up with her walking stick and set off as quickly as she could – and these days, that was really rather slowly – towards her house.

'Miss Reynolds – would you like any help?' said Martin, who had followed Matilda's progress and was now loitering just a foot or so from her arm.

'No, I'll be fine, thank you,' she said, finally reaching the back door and wrenching it open.

'I'll get my WD-40 on that later,' said Martin, holding it open for her. 'Should fix the squeak at least.'

Matilda nodded and walked into the house and down the hall passageway. When she reached the door to the lounge, she was taken aback to find three people squeezing into her front room. Two of them, Jamie and Tom, had moved some of her boxes away from the gas fire so they could take a look at both that and the back boiler behind it. It was strange seeing that fire again, for what must be the first time in at least five years, Matilda thought. In the early days in the house they'd spent their evenings sitting in two armchairs in front of that fire, starting with it on full to take the chill off and then gradually lowering it as the heat filled the room. Then later, when she'd been on her own, she'd sat there reading for many a night, until the fire had finally packed up, and she'd kept warm using a hot water bottle and her bedclothes. She went to bed when it went dark, anyway, so she slept for most of the coldest hours, rising at dawn like the farmer and the shepherd, keeping to nature's timetable. In the winter, she wore as many layers as she could fit on her small frame, and sometimes wore a blanket over her shoulders, too.

'So yeah, this is a Baxi,' said Tom, prodding around the gas fire. 'I've only seen pictures and diagrams of these. We don't fit these now. They're very inefficient. Are you sure she wants us to fix it?'

'Yes,' said Matilda, and the two men's heads snapped around to look at her. 'Yes please. I always got on well with it. That boiler and I understood each other.'

'OK,' said Tom, his face momentarily disturbed from its engineering reverie. 'I will do that.'

'Right, I'll leave you to it, then,' said Jamie, nodding at Tom as he headed for the door. To do this, he had to pass by Matilda, who had pressed herself against a leaning tower of phone directories. 'Sorry, Miss Reynolds,' he said as he squeezed by her, leaving behind him a very pleasant aroma that reminded Matilda of pine trees and mixed spice.

Now there were just two other people in her sitting room, and Matilda turned her attention to Constance, who was kneeling over a large cardboard box near the window. Beside her, Matilda spotted a black plastic bag, and she felt her heart begin to race.

'What are you doing, Constance?' she asked, following the path the younger woman had forged between several stacks of boxes, each step taking her several seconds as she calculated where she should place each of her feet, plus her new walking stick, which she was absolutely determined not to lose. It was so much more rigid and trustworthy than an umbrella.

'Oh, Matilda. Hello. I'm trying to make you a bit of space, so that we can put a bed in here for you. Mum has managed to find one from a local charity, but we need the room for it. We thought it would be easier for you to do things all on one level. And I've found some mould here, on the wall facing the street, so I'm going to get some gloves on in a bit and wash the wall down with bleach. It should help.'

'Stop,' said Matilda, who was trying her best to keep her voice calm. She knew, really did know that these people were just trying to help her. But the sight of her precious things being thrown willy-nilly into bags was just too much to bear.

'But I really think that we...'

'Just stop.'

'Oh.' Connie, who had looked positively energised up until that moment, now appeared to have had all of her positivity sucked out of her.

'I am sorry, Constance. I know you think you are being kind, but leave my belongings, please.'

Connie stood up and brushed her hands against each other as if wiping off dirt.

'Matilda, I know you're… attached to your things, but the thing is, you need room to move down here. And there isn't any, is there? You were seriously injured before because things fell on you, weren't you? I know you're angry that social services came in here and I get it, but they're right, it's not safe for you. Not safe at all. If you just let me clear some things out here, then I think you stand a chance of them changing their minds. There are a whole bunch of free newspapers here dating back decades that I think we could safely send to the recycling…'

Matilda shut her eyes and her mind spun back to the beginning of the 1960s. There was an enormous collage lying on the floor of the sitting room, far bigger than the dining table. The hundreds of tiny pieces – letters, images, cartoons, blocks of colour – had been cut out of hundreds of free newspapers and then glued individually onto a large piece of wood that Matilda had found dumped on the main road. The hands that cut and stuck those pieces had been lily white, unmarked, adored.

'Matilda?'

Matilda opened her eyes. Constance was still standing in front of her, her whole body one giant, infuriating question.

'*No.*'

'No?'

'*No*, you will not put any of my precious things in your blinking black sack.'

'But…'

'But nothing. I know it's impossible for you to imagine, but I need these things. They are a part of me. They are a part of my past. I will not let you get rid of them.'

'But it's just paper! Just bloody paper. A pile of newspapers, some of which are in pieces. There are mice droppings in here.

Come on! Just throw them away. It'll make you feel lighter, I promise.'

As Connie spoke, she picked up one of the newspapers, and a piece of paper cut into the shape of a snowflake fell out and floated down to the floor. Matilda followed her instincts and bent down to try to pick it up, before realising that she was too disabled to do it. As it landed on her filthy living room floor, Matilda felt her sorrow rise up and burst out of her. She was powerless to stop it now. Tears began to stream down her cheeks and her chest felt like it was squeezing the air out of her lungs.

'You... must... not,' she said through her tears.

Connie looked frightened then. She reached down, picked up the snowflake and presented it to Matilda.

'OK, Matilda, I'm sorry, really sorry. I didn't mean to upset you. I really am so sorry,' she said, rambling now. 'Look, how about I take these things upstairs instead? I'm sure we can move things around and make some room.'

Matilda took a deep breath and nodded. Yes, that would have to do for now, she thought. Just for now. But as soon as the council had given her the go-ahead to stay here, those newspapers were returning to where they belonged.

— 18 —

September

Constance

'Oh my God, it's so frustrating. She's living in a filthy house full of rubbish, and we're all busting a gut to help her, and she's refusing, absolutely refusing to let us throw even the smallest bloody thing away.'

Connie was pacing back and forth next to where Jamie and Martin were busy hammering, nailing and gluing a selection of junk from Martin's front garden into what apparently promised to be a feed store.

'I mean, she's facing eviction, she has mould on the walls, no heating, no means of keeping clean and she's so disabled now I don't think she can really look after herself, let alone the animals, and she's behaving like a… like a…'

'Like a scared old lady?' said Jamie, taking a break from his current task.

Connie stopped pacing and glared at him.

'No, like a stubborn old bag.'

Connie had just finished her sentence when she spotted Matilda coming out of the back door of the house. Whether she'd heard her or not, she wasn't sure.

'I've got to go over to Tom's now to pick up some tools,' said Jamie to Connie, noting Matilda's presence. 'Would you like to join me?'

'Sure, yeah, why not,' replied Connie, thinking that some time off the premises might help her calm down.

'Great,' said Jamie, a look passing between him and Martin that Connie didn't quite understand.

Connie followed Jamie out of the garden and onto the pavement, and they began walking together in the direction of Donna and Tom's house.

'Do you think she heard me?' asked Connie.

'Nah. Well, maybe. But she's old and deaf, isn't she? So probably not.'

They walked in silence for a few moments, Connie lost in her thoughts. Had she been wrong to push Matilda that far, she wondered. Was she being selfish, caught up with the heady high of actually having a purpose again? Was she... what would that counsellor she'd seen say... projecting her own issues on this frail old lady who obviously had her own mental health struggles?

It was a minute or two before Connie realised they'd walked out of the estate and onto the road leading out of the village.

'Where are we going?' she asked. 'We've missed Tom's?'

'Yeah, I didn't actually need to get anything from his 'ouse. I was just after an excuse to come on one of your famous walks with you.'

'Famous walks?'

'Yeah, one of your stomping-through-fields specials. Dean told me that 'e'd seen you the other day. Martin and I always wondered where you went and what took you so long, so 'ere we are. I'm 'ere to find out.'

The fact that her walks, planned so carefully to avoid prying eyes, had been noted and discussed anyway, infuriated Connie. She had been mad to think that coming back here would give her the privacy she needed. *Mad.* She forged on, lengthening her stride with the hope that she'd leave Jamie behind. With any luck, he'd bugger off.

'Are we speed walking?' he said, racing past her at a speed that wouldn't have looked out of place in the Olympics.

'No,' said Connie, coming to an abrupt halt.

'Ah, shame,' said Jamie, grinning at her like the proverbial Cheshire cat. 'I reckon I could do well at it.'

'Oh for fuck's sake,' said Connie. '*Why?* Why am I such a curiosity around here? Is it because I'm the resident black sheep, the local madwoman who only comes out of her house at dawn?'

'No, isn't that Matilda?'

Connie sighed and placed her hands on her hips.

'None of this is funny, OK? None of it. I moved back here for some peace. To be invisible. And you all seem to know all about me and I feel like you're all laughing at me behind my back.'

'No one is laughing at you, Connie.'

'Don't you mean "Posh Spice"?'

'Oh come on, that's affectionate. Liv 'eard you talking in the garden once and said you sounded posh, and it sort of stuck.'

'Who's Liv?'

Jamie made a face.

'Really?! Christ. You share a fence? She's new. Young single mum, two young boys?'

Ah yes, thought Connie. Little Miss Perfect. 'Oh yeah, her.'

'Yeah, 'er. She's nice. You'd like 'er.'

'Seriously, do you think I'm here to make friends? Do you think I'm enjoying this? Discovering that you've all been listening to me and that you seem to know all my secrets?'

'What sort of secrets?'

Connie examined Jamie's face. Was he lying? Or was there still a chance that he hadn't uncovered what she'd done? Connie decided to cling to that chance.

'Oh, just my morning walks, and stuff.'

'Stuff?'

Think, Connie, *think*.

'And my overdose. You all know about that, don't you? About me being taken to hospital. I'm sure you all watched, like it was a live episode of *Ambulance*.'

Jamie was no longer smiling.

'I'm really sorry, Connie, I didn't know about that. None of us know about that. Well, at least, Martin and I don't.'

Connie was incredibly relieved. If they didn't know about that – and judging by Jamie's face, he really didn't – then perhaps her secret was still safe. It would seem that her overdose and the ambulance called for her had been disguised well by the ambulance she'd called for Matilda. It was a relief that people locally hadn't known that and been prompted to ask more questions.

'I'm glad about that. It's not something I'm proud of,' said Connie. 'It was at my lowest point, you know. But I don't think I really meant it. To be honest, I'm not sure about a lot of things,' she said, still walking at pace up the road towards one of her favourite places, a gnarly, ancient oak tree beside a stream that was languid in summer and frothy and overladen in winter.

'I know fuck all about anything, so that makes two of us,' said Jamie, who had run to catch up with her. 'Seriously, jack shit. I failed all my GCSEs, so that was a bust, and now I'm renting a room off a guy who fostered me for a bit, because I 'aven't got anywhere else to go.'

'Martin fostered you?'

'Yeah, 'im and Janet were really kind, the best. I loved staying with them. But I 'ad to go when she got sick, like. I understood that it wasn't personal. But Martin let me come back last year, and that was great because I didn't 'ave anywhere else to go.'

Connie slowed down as she reached the gap in the hedge that led to her favourite tree. 'Down here,' she said, beckoning for Jamie to follow her. She was still processing what he had just said. She hadn't known that Martin and Janet had fostered. In fact, she hadn't even known that his name was Martin, so what had she expected? She was a stranger here, masquerading as a local.

Jamie squeezed through the gap behind her and followed her as she made her way to her tree. Because it was, most definitely, hers; she had claimed it as a young girl, and it would always be so. It was broad, balanced and solid, and there was a perfect seat in between its exposed roots which was an ideal place to hide, read a book or cry your eyes out, depending on your mood. Connie found the dip and sat down in it.

'Grab a pew,' she said. 'This is where I came, by the way. This place, and then I'd march through the field afterwards, to walk off my stress and... the darkness.'

'I didn't mean to pry,' said Jamie, sitting down a few feet away, to Connie's great relief. She would have freaked out if he'd been any closer. 'I'm really sorry. I was just taking the piss. Trying to make you laugh, like. You don't seem to laugh much.'

Connie looked down at the water, which was ambling between rocks, fallen branches and mud dams, destined, after many trials and tribulations, to join the River Severn.

'Nah, I don't. I used to, but not any more. There hasn't been much to laugh about recently.'

'Except me clambering over a wall and almost being eaten by a vicious goat?'

Connie smiled. 'Yeah, there is that,' she said. 'That definitely had comedy value.'

They both sat there for a moment in silence, focusing on the babble of the brook, the birdsong from the tree canopy and the distant sound of combine harvesters bringing in their crops.

'I 'ave depression, too,' said Jamie, finally breaking the silence. 'I've 'ad it for a long time, but I only got diagnosed a year or so ago, after I ended up 'omeless and I was given a bed by a shelter that 'ad a medical team that visited. They sorted me out, that lot, they were sound, really sound.'

'That's good to hear. What did they do that helped?'

'The medics? Oh, they gave me some pills, and they 'elped, definitely, but they also got me back in touch with Martin, and that got me a 'ome, so... It all 'elped.'

'Did Martin and Janet have any kids?'

'Of their own? Nah. But they 'ad loads of foster kids, masses of them. Some of them still visit. A couple of the girls are really nuts, they get off their 'eads a lot and turn up at Martin's door in the middle of the night, begging to be let in. 'E's proper patient with them, 'e is. I wouldn't be.'

So that was what Connie had seen. Not lovesick women he'd met at the pub, then, but stoned ex-foster kids.

There was a brief silence while Connie worked up the courage to ask about something that had been really bothering her.

'Do you still think I'm posh?' she asked, trying to keep her tone even, not wanting to give anything away.

'You're still bothered about that, are you? Seriously? It was just a joke. Martin and I just think you're obviously a cut above, that's all.'

'In what way?'

'Well, like I said, you don't 'ave a local accent any more, and you dress well. You 'ave nice clothes.'

Connie looked down at what she was wearing – a pair of jeans and white and blue stripey top, and couldn't see what he meant at all.

'I grew up here, you know that, don't you?'

'Yeah, I know. But you left, didn't you? Where did you go?'

Connie thought for a second.

'I went to London. To live with my dad.'

'Oh, right.'

Jamie didn't say any more, and Connie felt like she had to fill the silence, as if she had to explain.

'Mum was working loads. I spent a lot of time alone, you know? It wasn't her fault, but I was lonely, I was bored, I was confused. Plus we fell out a lot. Mum is… very house-proud, and I'm not. She had high standards, and I couldn't see the point of them. And London seemed so exciting, you know? Like my life could finally start.' As she explained why she'd left, Connie realised she wasn't even convincing herself.

Jamie frowned, and Connie realised what she'd just said.

'I'm sorry, I didn't mean that…'

'Yeah, you did though. And you're right, really, aren't you?

Nothing 'appens 'ere, does it? And there are 'ardly any jobs, and the jobs there *are* pay peanuts, and if you don't 'ave a car you're basically a prisoner in your own 'ome. I wish I'd left too, to be honest.'

Connie looked around her, at the beauty of nature that surrounded them, and wondered why she'd ever thought that leaving was the right thing to do.

'Yeah, well, I've been doing a lot of thinking about all of that, my decision to leave, and what that meant,' said Connie, 'and I've changed my mind. Look at all of this. Look at the amazing beauty of it. Doesn't it calm you? Doesn't it make you feel better? It does me. I came home after I… lost my job, because I knew it would help me heal. The countryside is amazing. It never changes. You can trust it. It doesn't betray you or argue back.'

Jamie stifled a laugh.

'Yeah, enough of that tree-'ugging bollocks,' he said. 'You're wrong, Connie. The countryside does change. It's changed a lot. Since you left, second-'ome owners 'ave bought up all of the pretty cottages around 'ere and basically turned villages into 'oliday rental estates, and local people like me can't even afford to rent the land for a caravan. Our old pubs are closing because there's no proper locals to drink in them, and our shops are shutting for the same reason. And developers keep building more and more 'ouses, but they're all really expensive, not for the likes of me and you. Living in Stonecastle is now like living in a theme park for rich people.'

That was the most Jamie had said to her since they'd first met, and Connie was struck by how passionate he was about it.

'It's really shit, isn't it,' she said. 'The roads get so much busier at weekends, and then seem to empty during the week.'

'Yeah, the weekend "country supper" crowd clear out on Sunday afternoons, back to their town 'ouses in Chelsea, or whatever. Leaving the likes of us to go and work shifts on Monday in the logistics warehouse we're supposed to be grateful someone 'as built near Worcester, or the chicken processing factory, or in the dark at a mushroom farm.'

Connie didn't know how to respond. If she needed a reminder that she absolutely did not live in the real world, this was it, and it made her feel incredibly guilty.

'Shall we head back?' she asked, deciding that action was better than words. 'They might be missing us. There's loads of work still to do.'

Jamie nodded, stood up and held out his hand. She took it without thinking and rose to her feet, trying to ignore the warmth she felt, which was awkwardly coupled with the shock and discomfort of having a man touch her.

'So what are you going to do about Matilda's stuff?' asked Jamie as they began the walk back to Roseacre Close, unaware of her reaction to what had been, after all, simply a kind gesture to help her get up. 'Will you just give up clearing out the 'ouse?'

'Yeah. I've told her I'm going to just move things upstairs for now,' replied Connie. 'I feel bad. I was really impatient with her, and I shouldn't have been. She's been a recluse for a long time, and it must be really weird having all of us in her house. And you were right. She's just a scared old lady, isn't she? Over the years I've made her out to be some kind of witch in my head, someone who wasn't really human. But she's just a woman, a woman with a few mental health issues, and God knows, I've got enough of my own to appreciate when someone needs to be left alone.'

It took Connie several hours and a lot of muscle power to clear a pathway on Matilda's stairs and move things from her living room into the main bedroom, which, while also full of clutter, still had a bit of room for Connie's neatly stacked boxes. When she'd finished doing that, she went back to her own house, grabbed some cleaning products, unplugged their hoover and brought it all back to Matilda's, where she zapped all of the cobwebs, wiped away mould, sucked up hundreds of dead ants and flies and swept up the thick layer of dust which had laid untouched on the sitting room floor for God knew how many years.

When she was finished, she surveyed her work. There was now a decent amount of room for the bed that Ellen had arranged to be delivered later, and the whole space smelled better, looked better and frankly *was* better for Matilda. The fact that the old lady would no longer be inhaling dust and mould spores made Connie feel happy. It was nice, she realised, to be given a chance to make a difference. On the other side of the room was the gas fire, which now had enough space in front of it for a seat and, crucially, it now worked. Tom and Gaz had left just a few minutes ago, having wrestled the back boiler into life. When early autumn gave way to winter, Matilda would be warm in here, and that was fantastic progress.

Happy with her work, Connie walked out into the hall, through the kitchen and into the garden. It had been transformed in just one day. The ground had been swept and the veg patches weeded; the animal shelters had been screwed together properly and their holes patched; and to her right, the pièce de résistance – Martin and Jamie had made an extraordinary-looking feed store, which had a raised storage area, so Matilda could reach things, courtesy of some bricks and the bath, and a solid room to keep the rain off, courtesy of parts of the old trailer. It was a strange-looking thing, undoubtedly, but Connie thought it would do the job. Next to it, she could see that the outdoor toilet was now clear of feed.

'You guys have done an amazing job,' she said, walking over to where Martin and Jamie were standing. 'You've worked so hard.'

'Ha, so have you, by the looks of it,' said Martin, looking Connie up and down. She realised then that she must look absolutely awful. She was hot, sweaty and dusty, and her clothes – the parts she could see, anyway – were filthy.

'Yes. The sitting room is looking a lot better,' she replied. 'You need to come and see.'

''Ave you shown Matilda yet?' Jamie asked, and they all turned to the bench at the end of the garden, where Matilda was sleeping. Her head was bent over almost ninety degrees, and it looked incredibly uncomfortable to Connie. Matilda had clearly needed the rest.

'I don't want to wake her,' she replied.

'We're going to have to at some point. We can't leave her there overnight,' said Martin.

'No, I know. How about we wait until the bed has been delivered and we've made it up? Then we can wake her, show her what we've done, and leave her to settle in.'

'I like that. Yes, let's do that. Right, Jamie, let's tidy up and make sure we've moved all of our tools. We can come back later when we see the charity delivery truck.'

Connie watched as the two men gathered their things, made a final check on the stability of the new feed store, and closed the door to the outdoor toilet.

'Tom said he'll be back in the morning with an electrician friend to fit an electric shower in there,' said Martin.

'It's amazing he's managed to persuade these guys to help for free,' said Connie.

'Yes. But there are good people around here. Good people. We help each other if we can,' replied Martin. Connie felt even more guilty than usual, for the assumptions she'd made about all of her neighbours. 'So yes, as I was saying, Matilda's got the drain outside the toilet, so water can just run off there, and I reckon she could probably use it when she's sitting on the loo. That'll make things easier, with her disabilities.'

Connie looked at the kind, thoughtful, hard-working man she'd only just got to know, and felt she needed to say something.

'Thank you so much for everything you've done,' she said. 'You didn't have to and it's been really hard work, and you don't know me from Adam, so...'

'Don't be silly. I did this for Matilda, anyway, not for you,' replied Martin, smiling. 'And Jamie's pleased we've managed to clear some of the front garden now. Every cloud, and all that.'

'I'll see you later then? When the bed comes?'

'Yep, we'll go home and have our tea, and we'll be back to help bring it in. When did you say the council were coming?'

'Friday, I think. I'll check with Matilda. When she wakes.'

'Great. See you later.'

Martin waved as he walked up the side passage, with Jamie following closely behind.

When they'd gone, Connie stood in the garden, her arms braced across her chest, breathing in the smell of agriculture – the scent of the leaves, of compost, of feed, of faeces, of animals – and smiled. And then she felt something nudge her hand, and she looked down to find Rory – no, Clarrie – looking up at her with intense expectation.

'Oh yes, it's dinner time, isn't it,' said Connie to Clarrie. 'I'm coming, little one. I'll feed you now.'

— 19 —

September

Matilda

Matilda had expected them to come early, so she'd made sure she was ready. She'd had a wash, courtesy of the new, slightly odd but very effective shower-over-toilet combination in the outside toilet, had put on her hospital-gifted tracksuit, which Ellen had kindly washed for her, and boiled herself a fresh egg for breakfast. When she'd fed the animals, she sat down on the chair in front of the fire and began to read. Connie had moved some boxes so her bookshelf was now accessible, and she was reacquainting herself with her favourites. Today, it was *Brideshead Revisited* that had caught her eye. She was fully immersed in Sebastian Flyte's Oxford when there was a knock at her front door.

Matilda pushed herself up with her stick, took a deep breath and shuffled to the front door. She opened it to find Caroline Goodman on her doorstep, along with the younger social worker, Daniel Symonds, and a man in his sixties with a round face and a moustache, wearing a sharp grey suit, who she didn't recognise.

'Hello, Miss Reynolds,' said Caroline. 'Can we come in?' There was no explanation as to why she'd turned up with reinforcements.

Matilda managed to force out a thin smile. 'If you must,' she said, retreating a few steps so they could enter. Normally she'd have told them where to go, but part of her was rather looking forward to showing them the improvements her neighbours had made.

'We're just going to take a look around the house, to check its condition, Miss Reynolds,' said Caroline, walking into the sitting room, leaving Daniel and the mystery man in the hall. Matilda knew that the sitting room was significantly tidier than it had been the last time she'd seen it. Matilda heard Caroline take a deep breath, and was quietly delighted. That must mean she was impressed. How could she not be? It had been painful, to be sure, but her neighbours had worked really hard for her, and she was genuinely grateful. The garden, in particular, was so much easier to get around and the feed store really did save her poor back.

'How is the boiler, Miss Reynolds?' asked Caroline.

'It's fixed. I had a lad from down the road fix it for me. Good as new.'

Caroline did not reply for a while. She looked at the wall behind the boxes, which Connie had wiped free of mould, and at the new bed, which had clean bedsheets on it, courtesy of Ellen.

'So your neighbours have helped you, is that right?'

'Yes. I'm very lucky. They realised I was in a pickle, and they stepped in. I'm so grateful. There's a lovely community here. Really supportive. Have you seen the garden? They did amazing things with...'

'We'll have a look out of the back bedroom window,' said Caroline, walking out of the living room, leaving a heady dose of her perfume, which smelled to Matilda like boiled sweets, in her wake, and climbing the stairs, flanked by the older man. Daniel, the younger one, stayed with her. They think I need a babysitter, Matilda thought. Hah.

'This room seems much more comfortable now,' said Daniel, interrupting Matilda's thoughts.

'Yes,' she replied, still thinking about the older man. Who was he? She assumed he must be some kind of surveyor or maybe even a builder, although he didn't look like one. What were they looking for upstairs? She hadn't been there for a long while, but Connie had told her that it was messy, but not damaged in any way, no leaking roof, or anything like that.

'My grandad had one like this.' Matilda nodded but didn't take the bait. 'Look, I'm sorry about... Caroline. She's new. Wants to make her mark. Isn't used to how we tend to do things.'

He's trying at least, poor lad. Imagine having to work with that woman. Must be absolutely grim.

They were taking ages up there, she thought, after several minutes had passed. Should she try to go up? She hobbled back into the hallway and looked up the stairs, with Daniel following her. Caroline and the older man were in the main bedroom, undoubtedly looking out over her back garden. They were talking, and she could hear what they were saying quite clearly.

'I hadn't fully taken on board what an amazing view these properties have, Caroline,' said the mystery man. 'It's quite the idyll.'

'Isn't it,' replied Caroline.

'How big is the site in total?'

'About five acres. The gardens are unusually generous.'

'Yes, they are. The houses are relatively small for their plots.'

'Yes, that was the style of the era. Plenty of outside space to grow produce. Now, of course, we maximise living space indoors. Times change. Have you seen all you need to see?'

'Yes, I have. Thank you. Thank you for letting me come along.'

'It seemed too good an opportunity to miss,' said Caroline, heading towards the stairs.

'How are things up there?' asked Daniel.

'As expected,' replied Caroline, walking back down the stairs, followed by the man.

'Thank you, Miss Reynolds, we're done now,' said Caroline, moving towards the front door. She's itching, just itching to get out, isn't she, thought Matilda. 'You have made positive changes here. There's no obvious sign of extensive damp, and your heating and hot water are now working, which is good. I'll update the social services team accordingly and I'll confirm that in a letter. OK?'

Matilda looked at Caroline and wondered how much it had hurt her to say that. She had come, undoubtedly, with the intention of telling her to sling her hook, and that must be disappointing for her, mustn't it? But as Ellen said, there was nothing about her living arrangements currently which could be said to be dangerous or a nuisance. And she was right, it seemed. Matilda's heart soared.

But just then, a look passed between the man-with-no-name and Caroline, and Matilda's blood ran cold.

Because there was something in that look that told her this was far, far from over.

'So she said you could stay?' asked Connie later that day as she leaned over into the new feed store and scooped out some grain for the chickens.

Matilda thought for a moment.

'Not in those words. She said that the changes were good and that she'd tell her team about them.'

'That must be good news, mustn't it?'

Matilda watched Connie sprinkle the grain on the ground and smile as Brian and the girls scurried over and hoovered it up. She really wanted to tell her that it was good news, because Connie had worked so hard on her behalf. Heaven knew, she wanted to believe it herself. After all, she'd made a promise that she'd never leave here, and she intended to keep it. And yet there was something about that visit that didn't make sense. Who was that man? And why had he been so interested in the size of the estate? She felt confused and unsettled.

'I think we'll have to wait and see,' she said.

As Matilda turned to look down her garden towards the distant hills, she heard a rumble of thunder. Yes, there was a storm coming. She was sure of it.

— 20 —

September

Constance

'You ready?'

Ellen was standing at the bottom of the stairs, shouting up for Connie, who left her room with great reluctance.

'For what?'

'The barbecue in Niamh's garden? To celebrate Matilda being allowed to stay?'

Connie blinked twice – her brain, pleasantly lubricated with vodka, slowly realising that it had forgotten something important.

Matilda had received a letter a week previously from poisonous Caroline saying that her housing now met the required standard for her to live in, provided her animals were not regarded by her neighbours as a 'nuisance'. She had smiled broadly after receiving that letter, and although she obviously couldn't skip these days, Connie had noticed a bit more of a spring in her step afterwards. And for the first time in ages, frankly, Connie felt proud. Although there had been some self-interest in her efforts, she'd undoubtedly done something good for someone else, and the effect on her had been quite visceral. She'd never taken those drugs she'd been given by the doctors, but she did wonder if this was what it might feel like if she did.

'Oh. Yeah.'

Martin and Ellen had decided to use the group effort on Matilda's house as a springboard for more community events, something that had taken a knockout blow during the pandemic and never really recovered. Connie had known the party was planned, but hadn't really registered when it was. Although, frankly, she had very little idea what day it was anyway.

'Yes. So. Are you coming?'

Connie looked down at what she was wearing. She'd been planning on going to feed the animals in a bit, so she was wearing her most scraggy jeans and a loose, greying, once-white T-shirt with a stain down the front from breakfast.

'I'm not dressed for it.'

It wasn't really about what she was wearing. She could easily change. It was really that Connie wasn't at all sure that she wanted to go and be sociable. She had managed it when they'd been sorting out Matilda's house, because she'd had a clear purpose. But just standing around talking to people – that would be different. It would mean trying not to answer questions, pretending to be normal and functioning, pretending to be someone she wasn't.

'You look fine. It's an outdoor meal in a garden, not The Ritz.'

'I've got to feed the animals.'

'You can nip over and feed them. It's right next door.'

'No one wants to see me there, anyway. They don't even know who I am.'

'Everyone knows that you played a large part in getting people together to sort out Matilda's place. You were the one who made it happen. Come on, Connie. Let's go and have a bit of fun. We never have fun, do we?'

Connie was running out of excuses. She looked at her mother, who'd changed out of her uniform into a bright red shirt and jeans, with matching dangly earrings. She looked happier than she had in a long while, as if a huge weight had been lifted from her shoulders. Connie sighed, ran her hands through her messy hair, and walked downstairs. She didn't want to ruin her mother's good mood.

'OK. I'll come. But only for a bit.'

''Otdog?'

Jamie and Martin were in charge of the barbecue, obviously. It was an unwritten law that men who'd never even consider cooking in a regular kitchen were attracted to grilling meat outdoors.

'Sure, why not,' replied Connie, accepting the blackened sausage and pre-sliced bun in a napkin from Jamie, who was grinning broadly.

'Ketchup and stuff is over there,' he said, pointing her in the direction of a trestle table playing host to a range of condiments, some paper plates and a large bowl of coleslaw. Connie walked over to it, picked up a bottle of American mustard and squirted it liberally. Then she headed towards the end of the garden, which sloped gently down towards a stream, beyond which a field rose sharply, the village church's spire just visible over its peak. She'd spotted a bench by the fence beside an apple tree which was laden with ripe fruit. Niamh's garden was long and thin, like her mum's and Matilda's, and Connie hoped she might be left in peace there.

She sat down with a sigh, crossed her legs, bit off a mouthful of overcooked sausage and observed the group of residents, who were gathering around the food and drink stations like bees around a honeypot.

'Hi,' said a female voice with a Brummie accent. Liv, aka Little Miss Perfect, was walking down towards her. Connie examined her. Despite being only about five foot two, Liv nevertheless had everything in extraordinary proportion – in fact, thought Connie, she had the perfect hourglass figure. Today, Liv was wearing blue ripped skinny jeans and a tight red and white spotty T-shirt, and looked like she could have just stepped out of the pages of a catalogue. Her long blonde hair was piled on top of her head in a doughnut bun, and her lips were bright red. 'You're Connie, aren't you? Jamie said.'

'Yep, that's me,' replied Connie, bracing her hotdog to her chest.

'We're neighbours, aren't we?' she said, sitting down next to her on the bench.

'Yes, we are,' replied Connie, feeling simultaneously both very shy *and* very guilty that she wasn't capable of being more friendly.

'I wanted to say, I hope my kids don't annoy you and your mum when they play out.' Liv was sipping what Connie thought might be cider from a white plastic cup. 'Sometimes they get so stir-crazy in the house that I just have to chuck them outside, you know?'

Connie didn't know, but she could imagine. She had certainly heard them playing, but only during the day, and they didn't bother her particularly.

'Nah, they're fine. Honestly, nothing could be worse than waking up at dawn to the dulcet tones of Brian the cockerel,' said Connie, smiling, noticing that Liv's boys were currently nearer the house stroking Snuggles, who actually seemed to be incredibly docile. His bark was clearly far worse than his bite.

'Oh, yeah! I hear him too,' said Liv with a chuckle. 'But I'm usually up then anyway with my youngest, so it's fine really. You are too, aren't you? I've seen you walk by sometimes, early. I quite like the view at that time of day. It would be great if I wasn't completely knackered.'

Jesus, does no one in this close sleep in, thought Connie.

'Know how you feel,' said Connie, although she didn't, of course. She usually just got drunk and slept all day, because she had sod all else to do. 'Also, I like walking when it's quiet.'

Liv laughed.

'Ha, it's always quiet around here. There's nothing to do.'

Connie was about to defend her childhood home, but then she realised what it must be like for Liv, a single mother with no car, in an area with hardly any buses. She remembered too how she'd felt just before she'd left, her teenage years spreading out before her in a place where she had few friends and even fewer prospects.

'Yeah. Great, isn't it?' said Connie, and Liv grinned. 'So what brought you here?' asked Connie, suddenly curious.

'It was the furthest away the council could get me from my ex,' replied Liv, matter-of-factly. 'He – my ex – lives in Droitwich. He knocked me about,' she said, avoiding Connie's gaze. 'So in the end I took the kids with me to a shelter, and then the council put us in a B&B and on the list to move into our own place. This was the first one that came up.'

'Have you got family in Droitwich?'

'Yeah, my mum's there, and I miss her. But I had to make a fresh start, you know? He kept saying sorry and I kept going back, and each time it got worse and worse. So I'm here to save me from myself, really.'

Me too, thought Connie, feeling a surge of warmth towards the young woman next to her.

'Well, you're very welcome,' she said, smiling.

'Thanks! I do feel welcome here. Jamie and Martin have been really good, helping me with stuff in the house that needs fixing, and lifts sometimes to town, for the food bank and that.' She paused to take a sip from her cup. 'I do want a job so that I can buy the boys nicer things, but I can't get free childcare for my youngest until he's two. It's a bit shit, you know... No, Max, stop that!' she shouted. 'Sorry... I need to go and sort that out.'

'Understood,' replied Connie, smiling, watching Liv run up the garden towards her eldest son, who was trying to pull some of Niamh's beautiful blooms out of the flowerbed.

'Would you like a drink?' said Martin, walking down towards her with a plastic cup. 'It's white wine?' Connie accepted it gratefully. 'And are you OK, here by yourself? I'm sorry everyone's stubbornly staying up there,' he said, pointing to the house. 'I suspect it's the free booze.'

'No, you're all right. I like it here,' replied Connie. 'I like my own company.'

'OK, suit yourself,' he said, smiling. He walked away to return to the drinks table. She was taking a large swig of wine when she saw that the elderly lady from across the road was making her way towards her. She was holding the hand of her husband, Colonel Mustard.

So much for being on my own, Connie thought.

'Hello duck. We haven't seen each other for years. I'm Jocelyn,' she said, standing a few feet away from the bench.

Jocelyn was not as Connie had expected. For a start, she didn't have a local accent. Instead, she was emphatically northern. And while from a distance she'd looked frail, up close she was upright, animated and joyful and her broad smile was emphasised by carefully applied red lipstick. 'And this is Brian.'

'Hello, love,' said Brian. 'I'm very pleased to make your acquaintance.'

'Nice to meet you too,' said Connie.

'May we sit down?' asked Jocelyn. Connie nodded, keen not to offend her, while also considering how soon she could politely make her escape. She didn't really want to talk to anyone, and yet it seemed she had no choice.

They sat in companionable silence for a few moments, before Brian spoke.

'We need to go home, dearest,' he said. 'I've got marking to do.'

This confused Connie, because Brian was well past retirement age. What marking could he possibly be doing?

Jocelyn stared straight ahead, and took a deep breath in. 'I know, darling. But let's just talk to Connie first, and then we can go home, all right?'

'Of course, dear,' he replied.

Jocelyn was still holding his hand, Connie noticed.

'Connie, love. You don't remember me, do you?' asked Jocelyn.

'No, I do,' she lied. 'You were my Brown Owl, weren't you?'

Jocelyn's eyes lit up.

'Yes, I was. It was fun, wasn't it? Our pack had fun.'

In truth, Connie's memories of her time in Brownies were sparse, but this old lady didn't need to know that.

'Yes, it was. I enjoyed it.'

'I'm so glad. You were a lovely little girl, you know. Quite quiet. Like now, I suppose? You like your own company?'

Connie shrugged.

'Yeah. Yes. I do,' she said politely, hoping that this would mean that Jocelyn would take the hint and stop talking to her.

'That's good. I wish I did. But I've never been very good at it. But luckily I always have Brian now,' she said, her voice overly bright. Jocelyn's face seemed to be frozen in a smile, and her hand was gripping Brian's even more tightly than before.

'He's becoming a bit of an escape artist, prone to wandering off,' she whispered in Connie's ear, unprompted. 'He got out the other day and the lady who runs the local shop had to call me. I had to ask Martin to go and collect him. I don't know how he walked all that way, it must be a couple of miles.'

And now Connie understood why they were always holding hands on the rare occasions they went out. Jocelyn was caring for Brian, who she realised must have dementia. Connie felt chastened. She'd thought she'd known these people, but it was becoming increasingly clear to her that she knew nothing about them at all.

And then Connie realised that they had no car in the driveway. How did this couple get their shopping? Did they ever leave the village? How did they visit the doctor's or the hospital? Connie knew how useless the local bus service was.

'If he does that again, just let me know and I'll go and get him.'

'I will love, I will. Thank you,' said Jocelyn, reaching into her pocket, pulling out a handkerchief and wiping her eyes. 'Everyone here is so kind.' Connie thought she might be on the verge of tears.

'Would you like a drink, either of you?' asked Connie, keen to do something, anything, to try to cheer Jocelyn up. And if truth be known, she also needed to do something to assuage her own guilt. 'Or food?'

'Do they have sherry?' asked Brian. 'Or gin?'

'Brian loves a tipple,' said Jocelyn, a smile returning to her beautiful face. 'But a white wine would be fine for us both.'

Connie nodded and walked back up the garden towards the crowd of locals, who were all laughing, slapping each other on the back or involved in intense conversations. She was struck by their cohesion, despite their obvious differences. They were a random group of strangers thrown together by chance, but they all seemed to have a place at the proverbial table, and occasional roles in each other's lives, as and when there was need.

For the first time ever, Connie could see the appeal of living in a community like this. It must be wonderful, she thought, to feel like your neighbours had your back, to feel they really knew you, and you them. It was something she had never experienced, and never would.

Just before Connie reached the drinks table, she turned around to take in the sun, which was setting over the hills. The valley below glowed gold.

Yes, she thought. Her own mistakes had put paid to that.

PART THREE

— 21 —

October

Constance

The day began like any other. Well, like any other of Connie's recent days, anyhow. She had returned to her regular morning walks, although she'd stopped leaving before dawn, as there now seemed little point in hiding. She checked her watch; it was 8 a.m. Matilda would be feeding the goats around now. She had recovered enough to do it, so Connie had switched to doing the evening shift instead, and that suited her. Having something to do at both ends of the day gave her structure, something which she hadn't had for quite some time. She had found that it was helping her. She was drinking a bit less and spending less time holed up in her room watching TV. Baby steps.

She turned left and walked up a narrow lane which had a broad strip of grass down the middle of it, the grass on the rest of the track kept at bay only by occasional farm traffic. The hedgerows either side of her were becoming more see-through daily, as the plants began to shed their leaves in preparation for the winter frosts. Through the hedge on the left, she could see a tractor pulling a large piece of red machinery on its back; probably drilling the winter wheat, she thought. Dean, who it turned out was actually friends with Jamie, had told her that. He'd told her a lot, actually, about farming, over the occasional drink in the only pub in a four-mile radius that still had relatively cheap beer and a regular darts night. She'd felt self-conscious at first, after their meeting in the lane, but he'd laughed it off and she'd been hugely relieved. Years ago, conversations like the ones she'd recently had with Dean would have bored her stupid, but there was something about the annual rhythm of farming, the symbiotic relationship between humans and nature, that she now found fascinating and reassuring. It was exciting to get to the age of twenty-nine and discover something completely new about yourself, she thought. Particularly given that she hadn't much liked all the things she knew about herself before.

The yearly rhythm of Matilda's little smallholding was also a welcome challenge. Connie had just finished harvesting the final runner beans of the season, and the pumpkins were now nearly ready for their annual Halloween outing. She was learning something every day. Last week, for example, she'd also dug up the potato tubers and sown seeds for broad beans, both under Matilda's watchful eye. It amazed Connie how well she and Matilda managed to rub along together, given how far apart they were in age, background and lifestyle choices.

Actually, thought Connie – what *was* Matilda's background? She realised that she didn't know. She'd been going over daily for a couple of months now, talking and occasionally sparring with her, but they'd never really spoken about much beyond the animals and the weather. That had been a relief, in many ways. But she *was* curious about how an intelligent woman like Matilda had ended up as both a hoarder and a hermit. She wondered if she'd ever tell her. Given their track record, however, she thought it was unlikely. For now, she was just grateful that Matilda had absolutely no interest in her own past, and so she had to keep her end of the bargain and refrain from pushing too hard.

After a sit-down by the stream and a few precious minutes of stillness during which she focused only on the sound of her own breathing and the myriad different lives in the natural world around her – that tree-hugging stuff, as Jamie would put it – she headed for home.

It was when she was passing the first house on the right in the close, number eight, that she realised something was wrong. Mr and Mrs Chicken were not at work, even though she was fairly certain they were on a week of day shifts. And when she passed Tom and Donna's house, she saw that Tom was outside in the front garden with his hands over his ears, looking for all the world like he was seeking shelter from a weapon of war.

She could see Donna through the front window of number seven. She was on her phone, ranting. Connie couldn't make out the exact words, but there was no doubt at all that she was absolutely furious. Then she caught sight of Connie, waved at her frantically and ran out of her front door, which Tom had left ajar.

'Have you been 'ome, Connie? You need to go 'ome. See your mum. Tell 'er to open the post. It's fucking outrageous, what they want to do. Fucking outrageous,' she said, before throwing her phone on the floor.

'Mum,' said Tom, his hands still over his ears. 'Please stop shouting.'

'Sorry, love,' said Donna, her anger abating when she saw its effect on her son. 'I'm sorry. You can come back in now. I promise not to shout.'

Connie could see that Donna, who had now picked up her phone from the ground and dialled another number, was not in the mood to talk about whatever was upsetting her, so she spun on her heels and walked home to number three as quickly as she could.

'Mum?' called out Connie, as soon as she'd turned the key in the front door.

'In here.'

Connie followed the sound of her mum's voice into the lounge. Ellen was sitting on the sofa with a letter laid out on her lap.

'What is it, Mum? What's in the letter?'

'Oh, Connie,' she said. 'I don't even know where to start.'

Connie sat down next to her mother, and read.

Dear Ms Darke,

I'm writing to you and all Roseacre Close residents to give you notice that the council has made the very difficult decision to put the close up for sale.

While the provision of social housing in rural areas is important, the council has concluded that it could provide many more units elsewhere in the county with the proceeds of the sale of this land, which is located in an area with high demand from property developers.

Furthermore, during a recent visit to the estate it was noted that at least one of the houses, which date back to the 1950s, is in a state of disrepair, and the council believes that footing the bill for remedial works potentially required across the close is not in taxpayers' best interests.

We appreciate that this news will be upsetting, but please be assured that we will provide you with suitable alternative social housing within the county.

We will also strive to give you as much notice as we can of your moving date when we have found a buyer.

Yours sincerely,
Joseph Richards
Head of Asset Management & Property Services
Severnside Council

Connie felt sick. She had never, *never* in her wildest dreams imagined that this might happen. Surely this couldn't be real? She'd lived in this house as a child. Matilda had lived next door pretty much since the estate had been built. How could they just pull the rug out from under everyone here? And what about the animals? Where would they go?

'Oh my God. Can they do that?'

'I'm guessing so,' said Ellen. 'They're the landlord, aren't they? They can do what they want.'

'But we... you... have rights, surely? You've been here so long, this place is yours, right? They can't just make you move.'

'I think they can, Connie. I really think they can. I've been looking online since this arrived, and it's getting really common for councils to sell their old housing stock. They make loads of money from it, and then they can put up new housing – flats and small houses on smaller plots – elsewhere, or on the same site, but closer together, you know? I guess they think that we aren't a good use of this space. I mean, our gardens are huge, aren't they? And there are two women living alone on this estate, in three-bedroom houses.'

'But... this is our home,' said Connie, feeling tears start to form. 'It's ours. All of ours. It's Martin's and Jamie's, and Matilda's, and everyone else who lives here. And what sort of place will they put you in, do you think? Will they give you something the same size, with the same garden?'

'It doesn't say so. It just says suitable. *I mean*, define suitable,' said Ellen, her head in her hands. 'You're an adult, so they won't even count you in the head count here, so they could easily just offer me a one-bedroom flat without any outside space, and tell me to lump it.'

Connie was struggling to retain a grip on reality. What she'd just read seemed so crazy, so out there, that she felt like she was having an out-of-body experience. Everything she had recently discovered that she really, really cared for seemed to have been cut loose and was now swimming around in a maelstrom in her brain: her bedroom, the scene of many a childish fantasy and early-teen angst; the view of the fields from the patio, where she and her mum had often eaten breakfast on sunny days; the open countryside that was within such easy reach for her walks every morning; the animals, particularly Clarrie, who was, obviously, the most precious of all; and, she realised with surprise, her new friends – the people she'd just made connections with here, people who had surprised her in so many different ways.

Yes. *Friends*. That's what they were. It hadn't, up until that moment, occurred to her that that was what they were, but now she had realised it, she cared more about them after this horrendous piece of news than she had even a few seconds ago.

'We can't let them do this to us, Mum,' she said, wiping her eyes with her sleeve and snorting to try to clear her nose.

'I don't think we even have the option of fighting it, Connie. Although I suppose we could talk to Citizens Advice or something? But none of us have the money to pay for legal advice, do we? Unless you...'

Connie could see where her mum's thoughts were going.

'*No*, Mum. I *cannot* do that. It would mean going back to my old life, and I just can't. Not now.'

There was an awkward silence.

'I love you, Connie, I really do, but you're as stubborn as a bloody mule.'

'I just can't, Mum. Not when I'm finally starting to feel better.'

'I get it, love, I do,' said Ellen, putting her arm around Connie and drawing her in for a hug. 'And I'm so delighted you're better. There was a time there when I really thought I was going to lose you, and you have no idea how glad I am that I didn't.'

Connie felt her mother's arms around her and cast her mind back to her childhood, when Ellen would come up to her room after she'd finished work and, finding her crying, gather her up and let her sob against her chest, for as long as she needed. And then later, when she'd been in that large, well-furnished room in Kensington, and her stepmother had tried to do the same, she'd practically flung her away, desperate to refuse her help, because she had been trying to cover for her husband's failure to parent.

Now that she had some perspective on her childhood and how her mum must have felt, Connie realised how little thought she had given to Ellen when she'd taken those pills in the summer. The fact that her mother had been such an afterthought, yet again, made her feel incredibly ashamed.

'I'm so sorry I put you through that, Mum. I really am. At

the time, I wasn't myself, right? I was a complete bloody mess. I haven't been myself for a long time.'

'I know that, love. And I know that I haven't always behaved very well, either.'

This was as close as Ellen had ever come to apologising for her own behaviour, and it made Connie squeeze her mum even tighter. She knew that she'd had her own struggles, and the two of them, each dealing with their own stuff, had been a toxic combination.

Ellen reached into her pocket and pulled out a tissue, handing it to Connie.

'You're a proper mum, you are,' said Connie, pulling away. 'You've always got a clean tissue about your person, ready for tears.'

'Yes, or a stray bogey.'

'Nice,' said Connie, managing a smile before blowing her nose.

'So, Miss Constance, if we're not going to let them do this to us, but we're not going to pursue the route I suggested, what *are* we going to do?'

Connie stared at the opposite wall, at the fireplace which used to be home to an old back boiler, and then saw beyond the wall, into Matilda's home, which had been improved beyond measure in a matter of days with the help of her neighbours. *Her friends.*

'We'll all get together, all of us in Roseacre Close, and we'll put our heads together and make a plan,' she said.

'All of us?'

'Yeah, even the sad-looking couple at the end who I don't know yet, and Niamh with her scary but strangely friendly dog, and Liv with the amazing arse. All of us.'

'Well, if we've got an amazing arse on our team, how can we lose?' said Ellen, laughing.

'Better than the absolute arse behind this ludicrous plan, Mum,' replied Connie. 'I'm not sure who it is yet, but I'm going to find out, and when I do, I'll make sure they know about it.'

'Fighting talk.'

'Yeah. A fight. That's what they're going to get. A fight.'

'I'll drink to that,' said Ellen, standing up. 'Now. How about a commiseratory cup of tea?'

— 22 —

October

Matilda

Matilda didn't hear the post being pushed through the letterbox, because she was sitting on the bench at the end of her garden looking out towards the horizon. The ancient hedgerows that divided the fields beyond the fence were just turning from deep green to russet and amber, and in the orchard at the bottom of a distant hill, the last of this year's apples were being shaken from the trees. The air, meanwhile, was dense with the scent of the last wild fruit – the season's final blackberries, sloes and rosehips were almost falling off the branch, ripe for the picking.

This time of year held a great number of memories for her, and she needed time to be alone with those memories. It had been this time of year when she'd first moved here, newly in disgrace, newly free, newly responsible.

She had been twenty-three years old, and all she'd known since childhood was the convent. She had decided to succumb to her school's desire to create nuns of its students, knowing that making her way in the outside world, an orphan with no means, would be very hard. And frankly, the nuns had made their calling seem almost glamorous. They had promised further education, nursing training, the opportunity for travel. These were all things Matilda had wanted, and the safety and security she had found in the daily rituals of the church had seemed to make taking her vows the obvious choice. She had taken them gladly, in fact, promising poverty, chastity and obedience with the certainty of a young woman who knew almost nothing, but thought she knew everything.

And then she had met Sister Theresa, and slowly but surely, the parts of life she had not previously understood had been revealed to her in glorious technicolour.

Back in the present day, Matilda closed her eyes and focused on the feeling of the ground beneath her feet, and on the sounds that surrounded her: the shuffling and squawking of the chickens; the clicks and licks of cats vying for pole position in front of their breakfast bowls; the rumbling of traffic on the road at the end of the close; the unmistakable sound of a tractor's diesel engine labouring up a hill; the bleating of the ewes congregating in a field nearby, newly returned from being dipped to rid them of disease.

'Matilda! Matilda! Are you there? Can you hear me?'

It was Constance. That child is far too dramatic for her own good, thought Matilda. Does she think I'm dead? I might be ancient, but I've not fallen off my perch yet.

'I'm here, Constance,' said Matilda, refusing to shout. She just didn't have the energy for it, and anyway, it was vulgar to raise one's voice.

'Matilda,' said Connie, running across the garden, dodging cats and chickens with what Matilda felt was impressive dexterity. 'Have you read your post this morning?'

'No, I have not.'

'Oh.'

'Why?'

'There's a letter in there you need to read. We've all had one. Everyone on the close. It's awful, Matilda. They're going to sell the estate and move us all on.'

Matilda had been feeling at peace with the world up until that moment, more at peace than she had in years, particularly given the letter from the council saying that she could stay put. She had been so relieved about that. That whole thing had made her feel so very ill. But now… she felt her mind shifting from the new stability she'd found towards the edge of the abyss it had been teetering on for decades. Surely this couldn't be true? I must keep calm, she thought. I need to be calm. *I must think*.

'Could you go and get the letter, please, Constance,' she said. 'I need to read it for myself.'

Connie ran into the house and returned to the bench within a minute. She handed the letter to Matilda in the manner of a faithful servant delivering a death warrant. Matilda slid her finger under the flap, ripped it open, removed the letter, unfolded it and began to read. As she did so, her mouth went dry. This was a nightmare, surely? She couldn't actually be awake?

Then she jumped, because Connie had put her arm around her shoulders. She had not been touched by another human – except for those blinking nurses of course – for years.

'Oh, sorry, Matilda, I'm so sorry,' Connie said, removing her arm, 'You looked so upset. I always do that when people look upset.'

Matilda took a deep breath to try to steady herself.

'I'm sorry, my dear, that was awfully rude of me,' she said, still feeling the warmth of Connie's embrace on her skin. 'I am not used to hugs. I've never really… been a hug sort of person.'

'Sorry, I shouldn't have presumed. I mean, I'm not that keen on being touched, either…'

'Don't apologise. It's perfectly fine.'

Connie and Matilda sat in silence for a few moments. Matilda was glad of the pause; she needed time to bring herself back from the edge.

'It was that woman who came to the house,' said Matilda, finally. 'That Caroline woman. Mark my words, she's behind this in some way. I knew there was something wrong when she visited. She had someone else with her, a man who seemed very interested in the estate.'

Connie raised an eyebrow.

'Who was he?'

'I'm afraid I have no idea, Constance. But I'd like to know.'

'OK. Well, it's something to go on, at least.'

Matilda swallowed.

'I can't leave this house,' said Matilda.

'Oh, I know how you feel,' said Connie. 'I can't bear the idea of Mum having to leave next door, either.'

'No, Constance, you aren't listening. I cannot leave this house. You will have to trust me on this.'

'OK,' she replied, sounding startled.

Matilda wondered whether she should tell her the truth. But then she hardly knew her at all, did she? While she was undoubtedly a kind girl, she was definitely a lost soul who had yet to find safe harbour. Who was to say whether she could trust her with her secret, should circumstances change?

'Right. OK, so you will be interested in hearing that I'm not planning to let them win, then?'

Matilda shot Constance an inquisitive look.

'Yes, of course. I don't intend to let them win, either.'

'Great,' said Connie, sweeping her hair back from her face. 'I've been talking to Mum about this. We need to galvanise everyone on this estate into action. And I mean, everyone. We need to arrange a meeting so that we can get our heads together. I'm not really sure, but I'm hoping that together we will be able to come up with a plan. Better together, that sort of thing.'

Matilda didn't reply immediately, because she was thinking. She had dealt with hostile authorities before, and by God she knew how to fight them.

'Yes. So, Constance, here's what we'll do. Tomorrow, you need to go around and knock on every door on this estate and tell them that we need to have a meeting. OK? I wish I could come with you, but I'm pretty useless these days, as you know. And you also need to get them to agree to a petition, and sign it. Start here in the close, and then we can ask others in the village to sign.'

'Do you think we need some sort of official advice?'

'Yes, that's a thought. Who are those people… that charity, you know, who people go to for advice? I read about them in the paper every so often.'

'Citizens Advice?'

'Yes, that's them. Could you call them?'

'Yes. They're on Twitter too, I think. I'll drop them a message.'

Matilda decided not to ask for a translation of this, and merely nodded.

'Right then. So, when shall we meet? How about next Saturday? That gives us four more days to think, and I'll get started on writing the text for a campaign leaflet that we can drop through people's doors. Could you Letraset that for me, or whatever you lot do these days with computers?'

Connie was still looking startled, and Matilda wasn't surprised. She was startling herself, frankly, but it was amazing what a shot of adrenaline and a real and immediate threat could do to a brain that had thought itself retired long ago.

'Yes, I will,' said Connie, who seemed to have pulled herself up a good few inches since she'd first arrived. Good girl, thought Matilda. It's wonderful to see some fighting spirit in you.

'Excellent. Great. See you tomorrow, then, Constance.'

That was Connie's cue to go, and she took it. She waved as she disappeared down the passage towards the gate, and Matilda tried her best to smile back.

As soon as she'd gone, however, her head sank into her arms, and she wept.

'I'm so sorry, my darling,' she said through her tears. 'I rather think I started this, letting the house get into the state I did, giving the council a reason to come in and see how wonderful our little home is here. They had ignored us until now, hadn't they? But I will do what I can to stop this. I promise. *Everything* I can.'

— 23 —

October

Constance

Connie had eschewed her usual morning walk in favour of several hours spent in front of her mum's laptop. It was astonishing how long it had actually taken her to create a basic table, to write a few sentences up the top and to tweak the font. It was as if she'd never used the bloody program before. A sign, she supposed, of how long she'd been out of work – no, make that out of society, really.

When the document was ready, Connie spent another half an hour wrestling with her mum's printer, which was almost out of ink and incredibly belligerent, bordering occasionally on psychotic. Did they make printers like this deliberately, she thought. To piss people off so they ended up attacking it with a sledgehammer, and had to buy another one?

Once she'd managed to produce one copy of the new petition that hadn't been chewed up or had half its text missing, Connie found a piece of cardboard and pinned it to it, popping a pen in her pocket. She didn't have a clipboard, so this would have to do. Then she took one final swig from her cup of coffee – she was having only a shot of vodka once a day at the moment, and she was proud of that – checked her reflection in the mirror, and headed off to Martin and Jamie's place.

She knocked on the door hoping that Martin, at least, might

be in. Matilda had told her to go around the close to drum up support, and she'd agreed, but Matilda hadn't said that she had to do it alone, had she? Despite her previous career, she'd always hated talking to people she didn't know. Cold calling had undoubtedly been the worst thing about her old job.

''Iya,' said Jamie, answering the door – fully dressed, this time. He was wearing a stained pair of grey tracksuit bottoms and a tight grey T-shirt with a giant hole under his right arm, and his dark hair was brushed back and still wet from the shower.

Oh my GOD he's hot, thought Connie, finally admitting to herself how physically attractive she found him, before doing her best to cast that thought aside. Because he was a man, and she was sworn off men. She was no good at relationships. No, this was just her hormones, after a long fallow spell, reacting to a man with broad shoulders, a wide jaw and a very muscular behind. Quite natural, in fact, to feel this way, she thought, and very easy to rationalise and ignore. And anyway, she was safe. She doubted he'd even looked at her twice, and even if he had, well, he wouldn't once he found out who she really was, would he?

'Morning, hi,' she said, sounding as if she'd just passed him on the street, rather than actually having sought him out. Jamie looked expectant. 'So, yes, well, after the letter yesterday...'

'Yeah, Martin was in bits last night,' replied Jamie. 'Never seen 'im like that before. Broke my 'eart.'

'Yeah, Mum was similar. Well, I decided that I'd put up a fight, and Matilda, well... it turns out she's even more of a battle-axe than we thought. She's basically cooking up some sort of war strategy, I think, and her first move was to send me out to get signatures from close residents on this,' she said, holding up her new petition, which Jamie took from her and began to read.

'*We, the undersigned, believe that Roseacre Close provides vital social 'ousing in a rural area with very little affordable accommodation, and we demand that the council take it off the market.*'

'Sounds good to me. 'Ave you got a pen?'

Connie dug into her pocket and pulled out the pen, and Jamie wrote his name and address and signature on the form, before handing everything back to her.

'Did you want anything else?' he asked.

'Well, the thing is... Are you free for a few minutes? I need to go around and knock on doors here, and I barely know these people.'

'You want me to come around and 'old your 'and, is that it?' said Jamie with a mischievous grin.

'No, well, umm, sort of,' said Connie, stumbling over her words like a nervous school girl.

'Yeah, why not. I don't need to go to work for an hour or so,' he said, grabbing some keys from a shelf beside the door and slamming it behind him.

Connie smiled with relief.

'What do you actually do for a job, by the way?'

She didn't want to tell him that in her fantasy *Gilmore Girls* world, she'd had him down as someone who worked for the council on the roads.

'Me? Oh, I work for the council as a groundsman and gardener. I keep all the public spaces tidy in town.'

One of my better guesses, then, thought Connie.

'Do you enjoy it?'

'Yeah, I do, actually. It doesn't pay very well, but I like being outdoors, and I like making things look nice.'

'Yeah, I get the being outside thing now,' said Connie. 'I used to think I hated it, you know. When I lived here when I was younger, I was bored. I begged Mum to take me into town all the time, but she was always working. That's part of the reason I left. I thought London had all of the answers. It didn't though. Or at least, it had the wrong answers.'

'Like what?'

'Oh, just stuff that made me really unhappy. Anyway, you've

only got an hour, so – which way first? Shall we try Liv, or the sad-looking couple at number eight?'

'You mean Sally and Nick?'

Yes, Jamie, obviously I mean them, thought Connie, mentally archiving their previous names, Mr and Mrs Chicken.

'Yes. They didn't come to the party.'

'No, not surprising, really,' replied Jamie with an expression on his face that Connie couldn't read. But before she had a chance to ask why, he said, 'Let's start with Liv. She'll definitely be in.'

'Sure,' said Connie, following Jamie out onto the street and down the footpath to the adjoining house, where Jamie rapped on the door. Connie could hear that the TV was on. It sounded to her like it was playing nursery rhymes.

'Oh, hiya Jamie, hi Connie,' said Liv as she opened the door, balancing a toddler on her hip.

''I there, Liv. And 'ello there again, little Kieran,' said Jamie, turning his attention to Liv's son.

'He's a bit snotty today, aren't you Kieran?' said Liv. 'He's a bit miserable. He won't leave me alone.'

'Aww, poor little thing,' said Jamie, who was now, Connie noted, playing peek-a-boo with Kieran.

'Have you come about the letter?' asked Liv.

'Yeah. Actually, Connie and I are 'ere to talk about 'er campaign to stop it 'appening.'

'Oh really? That would be *amazing*. I moved so far to come here, you know, and the boys have really only just settled at school and nursery, and moving them again just seems so… shit.'

'I've – we've – me and Matilda at number four – we've put together a petition for us all to sign, and a WhatsApp group to join, if that's OK,' said Connie, holding up the petition to show Liv. 'And we're going to have a meeting on Saturday at our place – I mean my mum's, number three – at three p.m., to talk about what else we need to do.'

'Yeah, I'm in,' replied Liv. 'As long as you don't mind me bringing the monkeys? I don't have any family near here, see, so they have to come everywhere with me.'

'No, that's fine,' replied Connie. 'We can put the TV on for them, maybe? And get them some snacks?' What *do* toddlers eat, she wondered. She decided that she'd have to google that.

'Sounds great. See you there,' said Liv. 'Bye Jamie, bye Connie. Nice to see you,' she said, before shutting the door.

'She's lovely, is Liv,' said Jamie as they walked towards number eight, the house opposite. 'A real diamond. 'Er ex, the boys' dad, was an abusive bastard. Did she tell you?'

'Yes, she did. Sounded awful.'

'Yeah. Anyone who's managed to leave all of their stuff and live in a B&B with two young kids for months without going mad deserves respect, I reckon.'

And I thought I had it hard, Connie thought. But I could have left too, couldn't I? *I* could have run away before it got bad, but I didn't. What Liv had been through, it really put her own situation into perspective. Connie realised that she had been wallowing in her own self-pity for a long time, but it was stories like Liv's that pulled her out of her own tiny, dark world, and she was now starting to see the light a little. And – *Posh Spice*. They weren't that far wrong, were they? She had been up there in her ivory tower, looking down on everyone. It had taken her a long time to realise it was they who should be looking down on her.

'Yeah, definitely,' she said, as they walked over the road. 'By the way, you do know that Posh Spice wasn't really posh, right?'

'Yeah. She was just rich.'

'And I'm not rich.'

'Fair enough,' said Jamie, not sounding entirely convinced.

As they approached number eight, Connie fell behind so that Jamie could knock on the door. She had never spoken to the couple inside, Sally and Nick, who she had, in her fictional world, decided worked in a chicken factory. Which was obviously, *obviously* going to be wrong, wasn't it?

'Jamie?' she said, just before he knocked on their door. 'What do these two do for a job? I see them going out together several days a week, both for days and nights. What are they doing?'

'Oh, they don't work any more,' replied Jamie. 'I don't think either of them've worked since the accident.'

'What accident?'

'Don't you know? I'm sorry, I thought you did. It 'appened about ten months ago. Their daughter, Maddie, was ten when she was 'it by a car opposite the primary school at picking-up time. She was crossing the road to get into their car. The guy who 'it 'er was driving a four-by-four far too fast, and 'e was drunk. ''E'd been in the pub all day. Anyway, Maddie is still alive, but she's in a coma. They make sure she's never alone in 'ospital – I think both sets of grandparents and Sally and Nick take turns being there, so that if she wakes, someone will be there.'

Connie could barely take it in. She hadn't even considered that there could be such pain on her doorstep. Her fictional world had never dived that deep into the darkness.

'Do you think she'll wake up?'

'I dunno. I'm not a doctor, am I? But if they 'aven't suggested to her family to turn the machine off, maybe there's still 'ope?'

'I hope so. I really do.'

'Yeah, me too. So, am I knocking?' Jamie said, his arm hovering near the door.

'Yes, sure.'

He knocked, and footsteps approached the door. There was a rattling of a chain and then Nick answered and smiled when he recognised Jamie.

'All right, Jamie? How are you doing? Haven't seen you in a while.'

'You too, mate. 'Ow are things? 'Ow's Maddie?'

'She's hanging in there, mate, thanks for asking. She's a fighter.'

'I bet she is.'

There was a brief pause, during which Nick glanced over at Connie and looked confused.

'Is this your girlfriend, Jamie?'

'Oh, no mate, this is Connie,' said Jamie, replying, Connie felt, a little too quickly for comfort. 'She lives down the way with her mum, Ellen? Dunno if you moved in after she left to go to London? Anyway, we're 'ere about yesterday's letter.'

'Oh yeah, that. We got back from the hospital last night and read it, and to be honest with you it felt like we were being knocked back into the worst of the days, you know, just after Maddie was hurt... I just can't imagine what it will be like to have to leave this house. I mean, we've got Maddie's room up there, with all her things in it. What if she wakes up, and we've moved and she doesn't recognise anything? What will we do then?'

Connie could see that he was about to cry.

'That's the thing. I've got this plan,' she said, judging that this might be the moment to do so. 'I reckon if we all club together, we can sort this out. We can make them keep the close. I've started this petition, Nick. Would you consider signing it, and joining our campaign? We have a meeting arranged at my – Ellen's – house on Saturday afternoon at three p.m. Will you come?'

Connie handed Nick the petition, and she watched him read it.

'Yeah, give me a pen,' he said, taking one and signing it immediately. 'I'm not sure about Saturday, though. We usually spend the day at the hospital...'

'We understand, mate,' said Jamie, jumping in quickly. 'Don't worry yourselves. Thanks for signing, though. We're starting a WhatsApp group, too. Can I add you?'

'Yeah, sure, of course.'

'Great to 'ave you on board, mate,' said Jamie. 'And Sally, too.'

'That's fine. Thanks for trying, both of you. Anyway, I've got to go, I'm sorry. I told Sally I'd bring her a cuppa in bed. She didn't sleep well last night, but she's managing a lie-in this morning. Let me know if there's anything we can do to help.'

'Will do,' said Jamie, just before Nick closed the door.

Connie didn't say anything as they walked away, still thinking about Nick and Sally, and how hard it must be for them both just to wake up every morning and function.

'Do you think it was wrong to ask them to join us? I mean, they have so much on their plate,' she said, thinking out loud.

'Nah. 'E lives here. 'E cares. 'E might not make it to the meetings, but I'm sure 'e's glad to be part of our group, trying to save the close.'

'You think so?'

'Yeah, I do. You 'eard him – 'e wants Maddie's room to stay the same, not to move 'ouse, and I don't blame him. 'E's been through enough. So that's another reason to fight the council, isn't it? To help Nick and Sally and Maddie.'

'Yes. *Yes*,' said Connie, slowing down and coming to a halt on the pavement outside her house. She felt mentally exhausted. Emotionally full.

'You OK, Connie?' said Jamie. 'Do you want to go to Niamh's another time?'

'You know what, Jamie, I think that might be good,' said Connie. 'I'm feeling a bit tired, all of a sudden.'

'Do you want to come round mine for a cup of tea? You might feel better after a sit-down,' he said.

Connie thought for a moment. Would she prefer to be alone? Her mum was out, and she could always retreat upstairs back into the safe, saccharin world of *Gilmore Girls*. Or she could, perhaps, face all of the emotions she now felt head on, and see if she could actually deal with them. Might that be better? Maybe?

'Yes, sure, why not,' she replied, following Jamie to the house he shared with Martin.

'Come on in,' said Jamie, turning the key in the Yale lock on the front door of number one. 'You'll need to take your shoes off, sorry, Martin's obsessed with that. I think 'is wife made 'im do it for years and 'e wants to keep doing it for 'er, like.'

Connie nodded and took off her trainers and looked around.

The decor was not as she'd imagined. She'd thought, given the state of the front garden, that it would be really cluttered inside, quite chintzy, but in fact the walls were painted in striking plain colours, lots of reds and blues, and covered in artwork and photos. The floor in the hallway was the original parquet tile, well swept.

'Wow, love what he's done with the place,' she said, meaning it.

'Yeah, I think it was mostly Janet's doing. She was an artist. The whole 'ouse is really colourful. My room is bright yellow. Makes me feel like I'm on 'oliday in Torremolinos,' said Jamie with a raised eyebrow.

'Oh, I like colour. My dad's place had lots of really striking, bold wallpaper in it. I loved it.' As soon as she'd said it, Connie wished that she hadn't.

'Do you see your dad much?' asked Jamie, walking through to the kitchen, with Connie following behind.

'No, not any more,' she replied, entering the kitchen, which looked out over an overgrown garden at the back, home to yet more items Martin was obviously intending to use for something, at some point, one day. The kitchen itself was relatively tidy, significantly more tidy, in fact, than Connie had expected. 'Oh, I like this kitchen,' she added, very keen to change the subject. 'I love the terracotta-coloured cabinets.'

'Yeah, it's a bit 1990s, but it works, doesn't it,' replied Jamie. 'Builder's tea OK? It's pretty much the only tea I make. Anything weaker just looks like piss to me.'

'You clearly aren't drinking enough water if your piss looks like that.'

They both laughed.

'Ah, so you *can* laugh,' he said, filling up the kettle and switching it on. 'Good to see.'

'Yes, I definitely can. There just hasn't been much to laugh about lately,' she said, looking down at the floor to avoid his gaze.

'Yeah, that letter was pretty shit, wasn't it?' he said, putting tea bags in two mugs.

'No, I didn't mean the letter,' said Connie, again immediately wishing she hadn't. Jamie raised an eyebrow.

'Do you want to tell me? A problem shared, and all that? The lads at work tell me I'm a good listener...'

'No... I...'

There was an awkward silence.

'It's OK. You don't 'ave to... I'm sorry... I don't want you to feel I'm pushing you...'

'No, I'm sorry. I shouldn't have said anything,' replied Connie, desperate for him to change the subject. The forcefield she had worked hard to erect around herself was vulnerable, and she knew that if she shared too much of her past, she might damage it.

'OK,' he said, walking through to a small conservatory at the back of the house and beckoning Connie to follow. He sat down on one of the two armchairs in the conservatory, which had houseplants covering every spare surface. 'Sorry that it feels like a jungle in 'ere – Martin is a keen gardener, so 'e uses this as 'is greenhouse.'

'No worries. I've come to like green a lot more in the past few months,' replied Connie, thinking back to glossy grey walls, lino floors and a yearning to escape. 'I used to think I hated living here, you know. But I think it was just me I didn't like.'

'So that was why you left? You felt trapped?' asked Jamie, sipping his tea.

'Yeah, sort of. Mum was working a lot, she always has. Dad and her did some sort of deal after I was born. Under it, he agreed to pay a monthly amount for my upkeep, but nothing for housing or other costs, like holidays and stuff. I don't think she minded at the time – she was young when she had me, and I reckon she just wanted to be shot of him – but I suspect she probably regrets it now. It's been hard for her.'

'So your dad refused to pay properly for 'er and you?'

'Yeah. Shit, isn't it.' She paused, shrugged and sipped her tea. 'They weren't married, and he weedled his way out of child maintenance somehow. Mum was naive. He got round it by putting me up at his place during the school holidays. He lived – lives – in this big house in London with his wife. They used to take me shopping for clothes and get my hair done, that sort of thing, and he used to take me out to dinner in the evenings, and I just… Well, it seemed so exciting. Much more than here. Mum and I were falling out all the time, you know. She is… quite difficult to live with. Two big personalities in one small space…'

'Big? Your mum seems pretty chilled to me.'

Connie snorted.

'Ha. Not at home. She's a complete perfectionist, can't bear for things to be out of place. It was a nightmare for a kid who just wanted to come home and relax. She'd come home and tell me off, we'd have a row and I'd storm off upstairs. And repeat. It was shit.'

'Sounds like pretty standard growing-up stuff to me. Actually, what am I talking about, I 'ave no idea. I was in and out of various foster 'omes, I 'ave no idea what normal looks like.'

'Sorry. That was thoughtless of me. I must sound super self-absorbed to you.'

Jamie put his mug down on a side table.

'Nah. You sound like every person who's 'ad a tricky childhood. It's not a competition, is it? We all go through our own shit and deal with it the best way we can. Anyway. Biscuit? Sorry, I should have offered earlier. Martin always does.' Jamie got up and walked towards the kitchen. 'Your mum must've missed you, though?' he called out, opening a cupboard.

Connie swallowed a mouthful of tea and thought about her mum's face on that sunny August weekend when she'd been driven away from the close. Her mum'd had tears in her eyes, but at the time, Connie had been far too excited about her move to London, about the promised new school, new life and new friends to care.

How must Ellen have felt, she thought, watching her only child leave her without so much as a backward glance? And how must she feel now, being used, essentially, as a refuge from the world, after being treated like that? Because Connie hadn't gone back to her dad's house, had she, when she needed a bolthole? The reality was, in fact, that she wasn't even welcome there. What a brilliant parent he'd turned out to be.

'Yeah. She even came to try to get me to come back once,' she replied, remembering her mum's tearful shouts, and her father's refusal to open the front door. 'But I didn't go. Dad told me that if I did, he'd never have me back to stay, and I just… I dunno. I feel bad about that now. Very bad,' said Connie, clasping her hands around her mug as if its warmth could somehow ward off the darkness she felt. 'I made the wrong decision, didn't I? I chose what I thought was exciting and new, but it was actually just scary and… it put me on the wrong path. I was an idiot.'

'She must be chuffed to 'ave you back now, then,' Jamie said, returning with a plate of biscuits.

'I don't think so, Jamie. I'm a mess. She's had a lot to put up with since I came back…'

'But you're in a good place now, aren't you?'

'Living in council housing that's soon to be razed to the ground and replaced with twenty four-bedroom second homes with double garages and a free hot tub?'

Jamie laughed. 'Ah, you see, you can laugh *and* you've got a sense of 'umour. Great progress. And yeah, we do live in council 'ousing, but it's fucking awesome council 'ousing full of great people, in the middle of some of the most beautiful countryside in the whole country. And we're going to lie down in front of those bulldozers and tell them to fuck off. Or something like that, aren't we? I think we're doing great.'

'Do you think we'll manage it? I mean, telling the council to go stuff themselves?'

'Dunno. Old Matilda seems pretty determined, doesn't she?'

'Yes, she does. In fact, it sounds to me like they'd have to physically remove her. She says that she can't leave. Not that she won't leave, but that she *can't*.'

Connie had been wondering about this for a while. She understood Matilda's reluctance to move – they all felt that way – but her response was different.

'Yeah, well, can you imagine moving all of that stuff?' said Jamie. 'It would take months.'

'Yes. You're right. Maybe it's just that. She can't imagine finding a place big enough for all of her clutter.'

'Yeah, I mean, the council will probably put 'er in a single-bed flat, won't they? Probably without a garden. Where would the animals go? That would break her 'eart.'

Yes, thought Connie. *And mine, too.*

As Connie placed her mug down on the coffee table and thanked Jamie for his hospitality, she made a resolution.

If I have to lie down in front of those bulldozers, she thought, I will.

I will do whatever it takes, because everyone in Roseacre Close deserves to stay in their home. Not just me, and not just Matilda.

Yes, she thought: the council must not win.

— 24 —

October

Matilda

Matilda had been searching for her typewriter for at least twenty-four hours. She needed to use it to draft a campaign newsletter and an agenda for the meeting on Saturday. Her handwriting wasn't legible these days, and she felt that Constance needed her support.

She'd last used her typewriter to write letters to her MP and to social services at least three decades previously, and she had no idea where she'd put it. She'd originally thought it might be in the sitting room, but she'd opened and searched through all of her boxes in there – a very slow, tough job for an old, arthritic woman – and found no sign of it.

Next, she'd hauled herself upstairs, grateful that autumn's arrival meant that it was no longer sweltering outside or in, because her body seemed to provide its own furnace. She'd already been through the boxroom and found nothing of note, so she was in her old bedroom, which was, she acknowledged, now much more of a junk shop than somewhere to sleep.

She surveyed the scene: there were several broken lampshades in here, two ancient bed frames, four old dining chairs, a selection of chipped crockery, a myriad of boxes of different sizes, and stacks and stacks of books. The typewriter had to be in here somewhere, surely. She sat down gratefully on one of the dining chairs and waited for her back to forgive her and for her breath to settle.

Once she felt herself to be back on an even keel, she decided to start with the box nearest to her. It was unlabelled, as most of them were, so she opened the lid with no idea what she'd find inside.

It was the handwriting she noticed first. It was her own, but a previous incarnation of it which had been hammered into her by the nuns, who had threatened the cane for those whose cursive was not up to par. She'd fallen short of their expectations once, but never again. It had been too painful a lesson.

Matilda leaned down and picked up the envelope, which was browning around the edges, and pulled out a letter written on thin, neatly folded lined paper.

October 1939

Dear Mother,

I hope all is well. How is Tilly? I think of her often. Is she eating OK? Is she catching all of the mice for you?

I am fine here. There is a lot of food, so you don't need to worry about that. The nuns have some cows, goats, chicken and sheep and we feed them. I was scared of them at first, but they are very friendly. And of course it means we have lots of milk and eggs.

I am working hard at my Latin and getting better at the Catechism.

I miss you. Have you heard from Father? And about Miriam? The nuns will not tell me where she has been sent. Please send me news.

Matilda

Matilda folded the letter and returned it to its envelope. Below that letter was one with very different handwriting.

November 1940

Dearest Matilda,

I am glad you are working hard and that the nuns are teaching you good things. Father Michael is pleased to hear of it, and that the school he recommended is working well.

I know you are worried about Miriam, but please don't be. Father Michael says he has found a good, safe place for her and she will be well looked after.

I miss you too. I will try to visit at Christmas, if I can get a few days' leave. The hospital is very busy now, and we are worried that things will get worse, if Adolf Hitler carries out his threats to the full.

Father has been writing to me twice-weekly. He is still training with the RAF somewhere near the south coast, and I'm afraid, my darling, I do not know where he will go after that. But I trust that God will take care of us all. With His grace this will all be over soon.

With love,
Mother

Matilda sat back in her chair, clutching the letter with both hands. She knew that the box was full of similar letters. She'd been sent them all in a bundle with everything else they had managed to salvage from the house after the bombing: a few ornaments; a carriage clock; a family photograph in a cracked frame. She knew that that particular photo was at the bottom of this box, but she didn't think she had the strength to look at it today.

In fact, she wasn't really sitting there in that cramped room on that old dining chair any more, anyway. Instead, she was at school – the convent school – in the dormitory she shared with five other girls.

'Look what Matilda has done to her hair. It's sticking up like a toilet brush.'

In an effort to tame a knot in her wild, tumbling curls, Matilda had simply decided to snip the knot out. It had seemed like a sound idea at the time, because no amount of teasing with a comb would work, and it was an ugly big ball of tangled hair which Sister Monica would undoubtedly notice in the morning. If she'd been at home, her mother would have applied cold cream or Vaseline and patiently chased each knot back to its source with her nimble fingers, but Matilda had nobody to help her here. The problem was, she'd snipped the knot off and that section of her hair had simply taken off into orbit, devoid of the length to weigh it down. And now Georgina had seen it. Perfect. She'd never hear the end of it now.

'Did you stick your fingers in a socket, Matilda?' said one of the other girls, sniggering.

Matilda threw herself into bed and pulled the blanket over her head. It was nearly time for lights out. They would have to stop taunting her soon.

'Matilda Reynolds?' It was Sister Elizabeth-Jane. She was far softer than Sister Monica, far less scary, so Matilda pulled the blanket off her head and sat up. If she was about to be told off for something, she might as well get on with accepting it. She was often being told off for a variety of sins, including being 'wayward', 'secretive' and 'a rule-breaker'. Matilda dreaded the next report the nuns would send home to her mother at the end of term. Her previous two had been appalling. Mother had cried.

'Could you please come with me, Matilda?' asked the nun.

Matilda swung her legs off her metal bed, slipped her feet into her leather shoes, grabbed her woollen dressing gown from the back of the chair beside her bed, tied it at the waist and walked towards Sister Elizabeth-Jane, who was standing by the door.

'Come with me, dear,' she said, turning and heading down the corridor towards the front stairs. But then Matilda came to a halt. She was not allowed down the front stairs. Use of the front stairs meant that you got a Black Mark.

'It's all right, dear, you can come with me this once. Come with me.'

Matilda thought Sister Elizabeth-Jane looked sincere, so it couldn't be a trap, could it? But if it wasn't a trap, why was she behaving so oddly? Despite still being unsure, Matilda decided that it would be best to follow her, to avoid being told off for something else, like ignoring an instruction. So she did so, down the front stairs and into the little sitting room at the front of the school, where the nuns on duty congregated, listening to the wireless, marking prep and drinking an inordinate amount of tea.

'Take a seat, dear,' said Sister Elizabeth-Jane, gesturing towards one of the wooden chairs in front of the fireplace. Sister Monica was sitting in the other one. Matilda was more confused than ever now. Was she going to be told off after all, by *both* nuns?

'Matilda, I have some news for you,' said Sister Monica, her tone as haughty as ever, but without the grumpy edge Matilda was more used to. 'It's not good news, I'm afraid.'

'Is it Miriam? Is she ill?' Matilda asked, her fear for her sister surfacing. And that wasn't hard, because it was just beneath her skin all of the time.

'No, dear, Miriam is fine, I believe. No. This is about your mother.'

Matilda dug her fingernails into her arm, hoping that if she inflicted pain on herself, she might be able to somehow spare herself the pain that was to come.

'I am very sorry to tell you, Matilda, that your mother has passed away.' Matilda dug her fingernails in deeper. *This couldn't be true, surely. It just couldn't be.* She had received a letter from her only the previous day.

Matilda wanted to ask a million different questions, like how, when, why, and if… But she was too shocked to speak.

Sister Monica filled the silence.

'We received a telegram with the news earlier. She died in last night's air raid. She was in bed and asleep at the time, they say. There had been a warning, but for whatever reason she hadn't gone to the shelter.'

'So, the house?'

'Your house took a direct hit, Matilda. I'm so sorry.'

Matilda felt the lump in her throat grow bigger and bigger until she let out a sob.

'We have tried to get hold of your father, Matilda. But we aren't sure where he is.'

'He's. Training. On. The. South. Coast. For. The. RAF,' she said, taking a breath between each word.

'OK. Well, we will keep trying.'

Matilda's tears were in full flow now.

'Where is Miriam?' she yelled between cries. 'She needs to know. I need to see her. I need to see Miriam.'

But neither woman answered her, and neither stepped forward to hold her as she cried. And Matilda knew at that moment that this was how things were going to be for her from now on.

She was alone.

And she could rely on no one but herself.

Matilda opened her eyes and was glad to find herself back in her old bedroom, her familiar aches and pains a constant reminder of the many decades that had passed since she'd first learned of her mother's death.

That news had been an earthquake in her development, a parting of ways. She'd had two options, essentially: she could either fold entirely and give up, or she could opt to keep going. She'd chosen the latter. The years she'd spent in the convent had been difficult, but they had also been the making of her. They had confirmed and affirmed her faith, and they had also given her safe harbour. She had hidden herself there until she had felt strong enough to strike out, her armour repaired.

In fact, her armour had remained intact until Constance and Ellen had broken their way into her life. And it had felt to her, at the age of ninety, that perhaps it was time.

Matilda turned to her left and opened a different box. However, there was nothing in it but a random selection of tapes, some of them with handwritten labels. She decided not to look through them now – music triggered emotions in her, and she'd had quite enough of that for one morning. But the next box she tried offered up what she was looking for.

Inside, covered with a now partially disintegrated duster that she'd used to clean it several decades ago, was her old typewriter. She summoned all of her energy and hauled it out, feeling her back howl as she did so. And then she saw that there was paper at the bottom of the box. She lifted out a piece, and fed it into the typewriter with unexpected ease, her muscle memory doing the work for her.

And right there, in her dusty, cramped old bedroom, she began to type, as she had done so many times, so many years ago, fighting for what she knew was right. They hadn't beaten her then, she thought, and there sure as hell was no way they'd beat her now.

— 25 —

October

Constance

'Honestly, Mum, I really don't think they'll notice if the mantlepiece isn't dusted,' said Connie, watching her mother buzzing around the lounge like a mosquito on a hot summer's night. Her mother's constant need to be doing, to be cleaning, to be tidying, to be organising, had always been exhausting to watch. She had to constantly fight the urge to yell at her to *just bloody sit down*, so they could both relax together for just a moment, face to face, stationary.

'They might. But even if they don't, I will. I was brought up to always put my best foot forward when we had guests, and I'm sorry, Connie, but I'm going to stick to that.'

Nana Jane, Ellen's mother, had definitely been a meticulous housekeeper, right up until the end. Connie had often gone with her mother to help out in Nana's bungalow, which had been in a nearby village, when she'd become too disabled to manage all of it. She still remembered watching Ellen ironing bedsheets and washing curtains, keeping up her mother's standards until the end.

Connie went into the kitchen, where she found that Ellen had assembled enough snacks to feed the five thousand. There were neat rows of cheese and ham sandwiches sliced into dainty triangles, a pyramid of freshly baked sausage rolls, a tower of chocolate ring biscuits that were more chocolate than biscuit, and a huge serving dish piled high with 'posh' crisps flavoured with caviar and gold leaf, or something similarly unlikely. Connie had tried to point out that it was the middle of the afternoon and most people would have just had lunch, but Ellen had not been dissuaded, despite the obvious cost to her in both time and money.

Despite her exasperation, Connie *did* understand why it was important to her. She knew that it had been a long time since Ellen had had anyone else in the house – certainly, it had been before she'd landed on her mother's doorstep and begged for shelter – and she understood that it was important for her to show that she, *they*, were still keeping their heads above water and soldiering on.

Ellen had been soldiering on for decades now, ever since Connie's father had abandoned her when she'd told him she was pregnant, and it was only recently that Connie had begun to appreciate the emotional and physical energy this had taken from her mother. How Ellen managed to remain so cheerful, still going to work every day without complaint and doing extra shifts to pay for unexpected bills and the occasional treat while her daughter's father lived a life of luxury in London, Connie didn't know. She doubted she'd have been anything like as sanguine.

Connie's thoughts were interrupted by the doorbell.

'I'll go,' she said, aware her mum would need a moment or two to hide the duster.

Connie opened the door to find Jamie on the doorstep.

'Are you ready?' he asked.

'Yep,' replied Connie, pulling on her trainers. She followed Jamie as he walked round to Matilda's house and knocked on her door. 'I suppose she didn't go for the wheelchair idea?'

'Nah. I told 'er that Martin 'ad found one and that she could borrow it, but she basically told me to fuck off. I mean, not using those words, yeah, but it seems that a stick is as far as she's going to go.'

Several minutes later, Matilda opened the door. She was wearing her purple tracksuit, which Connie knew her mother washed for her at least twice a week. Beyond that, no real effort to improve her appearance seemed to have been made; Matilda's hair had been somewhat rewilded since her return from hospital, her matted curls beginning to resemble dreadlocks once more. Despite the fact they'd installed an electric shower for her, it seemed that hairwashing was simply one effort too many. But never mind, thought Connie. The thing was she was managing to live alone still, and she seemed happy about it. Messy, greasy hair was nothing in the grand scheme of things.

'Hello, Constance, hello, James,' said Matilda, holding onto the doorframe with her left arm while she manoeuvred her stick down onto the step with her right. Jamie stepped forward and offered her an arm, which she took, and together they walked slowly up the garden path and back down towards Connie's front door. When they walked through into the hall, Connie could hear her mother talking to Niamh, the woman whose garden they'd used for their late summer barbecue.

'Oh God he's a horror, so he is. A complete horror,' said Niamh in a lilting Irish accent.

'Ah, don't worry about it. He only barks for a few minutes when you let him out. He's fine,' said Ellen.

'No, don't be silly, he's an eejit. Snuggles is an *eejit*. When he was a puppy, I almost caved in and returned him to the breeder, you know. I mean, he's full of love and kisses, but he's also absolutely batty.' Connie walked into the lounge to find Niamh sitting on their sofa, being plied with a platter of sausage rolls by Ellen. 'I only got him because I was *so lonely*. After my Frank died, I didn't know where to put myself, and Snuggles was a distraction, do you know. But what a distraction he is,' she said, taking a sausage roll, her eyes twinkling as she burst into laughter, 'yes, batty as hell. Oh, hello – it's Connie, isn't it? Lovely to see you again. Sorry I didn't get a chance to chat to you at the barbecue, it was all a bit of a whirlwind, in the event.'

'Honestly, that's fine,' said Connie, remembering that Niamh had been quite tipsy at the party, laughing heartily, her face full of warmth.

'Ah, it's so lovely to have you here, though, Connie. Back with your mammy. So lovely.'

Connie wondered what conversations she'd been having with Ellen.

At that moment Jamie came through the door with Matilda, who'd taken her time getting up the front steps.

''Ere you are, Matilda, we made it. This is the place to be this afternoon! Look at your audience. Do you want to come and take a seat over 'ere?' asked Jamie, leading Matilda to a high-backed armchair by the fireplace.

'Yes, that will be fine,' said Matilda, lowering herself down into the chair with Jamie's assistance.

'Would you like a cup of tea, Matilda? And something to eat? I have sandwiches, chocolate biscuits, sausage rolls…'

'Goodness, quite the spread,' said Matilda, still getting her breath back after the enormous effort it had taken to get her here. 'I'd love a cup of tea, please. Milk. Two sugars. Oh, and a chocolate biscuit?'

As Ellen beat a retreat into the kitchen to assemble Matilda's order, Connie examined Matilda's expression. For a woman who – by her own admission – had spent several decades living outside of society, she seemed to be coping surprisingly well with suddenly being thrown back into it. And was that a twinkle in her eye she could see? Perhaps. It certainly wasn't fear, Connie thought. Was she, possibly, even *enjoying* this opportunity to organise and to protest?

The doorbell rang. Connie left Matilda, Jamie and Niamh in the lounge and answered it, finding Jocelyn and her husband waiting on the other side.

Jocelyn had clearly made a significant effort for the occasion. She'd swept her silver hair up into a bun, was wearing both mascara and eyeshadow, a pair of grey linen trousers and a crisp white shirt, and had accessorised her outfit with purple drop earrings and a purple scarf. She looked put-together, efficient and glamorous, and Connie wondered what she'd done as a job before retirement. Maybe a teacher? Or a lawyer? She was a bit of a mystery, all told. Just another mystery to add to a close already riddled with mysteries.

'Hello, Connie,' said Jocelyn, her arm firmly linked with Brian's, her smile broad.

'Hello, Connie, nice to meet you,' said Brian, clearly not remembering her from the party. 'Lovely day for it.'

Brian was wearing smart grey trousers, a white shirt and a grey waistcoat with a red and white checked handkerchief neatly folded in the top pocket. He looked every inch the gentleman.

'Come in,' said Connie. 'Everyone's gathering in the lounge. I'll just go and get some more chairs for you all.'

As Jocelyn and Brian made their way into the lounge, Connie walked through the kitchen and out into the garden, where she yanked open their shed's wonky wooden door.

She hated the shed. She hated spiders and she hated mice, and she was pretty sure that both of them lived in there. She took a deep breath and was about to enter its damp, disordered gloom when someone tapped her on her shoulder. The shock made her jump out of her skin.

'Fucking hell! Will you stop doing that!' she said, when she saw who it was. She took a series of deep breaths to try to expel the adrenaline.

'I'm only wanting to 'elp,' said Jamie, laughing. 'You should see yourself. Proper got you there, didn't I?'

'It's not funny. You could have given me a heart attack.' In truth, being caught unawares triggered all sorts of unpleasant memories in her.

'Sorry. Do I take it you don't like spiders?'

'It's not that, it's the dust. I hate dust.'

'Yeah, right.'

'And it's a mess in there. I can't find anything, ever.'

'I'll do it, shall I? And fight off the big scary, 'airy spiders while I do it?'

Connie's mouth curled at the corners, despite her efforts to prevent it. Jamie returned her smile and went into the shed, returning a few seconds later with four folded plastic chairs.

'These are what you wanted, I presume?' he said, brandishing them at her.

'Yes.'

'I only 'ad to fight off four tarantulas and an 'umongous black widow for them, so all's good,' he said, walking back to the house with two slung over each arm. 'Aren't you going to thank me?' he said, turning round and grinning at her.

'Thank you, James,' she said, in her poshest voice, an imitation of the accent that her secondary school's headteacher, Miranda Deacon, had used during Friday assemblies. 'That will be all.'

'Yes miss,' said Jamie, doffing an imaginary cap at her before resuming his walk up the path.

After she'd watched him disappear into the house, Connie stood still for a moment, looking about her. The leaves on the gnarly old apple tree at the bottom of their garden were just on the turn; the ground around it, where she had sat sheltering from the sun during many childhood summers, was now littered with soft, browning apples which were gradually being devoured by grateful bugs. In the skies above her, a murmuration of starlings was swooping over the close, the collective movements of hundreds of birds a spellbinding tribute to what could be achieved when living creatures worked in harmony.

As she started to walk back to the house to join the others, Connie thought: I love this place. Yes, *I love it*. And I will not be parted from it.

'So I think that's everyone,' said Ellen, closing the door, having let Liv and her children in. 'Tom and Donna send their apologies, they're at work, and Sally and Nick are at the hospital, I think.'

'Cool. So are we going to chain ourselves to the doors of the council headquarters, or what?' asked Liv, sitting down on the second high-backed chair, balancing two children on her knee. The older one, Max, was playing a game on her phone, and the younger one, Kieran, was digging in a small plastic bowl of very posh crisps with great enthusiasm.

'It worked at Greenham Common,' said Niamh, now chomping on a chocolate biscuit from a plate that was being passed around.

'Were you there?' asked Matilda.

'I might have been,' replied Niamh, with a wink.

'Shall we get going?' said Ellen.

'Shall I note-take? I have a hundred words per minute shorthand,' replied Jocelyn, pulling out a pad of paper and a pen from her handbag.

'Yes please,' said Matilda, casting a curious glance over at her neighbour.

'I was a PA to a CEO for a long time,' said Jocelyn. 'For a cider company. But I left to take care of… my lovely Brian,' she said, smiling at her husband, who stopped the jigsaw puzzle he'd been doing and rubbed his finger on her palm. 'Many years ago.'

Connie felt a lump form in her throat.

'Thanks for offering, Jocelyn, that's great,' said Ellen, who was perching on one of the folding plastic chairs close to the door, in case any more drinks or snacks were needed. 'Do you want to start by telling everyone what they told you at Citizens Advice, Connie?'

'Sure,' replied Connie, who had caught the bus into Worcester the previous day to go and speak to an advisor. 'Sadly, it's not great news, really. The woman I spoke to had dealt with a similar issue over Kidderminster way last year, so she knew what she was talking about. So, the first thing the council will apparently need to do is to get their housing officers to find out what they think they'll get for this land, and how they can rehouse us all elsewhere. They have to be able to show that they're maintaining their overall stock of social housing, so the advisor reckons that they're probably planning to build a new block somewhere else, maybe on a city centre site, to make up for selling this place.'

'City centre?' said Niamh, her earlier jolly demeanour now absent.

'Yeah. I know,' said Connie. 'It's... crap. So yeah, there will be a feasibility study done on the sale, to, you know, try to justify it, and that's carried out by housing officers – council employees. Apparently, though, sometimes local councillors do try to get involved at this stage, leaning on officers to make the figures larger, that sort of thing.'

'So that might have happened here?' said Ellen.

'Yeah, it's possible. Anyway, once the feasibility study is done, there's something called a procurement process. Councils are supposed to put things on the open market and take the highest bidder, like you do when you're selling a house. But sometimes they do deals privately, without the open market knowing, in exchange for things that apparently benefit the council, like, you know, the developer building a new school, or something like that. And in that case, they just go with that developer.'

There was a pause while the assembled group digested what she'd said.

'So at what point do we, the residents, get asked what we think?' asked Niamh, rubbing the back of her neck.

'We don't,' replied Connie. 'We – you – are tenants. We don't have a right to anything.'

'Well I'm not,' said Martin. 'We bought our house more than a decade ago. They can't make me move, can they?'

The mood in the room seemed to lift. Connie suspected they thought this meant that they were saved; that the council wouldn't be able to sell an estate with one house that had to remain in it.

'Unfortunately, they can,' Connie said with a grimace. 'It's more expensive for them and it takes longer, but they can just slap a compulsory purchase order on you apparently and you'll still have to move. The only difference is that you'll get paid to do it. The rest of us will just have to go where we're told.'

Martin looked devastated.

'Sorry, guys, I didn't mean I'm special, or anything.'

'Ah, go on with you. We know that, Martin,' said Niamh. 'We'd all have bought our places if we'd had the cash. I wish I'd done that now, you know, with the death in service benefits I got from my Frank's pension, instead of buying that car and going to visit my cousin in Canada. But I just never thought they'd make me leave. Just never thought it.'

Martin looked relieved, and Connie saw Niamh give him a supportive wink and a smile. Martin's face glowed.

'So what you're saying is that we've got fuck all chance of saving this place?' said Jamie.

'Jamie, *manners*,' said Martin.

'Sorry, Martin. Sorry, Matilda, Sorry, Jocelyn and Brian,' said Jamie, with a cheeky smile on his face.

'And me,' said Niamh.

'Sorry, Niamh,' said Jamie. 'So Connie, you were basically told the council can just decide to do it… and we 'ave no say?'

'The council can, yes. But the advisor said that the council is made up of lots of different councillors, some from different parties, you know, and they all have to vote on it. So there's a chance that some of them won't, if we can persuade them.'

'So we need to write to local councillors, as well as our MP.'

'Yep.'

'How far along do you think this all is by now?' asked Jocelyn, still clutching the hand of her husband, who was enraptured by his puzzle. 'Is it already a done deal?'

'We need to find that out,' said Connie.

'You know, I think Sally used to work in planning,' said Martin. 'I'll go over later when they get back from the hospital and ask if she still has friends there. Maybe they could tell us?'

'Great idea,' said Ellen.

'Can't we, what's it called... tip off a journalist and tell them to go along to one of their meetings and ask them a question about it?' asked Niamh. 'I'm sure I've read stories in the local paper about that.'

'Yeah, we could try that,' replied Connie. 'But I made friends with some journalists when I worked in PR, and they told me that sometimes councils can avoid questions about stuff like this. Commercial sensitivity, they call it. So they might just dodge the question?'

'So, as I said before... we 'aven't got an... 'ope in 'ell?' said Jamie.

'Don't be downhearted, James. There is always a way. This is just the start,' said Matilda, her voice sounding deeper and more powerful than usual. 'As the leaflet says.'

Connie looked down at the leaflet, which she'd put together at some speed on her laptop last night after Matilda had given her two pages of text typed on an old manual typewriter. How she'd had the energy to even type it, Connie couldn't fathom – Matilda's ninety-year-old hands must have really struggled with it – but type it she had, and it was good stuff, if a little old fashioned. She'd suggested that they stage a march to the council offices to deliver the petition, tied in with a publicity campaign targeting the local papers and radio station, and the writing of letters to their local councillor and MP. Connie had suggested they add in social media, which the younger members of the group had agreed with, and the older ones had given the go-ahead just to avoid having to find out any more about it.

'Who will organise all of these things? The march, the media campaign, the letters?' asked Jocelyn.

'I can do the social media. I'm on it all of the time anyway,' said Liv. 'And I can do videos, if you need those – TikTok and that? I'm good at videos. And I think Tom does them too?'

'Yeah, 'e made up all sorts of great dances during the first Covid lockdown,' said Jamie.

'I can draft a letter to send to our MP, and give it to Constance for her to share with you all,' said Matilda. 'Then all you need to do is just sign it and send it off.'

'Or you can email it,' said Connie. 'It's free to email.'

'Yes,' said Matilda, nodding despite her obvious confusion. 'Yes, or… email.'

'Does anyone know any of the councillors? Or anyone at the council at all?' asked Ellen.

'That's where our Jamie works,' said Martin, sipping his tea from a china cup and saucer Connie hadn't even seen before. Where had her mother been hiding that?

'I'm only in the gardens and parks, Martin. Not in the office or anything.'

'Yeah, but I bet you hear things, son. I bet you hear lots of things. And you know people who work inside, don't you?'

'Yeah, I s'pose.'

'Well, then.'

'Well, keep your ear to the ground,' said Ellen. 'That's a good point Martin made. We need to think who we might know who can help us.'

Ellen shot a look at Connie, and Connie in turn looked at the floor.

'One thing I can do is press releases,' Connie said, still not looking at her mother. 'I'll write us one and send it to the local media.'

'Great, Connie. Good. Now, I think we should probably wrap this up soon,' said Ellen, noting that Liv's kids were getting restless. 'So shall we just decide on next steps? First, we need to get more signatures on our petition from local people.'

'I'll take it round the pubs and to the shop,' said Jamie.

'I'll take it to the church,' said Niamh.

'Great. We need an online one, too,' said Ellen.

'I'll make that,' said Connie.

'And I'll share it on the social media channels I create for us,' said Liv.

'Perfect. Then when we have lots of signatures, we're going to organise a march to the council office and deliver it.'

'I'll make the signs,' said Martin. 'I've got lots of wood lying around and that.'

'Great,' replied Ellen. Connie was spellbound by her mother, who appeared to be in complete control of the meeting. She had never seen this side of Ellen before. 'And Martin, you're going to talk to Sally about the council housing department.'

'Yes, I'll do that this evening,' he said.

'If you're not on the WhatsApp group already and you'd like to be, could you give me your number as you leave?' said Ellen.

Connie could see the confusion on the faces of the older generation.

'It's a messaging system for groups on mobile phones,' explained Connie.

'Oh,' said Niamh. 'I thought it was some kind of group therapy.'

'Ha, that too,' said Connie.

'What'll I do?' asked Niamh. 'I haven't got a job yet.'

'You, Nick, Sally, Tom, Donna and me, we are all the back-up team,' said Ellen. 'We can all use our skills in lots of different ways. For example, I could provide the catering for the protest. Or take letters to the post office. Or write emails on behalf of people if they don't have internet.'

'I know what I can do,' said Niamh, her voice suddenly quiet. 'I'm good at talking to people. People who are going through difficult times. It's something I've discovered I'm good at. I could be a listener, you know... for anyone here who's having a hard time, with all of this that's going on.' There was a short silence while the group processed this offer. 'Look, I'm serious. I know you guys have moaned about the mad parking outside my place in the past, but you know, don't you, that I've been hosting a weekly support group for bereaved women for years. And during that time, I've learned a lot. Got good at it. I like helping people.'

'How wonderful,' said Ellen. 'Then you can be our team counsellor. I love that.'

Connie saw Niamh's face light up and, yet again, Connie was in awe of her mother, who seemed to know exactly what to say to each and every one of them.

'Look guys,' said Jamie, as the excitement about the allocation of roles died down. 'I 'ear you with the march and stuff. But isn't that a bit... boring?'

Connie saw Matilda scowl.

'James, it's a traditional form of protest. Everyone in the town will see us. It will work,' she said.

'Yeah, I know. And I can see we need to take this petition to the 'all. But can't we do something else... bigger?'

'Like a stunt?' asked Martin. 'Like them protesters who stick themselves to things, and that?'

'I dunno about that...' said Jamie.

There was an awkward silence.

'I think for now, let's just get on with our current plans,' said Ellen. 'But Jamie, if you or anyone else here comes up with another form of protest, please put it forward. The more the merrier, I think. Right, then... Shall we end it there?'

Connie watched as, one by one, her neighbours – her new friends – got up from their seats and made their way back to the front door, writing down their phone numbers and other contact details on a sheet as they left. Ten minutes later, only Jamie remained, helping Ellen and Connie to return the house to order.

'That was awesome,' said Jamie to Ellen, carrying the four folded chairs back out into the garden. 'Really awesome. The council should elect *you*, that's what they should do.' As the kitchen door swung closed behind Jamie, Connie walked up to her mum.

'He's right, Mum,' she said, putting her arm around her mother. 'You're a natural leader. Amazing. You had us all sorted.'

Connie embraced Ellen, and it took her a while to realise that her mother was shaking. She pulled back and saw tears in her mother's eyes.

'Why are you crying, Mum? Please don't cry.'

'I'm not sad,' she replied. 'I'm happy.'

'Why?'

'Because you are proud of me,' Ellen said, doing her best to get all of the words out.

Connie pulled away and looked her mother straight in the eyes. The guilt she had been suppressing, carrying around unknowingly since her childhood, had been bubbling up to the surface over the past couple of months. She realised now that she had always underestimated her mother; dismissed her and taken her for granted; overlooked her in favour of her father and his conspicuous success. She had allowed her youthful frustrations with her mother's behaviour to cloud her judgement. But no more. It had taken her almost three decades, but she could see the truth now.

'Mum, I am prouder of you than you know,' she said. 'I love you. You're amazing. You took it all, all of the shit I threw at you, and you never held it against me. And that is amazing.'

'Of course I didn't. I'm your mum. I will love you, whatever.'

Connie drew her mother in for another hug.

'I know that, Mum. But I promise, I'll never take that for granted ever again.'

— 26 —

October

Matilda

'What time are they coming?'

'About midday, I think.'

It was 11.30 a.m. Matilda considered whether she should ask Connie to help her find her hairbrush. She wasn't given to using it often, but she thought that if she was going to be in the local paper, the newspaper that had been delivered through her own door for decades, she should probably at least try to brush her hair.

She was finding it difficult to adjust to a world that cared about her appearance. For so long she'd had her hair covered up, so it hadn't mattered, and when she moved in here, she'd rarely seen people anyway, and those that she had met, she hadn't cared at all about what they'd thought. But now she *had* found people she liked, she found that she *did* care. And frankly, it was a nuisance.

She had noticed how Connie held herself when good-looking lads like Jamie were around, how she pulled herself in and wore clothes that looked far from comfortable, and she wondered what that sort of pressure did to a person. She knew, because Connie had told her, that Connie plucked her eyebrows, and Lord knows, she probably stripped herself of hair all over the shop. But who for, thought Matilda. Really and truly, was it for herself? How much of this preening did women do simply because that was what society expected of them? Matilda was thankful that she had never had to bother with any of that. There was something delightfully rebellious about choosing to look like the proverbial witch. In fact, she decided, *I shall not* look for my hairbrush. I shall come as I am. They can take me or leave me as they please.

'So the plan is that you'll have the photos taken outside,' said Connie. 'With the animals. Are you OK with that?'

Matilda wasn't at ease with any of it, but she felt that it was far too late to back out now. And anyway, there was a battle to be fought, and she was determined to win it. If that meant inviting a gentleman of the press into her back garden, then so be it.

This whole campaign was going a lot better than she'd expected. Constance had adapted her suggested text (rather too much, in her opinion) and Liv had sent it out via computer to numerous local news outlets, some of which she'd heard of – the BBC local radio station was of course familiar to her – and some of which, like these apparently popular groups on something called the book of faces, she had not. But no matter. Things seemed to be well and truly picking up steam now, and this grisly event, the photoshoot, promised to get them even more attention.

'They're here,' said Connie, hearing a hard rapping at the door. 'Are you ready?'

'Yes, as I'll ever be,' replied Matilda, walking over to her bench, where Connie had agreed she could sit for the photos. Connie was going to bring them round the side passage and straight into the garden; they had agreed that they didn't want them writing anything about her house, which even Matilda accepted was a little cramped. 'Clarrie! Eddie!' she called, knowing they'd hear her and anticipate either a snack or attention, both of which they craved.

The goats were only a few feet away from her when Connie

emerged from the side path, accompanied by a young woman who looked to Matilda as if she was on work experience. Could this really be the team from the *Echo*? She had expected a middle-aged man wearing a mac and carrying a notebook or a Dictaphone, accompanied by another middle-aged man with a camera slung around his neck, not a whippersnapper in ripped jeans with an intelligent phone, or whatever they were called.

'Miss Reynolds, this is Amy,' said Connie. 'She's from the *Echo*.'

'Hello, Miss Reynolds,' said Amy, very loudly. 'As Connie says, I'm Amy. I'm a reporter from the *Echo*, and I'm here to talk to you about animals and this awful thing with the council.'

Clarrie and Eddie appeared startled by her volume, and backed away.

'I'm not deaf you know, child,' said Matilda, affronted by the young woman's assumption.

'Oh I'm sorry, Miss Reynolds, I'm used to my granny. She's about your age. She won't wear a hearing aid, and we have to shout.'

'Yes, well, my ears are one of the things left on me that work,' replied Matilda.

'I'll just go and get you a chair from inside, Amy,' said Connie, with something of a forced smile.

'Thanks,' replied Amy, smiling broadly in Matilda's direction.

Matilda had to admit that, despite her faux pas with the hearing, Amy did have a winning face. It was open, friendly, and she seemed kind. She reminded her of Theresa.

'Here you go,' said Connie, almost running back from the house with a chair, presumably to try to stop Matilda saying anything rude to the young journalist.

'Thanks,' said Amy, still smiling while she took a seat, placing her rucksack down on the grass beside her. Then she leaned down and unzipped it and pulled a spiral notebook out, unhooking a biro.

Aha, thought Matilda. At least I was right about *one* thing.

'I'm just going to take notes in shorthand while we chat, if that's OK?' said Amy.

'Fine by me,' replied Matilda, digging into a bag at her feet for a treat for the goats, who saw what she was up to and approached at speed.

'No problem,' said Connie.

'Can I check your names first?'

'I'm Miss Reynolds. Matilda Reynolds.'

'You don't need mine, do you?' said Connie.

'Oh, sorry. I thought you were both being interviewed?' said Amy. 'It would be nice to have you both. You know, two women of different ages, refusing to be moved…?'

'Well I… I dunno…'

'I don't want to do this on my own, Constance,' said Matilda, bristling. She did not want to be the focus of everything. And anyway, she knew she looked a bit unusual, and she suspected readers might warm to Constance's gentle beauty.

'Oh, OK,' said Connie with reluctance.

'Great. So it's Constance…'

'Darke. D-a-r-k-e.'

'Thanks, both of you,' she said, before becoming distracted by the goats, who were eating out of Matilda's hand. 'Awww, look at those lovely creatures,' said Amy. 'They're beautiful. What are they called?'

'Clarrie and Eddie.'

'Like from *The Archers*?'

This girl is going up in my estimation, thought Matilda.

'Yes, that's right.'

'And the chickens are called Brian, Jennifer and Ruth,' said Connie, and Amy laughed.

'Brilliant. Our readers will love that,' she said. 'Now, in your own time, could either of you tell me how all of this started?'

Connie spoke first, telling Amy about the letter from the council. Amy listened intently, her right hand scribbling away, seemingly independent of its owner. Then Matilda told them that they'd heard that the council had a preferred developer in mind for their site.

'It's called Orchard Developments,' Matilda said. 'Quite ironic, given that the firm probably spends most of its time demolishing orchards.'

'So how did you find out about Orchard getting the deal?'

Connie looked a bit shifty, and Matilda decided to step in.

'A... contact of ours, of our group, found out,' she said. 'But we have it on good authority.'

It had been a friend of Sally's in the council planning department who'd told them, confidentially.

'I'll look through the minutes of the recent planning committee meetings and see if I can see any reference to it,' said Amy.

'That would be helpful,' said Matilda.

'So they've already done the feasibility study?'

'Yeah, apparently,' said Connie. 'And the procurement process is being bypassed because they're allegedly going to provide what they call "planning gain".'

'Oh yes? What have they offered?' said Amy.

'A new village hall,' said Matilda. 'Which amounts to bribery.'

The village did need a new hall – the old mission hall built of corrugated iron in the Victorian era had been condemned and left to rot more than a decade ago – but allowing a guzzling, greedy developer to get away with just laying a few breeze blocks at the cost to themselves of about ten bob seemed a tiny price to pay for demolishing their homes, Matilda thought.

'Yeah, and we've also heard a rumour about where they want to put us all,' said Connie with a sigh. 'There's a new block of flats being put up near an M5 junction near Bromsgrove, on land previously occupied by a DIY store. One- and two-bedroom flats. It has "benefits" like cycle parking, a "landscaped" shared garden, mains drainage, and one parking place and one balcony per flat. Depressing isn't the word.'

Matilda didn't doubt that the flats would be built well and that someone would be glad to live there, but she was determined she would never be one of those residents. The very thought of being uprooted from her home and sent to that place, miles and miles away, made her feel physically sick. And it wasn't just her that would be adversely affected. Liv's children, for example, would have to change schools, just when they'd settled in to the local one; Sally and Nick would be moved ten miles further away from where their daughter was in hospital; Ellen was worried she'd have no room for Connie; Niamh was worried her wayward dog would hate not having a garden; and Jocelyn was deeply concerned that Brian, robbed of his familiar surroundings, would become too hard to care for at home. Even Martin, who at least owned his house, knew his chances of being able to buy somewhere else local were slim to impossible, due to the burgeoning market in second homes. In fact, there wasn't a single one of them who was prepared to just roll over and take whatever the council threw at them. Far from it, in fact. They were all preparing for war.

'So tell me, Miss Reynolds. When did you move here?'

'Just after it was built, in the late fifties,' Matilda replied, remembering the damp autumnal day when she'd arrived with just one suitcase, and had struggled to use the key that she'd been given because the lock had been fitted badly. The house had been empty and cold. She'd lit the fire in the living room and slept next to it that night, wrapped in her dressing gown and the towel she'd brought with her.

'Wow, so you've been here a long time. Are you from the area, originally?'

Matilda smiled.

'Has my accent left me that much? It probably has, I suppose. No, dear. I was born in Croydon. So I'm a Londoner, or at least, near enough. But I left when the bombing got bad. Instead of having us evacuated to who knows where, my mother took the advice of our local priest, and he sent me to a convent school near here, in a small village near Worcester. We were Catholic, you see. She thought it would be good for me.'

'Just you?'

Matilda's heart stopped. What had she said?

'Yes, just me.'

'You said "us", that's all.'

'Oh yes, sorry dear, I was confused. I meant we, the children who were evacuated during the Blitz.'

Connie looked at Matilda with curiosity. Matilda tried not to meet her gaze.

'Ah, I see. So you moved here by yourself?'

'Yes, that's right,' said Matilda, answering quickly to take possession of any thinking time. 'Although I haven't been alone, because I have the animals.'

Amy spent another ten minutes or so asking Matilda about her menagerie – their names, where she got them from, how she still managed to feed them at her age, and what they meant to her – before turning to Connie.

'What about you, Connie? How long have you lived here?' she asked.

Matilda saw Connie dig her fingers into her palms.

'Oh, I grew up here,' she said, her hands flexing as she did so.

'And you live here with your mum?'

'Yeah,' she replied, her feet tapping on the floor. 'I moved back in with her recently.'

'Saving for a deposit?' asked Amy. 'I'm doing that, too.'

'Yes, saving up,' replied Connie. 'Takes ages.'

'Sure does,' replied Amy. 'Particularly on what they pay local reporters these days.'

Matilda was unaware that Connie had any income to save. She also judged that she would like the interview to shift focus.

'Did Constance tell you about the march we're planning?' she asked.

'Yes, she did mention it. She said you've got a petition with a thousand signatures, that you've written to your MP, and that you're planning to deliver it to the council offices.'

'Yes, that's right,' said Matilda. 'Not that I can march any more. But I will definitely go there and sit.'

'And the next whole council meeting is in early December.' said Amy. 'I checked before I came. So you think that they might vote on this proposed sale then?'

'That's what we've been told,' said Connie.

Amy looked thoughtful.

'I'll ask one of my contacts, she's a councillor for the Green Party,' she said. 'She's always up on planning issues. She'll know. And have you heard back from your MP yet, by the way? Or your councillor?'

'Nothing so far,' replied Connie.

Amy nodded and continued scribbling.

'I'll chase it up with them,' she said. 'One more question before I finish,' she said. 'Why is it so important to you that you don't have to move? After all, the place the council is suggesting you move to is new, has better transport links, modern insulation standards – what is it about here that's so special?'

Matilda flexed her toes and felt the ground between her feet.

'This is my home,' she replied. 'It is beautiful. It is peaceful. It is mine. And my animals have room to roam and feed. If I move I'd have to… be parted from them. And I won't be parted from them. Ever.'

'And Connie?'

Connie took a deep breath and looked about her.

'There is something special about this place. It makes me feel better, honestly. Calmer. Happier. This countryside has… soul, you know? And yes, as Matilda says, it's our home. We are council tenants, or at least, my mum is. But no one ever expected to have to leave. And why shouldn't people in social housing be allowed to stay somewhere beautiful? Is the countryside destined just to be a theme park for the rich? If the council lets that happen, it will rip the soul out of this place, I promise you. None of the people who live here on Roseacre Close could afford to rent or buy somewhere here on the open market. Who will do the jobs the rich folk don't want to do? Who will bring in the crops, work on the till at the local shops or serve behind the bar at the gastropubs? We all have as much right to stay here as the old Etonians with their Range Rovers.'

There was a brief silence, while Matilda and Amy took in the strength of Connie's statement.

'Yes. I'm leaving in a box,' said Matilda. 'And that's also a promise.'

Amy smiled broadly.

'That's all I need, I think,' she said. 'I'll be back in touch when I've spoken to my contacts and looked through the council documents. Now, where shall we take the photo?'

'Can I stay on this bench?' asked Matilda.

'Sure,' said Amy. 'And if the goats want to be in it too, that would be awesome. Connie, do you want to stand behind her?'

Connie looked pained.

'Do I have to be in it?' she asked. 'I haven't really done my make-up.'

Matilda knew that to be an outright lie. She looked fine. Polished, even.

'Not if you don't want to, but it would be strange to quote you and not have you in the photo,' said Amy.

Matilda saw that Connie was thinking.

'OK,' she said, finally, her voice unusually high. 'I'll stand behind her, OK?'

Matilda had expected the reporter to pull out a huge camera from her bag, but instead she simply took out her phone, turned it on its side and pressed on the screen.

'OK, everyone ready?' asked Amy, as Matilda drew the goats in closer. 'Great. Smile.'

Matilda smiled, realising as she did so that this must be the first photograph of her that had been taken for years.

'Done! All good. Thank you so much, both of you, for your time,' said Amy.

'When will the story be up?' asked Connie, who looked to Matilda to be a little flushed in the face.

'Oh, this Friday, I think. That'll give me time to check with my source, chase your MP and councillor and look through all of the documents.'

'You have my email and our home phone number,' said Connie. 'Contact me whenever you like.'

'Will do,' replied Amy, putting her notebook and her phone back in her bag. 'Thank you so much for your time, both of you,' she said. 'I really appreciate it.'

Matilda watched Connie walk Amy back up the path towards the road, before turning her attention to Clarrie and Eddie, who were nudging her hand for another treat.

'Don't you worry, littl'uns,' she said, digging for treats in her pocket. 'I'm not going anywhere.'

— 27 —

November

Constance

'Do you prefer "Hands off our homes" or "Eff off Orchard"?' Connie said, holding up both of her sketches to the group.

'I don't approve of swearing,' said Matilda.

'Agreed,' said Niamh.

'It's not actually swearing,' said Jamie.

'It's suggesting it,' said Martin.

'I just think the second one is a bit confusing. I mean, what if people don't know you're referring to Orchard Developments?' said Ellen, prompting a scowl from Connie. 'I'm sorry darling, I'm only saying what I think. I just think you need to have an immediate impact, that's all.'

It was late on Saturday afternoon, and the core members of the *Save Roseacre Close* group were once again gathered in Ellen's front room, sipping tea and passing round a plate of Jammie Dodgers and Club biscuits.

'Yes, "Hands off our homes" works for me,' said Niamh. 'It does what it says on the tin.'

There was much nodding in agreement, and Connie was pleased that at least some of the hours she'd spent drawing the posters hadn't been wasted.

'So will we all have one of these?' asked Martin.

'Yeah, unless you want to make one of your own,' replied Connie.

'I'm going to make one of my own which says "The council are… a word beginning with C",' said Liv.

Jamie sniggered and winked at her. Connie saw him do it and felt her stomach contract. Damn it, she thought. Why am I incapable of ignoring men?

'Anyway. Yes, so that's signs sorted. We can all share cars on Monday, if that works? I think we'll have enough seats, if everyone here who has a car drives it and takes passengers,' said Ellen.

'Sounds good,' said Martin.

'Oh, I forgot to say. I got an email from a reporter at BBC Hereford and Worcester today. It looks like they might come on Monday, too.'

'Is that so? I love that radio station,' said Niamh. 'Particularly that nice lad, Gary, who does Sunday mornings. He has two cats.'

It looked to Connie like no one else could think how to respond to that, so Connie stepped in.

'Yeah, they're great. So Monday is a good focus for media attention. We need to make sure as many of us can go as possible.'

There were nods of agreement around the room.

'I'll come but I'm going to be more of a media liaison, I think – it's time the rest of you spoke about how you feel. We can't have too much about me,' said Connie.

'Don't be ridiculous, Connie. You're the lynchpin of our campaign. And you're much nicer to look at than me. We need you,' said Matilda.

'Yeah, we do,' said Jamie. 'We definitely do.'

Connie's heart sank. She had been hoping to get that decision passed with ease, in among all the other plans they were making. She desperately didn't want to direct any more attention towards herself, not after she'd stupidly let Amy take a picture of her. There must be no more pictures, she had decided that. And ideally, no more interviews.

'Yeah, well, we'll see,' she said, firmly intending to avoid being in the photo on Monday, anyway. 'How's the social media side of things coming on?' she asked Liv, keen to change the subject.

'Yeah, great, as it goes. I've joined all of the local Facebook groups and have shared our page on there, and we've got lots of likes. And Tom and I have been making little vids for TikTok of the countryside around an' that, and some of us lot. I collared Jamie yesterday and he did me a little dance, didn't ya?'

Jamie puffed out his chest and grinned. 'Yeah, I did. 'Ave you seen it yet, Connie?'

'I don't have a phone,' she replied.

'Really?'

'Yes, really.'

'Oh,' he said, looking crestfallen.

'I can show ya,' said Liv, reaching for her phone. 'Give me a sec.'

'It's OK, I'll look later,' said Connie, concerned that Jamie dancing might actually look quite appealing.

'How does doing a dance on this Clock thing help our campaign?' asked Matilda.

'Yes, I was wondering that too,' said Niamh.

'It's a way of getting people interested,' said Liv. 'You get lots of people watching a stupid chicken dance or something, so they follow you, and then next time you can show them a video of a protest. That's how influencers work.'

'Do I even want to know what an influencer is?' asked Matilda.

'I'll tell you later,' said Connie. 'Anyway. I had an interesting message from Amy, the reporter, today, which I wanted to fill you all in on. As you all know, she wasn't able to get anything concrete from her contacts before she ran the initial story on Friday, but she says that this councillor she knows, Yvonne Elvin, from the Green Party – she's come back to her and told her in confidence that she thinks there's something a bit murky going on. Amy can't write about this because she can't prove it yet – she'd get sued – but Yvonne reckons that another councillor has been – how shall I put it – *leaning* on the planning department to make sure that this sale goes through. Leaning with money. So she says.'

'I am not at all surprised,' replied Matilda. 'That woman who invaded my house... She was up to something.'

'This is so awful,' said Niamh. 'I can hardly believe it. And to think we vote for these people.'

'I've never voted in a local election,' said Martin, sipping tea. 'But I'm wondering if I probably should, next time.'

'What does that councillor, whoever it is, have to gain from bribing the planning officer, though? I mean, why bother?' asked Niamh.

'Usually, it's because they've got some sort of relationship with the developer. Like they're friends, play golf together, share a business, that sort of thing. That's what Amy is currently trying to work out,' replied Connie. 'She said she'd update me on Monday. She won't tell me the name of the councillor who she thinks is giving out bribes, but she knows who he or she is, I reckon. So fingers crossed she will get somewhere with her investigation.'

'I think it has something to do with the man who came to inspect my house,' said Matilda. 'I told you, didn't I, that Caroline brought some man with her. If we can find out who he is... If we can prove that there's skulduggery going on... surely we can get this whole thing overturned?'

'That's what I'm hoping. I reckon if we can expose corruption, we will win this. But we do need to prove it. We can't just throw out accusations. We'll get sued, then.'

'They can sue me if they like. I've got fuck all anyway,' said Liv, to a chorus of tutting. 'Sorry, my swearing sort of slips out,' she added. 'I do it all of the fucking time, see.'

'There you go. Nice and easy. Just the one step.'

'I'm not a child, Constance. I do not need encouragement to lift my leg.'

'Sorry,' replied Connie, containing her urge to snap back at Matilda. She was tired and anxious, but she knew that it never helped to share that with others. And Matilda was right; she had a patronising streak, and it was showing. 'Shall I leave you now?' she said. 'Are you OK for the evening?'

'Yes, I'm fine, thank you. Your mother brought me over a dish of fish pie earlier, so that will do me well.'

'Great, then. I'll see you tomorrow, when I come over to feed the animals.' Connie turned to leave.

'Yes,' said Matilda, before turning around. 'Actually, Constance – young Dean delivered some animal feed yesterday, and he included some local cider with it. He said he'd seen the article about us in the paper, and he wanted to give us a gift to cheer us up. I don't drink much, so – would you like a glass? We could perhaps sit out in the garden under blankets? I know it's a bit busy in the house...'

Constance was taken aback. Matilda had never invited her over for anything, not even a cup of tea. She only ever visited when it was her turn to look after the animals. And was she even in the mood for chatting, anyway? Her mind had been pleasingly full of strategy and organisational challenges to do with the campaign for some weeks now, but her anxiety was creeping back in. Taking part in anything public came with high stakes, and she was not a gambling woman. But on the other hand, she had that residual guilt about the fact that she hadn't tried to get to know anyone when she'd moved back to Stonecastle.

'Sure, why not. That would be lovely,' she said, before she could change her mind.

'Excellent,' said Matilda, beckoning her to follow.

'Shall I just pop home for some glasses and some blankets?' said Connie, visualising the state of Matilda's kitchen and knowing with certainty that she didn't want to drink anything from any of her glassware. 'And maybe hot water bottles?'

'Yes dear, that would be fine,' replied Matilda.

Connie walked home, put a full kettle on to boil, ran around the house locating the items she needed, filled the bottles and returned to Matilda's house fully laden in less than ten minutes.

'Here you go,' she said, opening the side gate and walking into Matilda's back garden, where she found her sitting on the bench at the far end of the garden under a blanket that was coated in grey cat hair.

'Thank you, dear,' said Matilda, accepting a hot water bottle and a significantly cleaner blanket.

'Where's the cider?' asked Connie.

'Oh, it's by the back door. I decided it was cool enough to leave it out.'

Connie nodded and walked towards the door, where she found a small cardboard box filled with large, unlabelled brown bottles. She removed two and returned to the bench and sat down next to Matilda, presenting her with one of the bottles.

Connie unscrewed the top of her bottle and sniffed. The sharp, tangy aroma of cider apples hit her nostrils and whetted her appetite. She filled the glass she'd brought with her, noting the cider's orange tint and opaque appearance, and took a sip. It was sweet and sharp all at once, and it fizzed on her tongue. It was delicious.

'Nice, isn't it?' said Matilda, pouring some into her glass as she did so. 'Dean's father used to bring me some every year about this time.'

'Do they make it themselves?'

'Yes. Well, several families do. They all clubbed together a while back and bought an orchard I believe, and turned it into a community endeavour. They pick the apples and press them every year, and there's a barn somewhere around here where they store their vessels for fermentation. They all get a share of the produce. It's great stuff, or so I remember. I haven't had any for years.'

'Tastes… strong,' said Connie, taking a large gulp and enjoying the feeling of warmth that was now spreading throughout her body.

'Yes. I rather suspect it is,' said Matilda, smiling. 'No one tests it.'

Connie took another sip and looked around her. It was half-past four, and already getting dark. It would be Guy Fawkes Night in a few days' time; the bonfire was currently being built on the village green. She had loved attending that event as a child, chewing on dark, brittle bonfire toffee and pretty pink candyfloss, watching old crates, large logs and the Guy that the local Scout troop had made transform into heat, light and tiny sparks that lit up the night sky. She wanted to go again, she realised. She wondered if Ellen would be off work then and able to come with her.

'Do you have any outside lights?' Connie asked, aware it would be pitch black within half an hour.

'No. But I do have candles. They are in the feed store. Martin and James put them in there for me, so I could find them easily if there was a power cut.'

'I'll go and get them.'

Connie walked over to the odd and yet strangely appealing upturned bath and trailer contraption that Martin had made, and found several household candles, a storm jar and a lighter on a small wooden shelf. She picked them up and returned to the bench, where she placed two candles in the jar and lit them. Both women sat in silence for a moment, staring at the flickering flames and sipping their cider.

'Everything looks prettier in this light, doesn't it,' said Connie.

'A good thing, in my case,' said Matilda, smiling. 'At my age, I need all the help I can get.'

'Me too,' said Connie, thinking of Liv's perfect figure, her contoured, perfect face and her glossy hair.

Matilda stopped drinking for a moment and turned towards Connie.

'You shouldn't compare yourself to others, you know, Constance. Everyone is beautiful in their own way. And the right person will always see that in you.'

Connie shook her head.

'I have yet to find them,' she said, laughing bitterly into her glass of liquid amber.

'You will,' said Matilda.

'I hope so.'

There was another pause while the two women drank their cider and stared at the candlelight.

'You remind me of my nana,' said Connie. 'Mum's mum. She died five years ago. She was good to talk to. She listened, and made me feel better.'

Connie noticed that Matilda was rubbing her eyes, and realised that she might be about to cry. She was astonished. She admired the control Matilda apparently had on her emotions. She had never seen her appear anything other than collected and determined.

'Oh I'm sorry, I didn't mean to upset you,' said Connie.

'You haven't. It was just a lovely thing to say,' said Matilda. 'You know, I have been on my own so long, I haven't had anyone to listen to for a long time.'

'You told Amy that you'd grown up in Croydon. I was surprised by that. I thought you'd always been here.'

'Yes, well, it does feel that way,' said Matilda, pulling a tatty handkerchief out of her pocket and wiping her eyes. 'I came here as a young child. I was sent to a convent school near Malvern.'

'And you never went back? To Croydon, I mean?'

Matilda shook her head.

'At the beginning, for holidays, yes. But later, no. There was nothing to go back to. My mother died in an air raid, and my father died fighting in the war. My mother's parents were already dead by then, and my father's parents said they were too old to care for us. So we stayed here.'

'We? I thought you were alone?'

Matilda took a large gulp of her cider, and Connie noticed her glass was finished.

'Could you get me another one of those, dear?' Matilda asked. 'I think I might need it.'

'Of course,' replied Connie, walking up to the back door, picking up two more bottles, and returning to the bench. Connie handed Matilda a bottle and waited while she composed herself. Matilda unscrewed her new bottle, poured some more cider into her glass and took a sip.

'No, I was not alone,' she said, after taking a deep breath. 'I had a sister. Miriam.'

Connie was shocked, although she realised she didn't have any reason to be. Why shouldn't Matilda have a sister? Why should she always have been alone?

'Was she older or younger than you?'

'Younger. Two years younger.'

'And you said *had*. I guess that means she's no longer alive?'

'You are correct,' said Matilda. 'She died a long time ago.'

'Did she live near here?'

Matilda took another large gulp of cider.

'When I was put into the convent school, she was put into an institution.'

'An institution?'

'Yes. They did that to handicapped people in those days. It was considered normal. Expected. Most didn't stay at home.'

'Your sister was disabled?'

'Yes, Miriam had epilepsy. It started off fairly mild when she was small, but it got worse and worse as the years progressed.'

'How did it affect her?'

'It was like a thief, coming to take a part of her away each time. And yet despite it, she had such spirit. She had the most wonderful smile. The most infectious laugh.'

'You must miss her,' said Connie, getting the strong feeling that Matilda did not want her to probe further, even though she really wanted to ask more about her.

'I do.'

'So while she was in the institution, you were at a convent school?' Connie said. 'How was that?'

Matilda raised her right eyebrow.

'Strict. Cold. Dark. But I had friends, you know, and it was reasonable once I'd got used to it. I hated it to begin with, but I felt safe there in the end.'

'Where did you go when you'd finished school?'

Matilda took another sip from her glass.

'Oh, I didn't leave,' she replied. 'I became one of them. A nun.'

Connie almost choked on her cider.

'You were a *nun*?' she asked, incredulous.

Matilda chuckled.

'Yes, I can imagine you can't see me in a wimple.'

Something about the word, or perhaps the way Matilda had said it, made Connie laugh, and that laughter proved to be infectious; soon Matilda was laughing too, and they both had tears in their eyes from an overdose of mirth.

'Goodness, I haven't laughed like this in a long while,' said Matilda, her nose beginning to stream. She pulled out her handkerchief again and blew her nose once more. 'Don't look so shocked. Nuns are women too, you know. Just human. Yes, I was a nun until my early twenties.'

'Why did you leave?'

Matilda stared at the candles, the flames dancing in her eyes.

'I got to a point where I realised my vocation had been born out of fear and duty. I had stayed there and taken my vows because I was too afraid to go out into the world, and I had felt, wrongly, I think, that my mother would have wanted me to do it. And also, I fell in love.'

Connie turned and looked at Matilda, who was still staring into the distance, her mind possibly light years away. She couldn't think what to say, or what to ask. *Did you? With who? How? When? Did it last?* She had so many questions, which she suspected Matilda wouldn't answer. But it turned out, in fact, that she didn't have to ask anything. Because Matilda wanted to tell her.

'She was called Theresa. She was a few years older than me. She was one of the nuns who I'd admired and wanted to emulate when I took my vows. She had a beautiful oval face and a smile like a pink bow. We became friends, very close friends, and over time I developed feelings for her. Are yòu shocked?' she said, turning to Connie for the first time since she'd started sharing her story.

'Shocked? No, not at all. But interested, yes. Please tell me more about Theresa.'

'It is not a story that has a happy ending, I'm afraid, my dear. What happened was that, in the end, I decided to tell her how I felt. And she didn't reciprocate. And that was the very worst feeling in the world. Or at least I thought so, until, that is, she went to Mother Superior and told her what had happened, and I was dismissed.'

'They threw you out?'

'Yes. What I'd done was a terrible sin, you see. Even though all I'd done was think things, and never actually done them… That was enough. I wasn't safe to keep in the convent, they said, and so I had to pack what few belongings I had, and leave.'

'That must have been really horrible,' said Connie, sipping her cider.

Matilda nodded and took another sip.

'Yes, it was. I had nowhere to go, no family, I hadn't yet passed my nursing exams… I had nothing. And the only community I trusted, the faith community, had cast me out.'

'I'm so sorry, Matilda.'

'Don't be, child. It was a different time, and I found my way.'

'So when did you move in here?' Connie asked.

'Oh, straight away. It had just been built, you know, and as I didn't have a bean, I went to the council, homeless, and they found me this place. And of course I've never left.'

'Wow. You are one interesting woman,' said Connie. 'Really interesting. I would never have guessed.'

'Oh, not that interesting really. I've seen and done very little. I'm just an old woman who found somewhere safe to hide, and stayed hidden. That's all.'

'And why,' said Connie, deciding that this might be the moment to ask her burning questions, 'do you keep all of those things in the house? And not throw them away? Forgive me, but it must be tricky to live surrounded by all of those things.'

Matilda was quiet for a moment. Connie wondered if she'd offended her.

'When Miriam and I were small, we had little in the way of food. Mother worked very hard but was paid very little, and Father didn't work much of the time, if at all. We were aware that dinner wasn't always on the table, and that breakfast was a treat, and I have never left that behind. I make sure I have plenty of food in now, just in case. And as for everything else, well, I suppose I am just very bad at letting go. I didn't have any possessions at all in the convent – as you probably know, you're not supposed to have anything to your name – and when I came out, I just felt like I couldn't throw anything I acquired away. That it would be a waste. I'm sure this seems like madness to you?'

Connie shook her head.

'No, I've definitely still got all sorts of things I should have got rid of years ago,' she replied. 'Both physical things and emotional things, if I'm honest.'

Matilda nodded. 'Yes, I'm not good at letting go of those sorts of things either. That's partly why I kept myself hidden for so long. It was easier than going out and risking getting hurt again.'

'I get that,' said Connie, opening her second bottle of cider as she did so, and pouring it into her glass. 'That's why I only went out at dawn when I came home,' she said, taking a sip. 'I decided that I was done with humans. That I'd had enough of being hurt.'

Matilda smiled. 'Well, we have that in common, at least,' she said. 'Although I think I forgot, when I was isolating myself, how good it can feel to connect, too. These past couple of months have reminded me that not all people are bad, that not all people will hurt you.'

Connie nodded. 'Yeah, I agree. Although there's still part of me that worries that they will, if I get too close to them. You know, that feeling that if you trust someone, they are bound to let you down? That's how I feel. I know it's stupid.'

'Not stupid at all. It's brave, letting someone in.'

'Yeah. Well, I have a history of letting the wrong people in. I don't trust myself any more.'

'Is that why you tried to kill yourself?' asked Matilda.

Connie's eyes widened. She couldn't quite believe that Matilda had asked her that, but then, Matilda had confided in her, hadn't she, so perhaps she should try to be as open as she could be?

'Yeah, I s'pose so,' she replied. 'I had a relationship break up. A really bad one. It was… very hurtful. I came here to escape it. I wanted to feel numb, to just exist, to not feel. So I took a lot of pills and drank a lot. And ended up in the back of that ambulance, as you know.'

'I didn't thank you at the time, Constance, for calling that ambulance for me. I should have. Thank you. I could have died if you hadn't done it.'

Connie shrugged.

'Of course I did. I wasn't going to let you die. You're my friend.'

Matilda's head snapped round. Her eyes were narrowing and her gaze was inscrutable.

'Do you mean that?' she said, her voice starting to slur.

'Yeah, course,' said Connie, realising that she *did* mean it. It had been a long time coming, their friendship – they had started off badly, for sure – but now, they were definitely friends, united by a common cause.

'Thank you, Constance. That means a great deal to me.'

'My pleasure,' said Connie, holding up her cider bottle.

Matilda looked at it for a moment before doing the same. The bottles clinked together.

'Cheers,' said Connie, taking another sip. 'Cheers to friendship.'

'Yes, cheers to that,' said Matilda.

'And to goats,' said Connie, looking over at where Clarrie and Eddie were sleeping. 'Cheers to them and their little furry chinny chin chins.'

'Absolutely,' said Matilda, chuckling. 'Cheers to them, too.'

— 28 —

November

Matilda

There was a freezing wind blowing, and the dark, low clouds above them threatened rain. It had been far from an ideal morning to march up the high street and sit outside the council offices holding a placard, but they'd no choice in the matter. They'd arranged it all in advance, and almost everyone had managed to attend – even Brian, who was sitting next to Matilda on a camping chair completing another large jigsaw on a tray.

'What time is Amy coming?' Matilda asked Connie, who was standing next to her. 'Did she say?'

'She said she'd be here before eleven thirty,' replied Connie, checking her watch. 'So about now. And the radio journalist guy, Russell, should be here soon, too.'

'Good,' said Matilda, pulling the blanket Ellen had given her further up and tucking it under her arms. They had been in position for about half an hour already. A few people had walked past them so far, some of them wearing ID tags which indicated they worked for the council, but no one had stopped to ask what they were there for, and they didn't look very interested, either, even when Ellen and Connie had led them in a chant of 'Hands off our houses. Hands off our homes.' Matilda was beginning to wonder what the whole point of remaining there was, despite having been the one to suggest it.

'It doesn't matter that there's hardly anybody here,' said Connie, reading her mind. 'We've delivered the petition by hand, and it's all about the publicity we'll get from the papers and the radio station. And also about those people inside knowing we're here. And they definitely do. And oh look! There's Jamie. He's chatting to the security guard. They must know each other. That's handy.'

Matilda peered into the far distance and saw Jamie was indeed outside the entrance to the council offices. He was wearing his gardening overalls, and seemed to be having a very relaxed conversation with the security guard. A minute or so later, he slapped the other man on his shoulder, grinned at him and walked towards where their group was standing.

'Alright, Matilda, everyone. 'Ow's it going?' he asked, his smile genuine and jolly, Matilda thought, despite the weather. She admired that. He had obviously spent the morning out in the cold, and it hadn't seemed to have bothered him.

'OK, thanks Jamie. Do you know that guy? The security guard?' asked Connie.

'Yeah, we see each other every day. 'E told me 'e saw you go in there with the petition and you'd been 'ere for a bit and that 'e'd been sent to keep an eye, in case you do anything naughty,' he said, his eyes twinkling. ''*Ave* you been doing anything naughty?'

Matilda noticed he was looking directly at Constance when he said that. Ease off, James, she thought. Be gentle with her, or she'll bolt.

'Chance would be a fine thing,' replied Liv, grinning. 'It's been dull as fuck.'

Liv was standing just the other side of Connie and was looking particularly pretty today. Liv had been blessed with a very pleasing face, and she was wearing a blue checked shirt which was a little tight, with some very washed-out jeans with rips in them, which Matilda thought must be very chilly.

'Oh look, there's Amy,' said Connie, her voice sounding overly light.

Matilda looked over to the right and saw the young journalist striding towards them.

'Hello, everyone,' Amy said when she reached them. 'Nice to see you again.' Matilda watched as Ellen and Constance introduced her to everyone she had not yet met, after which they returned to their original positions, and Amy came and stood opposite her.

'Hello again, Miss Reynolds,' she said. 'I'm so glad you were able to make it.'

'I wouldn't have missed it,' she replied. 'Even if it is a little cold.'

'Yes, isn't it? I'll try to be as brief as I can. Then you can pack up and go home, if you want.'

'Well, we need to stay and make our point,' replied Matilda.

'Yes, of course. I just meant that you'll have got the publicity bit out of the way, at least. Do you mind if we have a quick chat? And I'll ask Connie and Ellen, too. I need to talk to you all.'

Matilda nodded, and Amy attracted Connie and Ellen's attention and brought them over to join Matilda.

'So, I want to fill you in on what I've learned,' said Amy very quietly. 'I don't want to broadcast it to the whole group now in case anyone in the council offices hears, but please do fill people in after I've left. The thing is, I've managed to find out what the link is, between the developers and the council.' They all leaned in further, so they could hear what Amy was whispering more clearly. 'This goes right up to the top, I'm afraid. The man who runs Orchard Developments, David Sharpe, is the cousin of the leader of the council, Hugh Evans, and the partner of the new head of social services, too.'

'Caroline Goodman? That woman who tried to turf me out of my house?' said Matilda.

'Yes, that's her.'

'She brought some man round with her on her last visit to my house, did I tell you? He was in his sixties, had a moustache… Never introduced himself.'

They were talking about how big the plots were, Matilda remembered with a start; yes, he'd been eyeing up the view from her upstairs bedroom, hadn't he?

'Could be David. Might be him. Or might be Hugh, the council leader. They both have a moustache,' said Amy. 'If I show you a picture, would you be able to tell who it was?'

Matilda looked doubtful. She barely remembered where she'd left her tea cup these days.

Despite this, Amy picked up her phone and tapped away at it. 'If it was Hugh, Caroline could excuse that, arguing that he needed to assess the value of the estate. But if it was David… That's malpractice, bringing him along, definitely,' she said. 'Was it this guy?' she said, showing Matilda a photo on her phone. It was a picture of a white man, nearing retirement, in a suit. Frankly, it could have been anyone, thought Matilda. She tried desperately to picture the man who had visited her, but all she could see were his clothes and a blank, bland face.

'I'm so sorry dear, but I'm afraid I don't know. I sincerely wish I did.'

'That's OK, Matilda,' said Connie, rubbing her shoulder, trying to reassure her.

Amy put her phone away.

'I can't believe one of them, whichever one, was in my house,' said Matilda, feeling the anger shooting through her, from her feet right to the top of her head. 'Why didn't I ask who he was? Why did I let him in?'

'Don't upset yourself,' said Ellen. 'You weren't to know. That Caroline woman was really forceful, really unpleasant. I don't blame you at all.'

'So now you know what's going on… what's next? How do we expose him?'

'Well, the problem is, I have to be able to prove it,' said Amy. 'I have a source who's really certain that that's what happened, but I need actual evidence. And I'm not sure how to get it.'

'Isn't it a conflict of interest, the leader having a cousin who has a development company? Can't we get them that way?' said Connie.

'Well, the thing is, he did declare it,' said Amy. 'I've uncovered the minutes of the meeting where the council discussed the Orchard Developments bid, and the leader of the council absented himself from the meeting on the grounds that it was his cousin's business. He wasn't present for the vote. It was all above board, in that respect.'

'But he bribed the planning officials…' said Ellen.

'Yes, we think so. But again, we can't prove it,' said Amy.

'So are you saying that there isn't a thing we can do?' said Matilda, rubbing her arms to try to keep warm. 'He's going to get away with it?'

'Not entirely. There are a few other avenues I can try. And this campaign that you're engaged in may be enough to shame the council out of what they're doing,' said Amy, 'without me needing to go all Columbo. Have you heard back from your MP yet? His office said he was formulating a reply when I spoke to them last week.'

'Nothing yet. But we're hopeful,' said Ellen.

'Let me know when you hear. And yes, I'm going to speak to you all now and see if we can get you another front-page splash. If we shine enough light on this, they might back off. They don't want a bad reputation right now – it's an election year, after all.'

'Makes sense,' said Connie.

'Right, let's start with a photo,' said Amy, getting her phone out. 'Can you all look at me,' she shouted. 'Connie, where are you off to? Please come back in. Everyone knows you now from your last interview. You need to be in this one, too.'

Connie looked to Matilda as if she had been caught in headlights.

'Yeah, come on, Connie,' said Jamie. 'You're an essential part of our team. Come and stand over next to me.' Matilda watched as Connie walked over to him, and sensed her shock when he slid an arm around her waist.

'Great,' said Amy. 'Now, hold your placards up, yes, that's right… A bit higher, Martin. Thank you. Lovely.'

Matilda noticed that Connie appeared to be holding her placard so it covered most of her face.

The photos were taken swiftly, and then Amy took out her notebook and walked towards Brian and Jocelyn. At the same moment, Matilda saw another young person approaching their group. This time, it was a young man, dressed fairly casually and carrying a rucksack.

'Hi, everyone,' he said, with the confidence of a Redcoat at Butlin's. 'I'm Russell, I'm from BBC Hereford and Worcester. I'm here to interview you all and I'll be using a voice recorder and a microphone – is that OK?' There was a general nod of assent, and he put his bag down, pulled out his mobile phone and a small microphone. 'Hello there. I see that the lovely Amy is busy down the other end of the line. We see each other at events a lot, and know to work around each other. Can I start with you?' he said, making a beeline for Liv, who was holding Kieran on her hip.

Matilda saw Liv's face light up.

'Yeah, sure, no problem,' replied Liv, running her fingers through her hair.

'Great,' he said, smiling while simultaneously tapping at his phone. 'OK, good, I'm recording. Liv, I wanted to ask you some background first, if I may. Can I get your full name and age?'

'Yes, I'm Liv Mackay. I'm twenty-one.'

Only twenty-one, Matilda thought – and already a mother of two, living alone miles away from family.

'And how long have you lived in Roseacre Close, Liv?'

'Only six months,' she replied. 'I was in Droitwich before. But I had to move.'

'Can I ask why that was?'

'Yeah, well, my ex, he was controlling an' that.'

Matilda noticed that Ellen and Connie were also listening to this interview. She guessed they were wondering what 'an' that' meant, too, and coming to the same conclusion.

'How many children do you have? And how old are they?'

'Kieran here is almost two, and Max is four.'

'So Liv, now I understand you're being told you will have to move – that the council are going to sell the estate you live in and move you back to near Droitwich. How do you feel about that?'

Liv's face froze, and Matilda could tell that she was experiencing physical fear.

'I can't go back there, no way,' she said. 'The kids are settled now. I can't move them. Kieran loves his nursery, you know. And most of all, I can't let my ex get his claws into them again. He will… Well, I dunno what he'll do. But I'm scared, to be honest.'

Matilda could well imagine how Liv was feeling, how vulnerable she clearly was beneath her polished face and attractive clothing. She could see from their faces that Connie and Ellen felt the same.

'And the thing is, in Roseacre, we've got a community, you know?' Liv went on. 'It's full of really nice people, and I know they have my back.' As she was saying this, Matilda saw her shoot a look at James. It was abundantly clear that she was hopeful of something more than friendship from him. Matilda wondered how James felt about that.

'Thank you, Liv. That was really helpful. Now, Connie, isn't it? I recognise you from the article in the *Echo*.'

'It is, yes, but I'd rather not speak to you, if that's OK. I think it's time to let others speak. Can I introduce you to Jocelyn?' said Connie, steering the young man to the left, past Brian and his jigsaw puzzle, to where Jocelyn was standing. She was looking very glamorous today, Matilda thought; every inch the efficient, well-paid PA. Such a shame that she'd had to give up that job. She'd clearly been made for it.

Matilda watched Connie make the introduction and Brian shake hands with Russell. Then Connie walked back to where she was sitting.

'Why won't you talk to the journalists?' Matilda asked.

'Oh, I just think we need to widen out the narrative,' Connie replied. 'Show that other people are affected.'

Matilda looked to her left, where Sally and Nick were talking to Amy. She could tell from her serious expression that their awful family tragedy was having a significant impact on the young reporter.

'Yes, you might be right there,' said Matilda. 'But you're worth talking to, too, you know.'

'Oh, no. I'm single, unemployed, with no one depending on me. I'm not interesting at all,' said Connie, who Matilda was certain was looking in Liv's direction as she spoke.

'On the contrary, dear Constance, I find you very interesting indeed. You are a woman of many talents. And, I think – many secrets.'

— 29 —

November

Constance

Connie heard their letterbox clatter and ran to the door. She had been waiting for the paperboy to come for two hours. She'd got up so early, she'd almost considered heading out for a dawn walk, but had decided against it, worrying that getting back into that routine might trigger a return to her old ways. She'd had a few drinks since, to be fair – her night in Matilda's garden, for example – but she had not felt the need to sink into paralytic oblivion since she'd left hospital. Yes. She'd kept her head well above water of late, despite everything, and she was proud of that.

She leaned down to pick up the paper, which was sitting on the doormat, and unfolded it. Then she let out a shriek of joy. They were front page again, and this time the focus was certainly on the others. There was a montage of photos, of Sally and Nick far left, then Liv, then Matilda, and then Brian and Jocelyn. Underneath, the headline read: *The Locals Who Won't Leave*. Amy had done a wonderful job of summarising each of their situations, and why it was imperative that they didn't have to leave Roseacre Close. In fact, their individual stories continued on pages two and three. Three whole pages of coverage. This was even better than she'd expected. Surely, she thought, the council would have to listen now?

'Mum,' she said, racing up the stairs. 'Mum! We've smashed it.'

'Good morning, Connie,' said Ellen, sitting up in bed and rubbing her eyes as her daughter ran into her bedroom. 'You're up early.'

'I couldn't sleep. I was worried about the coverage, whether Amy would have been unable to convince the editor to run it up front. But she did! Look.'

Connie passed the paper to her mother, who ran her eyes over it and smiled.

'This is great,' she said. 'But no mention of corruption? Of the councillor who's been bribing people to get a dodgy deal?'

'No,' said Connie, sitting down on her mother's bed. 'No, Amy sent me a message yesterday. She's really frustrated, but she can't make accusations like that without proof. The paper would be sued. So our only option at the moment is this – shaming them into backing down.'

'It's not our *only* option.'

Connie shot a look at her mother.

'It *is*, Mum. I've told you. Look, don't ruin this for me. I was feeling really good just now, about how the campaign's going, and now you just seem to want to shut me down.'

'I'm only saying the truth.'

'If you're so certain it would fix it, why don't *you* ask him?' said Connie, feeling her pent-up anger about her recent history beginning to seep out.

'Don't be ridiculous, Connie.'

'Maybe that would be a grown-up thing to do?'

'Maybe it's not me who needs to grow up?'

Connie stomped out of the room and down the stairs, not turning around when her mother called after her, and in that moment became that child again, the one who had frequently shouted at Ellen and then stormed out across the fields, fuelled by incandescent rage. When she reached the hall, she grabbed her padded grey coat from one of the hooks on the wall, snatched her keys from the small table by the radiator, and slammed the door behind her. She would have that walk after all, she thought.

Connie was striding past Martin's house when a voice called out to her.

'Oy, Connie! Wait up.' It was Jamie. He was hanging out of the upstairs front window, his bare chest illuminated by a streetlight. His right arm was holding onto the window, and Connie couldn't avoid noticing how defined his bicep was. She briefly imagined what it might feel like to have his arm wrapped around her, before chastising herself and doing her best to look unwelcoming and fierce.

'Aren't you freezing?' she asked, noting that she could see her own breath.

'Yeah, course. But I wanted to catch you,' he said. 'Wait there.'

Connie considered walking on anyway – she was not in the mood for a friendly chat – but realised that the new version of her, the one who actually *had* friends, would not do that. So she stood still and waited, stomping her feet every so often to keep warm.

'Did you 'ear the radio bulletin at six?' said Jamie, walking out of his front door, pulling on a puffa jacket as he shut it behind him.

'The local BBC one? No. We don't listen to it very much.'

'Oh, right. Martin does. 'E likes to listen to the livestock prices. No idea why, 'e's never even worked on a farm. But anyway. I was up early for my shift, and I 'eard them play a long interview with Sally and Nick, and Liv too. It was great. Really great stuff.'

'Brilliant,' she said, trying to smile. 'There are three pages on us in the local paper, too.'

'Awesome. You've done a great job, Connie. You obviously know loads about PR. 'Ey, shall I come with you on your walk? I 'ave an hour until I have to leave for work.'

Connie couldn't think of a reasonable excuse why not, so she nodded and they set off together.

'It's not all me, you know,' she said, walking at pace up the road in the direction of the stream and her favourite tree. 'Mum is really involved. And Liv's been doing great work on social media.'

'Yeah, she 'as. She's really good at it. We 'ave loads of followers now. She did a video of Tom the other day that got two thousand likes. 'E was doing plumbing tips.'

'I dare you to try to explain that one to Matilda,' said Connie, laughing. 'She's baffled by it all.'

'Yeah, I don't blame 'er. It baffles me, sometimes.'

They walked in companionable silence for a minute. Connie looked around her, at the fallow fields, the bare hedgerows, the skeletal trees that marked ancient boundaries, and inhaled deeply. Even now, with the air full of rotting vegetation, damp earth and wood smoke, the scent of this particular piece of countryside made her feel at peace.

'So do you think we'll get the council to change their minds, with all of this media stuff?' Jamie asked.

'I don't know. I hope so. I mean, Amy hasn't been able to run with any of the stuff we know, but even without it, it looks dodgy that they're just going with the one firm, and not putting it up for tender.'

'I can't believe it's only a few weeks until the council vote on it.'

'Yeah, I know,' said Connie, dread pooling in her stomach. Despite all of their best efforts, things were not looking good.

They walked in silence for a few minutes, Connie focusing on her breath, which was immediately transformed into steam by the freezing air.

'Do you think we've done enough?' It was as if Jamie could read her mind, she thought.

'I dunno. Honestly, I don't. Maybe. Maybe not. I mean, we've contacted all the relevant people. Matilda's written a letter to our local councillor, Georgina Williams, by the way. I'm going to drop a copy round to everyone later. She's in the same party as the leader, unfortunately, but it's worth a try. We need to make sure she knows how we feel, when she's voting at the council meeting. After all, we could vote her out in the next election.'

'But with all of the wealthy second-'ome owners around 'ere, odds on she won't care about the votes of eight working-class 'ouse'olds?'

Connie shrugged.

'She might. After all, how many of those second-home owners actually vote here?'

'Yeah, good point.'

They had reached the break in the hedge which led to the tree by the stream. Connie walked through it, and Jamie followed.

'You OK, Connie? You seem a bit off this morning.'

Connie stopped and turned around.

'What do you mean?'

'You seem... less 'appy than I thought you'd be. About the radio and the paper.'

'I'm fine,' she said, resisting the urge to tell Jamie about the argument with her mother. She didn't want to go there.

'Connie?' Jamie was now close to her, she could smell his aftershave.

'Yes?' she said, glaring at him, hoping her expression might act like some kind of shield.

'I care about you, you know.'

'Do you?' she said, walking over to the tree and sitting down with her back to him.

'Yeah,' he said, walking in front of her and sitting down on the freezing cold ground so that they were face to face.

Connie bristled. As he got closer, all she could think of was running away, getting away from this moment, protecting herself.

'I do. A lot, as it 'appens.'

'I wouldn't, if I were you,' said Connie, avoiding his gaze and idly picking up fistfuls of grass and then releasing them, watching them fall from her hands like confetti. 'I'm not worth it.'

'I think you are,' he said. She met his gaze. Then she felt a magnetic pull so strong that she dug her fingernails into her palm to help her resist it. That pain wasn't enough, however; she found herself leaning forward, just very slightly. That was enough of a cue for Jamie, who leaned further in. When his lips met hers, Connie felt an electric shock shoot through her. This was what she'd been yearning for for weeks, even though she'd done her utmost to resist. And when Jamie put his arm around her and pulled her in, it was like an earthquake had taken her over, with her senses at the epicentre.

She was in freefall now. Out of control.

'*No*,' she said, pulling away abruptly, taking action before she was so far gone there would be no chance of coming back. 'This can't happen.'

'What do you mean? It *is* 'appening,' said Jamie, trying to pull her back towards him.

'No. I'm not who you think I am.'

'I think you're everything I think you are.'

Connie avoided his gaze.

'Well, you're wrong. And anyway, I know how you feel about Liv. I've seen you looking at her. And after what she's been through, she deserves someone like you, someone kind and… reliable… Anyway, she fancies you, she definitely does. I can't do this to her. It would be wrong. This is *all wrong*,' she said, standing up and beginning to march away towards the gap in the hedge.

'Don't you think I should choose who I get to be with?' asked Jamie, running to catch up with her.

'Yes, maybe. But it can't be me,' she replied, breaking into a run. '*It cannot be me*.'

— 30 —

November

Matilda

Matilda winced as she lowered herself onto the toilet. Her now ever-present back pain meant it was agonising to bend, and it was absolutely freezing – Martin and Tom had yet to install a heater in her outside toilet – but she had no choice. It was the third time she'd had to go to the toilet this morning, and she'd been up in the night, too. She wondered if she had a bladder infection. She decided, with great reluctance, that she might have to give the doctors' surgery a call.

When she had finished emptying her bladder, she washed her hands, pushed open the door of her outdoor loo and shuffled as fast as she could to the back door, keen to return to the warmth of her home. The back burner Tom had fixed was still going strong, and the living room, where she now slept in relative comfort, was a warm and inviting place.

She was almost at the telephone when she spotted the letter lying on the front doormat. Using her stick, she bent down slowly and carefully, grasping the letter firmly on her second attempt to get down that low. When she pulled it up, she saw it was from the House of Commons. Her pulse quickened. This was the reply they had all been waiting for.

Their local MP, Sir William Dugdale, was a member of the ruling party, but had been known, on occasion, to show some independent spirit. Given their difficulties exposing the wrongdoing in the council, they had all realised that their MP would be crucial if their campaign was to be a success. In their last meeting, Matilda had also suggested getting in touch with the Minister for Housing, but Constance had pooh-poohed that, arguing that they needed to cover the local area first. Matilda thought that she was probably right on that, but it did feel strange not to be pursuing all avenues at once, especially given that the full council meeting where they'd vote on the sale of Roseacre Close was only two weeks away. There really wasn't much time left.

Matilda tore open the envelope and unfolded the letter, which was on thick cream embossed paper.

Dear Miss Reynolds,

I was interested and concerned to read your letter detailing the situation you and your fellow tenants are facing. I had not been informed of the decision to sell the estate, and I will address the matter immediately with the leader of Severnside Council, so that I can understand the reasoning behind it. Should the procedure they have followed prove to be at fault, as you suggest, I intend to raise the matter with the Minister for Housing as a matter of urgency. I will update you in due course.

Yours sincerely,
Sir William Dugdale MP

Matilda's heart swelled. 'We're winning, Miriam,' she said, addressing the house which had, over the years, come to represent her sister to her. 'We are winning.'

Matilda opened her front door, took her keys from the hook Martin had installed on the adjoining wall several weeks ago, and walked out into the street. Who should she tell first? In truth, there was only one answer to that. She shuffled down her path and up next door's and rapped at Ellen and Connie's door.

'Oh, hello Matilda,' said Connie, who looked a little red in the face and in the eyes. Had she been crying, Matilda wondered. And if so, what about? 'How are you? Is there something wrong? We don't usually see you out and about.'

'No, well, I have news. Can I come in?'

Connie nodded, smiled and stood back to let Matilda inside.

'Is your mother here?' she asked, heading for the living room where she knew she could find a comfortable seat that wasn't too hard to get in and out of.

'Yes. I'll just go and get her.'

A few moments later, Ellen walked down the stairs. She was wearing her pyjamas.

'Oh I'm sorry, Ellen, did I wake you? I must admit I didn't check the time before I came round.'

'Oh, that's OK. I was just reading the news in bed. I did a late shift last night.'

'Shall I make some coffee, Mum?'

'Yes please, love. Coffee, Matilda?'

'I'd prefer a tea, if you have some,' replied Matilda, who had never drunk a cup of coffee in her life, and didn't intend to start now.

'Sure,' replied Connie, heading into the kitchen.

'I have news, Ellen,' said Matilda, before saying in a much quieter voice: 'But before I tell you what it is, I must ask – is Constance all right? She looks… off colour.'

'Does she? I must admit I've only just seen her this morning, and I didn't look very closely,' said Ellen, her hands clasped tightly on her lap. 'She's had a tough time of it recently. Very tough. But she's been a lot happier lately. I've been much less worried. Maybe she just has a cold coming?'

'Yes, perhaps.'

'Now, what was it you came to tell me?' said Ellen, seemingly very keen to change the subject.

'I had a letter this morning,' said Matilda, just as Connie walked into the room bearing a tray laden with three steaming mugs.

'Thank you, Connie,' said Ellen, taking a cup of coffee from the tray, before Connie moved on to Matilda, pointing to the mug that contained her cup of tea. She smiled and accepted it, and took a sip. It was a little strong for Matilda's tastes, but she decided not to mention it. Connie quite clearly didn't have a cold, and she didn't want to risk upsetting her further.

'Yes, so, I had a letter,' said Matilda. 'From Sir William Dugdale.'

Connie and Ellen both let out a gasp. They'd been waiting for at least three weeks for a response, and had almost given up hope of getting any reply before the council meeting.

'Wow, that's amazing. What did it say?' said Connie, sitting down on the sofa opposite Matilda and shuffling forward so she was sitting on the very edge of the cushion.

'It said that he is going to contact the council leader immediately to find out whether they've followed the proper procedure.'

'That's exactly what we need,' said Connie, beaming. 'Exactly. He needs to be made to answer for his decision making.'

'Yes. And if not, Dugdale says he'll take it to the higher-ups. The department for housing, the minister and so on.'

'Well that's great,' said Ellen, although Matilda wondered whether her smile was a little forced.

'Yes, that's wonderful,' Connie said, then paused for a moment. 'I suppose I'm only bothered that it might be a bit late now. What if the council takes ages to respond? And how quickly will Dugdale act after he hears back?'

'Well, I intend to write to him again in a day or so to chase things.'

'Sounds excellent,' said Ellen, hugging her mug of coffee.

Although their words were natural enough, the faces of her two friends seemed to be false. The atmosphere in the room was absolutely not what Matilda had expected when she'd entered the house that morning. She had thought they would be as delighted with the MP's letter as she had been – after all, it was a strong vote of support for their cause. Something else was going on here, that was clear. Did it have something to do with whatever had upset Constance?

'So will you tell the others?' Matilda asked. 'My back is giving me terrible gip today. I don't think I'll be able to do it myself.'

'Of course,' replied Ellen. 'In fact, why don't we have a little celebration right now? I made some flapjacks yesterday, and the others could all do with a bit of good news. Poor Niamh looked almost in tears when I saw her yesterday, worrying about how she's going to fit Snuggles into a one-bedroom flat. And we need to talk about what we'll do on the day of the big meeting. Lots to plan.'

'That sounds like a great idea,' said Matilda, wondering if she'd imagined the odd atmosphere. It seemed to have dissipated now.

'Yes, that sounds lovely,' said Connie.

'Yes. I'll send out a message rounding up the troops. Connie – could you go in person to Jocelyn's? She doesn't have a smartphone.'

'Yes, sure Mum.'

Connie left the room, pulled on her shoes, opened the front door and slammed it behind her.

Matilda watched as Ellen retrieved her phone from her back pocket and began tapping away on it. It was extraordinary, she thought, how much time people these days seemed to spend plugged into those things. Mind you, it *was* a sort of magic, given that they'd all probably turn up at the front door within a few minutes, without any physical effort on Ellen's part. She wondered how contemporary nuns had reacted to such modern technology. Did they each have a mobile phone now? Did they even use computers? Did they send emails? When she'd been in the convent, they'd been cut off from pretty much everything, aside from the occasional letter. How far had the modern world managed to penetrate that world, she wondered. Had it made life there easier for them, or even harder to bear?

'That's done,' said Ellen. 'Hopefully we'll get a good few coming round. This is definitely good news. Thanks so much for letting us know as soon as the letter arrived.'

'Well, we need to do all we can, don't we,' she said. 'Absolutely everything.'

'Yes, absolutely. Do you fancy a flapjack?' said Ellen, standing up and heading in the direction of the kitchen. 'I'm going to go and get some snacks sorted while we wait.'

Matilda was now alone in the lounge. Without anyone to distract her, she was more aware than ever of her aches and pains, particularly in her back and her stomach. The pain was beginning to affect everything. She hadn't had a proper appetite for a while now, and no, actually, she didn't fancy a flapjack. She felt bloated and grim. She was definitely going to have to brave the GP. She would ask Ellen if she could take her.

'All done. Jocelyn is coming over in a minute. She's just finding Brian a coat and hat,' said Connie, reappearing in the room. Matilda noted that Connie's coat was very damp, and realised it must just have started to rain again. Those humid, baking days of summer were long behind them. Winter had got them all within its grasp now, and it would not let go for another four months at least. 'I'll get it,' said Connie, hearing the doorbell and going to answer it. 'Come in, come in,' she said. 'It's grim out there.'

Jamie, Martin and Niamh crossed the threshold, lowered their umbrellas and undid their coats.

'If it's like this on the day of the council meeting, I think I'll bring waders,' said Martin.

'Me too,' said Niamh, smiling at him.

Matilda noted an increased intimacy between them. Could there possibly be something there?

'Did you enjoy Martin's cooking, Niamh?' asked Jamie with a

broad smile on his face. 'Niamh 'ad breakfast with us,' he added, for Matilda's benefit.

Goodness, Matilda thought. Not just friends, then.

'Jamie, I'd thank you to be quiet,' said Martin.

Niamh seemed to be blushing, which confirmed Matilda's suspicions.

'Sorry Martin,' said Jamie, still grinning.

Due to the immense revelation she was just digesting, it took Matilda a while to work out what else was unusual about this scene.

Jamie had not acknowledged Constance since he'd entered the house, had he? He hadn't even looked at her when she'd opened the door.

What on earth was going on there? It had of course crossed Matilda's mind that, as young single people of similar ages, there might possibly be something brewing there. But she knew that Liv was in the frame too, and Liv was definitely more attractive, classically speaking, and less fragile than Constance; less unpredictable. Did men like unpredictable women, mused Matilda. Probably not. And Constance had never really made obvious overtures in James' direction, not that she had seen, anyway. And although, as previously acknowledged, she was no expert in matters of the heart, Matilda did feel that one probably needed to make one's feelings clear, if one expected someone to reciprocate. Having said all that, then, what did this apparent frostiness mean? Had one made a play for the other, and had there been a refusal? Had James perhaps 'asked Liv out', as the jargon went? Was Constance feeling rejected? Matilda felt, on balance, that this was the most likely scenario. She looked like she was wrestling with disappointment, or a sadness of some kind. She'd try to ask her later, if they had time after this impromptu party.

The doorbell went again, and Constance leapt up to get it, keen, Matilda thought, to get away from James.

'Oh, hello. Do come in,' Connie said, stepping back as Donna,

Tom and Liv walked in, directing them to leave their coats on the stairs.

''Iya everyone,' said Donna, as Ellen returned to the room with a tray laden with sweet treats. 'That looks fab,' said Donna. 'Thanks so much for inviting us over, Ellen. I'm dying to know the news.'

Ellen sat down on the spare seat on the sofa next to Niamh, while they all listened to Matilda updating them on the letter from their MP.

'Well, this is wonderful news,' said Donna, as the doorbell rang again. Connie sprang up and went to answer it, and ushered Sally and Nick inside.

'You've just missed the good news, guys,' said Martin. 'Our MP is taking up our case. He's on our side.'

'Thank heavens,' said Sally. 'We were just with Maddie and I was telling her all about our campaign, and I was thinking at the time how much I hoped I could give her good news soon. We don't want her waking up and not having her home to go to.' Sally's eyes were rimmed with tears.

There was a respectful silence in the room as Sally and Nick found their seats. Everyone there, including Matilda, knew the chances of their daughter regaining consciousness were remote at best. The pain this couple had gone through was extreme, that was clear, and they all wanted to be supportive, without really being sure how.

'So what does this mean, then, in the grand scheme of things?' asked Nick.

'Well, it means that the council will be feeling the pressure,' said Niamh, looking at Sally. 'Right?'

'Yes, that's true. And the potential pressure from the MP will add to it, I expect. It's definitely a step in the right direction,' replied Sally.

'Well, thank you so much for writing to him, Matilda. And thank you also to Ellen and Connie. We wouldn't be here, fighting, without you,' said Donna.

'Hear, hear,' said Martin.

'Yes! Hear, hear,' said Niamh, squeezing Martin's leg. Brazen, thought Matilda. *Brazen.*

'It is all definitely a group effort,' said Matilda. 'And far from over. We need to keep the pressure on.'

'I'm making sure I send out reminders of the final meeting date on our socials every day,' said Liv, who was perching on the side of the sofa, next to where Jamie was sitting.

'Yes, great,' said Ellen. 'We need to keep drumming up interest. Amy is coming to the meeting to report on their decision – whatever that is – and I think her radio reporter friend will come too. I thought we could meet them outside the council offices with our signs?'

'Ellen… Can I say something?' said Jamie, and the room fell silent. He sounded serious.

'Yes, of course.'

'Signs and everything are great, but… You know I was talking about doing something a bit more… out there… to get attention, last time?'

'Oh yes?'

'Well, I've been thinking. And you can tell me this is rubbish and that's fine, but… This is about our 'omes, isn't it…'

'Yes…'

'And the whole council aren't going to come to us.'

'No…'

Where was this going?

'So I thought… Why don't we take our 'omes to them?'

There was stunned silence.

'Like, how?' asked Liv.

'Like, we take our furniture and rugs and pictures and stuff, and we set ourselves up on the green outside the council offices.'

'I love it,' said Liv, her face a picture of delight. 'We could decorate for Christmas, too, couldn't we? That would look awesome on Insta.'

'Hang on a sec,' said Ellen. 'How on earth would we do this? We'd need a removal truck, surely? And what if it rains?'

'I could put up a gazebo,' said Martin. 'I think we've got some stored in the old village hall, from the last fete.'

'And I 'ave a mate with a van,' said Jamie.

'But what about power, if we want lights?' asked Connie.

'I've got an old generator in my front garden,' said Martin. 'It still works.'

'OK. Well, this is an interesting idea. We could set up and spend the morning there, before the council vote. It would be eye-catching, wouldn't it?'

'The papers would love it,' said Connie.

'But it'll be a lot of work,' said Ellen, frowning. 'Let's have a show of hands. Who thinks Jamie's plan for the day of the council meeting is a good one?'

Matilda looked around. Every hand was raised, including her own. She didn't much fancy her belongings getting rained on, but then, she didn't think they would be keen on using *her* things, anyway.

'Well, that seems to have been carried! You're on, Jamie and Martin. Can you keep me posted on plans, and we'll work together as and when?' said Ellen.

'Yeah, course,' said Jamie, grinning as if he'd just been awarded straight As in his GCSEs.

'So, that's it then. The next time we all meet, it'll be December fourth – the day of the vote,' said Ellen.

'I can't believe it's so soon,' said Donna, as everyone got up to leave. 'If we lose, though… 'ow soon do you think they'll make us move out?'

Suddenly everyone fell silent and still. Even Liv's son Kieran was quiet.

'If the council votes in favour of the sale, we'll appeal it,' said Ellen, injecting energy back into the room. 'We will not give up, I promise you.'

'Yes, absolutely,' said Martin. 'We will not let the buggers win.'

Matilda scowled at him.

'Martin! Wash out your mouth with soap!' said Jamie, laughing, and Tom and Liv with him.

'Sorry, Matilda. Sorry, Niamh. Sorry, Jocelyn and Brian,' said Martin, with a smile on his face.

'Oh don't worry about me duck, I used to work in an office where they used to swear all of the bloody time,' said Jocelyn.

The much-needed mirth was interrupted by a knock on the door.

Matilda wondered who on earth it could be. All of their group was present. Was it one of those delivery drivers? Or someone asking for donations to charity? They came to her door occasionally, but she always refused to answer.

'I'll go,' said Connie, looking really rather keen to get out of the room. Matilda watched as she walked out into the hall and opened the front door. Then Connie's eyes widened and she crossed her arms, forming a protective barrier across her chest. She looked shocked, Matilda thought. And frightened.

'Well hello, Connie,' a male voice said. 'It's been a long time.'

— 31 —

November

Constance

'Alex?'

'The very same. I haven't changed much, though, I don't think. Unlike someone I could mention.'

Connie could not quite compute what she was seeing. Alex had never been to Roseacre Close. She had never even told him about it. The world he lived in, the world she had lived in with him, was miles away from here. In fact, it was so different, it was almost on another planet.

He was dressed in dark blue jeans, an open-neck pink shirt, a grey V-neck jumper and brown deck shoes. His dark blond hair, which was cut and styled weekly by a Turkish barber in Fulham at some considerable cost, was expertly coiffed. His wide blue eyes were slightly bloodshot. He was taking large swigs from a bottle of beer.

'You're pissed,' said Connie, her arms folded across her chest.

'I might be, yes. But you're... brown. What on earth have you done to your hair?'

Connie realised that everyone in the living room was listening to their conversation, so she stepped outside and slammed the door closed behind her. It was drizzling outside, and the wind was biting. Connie wished she'd had the forethought to take her coat from off the hook. But most of all, she wished she'd never answered the door. Her stomach was churning. Her worst fears were being realised.

'Yeah, I dyed it.'

'Doesn't suit you,' said Alex, who was now using their gate for support. Connie reckoned he must have been drinking for several hours. She knew that he was particularly unpredictable when he was drunk.

'Thanks,' she said, deliberately ignoring the jibe. 'Look, can you just leave, please, Alex? I have a new life here. I'm a different person now. I didn't ask for you to come.' Connie hoped she sounded braver than she felt. She just needed to persuade him to leave, somehow.

'No, that's right, you didn't,' said Alex, waving his bottle of beer in her direction. 'But I've come here to tell you…' he said, momentarily losing his balance '…that I am prepared to forgive you. That you can come back now.'

Despite the fact he was incredibly drunk, Alex still managed to deliver that line with a trace of menace.

Adrenaline surged through Connie. Pulling herself away from Alex and all that he represented had been a seismic shift in her life, and him coming here meant there was a risk she'd be pulled back in. He had done it to her before. She was weak, wasn't she? She was very weak. And he knew it.

'We're done, Alex. We were done long ago.' Connie was trying to remain calm, but beneath the surface she was melting.

'That's a matter of opinion. Anyway, don't you think I'm clever, tracking you down? You never told me where your mother lived – and I can now understand why, by the way – bloody hell, this place is a dump. But a friend of mine was having a mini break around here in a rather special Airbnb and he spotted your little face in your local rag, and although you've changed your surname and your hair, Con, you're fooling no one.'

Alex's words ignited Connie's rage. How dare he insult her home, she thought. *How dare he?*

'Don't you *fucking dare*. This place feels more like home than your overpriced flat ever did.'

'Ooh, you've got feisty,' said Alex, taking another slurp from his bottle, discovering it was empty, and then chucking it into one of Ellen's flowerbeds.

'Are you going to pick that up?'

'No.'

'You *need* to pick that up,' said Connie, the colour rising in her cheeks.

'No. You can pick it up yourself. I'd have thought that would be the sort of thing you're used to now.' Alex tutted and wagged his finger at her. 'How far you've fallen, dear Constance. So very far...'

Connie was no longer capable of rational thought, and all of her determination to control her reactions was forgotten. She lunged at Alex, anger filling her fists with iron and her heart with steel. She was about to make contact with his nose when she felt two arms wrap themselves around her and yank her backwards.

'Ooh, who's the grunt?' said Alex, looking Jamie up and down. Connie realised Jamie must have come out of the house while they were talking. She wondered how much he'd heard.

'He's a friend of mine,' said Connie.

'A friend, is he?' said Alex, his lips puckering, his whole face a jeer.

'Yeah, I am,' said Jamie. 'I am 'er friend. And you need to leave now.'

'Fuck off, *Farmer Giles*.'

'Just ignore him, Jamie. He's an idiot. Let's go back inside,' said Connie, who was now hyperventilating. She turned away and began to walk back to the house, and Jamie followed her, to her relief. This needed to be over, now.

'Does he know about you?' said Alex. Connie's blood ran cold. She spun around, and as she did so, she made a quick calculation. Was it worth bluffing? She decided it might be worth a try. What else did she have to lose at this point?

'He knows all he needs to know.'

'So not everything, then. Does he know where you've been? Or about those charming pictures and videos? Does he know what I might do with them if you don't come back with me?'

You absolute bastard. And you'd do it, too, wouldn't you? Alex had proved time and time again that he'd always carry out his threats.

'Mate, she's not going back with you, OK,' said Jamie, turning back around and walking up to Alex. 'She lives 'ere now. She doesn't need you no more.'

'*Any* more, Giles. It's *any more*. And why *wouldn't* she come back with me? She's a slut, and sluts keep coming back for more.'

'You absolute fucking prick,' said Jamie, fronting up to Alex, who was looking more drunk than ever. Connie wondered if Alex would even survive Jamie hitting him. He had never been a particularly bulky man, that was the irony of it all, and she reckoned that Jamie's muscular physique would overpower him easily. The temptation to let Jamie go at him was strong, but she knew, after all she'd been through, that violence was never the way forward. Even when you were backed into a corner.

'She's not who you think she is,' said Alex, his eyes narrowing as Jamie's face grew closer to his.

'Come on, Jamie, let's go inside,' said Connie, tugging at his sleeve. To her relief, he moved away with her, towards the front door.

'Yeah, you run along inside with Shrek,' said Alex. 'But make sure you have a think about what I said. You belong with me, Con. You always have. I miss you. I forgive you everything. You can come back.'

'Fuck off, Alex,' said Connie, finally finding her voice. Alex didn't flinch.

'I'm staying in the pub. The Plucky Duck. Come and see me there. I'll be waiting. If you don't… Remember what I said. I won't be able to hold onto those videos any more, I'm afraid. They're burning a hole in my SD card.'

'As I said, *fuck off*.'

'Right.' Alex raised his arm in her general direction, and began to walk away. 'But think on it, dear Lady Macbeth. Think on it. What's to be done?'

Connie watched him walk out of the close, her eyes locked onto him until he was out of sight. Her heart was thrashing in her chest, and she took several deep breaths to try to calm the jousting swords in her arms and legs. She'd known, when Amy had taken that photo, that she'd been running a risk that she'd be identified. But she'd never imagined that Alex would turn up here. And even worse, Jamie had heard and seen him. But how much had he heard? That was the question. Could the genie ever be forced back into the lamp?

'Are you OK, Connie?' said Jamie. 'You're shivering like mad.'

Connie hadn't realised that she was, but now she looked down, she could see that her arms and legs were quivering uncontrollably.

'Oh. Yeah. I'm really cold, I think.'

'Wait up, I'll go and get your coat.' Connie noticed that when Jamie pushed the door open to retrieve her coat from the hall, there was silence from the living room. She could safely conclude that they'd heard everything too, then.

Jamie returned with her coat and helped her to put it on. It was harder than it should have been, because her arms didn't seem to be doing what her brain was telling them to.

'There you go. Shall we go into Matilda's garden and sit down for a bit?' said Jamie. 'We could find Clarrie, and you can give 'er a cuddle. She'll calm you down. She's good like that.'

Connie nodded and let herself be led down the side passage into the back garden, and onto the bench. Jamie called Clarrie over, and she came willingly and placed her chin on Connie's lap, awaiting a scratch. Despite how traumatised Connie was, she felt her adrenaline starting to subside as she ran her hands rhythmically over Clarrie's head.

'Well, 'e was a…' said Jamie. 'I want to use a very bad word. But Matilda would be cross. So I'm going to go with… plonker.'

Connie laughed, despite the state she was in.

'Yeah, he's definitely a plonker.'

Connie rubbed underneath Clarrie's chin, and wished desperately that the goat could take over this conversation for her. Because it was going to be difficult, and she was going to have to lie.

''E's an ex of yours, then?'

Connie took a deep breath.

'Yeah. I was with him for a few years.'

'I'm guessing 'e must 'ave some redeeming features, otherwise you wouldn't've been with 'im.'

For about the thousandth time in the past few months, Connie castigated herself for ever being weak enough to fall for Alex's dubious charms. It was something she'd had a long time to think about.

'Yeah. Well, I knew him in another life, sort of. I think, probably, I should tell you something,' said Connie, still not really sure how much she was going to reveal.

'Alex was my boyfriend when I lived in London. As you know, I left here when I was twelve. I moved in with my dad and, unlike Mum, he had lots of money. He paid for me to go to this really posh school, and then I went to uni afterwards. I dropped out, though, because I was in a really bad place, mentally, and that's when I began temping. I ended up on reception at the PR firm Alex's family runs. He was… I don't know really… persuasive? He had so much money, and he wined and dined me and took me out to all the best clubs, all the places people went to be "seen". And I don't know, I'm kind of embarrassed now, but then, I really felt like I was becoming someone. I'd always felt out of place, but there I felt like I'd arrived, like my face and name were on the map. If there was a gallery being opened or a club night being launched, we were there, every time. I spent most of my time high, often on cocaine and amphetamines, mostly gifts from

Alex, and I never really ate, which Alex liked, because I looked like one of those starving models on the catwalk.'

'Shit.'

'Yes, it was. It was really, really shit. Anyway, our relationship went bad. Like, really bad. Really bad stuff happened, stuff I don't want to tell you, because I'm... ashamed.'

'You don't 'ave to tell me anything. But you don't need to worry, either. I'm unshockable, me. I've seen some real shit in my time.'

Connie raised an eyebrow.

'This stuff... I just don't want to... It would ruin everything, you know? I came here to get away from it all, to start again.'

''E said you'd changed your 'air colour.'

'You heard that, then?'

'Everybody did, Connie.'

Connie exhaled loudly.

'Yes, well, I did. I used to be blonde.'

'Sounds to me like you didn't come 'ere to start again, then. That Alex said 'e'd been trying to find you, and someone spotted your picture. Sounds like you came 'ere to 'ide. Were you 'iding from him, Connie?'

Connie thought for a heartbeat.

'Yeah. I was. I was hiding from him.'

'Well, you don't 'ave to do that now,' said Jamie. ''E's found you, and you've told him to fuck off. You told 'im where to go.'

'But he's got these pictures...'

'Were they from sexting? Naked ones, and that? Because there are a few of me floating around, let me tell you. I was mortified for a bit, but to be honest, it didn't matter in the long run...'

Connie wished so desperately that they were.

'No. Well, some of them were. But no. There were things he asked me to do. And I was out of my mind, you know? Completely out of it. I don't even remember doing them. But it's much worse than just naked pictures. You get my meaning?'

There was a brief pause while Jamie digested this information.

'Yeah, I do.'

Connie looked into Clarrie's eyes, and wondered what the goat would say to her at that moment if she could speak. She'd probably tell her to go and see Alex and tell him where to get off. And she agreed with her; that was the correct course of action. But then, if she didn't go with him, he had more secrets to divulge. And if he did divulge them, what would that do to her life here? Would there be anything left here for her?

'I'm sorry, Jamie. Alex is right. I'm not who you think I am. That's why I said what I said the other day. It wouldn't be fair for anything to start between us, because I'm not really me. Not the person you think I am. And after Alex... I just... can't...'

Connie started to cry. Hot tears rolled down her cheeks.

'Don't be so stupid,' said Jamie, putting his arms around her shoulders. Connie froze for a millisecond at his touch, and then relaxed, because this was Jamie she was with; Jamie, who cared for the animals, and cared for old people, and cared for... her. 'I've spent enough time with you by now to know the real you, the one beneath the surface. You're ace. You really are. It doesn't matter what 'e 'as on you. Just ride the storm out. It'll pass.'

Connie wished desperately that she could freeze time right there, with the arms of the man she was falling in love with draped around her, with the animal she loved nestling on her knee, but she knew, without a doubt, that everything around her was doomed to disintegrate, due to the secrets she still held close.

Because she was a selfish fool, and it was only a matter of time before they all found out the truth.

PART FOUR

— 32 —

November

Matilda

'It's not good news, I'm afraid.' Matilda looked closely at the woman sitting at the desk, her body turned away from her screen and towards her patient, a perfect picture of engagement and sincerity.

The doctor was probably only thirty, but already had lines forming at the sides of her eyes. She had a very stressful job, Matilda thought, a job where you held together the threads of lives which were threatening to unravel. It was no wonder it was taking its toll.

'You have cancer that started in your ovaries, but it has unfortunately spread quite widely. I'm sorry we didn't pick this up when you were in hospital over the summer. You must be in a lot of pain.'

Matilda felt the familiar ache in her back, which now felt like a sword stabbing into her vital organs. It was certainly going to have the same effect in the end.

'Not to worry, my dear. I kept it to myself. And this is what I expected to hear today.'

Her back pain, her tiredness, her lack of appetite: all her symptoms had contributed a strand to the whole damning story. A bladder infection had been very wishful thinking on her part.

When she'd managed to get them to make an appointment

for her over the phone, and not 'on the line' as they had tried to doggedly insist, the GP had taken more than a week to see her. Once they'd finally examined her, however, they'd sent her to hospital for tests within a week; remarkably spritely for the modern NHS. Not that a week here or there made any difference, apparently, at this stage. It had been far too late for far too long already.

'There are things we can do, Miss Reynolds, but I'm very sorry to say that nothing we do will stop the cancer from spreading. It's too late, I'm afraid.'

Matilda nodded, listening to the distant squeals of trolleys in the labyrinthine hospital corridors.

'Yes, I thought as much.'

The woman – Doctor Rachel Fung, her badge said – pushed her glasses further up her nose.

'Although it might not be a complete surprise, you must allow yourself a chance to take it all in. There are things we can do…'

'Yes, I know. But I don't want them.'

What would they achieve, in the end? Just a few more weeks of pain, postponing the inevitable?

'I would recommend we operate. We could probably remove most of it, and give you as much extra time as we can. And then there's radiotherapy…'

'No. I don't want it. Any of it. I don't want you messing me about.'

I'm coming, Miriam, Matilda thought. It won't be long now.

'It would only be a couple of days in hospital, most likely.'

'I want to stay at home, with my animals… and the people I… need. I want to be there, not here. I am old, Dr Fung, very old now. And I think it's time.'

'Just because you're in your later years, it doesn't mean you should be condemned to suffer, Miss Reynolds. If you do want to go home and stay there, I can arrange for nursing care to make you comfortable. There are some drugs we can give you to take the pain away.'

'Will they make me sleep all the time? Because I don't want that.'

Ellen and Constance had been so helpful, Matilda thought, but they absolutely should not have to care for a bedridden invalid.

'The nurse can adjust the dosage so that you're happy.'

Matilda pulled out her hanky and blew her nose.

'How long have I got left, doctor? Please be honest with me. I don't have time for platitudes.'

The doctor looked down at her shoes, inhaled and then raised her head to meet Matilda's gaze.

'Any figure I give is only an estimate. But I think, without treatment, just a month or so. Or perhaps, weeks.'

Matilda felt a lump form in her throat. Even though she had known, deep down, for a long time, that this was the ending God had chosen for her, she had still felt a stab of misery and anger when hearing the doctor's prognosis. It had been far easier when she had ignored her symptoms. Could she have managed until the end, not knowing? Perhaps that would have been easier. But at least she now knew how long she had to put her affairs in order, to shepherd those few lost sheep back into their pen, before night fell.

'Thank you for your honesty.'

'I always try to be honest with my patients, Miss Reynolds.'

Matilda tried to say something more, but simply managed a small grunt, because she was worried that if she opened her mouth, she might cry out.

'I'll get in touch with the relevant charities and NHS departments, and organise care for you at home.' Matilda nodded. 'Are you OK getting home, by the way? Do you need transport?'

Matilda shook her head.

'I have... a neighbour... here,' she managed to say, pushing herself up to standing and beginning the slow and painful shuffle back into the hospital corridor.

'Good. You will receive a letter in the coming week with more details of your care package and options.'

Matilda didn't turn around to thank her, because she felt too full of conflicting emotions to manage to do so. She did wonder whether the doctor might think her rude, but then she realised she probably was used to all sorts of reactions to that kind of news. Some people probably shouted in rage, or were numb with shock and unable to respond at all. Walking away and not saying thank you was the very least of it, most likely.

As the door swung closed behind her, Ellen, who was sitting opposite in a row of chairs, their usage still rationed by Covid prevention notices, stood up and took her arm.

'How did it go?'

'Fine, dear, fine.'

Matilda was too overwhelmed at that moment to tell her neighbour the whole sorry story. There would be time for that when she was ready.

'Did they find anything on the scan?'

'Only old bones, Ellen. Old, old bones.'

'That must be a relief for you. Thank heavens for that. Shall I drive you home and then we can eat the carrot cake I made? That would be a nice little celebration. And I can fill you in on the latest with our campaign, if you like?'

Ah yes, thought Matilda – that was one of those lost sheep. I need to live long enough to see it back to safety. The council meeting was in two more weeks. Surely she could manage that?

And then, of course, there was the other thing. Did she have time? Could she persuade them? As soon as they returned to the close, she would ask Ellen to find her the address, and she'd write a letter to them on her typewriter. And then she'd pray.

'Matilda?'

When they'd got back home, Ellen had helped her to light the gas fire in the lounge, and then Matilda had asked her if she could tell Constance she wanted to see her, before her evening duties with the animals. And now she was here and she had things she needed to tell her.

'Take a seat, Constance,' said Matilda, pointing to the other armchair, which Ellen had made sure was clear of debris.

'Sure.' Even with the warm light from the fire, Connie looked pale. Why was that? Was it because of that horrible young man who'd visited her? Was she back drinking again? Was she eating? And as she had those thoughts, Matilda was taken aback by how deeply she cared for this young woman, a young woman she hadn't even spoken to until so very recently.

Why did she like her so much? Well, they had far more in common than they had realised. They were both incredibly stubborn, instinctively insular, and, she thought, rather damaged. She was astute enough to realise that she didn't know the half of the injuries Constance had suffered, but then, Constance didn't know hers, either. But tonight she was going to change that.

'Are you OK, Matilda? Mum said she'd had to take you to hospital earlier.'

'Oh, it was just a routine thing. I am *fine*. Nothing to worry about.'

The poor girl doesn't need to hear my troubles.

'That's good,' said Connie, who was staring at the fire.

'But are you OK, dear? After that man came to see you yesterday? It must have been a shock.'

'Did Mum tell you who he was?' said Connie, her eyes wide.

'Yes, she told me that he used to be your boyfriend. That it was quite serious between the two of you.'

Connie let out a long breath.

'Yes, it was. For a long while.'

'That must have been very hard, that ending?' said Matilda, remembering the physical pain she'd felt when Theresa had rejected her.

'It was, because he made me need him so much. It was like an addiction, you know – I had to wean myself off him. But now that's done, I can see that he was very bad for me. We were very bad for each other, really.'

'So it was a complete surprise, him coming to see you?'

'Well, it was something I had dreaded. I thought he might find me eventually. I guess you heard him talking to me?'

'Not all of it. But I heard that you used to be blonde,' said Matilda, who had heard significantly more than that, but felt it best not to say.

'Yep. And I used to have a different surname, too. I used to use my dad's surname, and not my mum's. So in London, I was Constance Phillipson, not Constance Darke.'

'Why did you change it?'

'So that he – and lots of other people – couldn't find me,' said Connie, looking straight at her. 'I could lie and say it was done for a new start, and it was partly that, maybe, but it was mostly about hiding from everyone I'd known before.'

'I can understand,' said Matilda.

'Can you?'

Matilda chuckled.

'Yes, of course. That's why I shut my door here and didn't come out for several decades. I wanted to hide, too.'

'Why?'

Matilda wondered how much she should tell her.

'Well, I did something that some people disapproved of,' Matilda said.

'You mean, falling in love with a woman?'

Being reminded that Constance knew her secret gave Matilda a jolt.

'Yes, that was part of it. But also, I stopped being a nun, even after my final vows. In the Catholic community, that's, what would you say – a big deal?'

'Was it? Around here? Did people really care?'

'I don't really know. With hindsight, I can see that most people wouldn't really even have thought about it twice. But I was...

indoctrinated. I was convinced I had sinned dreadfully. I thought I was going to hell.'

'I see.'

A silence fell while Matilda wrestled with the truth.

'Yes, so there was that,' she said, finally. 'And then there was the other thing I did that made me fearful.'

There was a pause, during which Matilda could feel Constance's gaze boring into her.

Then, Matilda came to a decision. It was time to tell someone about it all. Why not? She was old. What could they do to her now?

'I stole my sister back,' she said, finally.

'You *stole* her?'

Matilda clasped her hands together and scrunched her fingers up into a ball.

'Yes. As you know, Miriam was handicapped, as we used to call it. Disabled, you'd say. Mentally, not physically. I don't know what she'd be diagnosed as having now, but as you know, she had epilepsy, which I think caused damage to her brain. She couldn't speak, and people said she was an idiot. That is such a cruel word, do you know that? It's used so freely, but it means a person of low intelligence – someone who is mentally disabled, that is.

'But she wasn't an idiot at all. She was so clever and interested, was Miriam, and she used to grab hold of my hand and take me places, to see dragonflies dancing on the pond at the park, or glow worms nestling in the ferns at dusk. She saw things I couldn't see, I swear, and she came alive when she was surrounded by nature. But I couldn't make Mother or Father see it. They kept her shut up at home, and when we were evacuated during the war, they sent her to an institution. I didn't know where she was for a long time, because the nuns wouldn't tell me, but I eventually befriended one of the older nuns, and she looked at my record and found a note on there. Bear in mind, I hadn't seen

Miriam then for more than fifteen years. I wrote immediately to ask the institution if I could visit and take her out for tea, but I was refused access. I wrote again and again, actually, but was always refused. They said she was happier without visitors. I was incensed. So once I'd left the convent, the very first thing I did was get a taxi to take me to see her.'

'To the place where she lived?'

'Yes. If you could call it living. It was such a beautiful place, you know – a Georgian mansion surrounded by wide green fields – but she was never let out to explore them, and the rooms she was kept in had flaking paint, nailed-down windows and stank of urine, and God knows what else.'

'So they let you in?'

'Goodness, no. I broke in.'

'You *broke in*?' Constance's eyes had widened.

'Well, not technically, I suppose. I waited until a man came to deliver milk. He propped open a side door and I went in behind him. And then I walked around until I found her. No one challenged me. But that might have been because I was still wearing my habit.'

'So you actually broke into somewhere disguised as a nun?' said Connie, with an incredulous look on her face.

'Yes, I did. And I know it sounds funny, doesn't it, but at the time I was very scared, and very angry. Because I found my poor Miriam locked in a room with bare walls, a few pieces of furniture and nothing at all to do. She had pulled out a lot of her hair, and was shrieking so loudly, I had to put my hands over my ears. But she stopped, all of a sudden, when she realised it was me. She came over to where I was standing and began to pat her hands all over my face, checking that I was who she thought I was. And when she was sure, she took hold of my hand and tugged. I could see that she wanted us to go out of the door. And I knew then and there that I couldn't leave her in that dreadful place.'

'So what did you do?'

'What do you think I did? I did what she wanted. We walked out of that room and down the front stairs, towards the main doors. I had noticed that the side door had a code, so I didn't fancy our chances getting back out that way. My decision to go out of the main doors was surprisingly easy to begin with – we just didn't see anybody – but there was a nurse on duty in a small room by the entrance, and she called out to me as we were about to go through the doors. "Sister," she said. "Can I help you? Why are you leaving with a patient?"'

'Did you reply?'

Even all of these years later, Matilda's heart began to beat faster as she told the story.

'I thought about lying to her and making something up, but in the end, I decided to tell the truth. I said, loudly, clearly, with confidence I did not feel: "She's my sister, and I'm taking her home." Then I told Miriam we were playing a game that involved running, so that she would run out of there with me. We both bolted. My taxi was still waiting outside, so I bundled her in there, and I asked the driver to leave immediately. The nurse who'd challenged me stood on the steps and watched us drive away.'

'They didn't come after you?'

Matilda ran her hand over her hair, as if brushing away the memory of the wimple she'd worn for so many years.

'I thought they might. I thought they would be able to find me – after all, they knew my name, and the council would have told them, I expect – but no one ever did.'

Matilda remembered how she'd felt in those first few days, jumping at the sound of cars parking outside the house, at knocks on neighbours' doors. But no one had come and, gradually, she had relaxed. But not enough to take Miriam out with her when she left the house. That had been too much of a risk. Instead, they had lived happily in their little house, tending the garden together, watching the wildlife and farm animals from the bench at the bottom of the garden.

'So you brought her with you? Back here?'

'Yes. It was the only place I had to go. But even though no one came to get her, I worried that we would be noticed if we went out, and someone would ask awkward questions. And Miriam, dear Miriam, with her suffering from that dreadful epilepsy, well, it was safer to keep her at home, in an environment both of us knew, where I could try to keep her safe. We had plenty to fill our days, anyway, because that was when I started keeping the animals. It was because Miriam loved them so much, you see. She was always so much more calm when around them, and seemed to have fewer fits. So I started with one goat – one of Clarrie's ancestors. She was called Lucy. Miriam adored her. And then we gradually acquired the cats from local farmers looking to get rid of unwanted feral litters, and chickens from another local farmer who was selling up his chicken shed.' Matilda paused and allowed her mind to travel back to a sunny but cold spring day, when Miriam had sat on the bench at the end of the garden wrapped in blankets, enraptured by a small black beetle that had landed on her hand. 'Yes, she was always so happy out there, surrounded by God's creatures.'

'I feel like that too, about the animals,' said Connie, feeling the fire's warmth bringing colour to her cheeks. 'When I came back here I was, I don't know, damaged, I suppose. Mentally. Something had happened to me that made me feel like I was frightened of animals. But it turns out that I wasn't. It was something else entirely. Mum was right, she tried to tell me so, but I didn't listen.'

'What happened?'

Matilda felt she knew what Constance was about to tell her, but she also felt that it might help her to tell it.

'I was attacked.'

'Ah.'

'It was... sexual. God, I feel so bad telling you this, you're probably not going to be able to look me in the eye again. Being a nun, and all.'

Constance was staring at her feet, refusing to meet Matilda's eye. Matilda felt anger burn up inside of her; not anger at Constance, of course, but anger that a man had made this clever, kind young woman feel this way.

'Oh child, don't be ridiculous. Nuns are human too, you know. We are not robots. We feel. We see. We know the world is full of evil. Please don't feel that way. I refuse to let you.'

Constance took a deep breath and looked up at Matilda.

'Thank you. That helps,' she said, running her hands through her hair. 'It's so hard to talk about. Yes, so… it was… rape. Not Alex, not the guy you saw. One of his friends. It was all so bad, I tried to pretend it hadn't happened. Like I could think it away, you know? And then later, when I came back here, I created my own story about it. I convinced myself I'd been trampled by a bull in a field. It sounds nuts, saying it now, but I think I felt like I could deal with it, if it had just been that.'

'I think that sounds very understandable,' said Matilda, who was fighting the urge to lean over and hold Constance's hand, which was a strange and unusual feeling for her, because she was generally averse to human touch.

'Thank you for saying that, but I know you're just being kind. I know I'm nuts. I've always been nuts. Both my parents have tried to get me to take antidepressants over the years, but I've always refused.'

Matilda nodded. She knew that doctors in the institution had given Miriam drugs to control her epilepsy, but they had sedated her and turned her into a kind of zombie. She had not given Miriam anything once she'd come home with her. It had been a decision born out of necessity, as she could never have registered her with a doctor. It had felt right at the time – she had so much wanted her sister to be awake and able to enjoy each day – but later, as medical advances occurred, Matilda had wondered whether she should have revisited that decision. Maybe it would have bought her more time? Maybe she'd have been more comfortable? Maybe, just maybe, she'd still be here?

'I am no expert, Constance, but I think those sorts of drugs are a bit better now? A bit safer?'

'Yes, they are, I think. But I am such an addict. I can get addicted to anything – to booze, to a person, to a feeling... I'm worried I'll get addicted to those pills, and never be myself again.'

'I see.'

'Do you?'

Matilda thought about the treatment the hospital had offered her yesterday. They had suggested radiotherapy and an operation to remove the cancer that was slowly but surely eating away at her insides, like a deathwatch beetle. Why had she refused? Well, because she was desperate to stay at home. And also, afraid of letting go, of losing control of herself.

'Yes, I do.'

'You must miss her.'

'Every single day. But I feel close to her here, in this house. That's why this house must remain standing, Constance. It cannot be demolished to make way for some money-making scheme. This was her last home. And it must always be her home.'

Matilda could see that Constance was smiling at her. Then she reached out and grasped Matilda's hand. The sweet, gentle shock produced by the touch of another human being flooded through her. So this is friendship, Matilda thought. What wonderful magic.

'I understand, Matilda. I do.'

'Thank you, Constance. That means more to me than you know.'

— 33 —

November

Constance

Connie switched on the radio and then immediately turned it off, because Mariah Carey's 'All I Want for Christmas' was playing, and she simply couldn't bear the sheer saccharin joy of it. Also, it was only the end of November. Surely the world deserved a little bit of respite before Christmas tunes had to blare out twenty-four hours a day from every single radio station?

Connie was tired and fractious. Since Alex had turned up on her doorstep, she'd been struggling to sleep. Memories she'd tried hard to suppress were torturing her. Her mind resembled a labyrinth, each blind alley populated by a monster of her own making. She knew that he still held a power over her that she could never escape from. It was quite possible that by now, after a couple of drunken days spent at The Plucky Duck, he had set off Chinese whispers about her which would eventually make their way to her door. She had been a fool to ever think she could escape what she'd done.

'Oh, hello, love. Couldn't sleep?' said Ellen, entering the kitchen and hanging her handbag up on a hook on the wall. She was wearing her uniform and had just returned from a night shift.

'No,' said Connie, opening the cupboard and pulling out a jar of instant coffee. 'Do you want a cup of coffee or tea?'

'No thanks, love. If I have one now I'll never get to sleep. Actually, come to think of it, I think I'll have camomile. Do we still have any?'

Connie peered into the cupboard and pulled a box out from the back.

'Yeah, we do. I'll make you one.'

Ellen wrapped her arms around Connie's waist.

'Thanks, love. Are you OK? Want to talk about it?'

Connie stopped making the drinks, turned round and gave her mother a hug.

'Thanks, Mum. I'm not OK, not really, but I think I've decided what to do.'

'So you're going to go and talk to him?' said Ellen, talking into Connie's ear.

Connie pulled away, and nodded.

'Yep. I've got to face him, haven't I? I mean, I can't hide here forever. I was stupid to think that I could.'

'You were following your instincts, Connie. You came home to me, and that meant the world to me.' Connie saw that there were tears in her mother's eyes, and so she leaned forward and gave her another hug.

'Oh bless you, Mum. How you can still feel that way about me, with all I've done, I'll never know.'

'It's called love, Connie. I love you. And you will get through this. We'll get through this together.'

'Are you sure? Are you sure I'm doing the right thing?'

'Positive.'

It was 9.30 a.m. when Connie left the house to walk the half a mile to The Plucky Duck. While she walked, she thought through what she was going to say. In many ways, she had been rehearsing this speech for at least a year. Although she had hoped to be able to disappear into the depths of the countryside, she'd also known, really, that Alex – and her past – would find her eventually.

It was the price she was going to have to pay for what she was about to say that had been keeping her up at night. When she'd come home, she'd given little thought to any kind of life she might make here. She had thought merely of existing, of marking time. Now, however, she had friends, real friends, as well as someone she felt very strongly about who'd said, miracle of miracles, that he liked her, too. But she knew she was about to have to destroy all of it, all of these newly formed links, and that reality was both frightening and devastating. Because that would undoubtedly be the price of telling the truth.

Connie pushed open the door of the pub and walked to the bar area, where she knew breakfast was served. The interior of the pub was relentlessly grey: grey floor tiles, dark grey walls, and grey, black and white prints on the walls, all showing Victorian farm labourers – who Connie doubted were in any way local, or even actually Victorian. She scanned the room. There was an older couple having a silent full English over in the corner in a booth, a group of construction workers chowing down on bacon sandwiches in the middle, and then over to the left – yes, that was Alex. He was on his phone, not looking around him. She walked right up to him without him even noticing that she was there.

'Hello, Alex.'

His head snapped up. He was looking a little the worse for wear, she thought with some satisfaction. He had stubble on his chin, his eyes were bloodshot and his hair was less vertiginous than usual. Connie wondered how his liver was doing, and how long it could keep up with this level of consumption.

'Well, hello. I knew you'd come eventually,' he said, pointing to the chair opposite him. Connie sat down without responding. A waitress dressed in smart black trousers and a tight white shirt came up to their table.

'Good morning, Alex,' she said, her smile broad and perhaps

just a little bit hopeful. Bloody hell, Connie thought. She's young and naive. Just his type.

'Good morning, Skyla. How are you?'

'Oh, all good, thanks,' the waitress said, studiously avoiding looking in Connie's direction. 'What can I get you?'

'Oh, I'll have a full English, please. And a flat white. And Connie? What would you like?'

'Nothing, thank you, Skyla. I won't be staying long,' replied Connie.

The waitress smiled her very best smile and turned away. Connie noted that Alex's eyes lingered just a little too long on her rear as she walked towards the kitchen.

'She's a bit young even for you, isn't she, Alex?'

Alex rolled his eyes.

'Oh for fuck's sake, Connie, give me some credit. It was only a bit of flirting. Nothing more.'

'Yeah, I can see that.'

Alex picked up his phone and began flicking the power button on and off, waking and putting his phone screen to sleep repeatedly.

'So, I've waited two days for you to come and see me. I'm guessing you've been trying to make up your mind, and I get that. It's a big thing, coming back.'

'You do realise that you're attempting to blackmail me to come back, Alex? Do you think that's somehow appealing?'

Connie watched as Alex blinked slowly and focused his attention directly on her, his long, curled eyelashes accentuating his deep blue eyes. She'd found that movement attractive, once. That ability to make her feel like she was the only woman in the room. Connie's palms were beginning to sweat. She needed to say what she had to say, and then she needed to get out of here.

'You must realise that the scars you inflicted on me are still healing,' said Alex, without irony. 'I was shocked and I'm still shocked. And I know that I'm not perfect, either. I should have… should have stopped Simon from doing what he did.'

'He raped me. Simon. He *raped* me. You knew what was happening, and you did nothing.'

'That's not strictly true. You had never said no to that sort of thing before. It was a reasonable expectation that you'd be fine with it…'

'You utter bastard,' she said, shouting.

Alex put his finger in front of his mouth and smiled.

'Shush, Connie, you'll be telling the people around here the truth next.'

'Actually, do you know what? I don't care any more, Alex. That's what I've decided. I'm not coming back with you. Ever. I don't care what you tell people. If you tell them everything, that's fine by me. But if you do, I'll tell them all about you, then, for good measure.'

Alex smirked.

'And you reckon they'll believe you? A slutty ex-jailbird, who changed her name and her appearance and ran home to Mummy? Fuck off.'

'No, *you* fuck off,' yelled Connie, pushing her chair back and standing up with force, almost colliding with the waitress, who had just returned with Alex's breakfast. 'We're done, Alex,' she said, gesturing an apology to the waitress as she stepped sidewards to get out of her way.

'Don't touch him with a bargepole, Skyla,' she added, heading for the door. 'He has piles, a teeny-tiny penis and a foot fetish. I advise you to always wear socks in his presence.'

— 34 —

November

Matilda

Someone was hammering at the door. It was early, Matilda thought. Far too early to be the postman, or Ellen or Constance. She swung her legs out of bed, found her stick and walked slowly to the hall. She turned the key and pulled it open. She was shocked to find Jamie standing outside, his hand still poised, seemingly about to hammer into mid-air.

'You've got to see this,' he said. He was holding something in his hand. Was it a letter? A newspaper? She couldn't tell in the dim light cast by the streetlamp, but it seemed sensible to ask him inside, to stop him waking up everyone else on the close.

'Come in, James.'

Jamie brushed past her and marched into her hall, like a debt collector barging in to reclaim goods. His weight was shifting from one leg to the other, as if he was about to do a round in the ring. What on earth had happened, she wondered. Matilda shut the door closed behind her, followed Jamie into the kitchen and flicked on the light.

'James, would you please tell me what you are here for? It's very early.'

'Yeah, I'm sorry to wake you, Matilda, but they weren't answering next door, and I really need to talk to someone about this.'

'Are you drunk, James? Have you been in the pub all night?'

'No, Matilda, I 'aven't been in the pub. I've just got up to do an early shift, and found this on our doormat. It's the tabloid Martin gets. The milkman just brought it. Look at the front cover. *Just look at it.*'

Matilda fumbled for her glasses, which were still, thankfully, around her neck on a cord, and put them on. As she adjusted to the light and the lenses, a huge headline came into focus. It read: *Tory minister's ex-con daughter hiding in council house.*

Underneath the headline was a photograph of a woman with streaky blonde hair and dark red lips, wearing not very much at all. It took Matilda a few moments to realise she was looking at Constance.

'Oh, goodness.'

'Yeah,' said Jamie. 'Orrible, isn't it.'

Matilda's head was beginning to spin.

'Come into the living room,' she said. 'We can sit down there. I need to read this article.'

Jamie followed her into the living room and sat down opposite her on the same armchair Connie had sat in just a couple of nights previously. He handed her the paper without a word.

The article continued:

> *The Orb* has discovered that disgraced former socialite Constance Phillipson, daughter of the Conservative Housing Minister Robert Phillipson, has taken refuge in a small council house in rural Worcestershire following her incarceration at Her Majesty's Pleasure.
>
> We can exclusively reveal that Phillipson, 29, who was convicted of Actual Bodily Harm for an attack on her ex-fiancé last year, and who served just three months of a six-month sentence, has now changed her name and appearance and is living with her mother in the village of Stonecastle.
>
> We are also now able to publish a series of photographs of Ms Phillipson, which show her scantily-clad, snorting Class

A drugs. Videos now circulating on social media, which *The Orb* has seen and verified, also show a graphic sexual encounter between Constance Phillipson and an unidentified man.

The Orb contacted Robert Phillipson MP's office for comment. A spokesperson replied: 'This is a private matter, and as such this is not something the Minister will comment on.'

Matilda looked up from the newspaper and saw that Jamie was chewing his cheek, his body seemingly unable to be still. And frankly, having read what she'd just read, she couldn't blame him. She suspected, however, that they might be upset about different things.

It wasn't the fact that Constance had been in jail that was bothering Matilda, although heaven knew, in normal times, that might have been enough. Nor the unmarried sex, which she had been brought up to abhor; she had learned of late that times had changed, and she should, if not actually change her views, try to ignore such things when they challenged her. No, what was bothering her was something quite different.

Constance's father was the Minister for Housing.

Surely that couldn't be true? Surely Constance couldn't have been hiding the fact that she was the daughter of one of the only people with the power to stop them all having to leave? Matilda felt her hackles rise. She had shared so many secrets with Constance, and she thought that Constance had shared all of her secrets with her. But apparently not. Not this one.

'Well, shall we go?' asked Jamie.

'What do you mean?' asked Matilda, wondering if she'd been speaking her thoughts out loud.

'I mean, we need to show it to 'er. She needs to see it and know it's out there. Because that bastard Alex must be behind this, and 'e's obviously full of shit.'

'Yes, yes, we do need to speak to her,' replied Matilda, trying to hide her rage. It was clear to her that James hadn't joined up the dots. She decided not to tell him now. She needed to gather her thoughts. She couldn't imagine why Constance had not told them about her father, but what *was* clear was that she had most likely held the key to their salvation in her hands from the very beginning and she had failed to use it, and that, Matilda felt, was an appalling betrayal.

'Did you say that no one was answering?'

'Yeah, no one answered when I knocked on the door.'

'What time is it?' asked Matilda, aware as she did so that she needed to at least pretend to be calm.

Jamie checked his watch.

'It's seven thirty.'

'I think Ellen will be home soon. She's on nights this week. Perhaps Constance is asleep?'

'I 'ope so. When she sees it, she will feel… she will be…'

James looked lost, Matilda thought. Adrift.

Matilda felt the urge to comfort him. She reached out and put her hand on Jamie's arm, and he didn't flinch or look repulsed, and Matilda was amazed. She was changing, and things around her were changing. Better late than never.

'I know. Look, James, why don't you go to work – you don't want to be late – and I'll make sure I catch Ellen when she gets home. I'll find out what this is all about, and you can come and see me later, OK? I'll be here when you get back. I'll find out everything I can.'

'Yeah, OK. That sounds like a plan. Thank you, Matilda. You're… ace.'

Jamie leaned over and gathered her into a hug. Matilda froze, not because the sensation was unpleasant, but because it was unexpected. She went stiff for a millisecond before she made a concerted effort to relax, and let his body actually touch hers. The hug didn't last long, maybe a second or two in reality, but that brief interaction had a profound impact on Matilda. She wished, as soon as it was over, that she could do it again. The very last person she had hugged had been Miriam, and even then her sister had not been one for hugging, although they had held hands often. But this hug, with a man she had zero attraction to – of course, she had never been attracted to the opposite sex – well, it had activated some sort of sensor inside of her, and she now felt warm and comfortable, and quite calm even, despite what she'd just read.

'No trouble at all, Jamie. No trouble at all,' she said.

'Wait a sec. You called me Jamie.'

'Did I? Goodness. I am getting modern,' said Matilda, with a smile. 'So, have a good shift, Jamie, and I'll let you know what I find out later.' Jamie moved towards the front door. 'And try not to worry too much. As you say, it may all be lies.'

Matilda sat in an armchair in the living room and read until she heard a car drive up, and next door's front door open and close. Then she found her stick and the newspaper Jamie had brought round, stood up, put a blanket around her shoulders and walked slowly and carefully out of the house and rapped on Ellen's door.

'Goodness, Matilda, you're here early. Do come in,' said Ellen, with a broad smile on her face. It was clear to Matilda that she had not yet seen the paper. Matilda was glad she'd had time to calm down. Mother Superior had taught her that anger bred anger, and calm bred calm.

'Yes, Jamie woke me up,' she said, crossing the threshold and heading into the living room, where she had her mind set on a high-backed armchair.

'Jamie? Is there something up with him? Or Martin?' said Ellen, following her in and plumping up a cushion to support Matilda's back, before helping her lower herself into the chair.

'No, Jamie is fine. Now look, Ellen. Will you please take a seat.' Ellen looked startled, but sat down opposite her as requested.

Matilda was not surprised at her response, but she couldn't think how else to begin this most delicate of conversations. 'By the way, is Constance in?'

'I presume she's asleep upstairs. What's the matter? Is she OK? Should I check?'

Matilda waved her right hand in the air, dismissing Ellen's concern.

'No, no, I'm sure she's fine. The thing is, Ellen,' she said, producing the newspaper from under her blanket, 'it's this. This news story. Jamie brought it for me to see.'

Matilda handed Ellen the newspaper, and watched as she digested its contents. Not having any children of her own, she was trying to imagine what it might be like for a mother to read a story like that about her child. Would she cry, or shout? Run upstairs in a rage, and yell at Constance? Dissolve into tears in front of her?

But as it turned out, Ellen did none of these things.

'We have been expecting this,' she said, and Matilda's eyes widened. 'I mean, not exactly this, but we knew that Alex would do something in this vein. It's very much his style. He's a dreadful piece of work, the very worst.'

'So he made up these lies to get back at her?'

Please, *please* let them be lies, thought Matilda.

Ellen ran her thumb and index finger back and forth along her nose.

'Not everything in there is a lie. But it's not the entire truth, either. Look, Matilda, I know how it looks. Just give me an opportunity to explain, OK? I need to tell you what happened, about how Connie came to be here. About how she got into this… mess. I don't know how much she's told you?'

'She told me that her former partner, Alex, was abusive, and that she came here to escape him. To start again.'

'Well, that's partially true,' said Ellen, closing her eyes. 'You know, I think, that Connie stopped living with me when she was twelve. She left here because her father was dangling a whole load of money her way, and she was nearly a teenager, you know? It was attractive, the life he was offering her. I don't blame her for that, although I do blame him. Anyway, yes, my ex-partner is a very wealthy man. So Connie moved in with him, he sent her to a very expensive school in London, and when she left school, she stayed on in the city. She met Alex when she was temping at the PR company his family run, and he was very persuasive, I think. He comes from a lot of money, and he threw it at her, and she was flattered. He's very charismatic, and very charming when you first meet him. I was pleased for her at first, because she seemed happy. But gradually, during our occasional meetings – mostly, when I'd have a day off and go into town to see her – I noticed changes. She was young, and yet she had dark circles under her eyes. She had what looked like scars on her forearms. She was getting thinner and thinner, so much so I worried that she was anorexic. And when she stopped returning my messages or answering my phone calls, I knew something was very wrong.'

Matilda noted Ellen's focus and emphasis as she was telling the story. This must be something she had said many times over in her head. What a weight this must have been to carry.

'I can imagine. What did you do?'

'There wasn't much I could do. I called around old friends of hers, but no one had heard from her. I tried to reach Alex, but he didn't respond. I even went into London to try to find her, but she wasn't at work – and no one was answering the door at her flat.'

'Goodness.'

'Yes. I didn't get much sleep that week. And I got even less when I got a phone call from the police, just after midnight on that Friday.'

Matilda took a sharp intake of breath. She had hoped that this section of the story was untrue.

'And what did they say?'

'They told me that Connie was under arrest for assault. That

Alex had walked into a police station with two black eyes and reported her for it.'

'And they believed him?'

Ellen smiled at Matilda.

'I am so glad you have leapt to that conclusion,' said Ellen. 'That's exactly it. I refused to accept what they were saying, but the police just kept going on and on about taking all assault seriously, and that they had Connie in for questioning, and that she'd asked me to find her a lawyer. I mean, I had no idea who to call, obviously. I'm not her father, I don't have lawyers on speed dial. So in the end, I rang him, my ex-partner. He immediately sent round this extraordinarily expensive brief who Connie tells me she was scared of. She was very... damaged at the time, and his masculine brashness, his pomposity, frightened her. Anyhow, she says Alex had some CCTV of the incident, so she was unable to deny it. But she had good reason to be angry... very good reason... She was raped by Alex's friend, and he knew, and he let it happen. I think she could have used that in her defence, but she said she told them she was guilty so they'd leave her alone. The lawyer tried to talk her out of it, of course, but she did it anyway. And so she was convicted and sentenced to... prison. As you already know, from what you read.'

'They sent her to jail for giving someone two black eyes?'

Ellen took a sharp intake of breath, as if gathering strength.

'She had a previous conviction for drug driving... she'd been given a suspended sentence for it. And so when this happened, she was sent to prison. It's automatic, you see.' Ellen sniffed. 'But yes, she was. It was... devastating. For her and me. I've never been so worried in my entire life. I thought she might try to kill herself in there.'

'But she survived.'

'Yes, she did. And as soon as they let her out, she came back here. She didn't have anywhere else to go, and I wanted to take care of her. She has always been vulnerable, mentally. She's had anxiety and depression since she was a child. I have tried and tried since she came home to get her to accept medication for it, but she simply won't. So she continues to try to treat it her own way, with alcohol, mostly. And recently, of course, with animal therapy. Your animals are the best thing that's ever happened to her. She's found a joy in them she has never found in anything else. I can't tell you how relieved I was when I first noticed the effect they were having on her.'

Matilda's heart sank.

'And then I came home from hospital, told her she wasn't welcome, and then she tried to take her own life. I almost killed her.'

'If it wasn't that, Matilda, it would have been something else. It has always been a risk. Please don't feel guilty. It's my fault for not getting her the right treatment, for not making her go away for help.'

'You did the right thing, Ellen. You brought her home to you. You love her, and she feels safe here.'

'Was it the right thing, though? Because I knew about those videos he'd made her take part in, and I knew he'd probably share them if she refused to go back to him. I wish now I hadn't encouraged her to tell him to go, to tell him it was all over.'

'What would she have done instead? Gone back to that hell she seems to have been living in? Golly, Ellen, no. You did the right thing by her.'

'But will she ever be able to live this down? I mean, you're shocked, aren't you, Matilda? I can tell by your tone, by your anger. Your view of her has changed forever, now, hasn't it?'

Matilda thought for a moment. Her friend had lied to her, and that was a major blow, given that she had only just let her into her life. But she also knew that when you were struggling to breathe, to move, to escape, sometimes you had to hide things you did from others. And she could appreciate that Constance's mental health troubles were an awful affliction and that the abuse she'd suffered had undoubtedly damaged her. And who would want to actively broadcast that they'd been in prison? It was understandable she had kept that quiet.

'I suppose it has, and everyone's will, but that's not a terrible thing,' she said, finally. 'She is still Constance. She is still our friend.'

'Yes, she is,' said Ellen, her eyes filling with tears. 'She is. She is very fond of you, Matilda.'

They sat there in silence for a moment, before a thought came to Matilda.

'So, the section about her father being a minister of government? For housing? That's not true, then?'

Ellen puckered her lips and inspected her fingernails.

'It is true. He is a minister. Not a secretary of state, but a minister, yes.'

'For housing?'

'Yes.'

In that moment, Matilda's empathy with Constance dissipated. For it seemed to her that Constance had hidden her father's role for entirely selfish reasons, to attempt to keep her prison sentence hidden from her new friends. And those selfish reasons might lead, she knew, to them all being kicked out of the place they loved, of the place that made them feel safe and secure. How could Constance have had that access to power, and not used it to try to put a stop to something that was causing limitless distress to her neighbours? After Matilda had confided in her about Miriam, and why it was so important that she should stay in her home? And what about Brian and Jocelyn, Sally and Nick, Donna, Tom and the others? Was their pain not worth a little discomfort on Constance's part? The absolute shame of it. *There just weren't words.*

'I think I should go now, Ellen,' said Matilda, her insides and her lower back screaming in pain as she stood up and began to walk to the door.

'Matilda...' said Ellen, getting up and walking towards her. 'Can I explain why she didn't go to him for help?'

'No, thank you, Ellen,' Matilda replied, too angry to say any more. As she was about to go out of the door, she heard footsteps, and saw Connie walking down the stairs, her long brown hair in a high ponytail, her thin body wrapped in a blue towelling dressing gown.

'Matilda? What are you doing here so early?' said Connie.

Matilda considered simply turning around and walking away, but she found she couldn't. Despite everything she had been taught, every sage instruction to remain silent in the face of provocation, she found that she simply *had* to say something.

'I came about this,' she said, throwing the paper in Connie's direction. It hit the third step from the bottom, and slid down onto the floor, the front page landing upwards, the lewd photograph clear for all of them to see. Connie's face went white.

'Oh my God...' she said, her hand flying to her mouth.

'It's OK, love, we'll sort it,' said Ellen, rushing to her side as she collapsed on the stairs.

'Yes, you get on with looking after her, Ellen, while the rest of us look forward to eviction,' said Matilda, almost spitting. 'I could forgive you all of it, Constance, except for the fact that the solution to our housing nightmare has been in your hands all of the time. All of it. And yet you did nothing. You have witnessed our pain and our suffering, and you could have put a stop to it, and you didn't. And that, I simply cannot forgive.'

Matilda turned away and walked down the front path. She heard the door slam behind her, but did not look back. When she had opened her own front door and closed it behind her, she sat down on her bed and wept.

— 35 —

December

Constance

Connie pulled the pillow over her head and stuck her fingers in her ears, but it was useless. Nothing could drown out the banging. They had disconnected the doorbell already, but that hadn't stopped the journalists. And then there was the yelling. 'Connie, have you got anything to say in response? Is it you in the pictures, Connie? How was your time in jail, Connie? Has your dad seen the videos?'

Her mother had tried reasoning with them, opening the door and telling them to leave Connie alone, but it hadn't worked; they'd just taken pictures of her instead, some of which had made it onto the inside pages of a few newspapers. They were like gannets in a feeding frenzy. In the occasional brief moment of lesser despair, Connie tried to reason with herself, having worked in the media world long enough to know that all obsessions faded – most of them within a few days. They'd go away eventually, she knew that.

But the videos – oh, the videos. The headlines might fade, but those unspeakable, desperate memories captured on Alex's phone would live on forever, watched by hungry naive schoolboys, lairy office workers in pubs, and desperate, pervy old men in dark, tobacco-filled living rooms. The fact she'd even taken part in the making of them now seemed mad, but she realised that it hadn't really been her. She hadn't been living in her own body for some time. Alex had been her macabre puppeteer. It was the only way she'd got through it. She'd disconnected from herself, not allowed her brain to engage, and allowed the drugs and alcohol he'd been giving her to make their own decisions. And when Simon had raped her, she'd shut herself off even more. It had felt easier than facing reality. She'd not gone to the police about it, because Alex had made her feel like it had all been her fault, that she'd somehow been complicit.

And when the police had come for her, not to defend her but to accuse her, she'd barely flinched. She'd sat through their questioning, her mind and body both dumb and numb. She'd taken one look at the lawyer her father had sent, his hair and build far too similar to Simon's, and thrown up in the wastepaper basket in the corner of the interview room.

She'd agreed with everything the police had said to get that whole session over with, and when she'd been sent to jail, she'd simply gone through the daily motions of living – eating, drinking, washing – and barely flinched. Even the noise of the place – a constant mid-level rattle and scream, reaching a satanic crescendo every few hours – had been bearable, because she hadn't really been there. She'd found solace in prison's routine and predictability, spoken to very few people, refused all medication offered, and avoided socialising. She'd spent most of her days lying in bed, sometimes reading, but mostly hovering in the space between sleep and waking, her brain willingly surrendering to unconsciousness. She'd dealt with her guilt and her anger in her own way, and when she'd come out, she'd returned to her mother's house to continue much in the same vein, with the addition of alcohol, of course, which had made a welcome and emphatic return to her life.

And then she'd met the animals. They'd done something to her brain that alcohol had simply never managed to do, and she'd found solace and calm, and something she might even describe as joy. And then of course she met Jamie, Matilda and the other residents of the close, and, in the campaign group they had formed, she'd found a purpose.

Thinking of them made her stomach lurch. What must they think of her now?

That look of bitterness and disappointment on Matilda's face haunted her, and as for the others – Sally and Nick, desperate to keep a home for their daughter to come back to, and Jocelyn, hoping against hope to keep Brian somewhere he found familiar – Connie couldn't bear to think about them. She knew her choice not to go to her father and ask for help would have made them angry. They would think her selfish. Was she? She hadn't gone to ask him for a number of reasons, and they had all seemed reasonable at the time.

Firstly, she had wanted to keep her new identity and her location secret, so Alex couldn't find her. Going to her father for help would have risked tongues wagging, because many of Alex's friends worked in Parliament. Hell, her father might even have *told* Alex, because he liked him, admired him, and saw none of his flaws.

It would also have meant that the residents of Roseacre Close would have found out who she really was, and she'd desperately wanted them to know the new version of her and not the tarnished original version, the version of herself which was tattooed with shame. She'd even allowed herself to feel a little proud of the new her, of her recovery from the depths of mental illness, of her new routine caring for the animals, of the part she'd played in their campaign.

And finally, she'd done it to protect her mother. Ellen had, of course, suggested that Connie should ask her father for help, but Connie had known that Ellen was only saying that out of love for her. With the benefit of hindsight, Connie could now see how terribly her mother had been treated by her father.

Ellen had met him when she'd taken a job working in a pub just off Westminster Square. He'd visited the pub every night for a week, bought her drinks and lavished her with gifts before she'd agreed to go out with him for dinner. She'd been only twenty-one, and he'd been thirty-five, and she'd been in his thrall. She'd never seen such wealth being thrown around, and he'd known that and used it. Her mother, newly moved to the capital and easily seduced by the apparent sophistication money bought, had felt herself to be in love. Because this was what love looked like in all of the fairy stories she'd read as a child – a handsome prince coming along and sweeping an impoverished girl off her feet – and naturally, they would live happily ever after.

Except, of course, as in Grimms' original stories, the fairy tale turned ugly. Ellen had got pregnant quickly, had told her boyfriend about it, confident that marriage would ensue, only to be sent packing to the countryside with a ridiculously small financial payoff and a broken heart so severe she had never really recovered. Connie knew that Ellen still bore the scar, and was aware that her mother's pride, let alone her own, would take a beating if she had to involve her father.

And so she had not gone to him for help, despite the fact that he might have been able to use his influence to force the council to give up the sale of Roseacre Close. Had that decision, bearing all of her reasons in mind, been selfish? Connie desperately wanted the answer to be no. After all, she knew very well what the consequences for her new friends would be if the sale of the close went ahead. And that was why she had put her heart and soul into the campaign, to try to gain them victory without her father's assistance. Just for that short while, she'd believed enough in herself to try to do it. Had that, in fact, been folly? Maybe. The thought of that made her reach for the bottle of vodka beside her bed. Her mother had not found all of her bottles. She still had three left and, after a period of relative sobriety, she was making her way through them now at speed.

In a mood for masochism, Connie reached down the other side of the bed for her mother's laptop, which she'd taken from her room. Ellen was out at work, and Connie would make sure she returned it before she got back. She turned it on and opened the Instagram app, looking for the account Liv was managing. She told herself she was just checking on the progress of the campaign, to check it was still running, but in truth, she wanted to see if there were any photos of Jamie. She ached to see him. She missed talking to him, laughing with him, sharing the same air with him. But she also knew that she was toxic, and she had told her mum not to let him in when he'd tried to visit her. She couldn't face his anger, too.

The most recent image on the Instagram account was of Clarrie, her head poking through a gap in the fence, a piece of grass hanging jauntily from her mouth. The second was Tom, proudly holding his plumber's kit, his mother Donna looking on in her nurse's uniform. Both of these photos were beautifully framed, clear and colourful; evidently Liv could take a nice photo. The third image in the grid, however, made Connie's heart stop.

It was a selfie, taken by Jamie, of him and Liv. They were standing in front of the Christmas tree in Liv's front garden. Connie knew she'd put one up there, because she could see it out of her bedroom window. It was strewn with bright white lights. Jamie's arm was around Liv in the picture, and he was grinning broadly into the camera. They both looked so happy. Liv, sweet Liv, who had gone through so much – well, she definitely deserved Jamie's special mix of loyalty, sincerity and laughter.

At least Jamie would now understand why Connie had been so keen to avoid getting involved with him. She presumed he'd seen the videos. Surely every man in the UK had by now. He'd probably never want to look at her, let alone talk to her, ever again. She was tarnished goods with a criminal record. She didn't deserve anything good.

Connie closed her eyes, and witnessed a familiar haunting.

She is shielding her face with her hands, but it isn't enough. The blows keep coming.

She scrambles around in the darkness trying to right herself, trying to crawl away, but it's no use. Every time she manages to find her footing, she's knocked over and the wind is pelted out of her.

Her lungs seem to have shrunk. She can't catch her breath, even though she keeps trying to take air in, trying to find room for some oxygen to ward off the asphyxiation which will surely come. She is panicking, truly panicking now. And the pain – the pain is searing; it's hot, it's constant. She has never known pain like this.

She decides to surrender. This is a fight she is going to lose – is already losing.

She closes her eyes, pulls her hands away from her face, and waits.

Connie opened her eyes. She was covered in a film of sweat, even though the heating was off and it was sub-zero outside. Her heart was racing. She felt nauseous and longed for oblivion. How long would she be forced to relive that rape? Never mind her weeks in jail – she was actually serving a life sentence, there was no doubt at all about that.

Connie shut the laptop, put it down on the floor, took another swig from the vodka bottle and hit the TV remote. Her own life had gone to shit, and she knew that it would never get better, so it was time to return to her safety mode. She would once again go out only in the hours of darkness; would live on a diet of trashy TV, carbs and alcohol; would endeavour never to think or feel. Her muscle memory found the button for Netflix, located *Gilmore Girls* and selected an episode at random.

For it was far, far better to live in a dreamy, alternate reality than the hell she had made for herself.

— 36 —

December

Matilda

Matilda turned her radio on and the sweet, melancholy sound of a cathedral choir singing 'In The Bleak Midwinter' filled the room. She stopped what she was doing and listened. The familiar carol, something she had sung at primary school and then annually during her years in the convent, spun memories out of thin air. Helping Miriam to hang a tiny glass bird off the branch of the silver Christmas tree in their tiny terraced house; going hungry on December 25th when her parents had simply had no money left to feed them; helping the convent cook, Mrs Jones, to bake mince pies for visitors; and hauling a tree into her new home in Roseacre, a gift from Dean's father, Don Collins, and decorating it with paper chains which she and her sister had made from recycled wrapping and newspaper.

It had been a long time since Matilda had celebrated Christmas. She had stopped when Miriam had died. After that, the only sign of the season for her had been lights strung from neighbours' roofs, the playlists on the radio and distant shrieks of children's laughter on Christmas morning.

It would be different this year, her final Christmas on earth. She had been invited to share lunch with several of her neighbours, including Ellen, Martin and Niamh. She had originally planned to accept the invitation from Ellen, but now... well, now she didn't think she could. Not after that last scene, where she'd said what she'd said and Constance had cried – well, that was something she couldn't quite get over.

And yet, she missed Constance. She missed her dreadfully. And the animals missed her too, although Ellen had taken over her evening feeding duties, so they were at least fed, and Matilda was still able to rest. She needed to rest a lot now. Judging by the increasing pains in her muscles and bones and her lack of appetite for food or activity, Matilda judged that it might not be long. She would not live to see next Christmas, that was certain.

Would Constance come to the whole council meeting, she wondered. It was in three days' time, December 4th. Their living-room-on-the-green protest, Jamie's brainchild, was planned for beforehand, and then they were all going in to watch the vote from the gallery.

Not that any of them really believed they were going to win, she thought. The initial optimism they'd felt after the letter from their MP had faded, and although Matilda had written again to prompt him, she had received no further reply. Amy, their friendly journalist, had said she was still working on the story, but she hadn't given them any further updates, so that lead also seemed to have gone cold. It felt like things were very much going the council's way, and this thought made Matilda feel even more unwell.

She pictured all of the lives on the close that would be changed forever if the sale went through. All of those individual existences so happily spent thus far on this tiny patch of English countryside, observing the seasons change from their kitchen windows: bulbs bursting through in spring, the feeding frenzy in the fields in summer, bringing in the fruits of autumn from the hedgerows, inhaling the sweet scent of burning wood in the winter. All of this, their intimate connections with nature and the wealth of the land they lived on, would be torn asunder.

She looked around her, at her cluttered and yet, thanks to her neighbours, still functional kitchen, and the memories it held.

This was the home she had made for Miriam. She would never leave it, not voluntarily. But of course, her cancer would see to that. She would be gone long before the bulldozers rolled in.

It was this thought that made her realise what she needed to do. Ignoring the cries of her body which longed for rest, she shuffled over to the front door, and picked up her blanket which was hanging at the end of the bannister. Just minutes later, she was at Ellen's front door.

'Oh, hello Matilda,' said Ellen. Matilda noticed a trace of dissatisfaction in her tone, and she wasn't surprised. They had not spoken when she'd come over in the evenings to feed the animals. It had seemed easier that way. Ellen was a mother defending her child, and that was undoubtedly a powerful thing.

'Hello, Ellen. May I come in?'

'Of course.'

Matilda mounted the steps and made her way to her favourite chair in the living room, without being directed there.

'What can I do for you?' Ellen had followed her into the living room and was standing a few feet away from her, the tabard she was wearing suggesting she was either just home from work, or about to go.

'Is Constance in?'

Any pretence Ellen had been making to put on a brave face suddenly fell away. The anguish she felt was etched in her features. Goodness, she looks exhausted, thought Matilda. How old must Ellen be? Fifty, perhaps? She had such a youthful face, but today she looked every year of her age.

'She is. She hasn't left the house since… the news,' she said, taking a seat on the sofa and putting her head in her hands. 'But I know what state she's in. She's refusing visitors. I've had to send Jamie away twice. I go in twice a day and take her food, but she's not really eating. She isn't getting dressed. I'm worried… that she won't recover this time.'

Matilda nodded. She remembered Constance's suicide attempt. She hadn't given much thought to how that had impacted upon

Ellen then, but she should have. To be someone's primary carer and to watch them falling into the abyss, but being unable to stop them doing so, that was one of life's most tortuous experiences.

'I must see her.'

'She won't leave her room, Matilda.'

'Yes. So I shall have to go up there. Could you help me, please?'

Ellen blinked.

'Up the stairs?'

'Yes.'

Matilda already knew how much this attempt would cost her, but she had no choice.

'She's too vulnerable to be shouted at.'

'I know that. I will not shout.'

'Or even to hear your criticisms again. She's taken them all on board. They're weighing heavily on her, I promise you.'

'I am aware of that, and I will not behave like that again. My reaction last time was a mistake.'

We all have secrets, Matilda thought. And reasons for keeping them.

'OK. But I have to go to work soon, so you can't be up there too long.'

'Understood.'

Progress was slow. Matilda managed a step every thirty seconds or so, followed by a lengthy pause to get her breath back. Despite Ellen's pressing need to get to work, she did not attempt to hurry her, and Matilda was grateful. She couldn't have gone any faster, anyhow. She felt the energy and life draining out of her with every step.

'Last step.'

Matilda made one final effort and reached the landing.

'She's in the small bedroom.'

The house was a mirror image of her own, although a lot tidier, of course. Matilda walked forwards for a few steps and pushed open the door to Constance's room. Ellen remained at the top of the stairs, watchful.

The curtains were still closed, so although the sun had risen at least two hours previously, Constance was living in twilight. There was a smell in the room that Matilda knew very well: stale body odour. It seemed that Constance was not only not getting dressed – she wasn't washing, either. Matilda looked at the bed. Constance was lying there beneath a mound of crumpled bedding. She did not acknowledge the fact that someone had entered the room. Exhausted beyond any measure, Matilda took a seat at the end of the bed, taking care to avoid sitting on her feet.

'Constance, dear.'

There was no movement. Matilda wasn't even sure she was awake. So she put her hand on her leg, and shook it gently.

'Constance. Please wake up. I have some things I need to say to you.'

A few seconds passed before the mound of bedding began to move, and Connie appeared at the top of it, her hair scraped up into a high ponytail, her pale face still bearing the half-moon shadow of eye make-up. Matilda watched as she turned over, put a pillow behind her back and sat up, leaning against the wall at the top of the bed. She was wearing a greying T-shirt covered in unidentifiable stains and her expression was blank.

'I thought you'd said all you wanted to say to me,' said Connie.

Matilda took a deep breath to try to dull the pain she felt all over her body.

'Not everything, no.'

'Oh.' Connie ran her hand over her face, as if trying to wipe it clean.

'I am worried about you, Constance.' Connie sniffed. 'I know you won't believe me, but I am worried about you.'

'Really?'

'Yes, I am. Because you are my friend. And I have been thinking a great deal since I last saw you, about what I said. I was angry, because I felt that you had betrayed my trust, not telling me who your father is. About what he might be able to do for us, in our predicament.'

'I couldn't tell you about him. I just couldn't. Or about... a lot of the other stuff.'

'Yes. You felt, I imagine, that we would not accept you if you told us that you had been in prison?'

'Yes.'

'And you hoped that you could come here and start again, and leave all of that horror you went through behind?'

'Yes.'

'I felt the same, for many years. I also came here to start again, to try to forget my past. And so I realise that we are more similar than I had ever considered. And that is why I am here.'

Constance did not respond, but Matilda felt that the expression on her face had softened.

'I am here, Constance, to try to persuade you to accept the help the doctors and your mother are trying to give you. I want you to take the medication they are suggesting.'

Connie's eyes widened. 'But I can't, Matilda. I will lose control of myself. I can't do that. Not again.'

'You will not. I believe that these antidepressants they prescribe nowadays are really quite clever. They are not the horrific drugs they tried to give my Miriam, and they are not whatever horrendous things that former boyfriend of yours got you to take.'

Constance pulled herself up in the bed.

'Why have you come here to tell me this? Why are you so bothered with what I do or do not do? I'm a fraud, aren't I? A liar. And it's because of me that everyone here is going to be turfed out of their homes, so that some developer can make his millions.'

'It's not your fault that's happening, Constance. You are not the reason the developer decided to try to do it, and I'm not even sure that your father's influence would work. We can't know that. The council don't have to do what he says, do they?'

'But they might have. And I didn't do it. I've been thinking about this over and over, and I can't think of anything else but how selfish I've been, how I just let my own stupid idea of rebirth or whatever it was I thought I was doing, ruin everything.'

'But Constance, you are not well.'

'I'm fine. My body works fine. I'm just my own worst enemy, that's all.'

'No, Constance, I believe your mind isn't well. Your mother tells me you have had ups and downs since you were a child.' Connie nodded. 'Some people, like Miriam, have diseases in their brains. Their bodies are perfectly ordinary, but their brains don't fire quite right. Yours is not epilepsy, Constance, but I do believe that it's a disease all the same.' Connie started to cry. She reached down to the floor and picked up a crumpled tissue and blew her nose. 'I have a disease, too, Constance.'

Connie stopped what she was doing.

'Of the brain?'

'No, mine is of the body. I have cancer. Cancer of the ovaries.'

Connie sat up and leaned forward so that she could see Matilda better.

'Oh God. I'm so sorry, Matilda. When did you find out?'

Matilda flicked her right hand, waving away Connie's concern.

'A couple of weeks ago.'

'And you didn't tell us? We could have helped you. We...'

'Yes, you are not the only person here who has been economical with the truth.'

Matilda and Constance sat in silence for a moment, staring at each other, acknowledging each other's pain and each other's dissemblance.

'I have felt it coming on for a long time,' said Matilda, eventually. 'I should really have gone to see the doctor a long time ago, but I refused to. I am inclined to fold into myself when I face a challenge like that, rather than facing up to it.'

'How bad is it? What treatment are they offering? Can they operate?'

'It is too late to make it go away, I'm told. It has spread throughout my body.'

'Oh, shit. That's just… Shit. I'm so sorry.'

'For the cancer or the swearing?' said Matilda, and Connie smiled.

'Both. But isn't there something they can do? Can't they give you chemo, or radiotherapy, or whatever?'

'I have said I don't want any of that. It would just postpone the inevitable, and I don't want to be in hospital for days on end… I just want to be at home. While I still can be.'

'Oh my God, this is just… so crap. This is my fault. Here you are, really sick, and you're going to be turfed out of the home you love. God, what a mess.'

'Me getting ill, and deciding not to have treatment, is not your fault.'

Connie wiped her eyes with her index fingers.

'Couldn't you have some treatment, just day treatment, to help you live longer?'

'I could, yes. But what for?'

'So that you can, I don't know, see some more chicks hatch, or see if Clarrie and Eddie produce another kid? All of the things you love the most, doing their thing?'

That's when Matilda had an idea.

'What if we made a deal, you and I?'

Connie raised an eyebrow.

'Like what?'

'How's about if I go back to the hospital and say I'll have some of this treatment they're offering for my exhausted body – you go to see a doctor and agree to take some medication for your exhausted mind?'

Matilda heard Connie swallow.

'You drive a hard bargain, Matilda Reynolds,' she said, wiping her nose with the tissue.

'Yes, I'm hard as nails, so they say.'

'I'll think about it.'

'Good. Now, I need to go, because your mother needs to get to work.'

Matilda located her stick and was about to try to stand up when she felt Connie's arms wrap around her waist. And just as she had felt when Jamie had hugged her, the impact of this unexpected embrace was far more than she could quantify. There was a warmth and a reassurance that felt like an injection of adrenaline. She looked down and grasped Connie's right hand with her own, and squeezed it.

'Understood, Matilda.'

'Excellent. I shall see you soon, Connie.'

Constance let go and Matilda pushed herself up and walked to the door, where Ellen was waiting. It was clear, even in the dim light, that she had also been crying.

'Now, young lady, why don't you have a shower and get dressed?' Matilda said, turning to say goodbye. 'You'll end up looking like me if you're not careful.'

As Matilda began the lengthy descent down the stairs, she was certain she heard Connie laugh.

— 37 —

December 2nd

Constance

It was 5:30 a.m. Connie's alarm had just gone off. She fought the desire to hit it or throw it out of the window. Her days of getting up at this time of day with regularity were long behind her. But today, despite the fact that she still felt like death warmed up and that every sinew in her body wanted to remain in bed with the duvet pulled over her head, she knew she must get up and get out. Because for the first time in a long time, she had something important to do.

She slipped out of the house before her mum woke. She left her a note on the kitchen surface telling her where she'd gone. Ellen had been on a late shift and wouldn't come down for breakfast until at least nine, so Connie was confident that she'd be on the train and long gone by the time she read it.

It was sub-zero outside, so she grabbed her warmest coat – a long grey puffa, which both looked and felt like wearing a duvet – and buried her chin in the collar. The first bus – one of only three in the morning – left at 6.30 a.m., and she would be in time to catch it. As she walked past Martin's house, she allowed herself a glimpse at Jamie's bedroom window, just on the off chance he might be awake early, too. The window was dark, however, and the curtains drawn.

She was trying very hard not to think about him, so she

tilted her head downwards and focused on the icy path in front of her instead. She reached the bus stop at twenty-five past six, then took a moment to look upwards at the stars. Several days of freezing fog had given way to a clear, cold night, and this far out of the city, the absence of light pollution ensured a wonderful view of the cosmos. She had always been a big thinker, even if those big questions unnerved her, and gazing up into space made her think about God. She had never been a church-goer, and she had no idea what had made Matilda spend her life in prayer for so long, but looking up there did make her believe in something, something bigger than herself. I mean, she thought, if this universe was the result of a random explosion, where did that explosion come from? What started it? Where did the parts come from? And if there's an end to this universe, logic said there must be another one beyond it, and another one...

Connie's slightly hungover, slightly exhausted thoughts were interrupted by the arrival of the bus, which she was relieved to see was both on time and empty. She was not in the mood for polite small talk with anyone, and she knew she looked a mess. She'd had a shower, because who was she to argue with Matilda, but she hadn't made an effort with her face or hair, because really, he didn't deserve that.

'One to the station, please,' she said to the driver, who looked pretty rough, too. She hoped the driver was feeling more awake than she was, or they were both in trouble. Connie paid and then found a seat at the very back of the bus, just in case the driver felt like being chatty. As they sped along the empty B-roads, Connie looked out at the houses they were passing. You could tell the ones that were occupied by people who lived there all of the time, because they were the ones currently sporting 'Santa Stop Here' posts and lit-up reindeer in their front gardens, or with strings of coloured lanterns hung around trees and bushes. The holiday rentals were dark and empty at this time of year, ahead of a two-week flurry over the Christmas period, during which

The Plucky Duck would be rammed and most likely run out of both gin and craft beer.

'Station,' said the driver, her voice a little lighter, probably due to the sight of an open coffee cart beside the stop. Connie got off the bus and headed to the ticket machine, where she bought a day return, and then walked onto the platform. There was a train due in ten minutes. She was relieved it had worked so well. If she had missed the first bus, she would have had to wait another couple of hours, and possibly face her mother, and explain what she was about to do.

Connie considered buying a coffee from the cart, but she decided she would wait until she got there. She needed food, too. She was hungry for the first time in days, but she didn't think a Danish pastry wrapped in plastic would really cut it.

The train arrived on time and she sank into a seat and closed her eyes. When she opened them, the train was pulling into Paddington. She had been asleep for more than two hours and, aside from a small amount of dribble underneath her chin, she felt better for it. She wiped herself clean with a tissue and sat up straight, gazing out at the graffiti beneath the bridges, at the hidden canals, at the utilitarian backs of elegant Georgian terraces. When she had been younger, this part of the journey had always filled her with excitement. She had craved the city when she had been denied it. But times had changed, and she had changed. London no longer gave her joy.

Connie was almost glad to exit the train and immerse herself in a crowd of people. One benefit of the capital was the sheer variety of people – it was such a diverse, accepting city that you could dress up like a peacock on your commute and no one would even look at you. Today, she needed that. She needed to feel invisible, because she didn't want to be here. She pulled a baseball cap out of her bag and put it on, tugging it down low. She needed to do what she'd come here to do and then she needed to get out of the city quickly, leaving no trace.

Connie entered the tube and took the Bakerloo line, changing for the Jubilee at Baker Street. She was in Westminster within twenty minutes. She checked her watch: it was 9 a.m. He would be just arriving in the office about now. She turned right out of the station, walked to the entrance of Portcullis House and entered through the revolving door.

'I've come to see Robert Phillipson,' she said to the receptionist.

'Do you have an appointment?'

'No.'

'I see. I'll have to speak to his PA. Who shall I say is visiting?'

'I'm Constance Phillipson,' she said quietly, her face burning, because she knew everyone in this building would have seen both the story and the videos. 'His daughter?'

'Oh, right,' said the receptionist, who, if she recognised her, was kind enough not to give it away. 'I'll just call up. Give me a minute.'

A few minutes later, the receptionist called her over.

'He says he's coming,' she said. 'He's asked if you'll go and get a seat in the meeting room just down that corridor' – the receptionist turned around and pointed to her right – 'and he'll meet you there?'

So he's too ashamed of me to meet me in his office, thought Connie. How loving. How kind. How fatherly.

Connie nodded and tried to smile, because it wasn't the receptionist's fault, and waited as a security guard let her through a security door and led her to the room her father had chosen.

It was small and simply furnished, with a large glass table and six high-backed metal chairs. There was just one picture hanging on the walls, a long, rectangular canvas daubed with multiple shades of purple. The only natural light came from a window which overlooked a small courtyard, and the bottom half of the window was frosted for privacy.

Connie took her coat off and was just about to sit down at the table when her father walked into the room.

He was a tall man, his grey hair parted at the side and expensively cut. He was wearing a long, camel-coloured wool coat, grey trousers and a pair of shiny brown brogues. He spotted Connie, raised his eyebrows in acknowledgement and walked over to her.

'Hi, darling,' he said quietly, unbuttoning his coat to reveal a grey suit jacket, a light pink striped shirt and a grey tie. 'What a nice surprise. Would you like something to drink? I've ordered some coffee, water and some pastries. They should be here shortly.'

He leaned in to kiss her, but Connie refused to reciprocate and sat down in one of the chairs. Robert looked startled for a brief moment but recovered quickly.

'I would like that, yes,' she replied. 'I haven't had breakfast. And of course it's a surprise that I'm here. Although I imagine it isn't a *nice* one? We haven't spoken in months. You didn't even call Mum after the article ran. After the videos...'

'Yes. Dreadful. How have you been?' he said, sitting down just as the door opened and a man in a suit entered carrying a tray.

'How do you think I've been?' she said, as the man lowered the tray onto the table in front of them. She was enjoying the obvious discomfort her father was feeling about the fact that she was *making a scene* in front of his staff.

'I imagine it has been very hard,' he said, as the man retreated back into the corridor and the door closed behind him.

'Yes, it has.' *Jesus*, Connie thought. Could you be any more detached from reality?

'Why didn't you visit me in prison?'

'I didn't realise you wanted me to.' Robert clasped his hands together, his thumbs circling each other like an executive toy.

'You're my father, of course I wanted you to.'

'Constance, if you remember, you stopped returning my calls long before your trial, and you said some genuinely hurtful things to me and Melia.'

This was true, of course. After the rape, and the argument to end all arguments with Alex, Connie had been like a wounded animal, striking out at everyone who tried to come near her. Melia, her stepmother, had made a few clumsy attempts to try to 'help' her, and she had been rebuffed. Connie had made the mistake of expecting her father and stepmother to behave like ordinary parents, who absorbed every blow thrown at them and still stood firm – unconditional love in action. Instead, they had simply withdrawn and left her to it, and it had been her mother, who she had abandoned years previously, who had stepped up and been there for her when everyone else had fallen away.

'Anyhow, I'm glad you're here now. You look different,' he said.

'Yes, I changed my hair back to my original colour.'

She'd done it to hide her identity, and she was incredibly glad of that now. She would bury her old life if she could. Just being in central London was enough to make her skin crawl.

'Suits you.'

'Do you still feel sorry for Alex?' said Connie, grabbing a cheese croissant and eating it greedily.

Her father's thumbs stopped circling.

'I am sure you were both to blame for what happened.'

Connie felt bile rising up from her stomach and stopped eating.

'Bloody hell. He abused me, Dad. He gave me drugs so I'd do what he wanted. And it's him who leaked the videos, you know that? He did it because I refused to go back to him. Is that the sort of behaviour you expect from your golden boy?'

'Are you certain?'

'Of course I am.'

'Well, that puts a different spin on things,' he said, taking a coffee from the tray and sipping it.

'Who did you think had leaked them?'

'I wasn't sure. I wondered if it was one of your other boyfriends.'

'They weren't my boyfriends, Dad. *Alex* was my boyfriend. *They* were his friends. He got me high and shared me around.'

'Keep the volume down, please, Connie. Unless you want the whole building to hear?'

'I don't really care if they do, Dad, but I am sure *you* do,' she said, resuming her breakfast, and taking a coffee from the tray.

'I just want this all to die down so that you can get on with your life.'

'No, Dad, you want all of this to die down so that you don't get asked awkward questions by journalists outside your front door.'

Her father slammed his coffee cup down on the table.

'That's not fair, and you know it. I have tried very hard over the years to protect you, to send you to the best school, to support you when you were floundering and unable to support yourself. Can you imagine how hard it's been for me, cut out from your life for more than a year, worrying daily whether you were alive or dead?'

Connie examined her father's expression. She knew that he was a master of spin. She had watched him in action at press conferences and in the Commons. He seemed sincere, however. Even a little choked.

'Well, I'm still here, Dad. Mum has been looking after me.'

'How is your mother?'

'About to be evicted.'

'Goodness,' he said, picking up his coffee. 'Why?'

'The whole estate is being evicted, because the council are selling it to a developer. Didn't you read about it? It was in some of the articles.'

Admittedly quite far down, thought Connie. Her fight for justice in rural England was clearly far less interesting than sex videos featuring a woman convicted for punching her boyfriend.

'No, I missed that, and I'm sorry. When will she have to move? Are they rehousing her? They should be.'

'That's why I'm here.' Her father's eyes widened. I'm hardly here for a heartwarming reunion, Dad, she thought. That would be delusional. 'The council are voting on the sale on December the fourth. That's two days from now. I've been leading a campaign to try to stop them from doing it. It's all grim, dirty, dodgy. The developer is related to the leader of the council. We suspect that someone was taking backhanders.'

'That's quite the allegation. Can you prove that?'

Connie shifted in her seat.

'No. I can't.'

'I see,' he said, taking another sip. Connie noticed he'd accidentally spilled some coffee on his tie. She didn't tell him. 'I can't just go and accuse people of doing something like that, Constance. If that's what you came here for.'

Did her father's top lip just quiver slightly, or was she imagining it?

'I don't want you to accuse anyone of anything, Dad. But isn't there something you can do? Can't you call up the council leader and insist they pause the sale, pending an inquiry, or something like that? You've two days. There's still time.'

'An inquiry into what? No wrongdoing has been committed.'

'I can't prove it yet, but it's all wrong, Dad. Something is wrong here. Social services came round to see our neighbour, because she was struggling, and we think they brought the developer with them to scout around her house. Surely that's illegal? Or at least, unethical?'

Her father picked up a napkin from the black plastic dispenser on the table and mopped his mouth.

'It would be, yes. But this is all conjecture. I mean, you have no evidence…'

'Can't you just trust me, Dad? I'm your daughter. I wouldn't lie to you.'

'Wouldn't you? You have lied to me many times, Constance.'

Slipping out of the house after bedtime, just to scare them; stealing from his alcohol cupboard and giving it to girls at school to try to buy friends; pawning her stepmother's diamond earrings to pay for new clothes that she didn't even need. The litany of

Constance's crimes ran around her brain and refused to leave. Jesus, she thought, I have so many sins to absolve myself of.

'I am not lying to you now.'

'That's as maybe, Constance, but the fact remains that I cannot interfere with council planning decisions if they have followed proper procedure.'

'But they haven't.'

'So you say.'

They sat in silence for a few moments. Connie tried to focus on the delicious food she was eating and not the ugly images dominating her thoughts. Would she ever be free of them? Maybe Matilda was right. Maybe those tablets Matilda had persuaded her to take might be able to dull her fears and dent her gargantuan guilt?

Matilda. Yes, there was another reason to feel guilty. She was dying. Her friend was dying, and she had been too selfish, too caught up in her own nightmare, to realise the importance of the small but significant card she had to play. That was why she was here. She was doing this for her friends. It was of no benefit to her, because she was certain they'd never forgive her, or be able to look her straight in the eye ever again. In fact, coming back here was risky. What if she was recognised? What if she found herself alone in a lift or in a railway carriage with a man who'd seen those videos and wanted a piece of the action for himself? The thought of that made her shake.

'Connie? Are you OK?'

Even her father had noticed.

'I think I need to go,' she said, grabbing her coat from behind her and getting up to leave.

'OK. Shall I call you a cab?'

Connie shook her head. She didn't want to accept anything from her father ever again.

'Look, I'll see what I can do, OK? I'll look into this thing at the council.'

Connie glared at him. She'd heard promises like this before.

I'll make sure your mother is well looked after, Connie. I'll come to see the school play, Connie. I won't make you stay in this clinic if you don't want to, Connie.

'Yeah. Whatever. I need to go now,' she said, suddenly wanting nothing more than to be many, many miles away from her father.

'OK,' he said, his expression not hiding his relief at her departure very well. 'Well, take care, darling. I am pleased to see you again and, as I say, I'll look into the council project. I am genuinely sorry to hear that your mother may have to move. I know she is very settled there.'

Settled? Connie knew that Ellen had fought tooth and nail and had managed to pay her rent on her carer's salary, while her ex-partner owned a raft of investment properties in the capital that provided him with the monthly income of a Premiership footballer.

Connie resisted the urge to slap him. Instead, she pulled on her coat and walked away, and did not look back.

— 38 —

December 4th

Matilda

'Do you think you'll manage today?'

Matilda nodded.

Ellen was looking at her with the concerned expression someone gave you when you had told them that you had cancer, a look that suggested part of you had already died. She was touched that she cared, naturally, but she was determined that she was going to get out of the house, today of all days.

'What time are we leaving?'

Ellen checked her watch.

'Half an hour. Ten fifteen.'

'Is Connie coming?'

Ellen shook her head and sank into the chair opposite Matilda.

'No, I don't think so. She hasn't even come downstairs yet.'

'Do you know who she saw when she went to London?'

'No. She said she'd gone there, but I don't know who it was she saw. She wouldn't tell me when she got back. *God*, I was just so pleased that she did come back, I didn't want to ask.'

Of course, Matilda thought. Connie leaving for London would have brought back memories of her departure aged twelve, when she'd left her childhood home, apparently for good. Poor Ellen. Yesterday must have been torture.

'Do you think she went to see Alex?'

'Maybe. But if she did, at least she came back afterwards. That man is disgusting. I wish she'd press charges against him for leaking those videos.'

'Yes, I wanted to ask you about that, without Connie listening. Not about the recent stories, but about the rape that she had to endure. Why didn't she report that?'

Ellen bit her bottom lip and exhaled sharply.

'I have asked her that myself. It was clear that she dealt with the whole ordeal by suppressing how she felt, by pretending it hadn't happened. She eventually persuaded herself, once she'd moved back here, that she'd been attacked by an animal, one of the bulls in the fields. It was displacement, a way of rationalising what had happened.'

'Couldn't she report it, even now?'

'Yes, she could. But she doesn't want to, and as much as I wish it wasn't the case, I agree with her. Have you seen the conviction rates for sexual assault? The burden of proof they demand? The cross-examination at the hands of a male barrister in court, opposite the man who did it? No. She needs to find a way to move on from it now. I don't think there's any point in looking back.'

'Poor, poor Connie.'

'Yes,' said Ellen with a sigh. 'But there's one speck of light, and I believe I have you to thank for that. She told me last night that she's going to make an appointment to see the GP, about finally taking some antidepressants.'

Matilda smiled.

'Oh, that is wonderful. But I was wondering… Why was she so reluctant to take them?'

'Oh, her father sent her to a mental health clinic when she was a teenager. She thought she was only going to be there for a day, but in the end she was in there for two months. She was fourteen and petrified, and too unwell to just refuse and walk away. If I'd known how terrible it was, I'd have done something, but she wasn't allowed to make phone calls and her father had convinced me that it was the very best place there was. I understand they put her on some medication there which gave her terrible side effects – night terrors, sweats – and so she's been reluctant to go anywhere near anything similar ever again.'

Matilda imagined how Connie must have felt, shut up in a building with only her own terror for company, plied with drugs by people she didn't know; the similarity with Miriam's plight was not lost on her. She could well understand why she had been so determined not to go down that road ever again.

'When are you going to the hospital for your discussion about treatment?' asked Ellen.

'Oh, soon, I believe. I take it from the speed the doctor is moving at, I really don't have long, in any case. But I'll do it for Connie. I think I owe her that.'

Ellen looked surprised.

'But I thought you would still be angry with her, about not going to ask her father for help?'

Matilda sniffed.

'If ever there was a time to trot out the phrase "Life is too short", Ellen, it's now. I have very little time left. And I have Connie to thank for calling the ambulance and saving me when I fell, twice, and for...' Matilda felt a tear gather in her eye, and her throat tightened '... and for bringing laughter and love back into my life. It had been a long time. But I'm so glad I had some of it again, before I pop my clogs.'

'Oh, you, stop it. You'll set me off,' said Ellen, sniffing. Then, the doorbell rang. 'That'll be the others,' she said. 'I think it's time.'

The journey to Worcester was uneventful, if slightly uncomfortable, with five people – Ellen, Matilda, Jocelyn, Brian and Niamh – all squeezed into Ellen's tiny hatchback. Liv and her children, Donna, Sally and Nick were coming in two other cars, and Martin, Tom and Jamie, meanwhile, had gone into town early as the advance party, to set up the mock sitting room on the green, ready for their arrival.

They arrived outside the council offices at 11 a.m.

'Goodness me,' said Niamh, from her position in the rear right seat, as Ellen pulled the parking brake. 'Would you look at that?'

Ellen, Jocelyn, Matilda and Brian all followed her gaze, and took in the brightly lit gazebo set up on the green in front of the council building.

Under it was a three-sided room made of wood. All of its walls had been wallpapered, and there were even paintings of rural scenes hanging from a picture rail. Inside the three walls was a standard lamp, a small TV on a round brown table, two comfortable armchairs and a side table which was playing host to a small Christmas tree covered in multicoloured jewel lights, topped with a star.

'Oh good, he managed to use some of our paintings,' said Jocelyn with pride. 'I donated them to the cause.'

Matilda waited for Ellen to open the passenger door, give her her stick and help her stand, and then they walked slowly over to the gazebo, where Jamie and Martin were waiting.

'This looks amazing,' said Ellen when they reached it. 'Well done, guys.'

'Our pleasure,' said Martin, beaming. 'Now, Matilda, would you care to take a seat?'

Matilda nodded and let him help her sit down in one of the two armchairs. It was comfortable, but of course not in any way warm, so she was grateful for the blanket Jamie brought and draped over her knees.

'How long did this take you?' said Ellen.

'Oh, a couple of hours,' replied Martin.

'Didn't anyone in the council office try to stop you?'

'Nah. Well. I know the security guard, see,' said Jamie with a wink, as their 'tame' journalist, Amy, walked up to the gazebo. She was dressed in a bright red long coat and matching woollen hat. At her side was that radio journalist, Russell. Matilda wondered whether there might be something going on there, and concluded that there might be. If so, that was a very nice thing to happen to a very nice girl, she thought. Amy's support for their campaign had given them such hope and such focus. It was wonderful when good deeds were repaid.

'Hello, everyone,' said Amy. 'This looks amazing. I'll take loads of pictures. It'll really spark interest on social media.'

'Thanks,' said Jamie, grinning, as the rest of Roseacre Close arrived, complete with folded chairs for the older residents, and an assortment of blankets.

'How are you all feeling?' asked Amy.

Matilda looked around at the assembled throng, who were all wearing their smartest clothes and their most anxious expressions. Tom was wearing a suit which seemed to be two sizes too small; Brian looked incredibly dapper in a suit, waistcoat and matching handkerchief, and Jocelyn looked polished and glamorous by his side; Liv's hair, meanwhile, seemed to have grown about five inches since she'd last seen her, and her lips looked bigger, puffier. Matilda wasn't sure she liked the change, but she expected that said more about her extreme age than Liv's fashion sense. Jamie, who was standing next to her, was wearing tight black trousers and a tight black polo neck, and looked, Matilda thought, rather dashing, even though she was no expert at all in these matters.

'Good,' said Ellen. 'We're feeling good, I think.'

'Determined,' said Nick.

'Fired up,' said Jamie, walking towards the back of the gazebo, for a reason Matilda couldn't fathom.

'Angry,' said Niamh, as a smattering of Christmas shoppers spotted what they were doing and walked in their direction.

'OK,' said Amy. 'Well, what I suggest is that I take photos and get a few quotes from you here – Russell will do the same – and then when it's time, we can all enter the chamber together.'

As she said that, music blared out from behind Matilda. It was something to do with a past Christmas, and donating a heart. The shoppers seemed to like it, however, as they were now emboldened to come up and find out what the fuss was about.

'Love it,' said Liv, as Jamie reappeared. Matilda *didn't* love it, but decided to keep her counsel.

'Is that too loud? We don't want to scare people away?' he asked.

Matilda saw Liv shake her head.

'Nah, it's great.'

'Yes, that works, Jamie, thank you,' said Ellen. 'And I've got something for anyone who comes to see us,' she said, opening up a bag for life she'd had over her shoulder, and pulling out a large blue tub. 'Chocolates. I thought we could give one to anyone who comes to talk to us. Especially if they work for the council. We want them to feel guilty.'

'Ah, great,' said Niamh.

'Can you do photos now, actually?' said Liv. 'The kids might get bored and make trouble. And I'm worried I'll rub my lippy off.'

Amy smiled and went over to take pictures of Liv and her children in front of the Christmas tree. They were both dressed in matching Christmas jumpers, and looked absolutely angelic holding the placards the group had made for them, which read: 'Santa, stop Orchard from stealing our home'.

Russell, meanwhile, came over to Matilda and Ellen. 'Hi, guys. Is there no Connie today?'

'I'm afraid not,' said Ellen, not missing a beat. 'She's poorly. Flu.'

'Oh, I'm really sorry to hear that. Given that she's been such a driving force behind this campaign, it would have been great to have got her thoughts.'

'Yes, it is a shame. But as you know, we have all played our role. Matilda here wrote the letters to our MP Sir William, who has been supportive, and Liv over there did all of our social media.'

'Yes, it's been a very impressive campaign,' said Russell,

holding his microphone and pressing record on his phone. 'So tell me, both of you, how you're feeling now that decision day has finally arrived...'

An hour later they had finished their interviews, posed for their photos, made some strange-looking videos (strange, at least, to Matilda) and handed out chocolates to a variety of Christmas shoppers and council workers, and they were all now becoming increasingly aware of the clock on the council office tower.

'I'll ask my mate in security to keep an eye on the gazebo while we're gone,' said Jamie, noticing that the time had come for them all to go inside for the meeting.

'Shall I take your arm, Matilda?' said Martin, and she gladly accepted his help, as she made her way slowly behind the rest of the crowd, across the green to the council building.

By the time they reached it, the atmosphere in the group had become noticeably more subdued. The Victorian red-brick building, with its steeply pitched roof and black cast-iron railings, reminded Matilda of the convent, and it was clear that it also inspired awe, and perhaps some trepidation, in the others, too. Matilda certainly felt anxious now. In less than two hours, they'd know the fate of Roseacre Close. And as things stood, it didn't look too hopeful, no matter how successful their stunt had been at drumming up support.

'We need to go in and find a seat. I wonder where the ramp is?' said Ellen, eyeing the steep flight of steps up to the entrance. They all knew Matilda would never manage those. 'They said there was one, when I called up. And a lift?'

'It's on the left-hand side,' said Amy. 'I'll take you.'

'I'll take everyone else through the front entrance, then, and see you there?' said Russell.

'Yes, brilliant, thanks Russ.'

Amy led Ellen and Matilda around to the accessible entrance, helped Matilda up the ramp and then located the lift.

'Where's Connie?' said Amy, pressing the button to call the lift.

'Didn't Russell tell you? She's poorly,' said Ellen, her arms folded across her chest. Matilda understood. Given how Connie had been treated by the media in the past few weeks, she could well understand why Ellen might be defensive.

'Oh, that's such a shame,' said Amy. 'This is a big day.'

'Well, she's had a hell of a time. As I'm sure you know.'

'Yes, I have read about it. And those videos, the poor girl… Whoever leaked those should be in jail.'

Ellen nodded.

'She won't speak to you about it, you know that? I know you probably just see everyone as fair game for a story, but she's had enough. She won't be giving you an exclusive, or anything like that.'

There was an awkward silence for a few seconds. Then the lift arrived, and Ellen helped Matilda inside.

'I didn't mean anything like that,' said Amy, following them in as the lift doors closed. 'We're not *all* vultures, you know, we journalists. Some of us do have integrity and a conscience. And, you know, I was sexually assaulted at university by someone I knew, so… there is no way in hell I'd try to make entertainment out of that.'

Ellen stared hard at the floor of the lift, clearly startled.

'I'm sorry, Amy. I didn't mean to offend you.'

'That's all right. I know you must have been through hell this week. I just wanted to make it clear that I'm on your side, OK? As a human, not just in terms of my job.'

'Thank you. I appreciate that.'

'No problem,' said Amy, walking out of the lift and gesturing for them to follow. 'It's this way.'

*

The wood-panelled chamber was already filling up when Ellen and Matilda arrived at the viewing area, which was a balcony that overlooked where the councillors would sit. The others had already arrived and taken their seats, but they'd left a space at the front right for Matilda, Ellen and Amy. Above them were vaulted ceilings, and beneath the roof line were a row of beautiful stained-glass windows. The room reminded Matilda more of a church than a place of government.

'Do you come to many council meetings, Amy?' asked Matilda, after she'd sat down and made herself comfortable.

'Yes, at least once a month for the full meetings, and to lots of committee meetings, too. It's our bread and butter at the paper. They have some right argy-bargees sometimes. Swearing, shouting, the lot.'

'Goodness. Will we see any of that today, do you think?'

'Possibly,' said Amy, with a twinkle in her eye.

There was a flurry of activity, and a man in his fifties with a moustache and wearing a gold chain around his neck walked into the room below and took a seat behind a raised desk equipped with microphones. He was flanked by a woman and two other men.

'Welcome, everyone, please sit down. We'll begin formal proceedings in a few minutes.'

'That's Hugh Evans, the council leader,' whispered Amy. 'Sitting with him are the deputy leader and two of his committee chairs.'

'Is one of them from the planning committee?' Matilda asked quietly.

'Yes,' said Amy. 'The man on the right, the one with the red hair. He's called George Lansdale. And sitting over there at a different desk, that's the man who runs Orchard Developments, David Sharpe, along with the chief planning officer, Helen Sweeney. They are there so members can ask them questions later.'

'Where does our councillor sit, the one for Stonecastle?' asked Ellen.

'Georgina Williams? She'll be in the rank and file on the floor. She has dark brown hair cut in a short bob. Let me see...' she scanned the room, 'that's her, sitting on the far right beside the fire exit.'

Matilda couldn't see that far, but she wasn't in the slightest bit bothered. In fact, it didn't really matter whether Georgina Williams was present or not, because she had been absolutely useless. She had replied to Matilda's letter with a non-committal 'I'll see what I can do' and there had been radio silence thereafter, despite prompting. She was either in on it with the leader, Matilda thought, or just genuinely bad at her job.

'Do you see the woman with brown curly hair, who's sitting second row from the front?' said Amy. 'That's the councillor I know well, Yvonne Elvin. She represents a ward on the outskirts of Worcester, and she's with the Greens.'

'Yes, I remember. You said you were going to speak to her about our case. Did she ever come back to you on that?' asked Ellen.

Amy was about to reply when everyone turned around abruptly to look at a new arrival on the balcony.

Matilda was astonished – and delighted – to see it was Connie. She had her hair tied back in a ponytail at the nape of her neck, and was wearing black trousers and a long grey coat. She was looking straight ahead, studiously avoiding meeting the eyes of anyone from their group. There was an outburst of whispering and Matilda thought she saw Connie wince.

Ellen, however, let out a cry of joy when she saw her and walked over and hugged her daughter. Then the council leader began to speak and Connie sat down on the other side of Amy. Matilda wished she was closer so she could hold her hand. She knew how hard it must have been for her to work up the courage to come here.

'Good morning, everyone, and welcome to this meeting of council,' the leader began, before going through the formalities, which included noting absences, telling people to turn their mobile phones off, reminding councillors to mute their microphones if they weren't speaking, and noting that the session was being recorded so that it could be accessed both on the council website and on YouTube.

'Right, now that all of that is over, we need to move on to the next item in our agenda, which is conflicts of interest. Please disclose any that are relevant, as per our standing orders.' There was a brief silence, before the leader moved on. 'OK, thank you. None. Our next item is for any petitions from members of the public in accordance with Standing Order Eighty-Four. Do we have any?'

There was silence in the room.

'None received. Right. The next item is members' question time.'

'Roseacre Close is up for discussion after this,' whispered Amy.

Matilda's heart was beating faster and her mouth was dry.

'Now as far as I know, we don't have any members' questions…'

'I have one,' said a woman's voice, and the look of surprise on the council leader's face was so marked, even Matilda could see it from her position in the balcony.

'That's Yvonne Elvin speaking,' said Amy, who Matilda noticed now had a broad smile on her face. 'The councillor from the Green Party.'

'If you have a question, Councillor Elvin, please stand up,' said the council leader.

Matilda saw the woman with the curly brown hair do as he asked. She was quite short, Matilda thought, and middle-aged, and she was wearing a purple shift dress and a royal blue cardigan.

'Yes, thank you. I apologise for not giving you warning of this question in advance as I would normally do, but I'm afraid that was not possible on this occasion. What I want to ask, of the leader and his cabinet, is why you, Councillor Evans, are so keen on the proposed sale of Roseacre Close, which is item six on our agenda today. So keen, that you paid a housing officer to assess Orchard Developments' sale favourably?'

'Oh my God,' whispered Connie, and Matilda could hear similar mutterings across the crowd in the balcony, and from the floor below.

'That is an incredibly serious accusation, councillor,' said the council leader. Even from where Matilda was sitting, she could see his eyes had visibly widened. 'And it is absolutely untrue. I submitted a form declaring my conflict of interest – that is, my familial relationship with David Sharpe – at the appropriate time. However, I have no financial interest in it whatsoever.'

'Then why, Councillor Evans, have I spoken to a source who tells me that you paid a housing officer to influence their assessment of Orchard Developments' bid?'

Councillor Evans appeared to have changed colour. He had started out looking like milk, Matilda reckoned, but now was the colour of raspberry yoghurt. Matilda's gaze moved toward the side table, where his cousin, David Sharpe, was sitting staring fixedly ahead. Hugh Evans glanced over to the corner of the room, where the council secretary was typing up everything he was saying. Matilda looked to her left, and saw that Russell was also recording the meeting on his phone.

'If such evidence exists, you must submit it to the relevant authorities, Ms Elvin,' said the woman sitting to the left of Hugh Evans, stepping in because the council leader appeared to have been struck dumb. 'Have you done that?'

'She's the deputy leader,' whispered Amy.

'I haven't, Councillor Fein, due to confidentiality. My source says that the housing officer in question is frightened of losing their job.'

'In that case, we cannot consider it, as I'm sure you know. It is pure hearsay.' A sigh of frustration came from the balcony. Surely, Matilda thought, it can't end like this?

'Do you have a follow-up question?' asked the deputy leader, her voice curt.

'Yes, I do, thank you,' said Yvonne Elvin. 'I wanted to ask, Councillor Evans, why it was thought appropriate that your cousin, David Sharpe, CEO of Orchard Developments, should accompany the council's head of social services, Caroline Goodman, during a welfare check on a vulnerable tenant in Roseacre Close?'

'That's absurd, Councillor Elvin,' said Hugh Evans. 'That would never happen, clearly. Please can you explain why you are making this accusation?'

'Because I am confident that it happened, Councillor Evans. Because a council officer who was also present has given me a sworn affidavit saying that it is true.' Yvonne Elvin held up a piece of paper and showed it to the people nearest to her. 'This document is signed by social worker Daniel Symonds and endorsed by a solicitor, and it states that he was present at the house of a Roseacre Close tenant in August this year, with Caroline Goodman, the recently appointed head of social services and – crucially – also David Sharpe. Symonds noted that Goodman and Sharpe seemed to know each other very well. Why is this, Councillor Evans?'

The deputy leader and the committee heads were staring at Hugh Evans, whose face had now progressed from raspberry yoghurt to strawberry jam, and then he proceeded to say something no one except those closest to him could hear.

'I'm sorry, Councillor Evans, you need to turn your microphone on,' said the deputy leader, her own face now the colour of chalk. Hugh Evans pressed a button in front of him.

'Right, yes, as I was saying, well, that's because David Sharpe and Caroline Goodman are partners.'

'Business partners or life partners?' asked Yvonne Elvin.

Hugh Evans cleared his throat.

'Life partners.'

'So there we have a clear breach of protocol and ethics, and something that lays the council wide open to accusations of things as heinous as corruption, do we not? And I would suggest, therefore, that the entire process of determining the benefit of the sale of Roseacre Close, which conveniently sidestepped the tender process in favour of one bidder, has been brought into question?'

Matilda saw the deputy leader lean over and whisper something in Hugh Evans' ear.

'Well, I must thank you, Councillor Elvin, for bringing this matter to our attention,' he said, after clearing his throat. 'I think the best course of action is for all documentation and decisions relating to the sale of Roseacre Close to be withdrawn, and for us to launch an inquiry to find out how this unfortunate incident came about. Clearly, there are serious questions to answer.'

'So you will not be selling Roseacre Close on this occasion?' said Councillor Elvin.

'I can confirm that we will not be proceeding with this sale,' said Hugh Evans, who now looked to Matilda like he needed someone to lie him down, lift his knees into the air and fan his face.

A roar erupted from the balcony.

If Matilda had been able to do so, she would also have leapt up into the air and thrown her arms around whoever was next to her. As it was, she simply held out her hand, and Connie took it.

'I'm so sorry, Matilda,' said Connie, as the rest of their group whooped with joy. 'I'm so sorry I didn't try harder.'

'Don't even think about it for one more second, Connie. It doesn't matter in the least now.'

'Can we please ask for quiet up in the visitors' gallery,' boomed Councillor Hugh Evans, in his most disapproving voice. 'We need to continue the meeting.'

The residents of Roseacre Close all stopped talking, as good citizens should, and sat back down.

Then Connie whispered to Amy, 'Shall we push off? We don't need to stay for the rest, do we?'

'Good idea,' she whispered back, and gestured to the others that they should follow. It took a while for them to move, however – Brian, for example, was keen to stay, as it turned out that he'd been a parish councillor in his younger days, and he seemed to be reliving his career highlights – but one by one, and to much tutting from the councillors below, the residents of Roseacre Close filed out of the room and into the corridor outside.

'Oh. My. God. We did it!' shouted Connie as soon as the door to the balcony closed behind them, and flung her arms around her mother, who gripped her tightly, tears streaming down her face. Then Martin helped Matilda onto a chair, before giving her a kiss on the cheek, something that she did not find *entirely* unpleasant.

'So, we did it, Miss Reynolds,' he said.

'We did, Martin, we did.'

'Do you know how all of that came about? That Yvonne Elvin woman, standing up and saying that stuff?'

'I don't, but I think I know who could tell us,' said Matilda, looking squarely at Amy, who was locked in an embrace with Russell.

'Good idea. I'll go and get her.'

Martin returned with both Amy and Russell a few seconds later.

'Did you know that was going to happen?' asked Matilda.

'I might have,' said Amy with a grin. 'Well, more accurately, I had an inkling. It was tough going, trying to get Yvonne to go for it, but in the end it was Russell who cracked it. Guess who plays rugby with Daniel Symonds?'

'Brilliant,' said Martin. 'It was his testimony that did it.'

'Yeah, he was amazing, doing that for me,' said Russell. 'He also convinced the housing officer to talk to Yvonne, confidentially. Daniel knows he'll never get promoted here now, but he says he's done with it anyway. He hates working here. He's looking for a new job. So he felt like it was the right thing to do.'

'We should all send him a letter of thanks,' said Matilda, remembering the berating she'd given him when he'd come to visit her in hospital. She had been very intolerant, really, of a young man just trying to do his job. She felt she might send him a personal letter of apology, too.

'Is that Daniel you're talking about?' said Connie, who'd walked over to join them, and picked up the tail end of what Russell had said.

'Yeah. He's cutting his ties here.'

'That statement was amazing,' said Connie. 'Simply amazing.'

'Yes. And Russell persuaded him to do it,' said Amy.

'Really? Awesome,' said Connie, taking a deep breath and pulling Amy aside, but remaining close enough for Matilda to hear what was said.

'Did you get wind of anything coming from central government, about the plans?' Connie asked Amy. Although she didn't mention him by name, it was clear she was referring to her father.

'No, I'm afraid I didn't, lovey. I mean, Sir William, the local MP, gave me a quote in support, but I never heard anything from the ministry, and Yvonne didn't mention anything, either.'

Matilda saw Connie's shoulders drop.

'Oh, OK. I just wondered. Thank you.'

'No worries at all. Now, I need to go and file this story asap. Please excuse me.'

Amy walked away and Matilda then looked around to see Jamie approaching. But he clearly wasn't coming to talk to her – he was coming to see Connie.

'Con,' he said, his voice low, almost a whisper.

'Jamie,' she said, bracing herself against the wall, her arms crossed.

Matilda realised they would both have preferred privacy, so looked down at the floor, feigning interest in her shoes.

'You wouldn't see me.'

'I'm sorry, Jamie. I haven't been well…'

'Yeah, I know.'

Was he going to say anything about the newspaper article, Matilda wondered. Or would she?

'It wasn't that I didn't want to see you.'

'Oh.' Matilda registered a glimmer of hope in Jamie's tone. He cares for her still, she thought. He definitely does.

'Look, I'm so sorry. I'm absolutely knackered. I dragged myself out of bed for this, and I'm glad I did, but… I need to go home now,' said Connie, her voice almost robotic. 'I'm sorry. We can talk later, yeah?'

'OK. Right. Yeah. Rest well, Con,' said Jamie, turning and walking off to help Liv deal with her children, who were running up and down the corridor, spraying Cheerios in their wake.

Now that Jamie was gone, Matilda took her chance to speak to Connie without being overheard.

'You went to see your father, Connie?' she said, as Connie took her arm and led her in the direction of the lift.

'I did.'

'You didn't have to do that. I know you are feeling very low at the moment. That must have been very hard.'

'I needed to try, for you all. I should have done it a long time ago. But guess what, though? I did it, and it didn't help at all. He could have called in favours or something, couldn't he? But absolutely bloody nothing. He's always been like that. Sorry for swearing, by the way.'

'I think he deserves it,' replied Matilda.

'Yeah, I reckon so.' Connie squeezed Matilda's hand. 'Now, I feel like going home to hide again. All of this celebrating has worn me out. And you must be feeling very tired, too?'

Connie was right. Matilda was absolutely exhausted. She had got through the morning on sheer adrenaline, but her levels had now simply fallen off a cliff and she was struggling to stay awake.

'Right, Brian and Jocelyn are coming with Mum. Let's go, shall we?' said Connie, pressing the button to call the lift. 'Let's go home.'

— 39 —

December 21st

Constance

The longest night of the year was now two hours old. The countryside around Roseacre Close was frozen solid, the fallow fields unyielding, and once burbling streams imprisoned under inch-thick ice. The insipid winter sun had been unable to bring the temperature above zero for several days, and tonight, hoar frost was forming under a clear sky, leaving its thick, feathery down on leaves, tree trunks and blades of grass, its intricacy and delicacy making it even more beautiful than snow. It was the sort of night that called for a hot meal and a warming drink, and Ellen was making sure they had both in abundance.

'Can you get the sausage rolls out of the oven, Connie? I need to check on Matilda. She's napping by the fire.'

'Yep, sure.' Connie stopped staring out of their kitchen window, took the gloves from her mother and opened the oven, the blast of hot air and delicious smells making her mouth water. She was feeling a lot more hungry since she had started taking Sertraline, not strictly a side effect, per se, but more, she thought, a reaction to feeling more on an even keel. She'd felt a bit woozy on the tablets for the first few days, and had almost given up – memories of her incarceration in the mental health clinic coming back to her – but once that feeling had faded, she had definitely begun to feel better. She'd also been put on the waiting list for counselling, though she'd been told it might be a few months yet before she received it, and she was set to start AA meetings in the New Year. She wasn't out of the woods yet, definitely not, but she thought that the darkness might not be *quite* so dark now – and that was something worth celebrating.

Celebration was tonight's theme, in fact. A celebration of Christmas, of course, but also of their mutual triumph, the salvation – at least for now – of Roseacre Close. This was the first time everyone had been in the same space since they had gathered in the corridor outside the council chamber.

Lots of celebratory memes had made their way around the close's WhatsApp group since, plus plenty of speculation about the political future of the council leader, whose record Amy and Russell had been busy excoriating in their respective news outlets in the preceding days. Connie had only seen these things over her mother's shoulder, however, as she was still not keen to re-enter the world of smartphones, which had functioned as a conduit for Alex's abuse. Buying one felt like inviting her old world back in, and she still felt too vulnerable to do that, particularly as she was fairly certain that those horrific videos would haunt her for the rest of her days. She also knew, however, that she couldn't avoid them forever, and that public obsessions faded. The headlines about her were already lining bins or providing firelighters across the land. Still, she wouldn't get a smartphone yet. One day, perhaps.

For now, she felt comfortable and safe in the small, predictable, ordered world she was inhabiting. She had plenty to keep her occupied. She was looking after the animals by herself and was likely to need to acquire some more gardening skills, too, as Matilda was growing weaker by the day. She was due to begin a short course of radiotherapy in January, which her doctors felt might prolong her life, without absolutely obliterating her final months.

Connie and Ellen had promised Matilda that they would do everything they could to keep her at home until the end, so they had been speaking to cancer charities and the local hospice about providing care, and their plans were shaping up well. Matilda had initially been resistant to any invasion of her privacy, but faced with the alternative – a bed in a nursing home miles away – she had conceded. She had even agreed to social services sending a carer to visit her daily to help her wash, go to the toilet and prepare food. The carer they had sent had turned out to be one of Ellen's friends, a warm, kind and funny woman called Fran. Which was just as well, thought Connie, because you definitely needed a sense of humour to deal with Matilda.

Connie felt a blast of cold air as her mother answered the front door.

'Come in! Come in! Just leave your coat over the bannister. Connie, could you please get Niamh and Martin a drink?'

Connie saw that her two neighbours, the widower and the widow, were holding hands, and that they both had a rosy glow in their cheeks which couldn't be entirely attributed to the chilly weather. She was delighted for them both.

'Sure. What would you like?'

'Something wet,' said Niamh.

'Warm or cold? We have mulled wine on the hob, or there's some beer in the fridge.'

'Ooh, mulled wine, I haven't had one yet this year. I'll have one of those.'

'One for me too, please,' said Martin.

'Sure. Two mulled wines coming up.'

Connie found two glasses and ladled out two full glasses of the spicy, warm red wine and handed them to her friends.

'Thanks, Connie, love,' said Martin.

'Yes, thank you,' said Niamh, before an uncomfortable silence ensued.

They're thinking about the videos, Connie thought. They can't get that image of me out of their heads.

'Er, Connie, love...' said Martin, after a slurp of wine, clearly uncomfortable with what he was about to say.

Come on, both of you, let's get it over with.

'What Martin is trying to say is thank you,' said Niamh, cradling her mulled wine like it was a hard-won university degree. 'We've lived opposite each other for years, waved at each other when we put our bins out, exchanged cards at Christmas, but we would never have actually got together if it hadn't been for you, and your campaign to keep us all here, in the close.'

Blood rushed to Connie's face. Their gratitude was entirely unexpected and, as far as she was concerned, entirely undeserved, and yet it meant so much to her.

'You guys, honestly, it was nothing to do with me. It was Matilda, really. She was the one who said that we had to fight. I just helped her.'

'Oh don't be silly, woman. You, your mum and Matilda changed our lives. We can't thank you enough,' said Niamh.

'I should've done more. I should've gone to see my dad sooner.'

'I read those papers, love, and he sounds like a right tosser, if you don't mind me saying so,' said Martin.

'Martin!' said Niamh, playfully digging him in the ribs.

'Sorry, love, but I call a spade a spade. He should have stepped in and looked after you, like your mum has. I've looked after loads of foster kids over the years, and some of them have come from families with plenty of money, but with absolutely no love and no sense. He's a type I know well, I'm afraid. I don't blame you at all.'

'Well, thank you, both of you. That means a lot.'

'Don't mention it, Connie. Now, I need a seat, Martin, because these heels are absolutely killing me.'

'Right you are, love,' said Martin, following her into the living room. 'See you in a bit, Connie.'

Connie smiled as she watched them go. They were two thoroughly lovely people, and she was so pleased they'd found each other. Then she looked down at the mulled wine, and considered pouring herself a glass, before deciding that it would be a terrible idea. She had managed to cut down, and she definitely felt better for it.

Then the doorbell rang again, and Connie saw Ellen let Jocelyn, Brian, Donna and Tom into the house. Jocelyn was wearing a deep red velvet dress and dangly red bauble earrings, and looked gorgeous. Brian was wearing his usual chinos and blue checked shirt, but with the addition of a bright red waistcoat. He was holding on tight to Jocelyn's arm, but looked remarkably at ease. A testament, Connie thought, to how much time he'd spent in their house with this particular group of people.

'Hello Connie,' said Jocelyn, accepting two glasses of mulled wine that she had offered them after they'd deposited their coats. 'We won't stay long, I don't think, because Brian gets so tired so early, but it's lovely to be invited and to have a reason to celebrate.'

'Understood. It's nice to see you both, though.'

'Nice to meet you, Connie,' said Brian.

'Lovely to meet you too, Brian,' said Connie, watching as Jocelyn gently steered him into the living room.

'All right?' said Tom, walking into the kitchen looking mostly at his phone.

'Drink, Donna?' said Connie.

'Oh, yes please. Crap day today. One of my patients died.'

'I'm really sorry to hear that,' replied Connie, passing her a mulled wine.

'That's OK. It goes with the territory. And no, Tom, you can't 'ave one of these.'

'I'm seventeen, Mum. I'm not a child.'

'Even so. While you live under my roof, you will obey the law.'

'It's not illegal to drink at 'ome, you know, when you're a child, as long as you're over five. That's what the actual law says.'

'Stop being a clever dick, Tom.'

'But I am clever, Mum. You keep telling me I am, and that it's a good thing. Why should I stop now?'

'Kids, eh. So literal,' said Donna, taking a swig of her drink and running her hands through Tom's mop of light brown hair.

'Get off, Mum.'

'Right you are,' said Donna. 'I suppose you could 'ave 'alf of one, maybe,' she said, and Tom's face lit up. Connie poured half a glass of mulled wine, and handed it to him. Tom grinned and quickly walked away with it, in case his mother changed her mind.

'Tom seems chipper,' said Connie.

'Yes, 'e does, doesn't 'e? 'E's 'ad a good week at college. 'E's got a great supervisor who's giving 'im more responsibility and teaching 'im more things, and 'e gets lots of praise. I think it's the first time 'e's actually 'ad someone saying nice things to 'im in a learning environment. It makes the world of difference.'

'I can imagine. It must have been tough when he was at school?'

'Yeah. Lots of tears, lots of storming off, lots of fruitless meetings with the SENCO who said all of the right things but did none of them. 'E almost got expelled once. It was rocky.'

'And really hard, I guess, doing it by yourself?'

Donna leaned against the kitchen counter. Connie noticed her glass was empty, so she took it and refilled it from the steaming saucepan on the hob.

'Yeah. 'Is dad buggered off years ago and 'as nothing to do with 'im. I've 'ad to work since 'e was tiny to afford our rent and our bills. I felt bad, not being around for 'im more, because what 'e needs is routine, not lots of chopping and changing of childminders and after school clubs. 'Is behaviour was partly because of that, I reckon.'

'That's not your fault, Donna.'

'Yeah, well. It is what it is,' she said, staring into her glass.

'Well, I'm really glad it all seems to be on a more even keel now.'

'Yeah, it's a relief. And 'ow are you doing, Connie? After that 'orrible thing with your ex?'

Connie felt a jolt of electricity run through her. She had expected this conversation, had thought that Niamh and Martin were going to ask about it, but had so far been lulled into a false sense of security. Actually having the whole nightmare raised was like being given an inoculation, a tiny, concentrated burst of the horror starting off small, and then gradually multiplying as it made its way around her body. Whether she could fight it off was yet to be seen.

'I'm doing OK, thank you,' she said, deciding to keep her answer brief, to try to persuade Donna to move on. 'I feel a lot better than I did.'

'That's good. I've been meaning to say, since I read that 'orrible story and spoke to your mum about what 'ad been going on, that I know 'ow it feels.' Oh shit, thought Connie, Mum has been telling people things. This is not good. I want to forget about it, not be reminded of it every time I see someone. 'I mean, not about the videos being leaked and stuff, but my ex, Tom's dad – 'e was controlling. 'E used to belittle me most of the time, tell me that I wasn't good for anything. And then there were occasional bouts of telling me that I was amazing, and the best thing that ever 'appened to 'im, you know, all that shit. 'Ot and cold, 'ot and cold, just enough 'ot to keep me 'ooked. So I know 'ow it goes.'

Connie nodded, but couldn't think what to say in response. It was definitely sounding familiar.

'Sorry, I know it's tough to talk about it,' Donna added. 'I never talk about what 'appened to me, either, so… You don't need to say anything. I'll just take my drink into the other room, eat a day's worth of calories in the form of chocolate and crisps, and we won't speak of it again.'

Donna made to leave. Connie took a deep breath, and addressed the elephant in the room.

'But I went to jail. You didn't go to jail.'

'No, I didn't. But if 'e'd done to me what your ex did to you, I might've, sweetheart. I might've.' They held each other's gaze for a brief moment, and then Donna smiled. 'Anyway, there are snacks to be eaten. As I say, we don't 'ave to ever talk about this again, if you don't want to. Up to you.'

Donna walked into the living room, and Connie fell back against the kitchen counter, the shock and relief of addressing her deepest fears overwhelming her. She had spent so long hiding her past, hiding who she had thought she really was. But the past few months had revealed facets of her personality she had never previously considered, and she was just beginning to see that perhaps Alex had manipulated her to such an extent that she'd never really been herself when she was with him. Now, however… now was a different matter. Day by day and interaction by interaction, she was discovering who she really was. And it was so much less frightening than she'd thought it might be.

'Connie, my love! The most amazing news,' said Ellen, breezing into the kitchen and opening the cupboards to take out bags of crisps and chocolates to replenish bowls in the next room. 'Martin and Niamh told me that they bumped into Sally and Nick earlier, and they apologised for not being able to come. Apparently Maddie has started to respond, so they have to be in the hospital. I mean, she's not exactly awake and sitting up, but she has started to respond to hand squeezes and other stimuli. Isn't that amazing?'

Connie thought about the pain they'd been through, of the absolute agony of seeing their daughter alive and yet not alive, of having their skipping, giggling, adventurous daughter's life ripped from them in an instant by a man who'd been too tight to call a cab. Imagining their relief now, albeit tinged with fear – for Maddie's battle was far from over, of course – tipped Connie over the edge. She began to cry.

'Oh baby girl. Come here,' said Ellen, pausing her search for snacks, and pulling Connie in for a hug. 'It's OK. I know this is probably all overwhelming. You can go upstairs and watch *Gilmore Girls* if you prefer.'

'I'll be fine in a minute,' said Connie, as Ellen rubbed her back. 'And I've just realised that I've trapped you in the kitchen. You should go into the living room. Matilda's asleep on the sofa. You could keep her company. I can take a shift doing drinks.'

'It's OK, Mum, I quite like it in here. It gives me an opportunity to talk to people without, you know, having to make small talk. Which as you know, I'm not very good at.'

'Maybe not right now, love, but eventually. But you don't have to go in there if you don't want to. It's entirely up to you.'

'Mum?'

'Yep?' said Ellen, pulling away, but remaining close by.

'I don't know how you've managed to keep the money coming in – I have contributed nothing since I've come home – and you work so hard...'

'Yeah, that's called being an adult, hon. You'll get the hang of it eventually.'

'Mum!'

'Sorry, love. I am joking, you know. I know it's hard. You've had a horrible time. But you'll get there,' said Ellen, helping herself to some mulled wine.

'I think I should try to get a job now.'

Ellen froze.

'Are you ready, do you think?'

'Yeah. Something local, though. Something I can do and still help Matilda with the animals. Maybe something outside. I love being outside.'

Ellen put the ladle down and took a sip from her glass.

'Do you think you'd fancy something to do with farming? I was helping Mrs Collins the other day, do you remember her? Dean's mother. You went to school with Dean? Well, anyway, Dean's dad Don is retiring and Dean needs more help on the farm. She said he was struggling to hire someone, because a lot of the people who used to come and labour on the farm were EU residents. And they've all gone back home.'

Connie almost choked on her drink.

'You're kidding. Farming? What do I know about farming? I'm a clumsy townie.'

'Ex-townie. You're going to stay here now, right?'

'Yeah. I am. But…'

'Why don't you just talk to him?'

Dean, who had almost run her over in his tractor. Dean, who delivered food and farming essentials to Matilda. Dean, who had told her so many stories about his farming life in the pub. Dean, who was friends with Jamie.

'Yeah, OK.'

'Great. How exciting. You can see what he needs, and if you can help.' Connie felt a seed of hope start to grow inside of her. 'Now, I need to go and make our guests welcome. Are you OK staying in here?'

'Yep,' said Connie, grabbing a cloth and beginning to wipe down the kitchen surfaces, hoping that her mother would be happy to leave her if she looked busy.

'Cool. See you in a bit.'

Just after Ellen had walked into the living room and shut the door, the front doorbell rang. Ellen did not return to answer it – it was clearly too loud in the living room for her to hear – so Connie walked over to the front door and pulled it open.

Jamie and Liv were standing outside.

'Sorry, sorry! I managed to get the teen sister of one of Max's school friends to babysit, but she was late,' said Liv.

Connie tried to focus entirely on Liv. It was far easier that way. She knew that if she looked at Jamie, she might betray how she felt, and she had to make sure she never did that. She didn't want to get in the way of their burgeoning romance, and she knew she had lied to Jamie repeatedly. And those videos… He was probably furious with her, and she didn't blame him for that.

'No worries at all. Come in, leave your coats on the stairs.

There are lots of drinks in the kitchen – mulled wine on the stove, beer in the fridge.'

Liv and Jamie brushed past her as they entered the house, and then Connie realised that the noise, the heat and conversation inside was getting the better of her. She was feeling a little bit better, yes, but not quite well enough for this. She smiled what she hoped was a genuine smile in Liv's direction, grabbed her coat, hat, gloves and keys and pulled the door closed behind her.

No, she didn't want to hide in her bedroom, because that felt like teenage behaviour, and besides, it was the outside, the countryside, the plants and the animals that coexisted with her in this beautiful place, that had helped her heal. It was normal, natural, she thought, to want to be in their presence.

When her eyes had adjusted to the mustard light coming from the streetlamp, Connie realised that the concrete beneath her feet appeared to be studded with diamonds, and each blade of grass on their front lawn looked like a microscopic silver sword. Each footstep she took felt like sacrilege, a destruction of precious and ephemeral beauty. And yet walk on she must, because she wanted to outrun the streetlights so that she could see the stars.

Then Connie heard a door slam, and footsteps running on the ice.

'Con, *Connie*. Wait up.' Jamie was running towards her, his feet slipping as he did so, making him look like an incredibly clumsy figure skater.

'OK! Please don't slip and break your neck.'

'Yeah, OK, good point,' said Jamie, slowing to a walk. 'These trainers never 'ad much grip in the first place, but now they're basically bowling shoes.'

Jamie drew level with Connie, and she looked at him properly for the first time that evening. He was clean-shaven, and his hair was hidden under a red, slightly wonky woollen hat with a large blue pom-pom standing proud at its tip.

'Like my 'at, do you? It was made by Niamh. She's going

through a knitting phase. I'm sure I can get 'er to make you one if you're jealous.'

'It's lovely,' said Connie. 'But I already have enough hats.'

'That's a shame. She's threatening to move on to jumpers next.'

They walked side by side in silence until they had left the close behind and were on the road that led out of the village.

'Connie?'

'Jamie…' Connie had imagined for some time now how the conversation that was bound to follow might go. Because they had to talk about all of the secrets she'd kept. They *had* to if they were ever going to be able to get on. And they *had* to get on, because they were neighbours, and they were friends. 'I'm sorry I told Mum I didn't want to speak to you.'

'I was worried about you, Con. Really worried.'

Connie was startled. This wasn't what she'd imagined he'd say.

'Were you? Really? You weren't angry with me for not telling you the truth?'

'What would I be angry about, Con?'

'You know… I went to jail… I didn't tell you who my dad was… Those videos…'

'Yeah, well, it was a shock about your dad, I'm not gonna lie. But I get it. I 'eard that you went to see 'im, and that 'e did jack shit. 'E's a twat. I don't blame you. But it was the way you must've felt, seeing what that bastard 'ad said about you in the papers… I thought you might do something stupid again…'

'Oh,' said Connie, who was struggling to compute how she could have got everything so very wrong. 'You know, you're a far, far better person than me, Jamie. Because if I'd just discovered that someone I liked had lied to me about who she actually was, where she'd been for the past year, and discovered that she'd taken part in some pretty disgusting videos that all of your mates have undoubtedly seen and shared… well, I'd have run for the hills. In better shoes.'

Connie shot a glance at Jamie and saw a glimmer of a smile.

'Do you think the council will really leave us alone now? The close, I mean? Will they try again?' asked Jamie, as they continued to walk deeper into the countryside.

'I dunno. Maybe. But if they do try again, all I know is that we'll be ready for them, won't we?'

'Yeah. We will.'

Suddenly, the hedges either side of the narrow, single-track road they were walking on seemed to Connie to be moving inwards. She felt like they might be about to asphyxiate her. She spotted a gap in the hedge to the right and ducked through it. Jamie followed. They found themselves at the entrance to a large open field which sloped down into the valley. On the other side, several miles away, twinkling lights marked out the site of one of the newest developments in the area, a huddle of thirty three-bedroom homes that were attached to a village which had neither a primary school nor a doctor's surgery.

Connie looked away from the houses and up to the stars. The sky was gigantic and sparkling. Before she could think about what she was doing, Connie threw her arms out and her head back, and began to spin, watching the universe dance in front of her eyes. Then Jamie started to do the same, and the two of them spun around and around like whirling dervishes, faster and faster, until the inevitable occurred; someone's foot stumbled on a frozen sod of earth, and that foot collided with another foot, and then Jamie and Connie, locked in a tornado of their own making, fell into each other with force.

'Ooof. Sorry. So sorry,' said Jamie, just managing to catch and right Connie before she tumbled onto the frozen earth.

'That's OK. It was my fault. I started it,' said Connie, realising that her face was now only centimetres away from Jamie's. She waited for him to let go of her, for him to stand back and brush the frost and dirt from his hands, but he did not.

'Jamie?' she whispered, barely able to speak.

'Yeah, Con?'

'I'm really sorry.'

'For what?'

'For making things complicated. For not telling you the truth earlier. For getting in the way between you and Liv. You should be at the party with her, and not out here with me.'

'You think we're together, don't you?'

Connie felt her stomach lurch.

'You're not?'

'Nah, we're not. I mean, she's lovely looking and all, but she reminds me of the girls Martin fostered. She's their age, right? She's sweet and kind, but not my type. We've been 'elping 'er because 'er benefits don't go very far and she isn't very 'andy with DIY. But she's not my girlfriend. Anyhow, she's got some new bloke she's met on Tinder. 'E's built like Popeye on spinach, 'as the energy of a teenager on speed and 'e's coming to see 'er again on Christmas Eve.'

'Oh.'

Jamie's arms were still around Connie's waist and their warmth was making Connie feel dizzy.

'And look, I did find it 'ard, finding out about all of those things you didn't tell me about. I was angry you 'adn't trusted me enough to tell me the truth, and I was so bloody angry with that Alex, Martin 'ad to stop me 'eading over to The Fucky Fuck to tell 'im what I thought.'

Connie smiled briefly, despite herself.

'Weren't you disappointed in me? That I'm damaged goods?'

'Mate, we're all damaged goods, every single one of us. We've all got a past. I'd never judge you for that.'

'Mate?' said Connie, looking up at Jamie with a coy smile.

'Nah, you're not my mate,' said Jamie, his eyes melting into Connie's.

'Then what…?'

Connie didn't manage to finish her sentence, because Jamie was kissing her, and she was responding like a starving animal. She felt a heat rise up from within her, a heat she had never, ever felt when she was with Alex. She wrapped her arms around him and pulled him even closer to her, eager, after so long, to lay claim to every inch of his skin and sinew.

'I'm sorry, is this too much?' he said, pulling away. 'We can take it slower if you want.'

'No,' said Connie. 'I want more. More of this.'

'Your wish is my command,' he said, picking Connie up and slinging her over his shoulder. Connie shrieked with shock and joy.

'What on earth are you doing?' she asked, her head dangling over his back.

'I'm taking you back to my place so that we can do more of this, without risking frostbite or a broken leg,' he answered.

'That sounds very sensible,' she said, feeling the blood rush to her head as she inhaled the scent of him, a mixture of woodsmoke, dust and deodorant.

'Jamie?' she said, as he stumbled slightly on the icy road.

'Yes, Con?'

'Don't you think it might be safer if you put me down?'

'Yeah, well, possibly,' he said, placing her down gently on her feet. 'But I can still 'old onto you firmly, can't I?' he said.

'Of course. In fact, that's very much encouraged. Please do as much of that as you like.'

—40 —

April 1st

Matilda

Miriam's hands were dirty. She had been making a mud castle in the garden, creating turrets out of slate and stone and doorways out of matchsticks. When Matilda had walked out to find her like that, mud smeared up each arm and over most of her cotton dress, she had just laughed, and Miriam had laughed with her. There would be time to clean her up later. Now, Matilda got on her hands and knees and joined in, burying her arms up to her elbows in the earth, warmed and dissolved by summer rain.

'Miss Reynolds? Matilda? It's Violet. Your nurse from the hospice. I'm just going to give you a quick clean up, OK?'

Matilda wondered briefly why Violet was playing in the garden with Miriam, but she decided not to pursue that thought further. She was having too much fun.

Another day, suddenly. It was raining, and it sounded as if millions of imps were dancing on the corrugated plastic roof of their lean-to. Miriam's nose was squashed up against the window and her breath was making circles of condensed steam on the glass.

'Matilda, can you hear me? It's Connie. Jamie and I are here, and so is Mum. We're here with you. We hope you're comfortable. The nurse has given you some painkillers, and she says you should be comfy, so we hope that's true.'

Remember your mercy, Lord, and the love you have shown from of old. Do not remember the sins of my youth. In your love remember me...

Now it was winter. Miriam had woken up at dawn when the ethereal light cast by the sun first meeting the snow had infused through their thin cotton curtains. She had plunged down the stairs and out into it, Matilda running after her with a warm coat and hat, donning wellington boots on the hop. They had built a snow woman, all curves and smiles, her eyes coal, her ears leaves, her nose a carrot that the goats had eaten within minutes.

Relieve the anguish of my heart and set me free from my distress. See my affliction and my toil and take all my sins away...

'I don't think it will be long now. Can you hear that noise she's making in the back of her throat? That is sometimes called the death rattle, but really it's just a sign that she's so relaxed, so at peace, that she is no longer even trying to clear her throat. If you want to tell her anything, now is the time.'

Miriam! Don't look at me like that. We can't eat the Christmas cake yet, we've a week to go.

'Matilda? It's Connie. I just wanted to say... oh God... lots of stuff really, but mostly I want to reassure you that we will make sure the animals are OK. We'll find somewhere wonderful for them to live. I'm even trying to persuade Mum to let us keep the goats in our garden.'

Yes, let's dance instead. Let's dance all night.

'And... thank you, Matilda. Thank you for being my friend. You are amazing. I love you.'

Matilda gathered Miriam into her arms, and they danced, oh, how they danced.

I love you too, Miriam. I love you so very much. I will never let you go.

— 41 —

April 25th

Constance

'Now, first we need to lift up the front loader. Lift the joystick gently – yes, that's right – and now slide the stick into neutral, and select the tortoise range on the gear box – we don't want to race around 'ere. Good, yes, that's right. You're off! Nothing to it, eh?'

It was the end of Connie's first month on the farm and her first day on the tractor. They would soon need to spray fertiliser on the grazing fields and top-dress the cereal crops, so she needed to learn how to use the equipment. Every day had been a steep learning curve since Dean had taken her on and she was mentally and physically exhausted every night, but she was absolutely loving it. Being outside every day, working in harmony with the seasons and the land, made her feel grounded and alive. This, she realised, was real-world meditation; you had no option but to live in the moment and respond to the nature that was all around you.

'Thanks, Dean. Thanks for being so patient with me.'

'No bother, Con. This is good for me, too. I mean, there's a very good chance you're going to stick around and live local for years, right? Not 'op on a flight 'ome when you've 'ad enough? It feels nice, to be honest, training someone else local on 'ow to manage the land…'

'Yeah, I'm not going anywhere,' said Connie, stepping down from the tractor, with Dean following behind her. Her tractor driving lesson would continue tomorrow.

'Are you still living with your mum, or are you and Jamie looking to find your own place?'

Connie grimaced.

'We'd love to get our own place, obviously – I think Mum and Martin have both had enough of us, to be honest – but we can't afford anything that's on the market around here. There are hardly any rental properties, anyway. Most of them are holiday lets. And we've put our names down for a council house, too, but there are hardly any of those now. You know how it is.'

'Yeah, I do,' said Dean, rubbing his ginger beard. 'I wish I could offer you something on the farm, but we 'ad to sell off our last tied cottage a while back, to make ends meet. We barely make a profit as it is.'

'Yeah, I know, I get it. Thanks, though. I know you'd help if you could.'

'Yep. I would. You and Jamie are great together. I'm so chuffed for the pair of you.'

'You're going soft, Dean,' said Connie, grinning as she grabbed her bike from the barn. 'I'll head off then. See you tomorrow.'

'Bye, Con.'

Connie sped down the country lanes where she had walked in the early hours less than a year ago, the ghost of her old life being exorcised as she pedalled along. She pulled into Roseacre Close about ten minutes later.

'I'm back, Mum.'

'I'm in the dining room,' replied Ellen, almost singing.

Connie walked through to the room, which was much more of a study and workroom than somewhere to eat these days, and found her mother sitting at her sewing machine.

'What are you making?'

'Oh, I got a new pattern I want to try. My tutor suggested I should have a go at something more ambitious.'

Ellen had started attending evening classes, taking up hobbies that she'd enjoyed many years previously but had parked due to motherhood and the necessity to keep a roof over their heads. With her tenancy now secure and her daughter in employment, Connie – and Matilda, in the months before she died – had persuaded her that now was the time to spread her wings. So far she'd tried cookery, pottery and sewing classes, with the latter in particular proving to be a hit. She'd made Connie a beautiful skirt, as well as a brand-new pair of curtains, fully lined, for her bedroom. The days of the streetlight shining onto her in bed were well and truly over, and she was not unhappy about that at all.

'What did you want to be, when you were a kid, Mum? What was your ambition?' asked Connie, pondering the joy she had found in a job that she would never previously have given a second thought.

'Oh, I wanted to be in *Starlight Express*, love.'

'*Starlight Express*?'

'It was a musical. Andrew Lloyd Webber. We went to see it on a school trip. They all pretended to be trains and raced around on roller skates.'

'Were you good at skating?'

'Absolutely dreadful.'

'So you don't regret not becoming a West End performer, then?'

'I think the world is a better place for not having to see or hear me do it. I sing like a hippopotamus with wind.'

Connie laughed and sat down at the table opposite Ellen.

'Seriously, though. Having me. It must have scuppered your ambitions? I must have seriously cramped your style.'

Ellen stopped what she was doing.

'All I had managed to do by the time I had you was to travel to a city I didn't like and find a job in a bar I hated. But having you, and finding that I had to do it by myself, meant that I came home and came here, and that was the right thing for me. I don't regret any of it. How could I regret having you, you silly thing?'

'And then I left you. I buggered off without a second thought,' said Connie, staring at her hands in her lap.

'Yes, you did. But you were almost a teenager, and I recognised a lot of me in you. I yearned for independence at that age. I knew you'd come back.'

'I didn't think I ever would.'

'No, well, it just goes to show, doesn't it, that your mother knows best.'

'Were you lonely, when I left?'

'I was, for a while, of course I was. I used to go up to your room and cry.'

'Oh, *Mum*. I'm so sorry.'

'Yes, well. But then I met a chap in the pub one night, and we had lots of fun, and I changed jobs and became a carer here, and made lots of friends, so...'

'You met someone in a pub?'

Ellen smiled.

'Yes, I have met lots of men over the years, darling. You don't think I've been celibate all of these years, do you?'

Connie was shocked, and then she chastised herself for being shocked. Her mother was only in her early fifties. Martin and Niamh had found each other in their sixties, after all – she realised she had absolutely failed to see her mother as a fully functioning human being for all of her life thus far, and she knew that had to change.

'I didn't know. Sorry, Mum.'

'Don't be sorry. I didn't tell you because I've never found anyone special enough to bring home, to disrupt my life here. But that doesn't mean that I haven't had a good time, or that I've been lonely.'

'OK. Understood.'

'You don't need a partner to be happy, you know, Connie.'

'Yeah, I know.'

'Not that I want you to dump Jamie, by the way. He's lovely. Definitely keep him.'

Connie smiled.

'I plan to! Right, I should get off. I need to go and check on the animals. Jamie's already there, I think, and I don't want him thinking I've left him to do all of the work.'

'Yes, you go. But, oh, before I forget, you have a letter. It's from the council.' Connie's heart lurched. Since Matilda had died, they'd been waiting for the council to let them know when they'd have to clear her belongings out, and when they'd have to find somewhere for the animals to go. They'd assured Matilda they would try to rehome them personally, rather than calling in an animal charity, but it was going to be a big job, and one that Connie was dreading. Saying goodbye to Matilda had been horrendous, and saying goodbye to the animals was a further, unbearable wrench. They were all she had left of her friend.

'And before you ask again, Connie, it's still a no to the goats. We can't look after them. They'll eat all of our flowers. Can you ask Dean if he knows anyone? Or maybe he could take them?' Connie shook her head. She'd tried that. She'd cried when he'd said he didn't have the room for them. In fact, she had cried a great deal since Matilda's death and it had exhausted her. Today, she decided, she would not cry. Matilda would want her to grasp the nettle and get on with things, as she had always done.

'Oh, Connie, love. You'll definitely find somewhere for them, I know you will. The letter's on the side in the kitchen.'

'Thanks.'

'Oh, and wait a sec, actually. I have something else for you.'

Ellen stood up and walked over to a small metal filing cabinet which sat in the corner of the room. She dug into it and pulled out a small rectangular white envelope and handed it to Connie.

'Matilda asked me to give you this when a letter arrived for you from the council.'

'What is it?'

'I don't know, Connie, do I? I haven't opened it. It's for you. She made me promise not to say anything about it until now, and you know Matilda, she was pretty scary, so I did as she said.'

Ellen smiled, and so did Connie, despite the fact that she was dreading its contents. She had already said goodbye to Matilda. Would this letter feel like saying goodbye all over again?

'Thanks, Mum. I'll take the letters next door and read them there, if that's OK.'

It felt fitting to Connie to read Matilda's words in the home she had loved.

'Yes, sure. But come back and tell me what she says later. I'm desperate to know.'

Connie clasped the two letters close to her chest as she pushed open Matilda's side gate and walked into her back garden. Jamie was there, as she had anticipated, refreshing the water in the tubs.

'All right, Con?' he said, spotting her. 'I've missed you. Where've you been?'

Connie walked over to him and kissed him on the lips, lingering a second or two longer than was strictly necessary.

'Sorry, I got talking to Mum. And she gave me these,' she said, showing Jamie the letters.

'Is that one from the council? Do you think that's the marching orders we've been waiting for?'

'Yeah, well, I suppose they'll want to get someone else in soon. There's such a shortage of social housing.'

'Why've they written to you?'

'What do you mean?'

'I mean, you're not 'er next of kin, right? Shouldn't they be writing to a lawyer, or some distant relative, or something?'

'She didn't have any relatives still alive, apparently. And she said she gave them my name as a contact, for after she'd died.'

'Oh, right,' said Jamie, washing his hands under the garden tap. 'So who's the other letter from?'

'Matilda. Apparently she wrote it a while back and told Mum to keep it until we heard from the council.'

'Christ. Old Matilda from beyond the grave. She never shuts up, that woman,' said Jamie with a wink.

'Shall we sit down and open them? On the bench?'

'Yeah, why not.'

Connie and Jamie walked to the end of the garden and sat on Matilda's favourite seat. It was half past seven and the sun was sinking beyond the distant hills. In the field at the bottom of the valley, newborn lambs were nudging their mothers for milk, and the land beyond the gate was being prepared for its summer crop.

Connie felt a surge of pride that she had preserved the status quo here, for now at least. There was no telling what the future might bring – the white stone-clad houses she could see in the distance on the new estate were an unwanted visual reminder of what they were up against – but for now, Roseacre Close would remain intact and the people she loved within it.

'Which one will you open first?'

'I don't know. The council one, maybe? Save Matilda's final words for… last?' said Connie, holding back tears.

'Good plan.'

Connie ripped the envelope open and unfolded the letter.

Dear Ms Darke,

I hope this letter finds you well. Please allow me to extend our condolences to you on the loss of your friend, Matilda Reynolds.

I am writing to let you know that Miss Reynolds expressed a wish before she died that you should be allowed to inherit her tenancy for 4, Roseacre Close.

As you may be aware, it is common for tenancies to be

passed on between families who have a long-established tenancy on a council property. In this instance, of course, Matilda Reynolds had no partner or children to pass her property on to. However, she made it clear in correspondence to us that she views you as family, and that your ongoing care for her animals has given you a direct link to the property.

Our housing guidelines state that, in exceptional circumstances, succession rights can be granted to non-family members who have a direct link such as this.

We are also aware that you and your partner work locally, and are on the waiting list for council housing.

It is for these reasons that we have, on this occasion, decided to allow you to take on the tenancy of 4, Roseacre Close.

Your tenancy of the property can begin as soon as you wish. Please get in touch with us to proceed with the paperwork, and let us know if you identify any maintenance issues when you move in. I understand the property has not had remedial work carried out on it for many years.

Yours sincerely,

Joseph Richards
Head of Asset Management & Property Services
Severnside Council

'Oh my God. She's left me the house.'

Connie stumbled over the words. She felt tears form, and this time she didn't try to hold them back, because these were tears of joy. This house, this place where she felt so at peace, was to be hers, and so were the animals that lived there.

''Ang on. Isn't it a bit... dodgy? I mean, shouldn't they give the 'ouse to someone further up the list than us?' Jamie asked her gently, noting how happy she seemed.

'Yeah, maybe,' she said, feeling her joy subside. Jamie was

right. Was she being selfish again? As if reading her mind, Clarrie wandered over from her feeding trough to the bench and stood next to Connie, begging for a scratch.

'I dunno, you know. 'Aving said that, it's what she wanted, isn't it? And she'd been 'ere since it was built,' said Jamie, after a lengthy pause. 'And we could keep the animals 'ere, couldn't we?'

'And there would be two of us here, wouldn't there? Not just me?'

There was a pause while Jamie took in what she'd just said, and Connie held her breath.

'Are you asking me to move in with you, Constance Darke?'

'Yes, I am, James Donald. I am.'

'I accept,' he said, throwing his arms about Connie and holding her tight until Clarrie nudged them, eager for attention. 'Yeah, all right, Clarrie, all right. We'll stop for now. But later, behind closed doors, you ain't stopping me then. All right?'

'She's a goat, Jamie. A goat.'

'Yeah. A clever, difficult goat, and we're stuck with 'er. She reminds me of someone, you know. Women, eh. Poor Eddie. It must be terrible, being with 'er all of the time.'

Connie dug her elbow into Jamie's ribs, her face one broad smile.

'So are you going to open Matilda's letter now, then?'

'Yep,' replied Connie, running her hands over the paper, imagining Matilda's own hands doing the same. It was when she turned it over she noticed that Matilda had written, in large, sloping, block capitals:

PLEASE LOOK AFTER THIS GOAT.

Connie laughed, took a deep breath, opened the flap at the back and pulled out a typed letter on thick cream paper.

— 42 —

April 26th

Constance

Connie had cycled the short distance to Dean's farm in a daze. She had barely slept the night before, the contents of Matilda's letter churning in her mind.

It had begun as she had expected it to begin, before taking a very unexpected turn.

Dear Connie,

By now, you will hopefully have been told that you are to be offered the continuing tenancy of 4, Roseacre Close. I hope that I have managed to persuade the council, who were initially reluctant to do so, that you are a fitting and deserving new tenant. This will, I'm afraid, mean that you will also inherit two obstinate goats, many, many cats and some rather elderly chickens. I hope you will keep them and love them, but in the end, that must be your decision. You have your own life to lead.

I'm afraid I have nothing in monetary terms to leave you, and I assume that you may wish to clear out many of my belongings. What you do with them is up to you. After decades of holding onto them, I have realised, very belatedly, that it was only the memories that they held that made them special, and I've taken those with me to where I'm heading next.

I want to thank you, dear Connie, for the past year, the last year of my life, and the fun and laughter you brought to it. I spent so long living in fear and in grief, and it was so wonderful to be reminded of the immense power of friendship, before it was too late. You are a remarkable young woman and I know your mother is very proud of you.

Finally, there is one more piece of information to impart, and I appreciate that this will come as a shock, for which I apologise...

Connie tried to focus on breathing, on moving her legs and propelling herself along the road. It was easier than allowing herself to think.

She was still trying to process what Matilda had written. Her initial shock at the revelation had made her feel nauseous, and Jamie, poor Jamie, had had to rush next door to get her a glass of water. He had been shocked too, of course, although he was obviously far better at controlling the contents of his stomach than she was.

The letter had meant that her utter joy at being left the tenancy of the house had been replaced almost immediately with unease. She hoped that Jamie had slept better than she had last night. Could it really be true? *Could it?* She knew that Matilda was unusual, alternative, a rebel. So, perhaps it really *was* true. And if so, what on earth were they going to do about it? They couldn't ignore it, could they?

Connie pulled into the farmyard. Dean wasn't out yet, which wasn't a surprise. She was early. She made her way to the office and pulled the door open, intent on putting on the kettle for her second cuppa of the day. She was astonished to find Jamie inside, in the midst of what looked like an intense conversation with Dean.

'Mornin', Con,' said Jamie, managing a smile, although she could see that he had also obviously slept badly.

'Morning,' she said, trying to smile in return.

'I couldn't sleep, so I came to ask Dean for 'elp.'

Connie raised an eyebrow.

'You told him?'

'Connie, my family've, well, sort of looked after Matilda for decades,' said Dean. 'We're the only people who 'ave, right? We've kept a lot of 'er secrets. Grandpa and Dad knew Matilda's sister was there, didn't they? And they never told anyone. I won't tell anyone anything now. Swear to God.'

Connie nodded. She trusted Dean, of course she did. But this was such a big thing. If they decided to keep Matilda's secret, Dean's promise to keep schtum would be seriously challenged.

'Did they know Miriam died?'

'Yeah. They did. But Dad says 'e doesn't know anything about 'ow she died, or what 'appened afterwards. 'E was too young then to 'ave been involved. Maybe Grandad knows more. But 'e'll be asleep now. I will try later, though. When 'e wakes up. 'E sleeps a lot. 'Is heart's not so good.'

Connie sank down into Dean's office chair and put her head in her hands.

'Do you think we should call the police?' she said.

'Maybe,' replied Jamie.

'But they'll tear your place to bits, won't they, and if they find something, it could trigger all sorts of stuff,' said Dean. 'You won't be able to keep it secret then. Everyone will know.'

'Do you think the council might think twice about handing on the tenancy, if there's some sort of investigation going on?' said Jamie.

'Urgh. Don't know. Maybe,' replied Connie, Jamie's suggestion an entirely unwelcome addition to her addled brain. She was already struggling to think straight.

No one spoke for a moment while they all considered the dilemma they were facing.

'I think we need to know what we're dealing with,' said Connie, running her fingers through her hair. 'If it's... what we think it is, and we *know* it is, then we can decide what to do. Whether to tell or to keep quiet.'

'Yeah. That's what I thought. That's why I came to see Dean,' said Jamie. 'I need someone to 'elp me dig.'

They were all standing at the end of Matilda's garden, near the fence. It was a glorious morning. The sun was rising, its rays warming the chilled fields, the bulbs and seeds beneath them pushing their shoots through the earth after their long winter slumber.

Jamie and Dean had lifted the bench away from its usual spot and rested it against the fence that bordered Ellen's garden.

'So you think she's... 'ere?' said Dean.

'Yep,' said Connie, having to make a conscious decision to breathe as Matilda's letter somersaulted around her brain. 'Are you sure you're OK with this?'

'Yeah. I've buried loads of our pets. Sheep dogs, and that.'

'But 'ave you dug any up?' said Jamie.

'By mistake, sometimes...' replied Dean with a shrug.

'Right. Well. No time like the present,' said Jamie, taking his hands out of his pockets and picking up one of the two spades that were resting against the fence. 'Better get going before I change my mind.'

Then Dean took the other spade, rested his foot on top of it, pushed hard and broke the soil.

Connie held her breath and thought about Matilda's letter.

I told you that I brought my sister, Miriam, home with me to live. You never asked me when she died, and I was grateful for that, because that terrible day was a festering wound in my memory. However, I must tell you about it now, because I need to let you know something very important.

Miriam lived with me for a wonderfully happy decade. I saw her through from her late teens to her late twenties and her glorious, joyful innocence lit up my life. Her days were, however, pockmarked with epileptic seizures, which varied in strength and severity. I learned to manage them as best I could, but each time I could see that they were taking their toll on her brain and on her body. And yet, I didn't want to medicate her as they had done in the institution, because I knew that those awful drugs would sap the life out of her. And so I let that dreadful disease rip through her and, one day, my decision came back and stabbed me in the heart.

I was asleep, Connie. I was asleep, and I didn't know that she needed me. When I woke up on that dreadful morning, I found Miriam face down in bed, stone cold. She had died in the night. Of what, I will never know. Was it asphyxiation during the seizure? Was it a heart attack? Frankly, it really didn't matter. She was gone, and I was distraught beyond measure. So I hid myself away, and shut the world out.

But the thing I need to tell you, Connie, is that I did not let them take her.

I could not bear to be parted from her again.

So Miriam, my Miriam, is in the garden, beneath the bench that looks over the fields. It was her favourite place to go, and mine, too. I would often go and talk to her there, after she'd gone. That is why I could never leave the house, because I could never leave her there on her own.

I must promise you that she will not give you trouble. She loved this place, as I did and you do, and her presence will only ever be a joyous one.

And one final thing. I know I asked to be cremated, and I am assuming you have done as I asked. But would you please scatter my ashes beneath the bench, so that the rain will send me down to be with her? Then you can talk to us both there, if you wish. I promise we will endeavour to answer you if we can.

With much love,
Matilda

'There's something 'ere.'

Connie forced herself to look up from her feet to where Dean and Jamie stood, shovels in hand, an intense expression on their faces. She felt sick. What would Matilda have wrapped her in, she wondered. Sheets? Towels? And how had she managed it by herself? She was younger then, of course, but even so, lugging Miriam out here and digging a big enough hole must have been utterly exhausting.

'What does it feel like?'

'Dunno. Solid. 'Ard.'

'Bone?' said Connie, feeling bile rising in her gullet.

'Dunno,' said Jamie. 'But maybe I should just use a trowel now, to see what it is. Don't want to... disturb the site too much.'

God, he sounds like he's in a police drama, thought Connie, before realising that it *would* be a real-life police drama, if they reported the body buried in their back garden to the police. *My God, Matilda, what on earth have you left me to deal with?*

Connie watched as Jamie took hold of Ellen's garden trowel and removed more earth from the hole he'd dug. He was going slowly, pressing the trowel down rather than jabbing it, out of respect, she imagined, for what lay beneath. Dean had stopped digging at his end and he was watching Jamie too. It was impossible to take your eyes away, Connie thought, despite what you might be about to see.

'I've got something,' said Jamie.

Connie and Dean approached the hole Jamie had dug and stared down into it. They watched as Jamie brushed away some loose soil from a solid object beneath.

'It's a tin. A biscuit tin,' said Jamie, the relief clear in his voice. '*Digestive-bloody-biscuits.*'

At that moment, Dean's phone rang. He picked it up and walked to the fence at the end of the garden. Connie, meanwhile, was staring at the biscuit tin.

'Do you think that's… it?'

'Dunno. 'Ow can it be? I mean, she wouldn't've been able to get 'er cremated, would she? The authorities didn't know she was 'ere. No one did. She'd've 'ad to own up to having 'er 'ere.'

'So what's in the tin, then?'

'I dunno. Did she 'ave jewellery or something? Maybe she buried it with 'er to keep it safe?'

'Only one way to find out,' replied Connie, raising an eyebrow.

'OK, Con. On your 'ead be it,' replied Jamie, levering the box out of the ground and resting it on the grass.

'So shall we open it, then?' she said, staring at the rusty, dented tin.

'We could, yeah.'

'Should we, though?'

'Yeah, why not. How bad can it be?'

Jamie was about to take the shovel to the lid of the box.

'*Don't open that. Leave it,*' shouted Dean, running towards them.

Jamie sprang away from the box as if burned.

'OK mate, sure, I've left it,' said Jamie.

They all stood around the box staring at it for a second, before Dean spoke once more.

'That was Mum on the phone. Grandad woke up. I just spoke to 'im. 'E says that they buried Miriam's ashes under the bench. In a tin. A biscuit tin.'

'Her *ashes*?' said Connie, brushing her hair off her face with an agitated swipe.

'Yeah. Apparently a farmer Grandad knew 'ad a sideline as an undertaker and 'e 'elped Matilda get Miriam cremated without going through… official channels. Don't know 'ow. 'E was a bit vague about that. But 'e said they brought Miriam back 'ere in a biscuit tin, and then 'e 'elped Matilda to bury the box under the bench.'

Connie felt relief surge through her and then she started to laugh.

'Typical Matilda. Withholding information to the last,' she said, relief bringing tears to her eyes.

'Yeah, she really 'ad me going there for a bit,' said Jamie, rubbing the back of his neck. 'Bloody Matilda,' he said, his tone indicating immense understatement.

'God, yeah. Well, all's well that ends well, I suppose. And at least you didn't open it up and scatter Miriam all over Worcestershire. It's a bit windy today,' said Dean.

'True, that,' said Connie.

They all stood in silence for a moment, contemplating the life of the woman who had once sat on that bench and enjoyed the same view they were enjoying, before spending eternity in a box meant for biscuits. Connie wiped her eyes with her hands, her laughter finally beginning to subside.

'Well, I should go and get on with the day. Lots to do,' said Dean, making for the gate. 'Are you all right to fill the 'ole back in by yourself, Jamie?'

'Yeah, no bother.'

'I'll be back at work in a bit,' said Connie, walking over to Jamie and taking hold of his hand.

'No rush. You've 'ad a bit of a shock,' said Dean, winking as he walked down the side of the house and out of sight.

'Shall we sit down?' said Connie. 'I know it seems a bit ridiculous, but I was genuinely a bit scared there. I thought we'd have the police digging up the whole garden, asking all sorts of questions.'

'Yeah, let's sit. And you know, obviously I'm a big, strong man and never bothered by anything, Con, but even so...' said Jamie with a smile.

'That's why I like you so much, Jamie,' said Connie, as they sat down on the bench and looked over the fields. 'You're not afraid to show your softer side.'

'Ain't nothing soft about me.'

'Whatever you say, James,' she said, grinning.

'Are you bothered about 'aving the ashes there, though, Con? I mean, we could ask the vicar about moving them to the churchyard...'

'God, no. Once you've come to terms with Matilda's madhouse and all of her funny ways, I don't think anything would bother you. And anyway, I think we're going to need to carry Matilda's wishes out and have her ashes here too, aren't we?'

'Yeah, why not,' said Jamie, reaching for her hand and squeezing it. 'We'll 'ave the pair of them as 'ouse guests.'

'Yes. They'll be easy to put up with, I reckon. Easier than these two lumps,' she said, noting the arrival of Clarrie and Eddie, in search of food, as always. 'And anyway,' she continued, 'there's love here, you know? Lots of love in this garden and this house. Matilda poured her love into it. It feels fine to me. It feels right to keep them here.'

Jamie and Connie watched the shadows shrink across the valley and heard the birdsong build with the morning sun.

'Yes, there's love 'ere, all right,' said Jamie, pulling Connie closer to him, and simultaneously scratching beneath Clarrie's chin.

'Yes,' said Connie, her head nestling against his neck, her hands intertwined with his hands. '*Yes.*'

Author's note

I grew up in rural Worcestershire, surrounded by the countryside I describe in *The Women Who Wouldn't Leave*.

It's a beautiful area, but often overlooked in favour of the ever-popular Cotswolds and the wild gorgeousness of Wales. I do recommend you visit, however, to enjoy the ancient, glorious Malvern Hills and the historic towns of Great Malvern, Pershore, Upton and Worcester, with Ledbury, Hay-on-Wye, Gloucester and Hereford all also within easy reach.

That being said, the area is grappling with many of the issues featured in this book, including rural poverty, a lack of social housing, shrinking public transport provision and the negative impact of second-home ownership. If you do visit, I recommend frequenting the many brilliant independent restaurants, pubs, hotels, farm shops and boutiques, happy in the knowledge that you are supporting the local economy.

One important note: Stonecastle and Roseacre Close exist only in my imagination, and Severnside Council luckily does not exist. If there are any MPs, councillors or officers working in Worcestershire with names similar to those in this novel, I promise this is entirely coincidental.

And finally – I spend far too much time on social media. Please do come and say hi!

Website: www.toryscott.com
Instagram: VictoriaScottAuthor
Facebook: VictoriaScottJournalist
Twitter: @toryscott
Tiktok: VictoriaScottAuthor

Acknowledgements

As ever, I would like to thank my agents, Northbank Talent Management, for always having my back and cheering me on, and also the fabulous team at Head of Zeus for believing in this book, editing it brilliantly and producing its stunning cover.

A huge thanks as always to my wonderful author friends, who offer support, advice and much-needed humour. This job of ours is amazing but also rather lonely and occasionally frustrating, and they *get* it.

Finally, I'd like to thank my amazing husband Teil and brilliant kids Raphie and Ella for putting up with me locking myself away in my study for hours and hours and being generally quite boring, and occasionally actually rather grumpy.

And you know, it takes a (talented) group of villagers to produce a book. So here, in the grand tradition of TV and film, are the production credits for *The Women Who Wouldn't Leave*:

Literary agents:
Hannah Weatherill, Diane Banks, Elizabeth Counsell and Natalie Christopher at Northbank Talent Management

The Head of Zeus team:
Editor: Rachel Faulkner-Willcocks
Assistant Editor: Bianca Gillam
Copy editor: Rhian McKay
Production: Emily Champion

Cover design: Jessie Price
Design support: Meg Shepherd
Marketing: Amy Watson, Jo Liddiard
Social media: Zoe Giles
Publicity: Ayo Okojie
Sales: Karen Dobbs, Dan Groenewald, Victoria Eddison
Digital sales: Nikky Ward

About the Author

VICTORIA SCOTT has been a journalist for almost two decades, working for a wide variety of outlets including the BBC, Al Jazeera, *Time Out*, *Doha News* and the *Telegraph*, and she is also a Faber Academy graduate. She lives near London with her husband and two children, and works as a freelance journalist, media trainer and journalism tutor. Her first novel, *Patience*, was the Booksellers Association Book of the Month and LoveReading Debut of the Month.